Aeolian
Visions/Versions

Modern Classics and New Writing from Turkey

Edited by

Mel Kenne, Saliha Paker and Amy Spangler

Milet Publishing
Smallfields Cottage, Cox Green
Rudgwick, Horsham, West Sussex
RH12 3DE England
info@milet.com
www.milet.com
www.milet.co.uk

Aeolian Visions / Versions: Modern Classics and New Writing from Turkey
Translated by the Cunda International Workshop for
Translators of Turkish Literature (CWTTL)

Editors: Mel Kenne, Saliha Paker, Amy Spangler
Assistant Editors: Arzu Eker Roditakis, Nilgün Dungan

First English edition published by Milet Publishing in 2013
Copyright © Milet Publishing, 2013
ISBN 978 1 84059 853 7

Images of Sunday (page 213) and Monday (page 219) from *Une Semaine de Bonté* (1933)
by Max Ernst: Copyright © ADAGP, Paris and DACS, London, 2013
Permissions acknowledgements for previously published material
can be found on pages 399 and 400

Funded by the Turkish Ministry of Culture and Tourism TEDA Project

Book design by Christangelos Seferiadis
Printed and bound in Turkey by Ertem Basım Yayın Dağıtım

In memory of Şinasi Tekin (1933–2004),
Professor of Turkish Studies at Harvard University,
who opened up the path to CWTTL's home in Cunda

Contents

Editorial Notes

Throughout this anthology, we have retained the Turkish for several types of terms, including personal names, honorifics and place names, among others. We have used the English spelling of Istanbul, rather than its Turkish spelling, İstanbul, because the English version is so commonly known. For the Turkish terms and other foreign language terms, we have used italics in their first instance in each piece and then normal text for subsequent instances in the same piece. We have not italicized the Turkish honorifics that form part of a name—in the case of this book, Abi and Hanım—to avoid splitting the name visually with a style change.

We have italicized the English titles of books and longer poetic works even if they have not been published in full in English, rather than using the standard quotation marks for titles of unpublished works, so that the style of the English and Turkish titles is the same. We felt this would make the relationship between the two titles clearer.

The translators represented in this volume write primarily in British English or American English. In this edition, we have aimed for a "mid-Atlantic" pitch, using terms and idioms from both dialects, but mainly US spellings.

Guide to Turkish Pronunciation

Turkish letters that appear in the book and which may be unfamiliar are shown below, with a guide to their pronunciation.

c   as *j* in *just*
ç   as *ch* in *child*
ğ   silent letter that lengthens the preceding vowel
ı   as *a* in *along*
ö   as German *ö* in *Köln*, or French *œ* in *œuf*
ş   as *sh* in *ship*
ü   as German *ü* in *fünf*, or French *u* in *tu*
ˆ   accent over vowel that lengthens the vowel

About This Book

Within these pages you will find a sampling of English translations representing powerful and diverse voices of Turkish literature from the last fifty years. You will also find something rather different from a typical anthology of literature in translation. For this collection represents a highly collaborative effort that has taken place over several years: the Cunda International Workshop for Translators of Turkish Literature (CWTTL). The CWTTL is an intensive translation workshop held each year on Cunda, a small, sunlit, windblown island off the Aegean coast of ancient Aeolia, in northwestern Turkey. All of the translations in this collection were either produced by the poetry and prose groups at CWTTL, or presented at the CWTTL by participating translators as works-in-progress, and they were selected and compiled collectively by members at our workshop in 2012. Our selections were based on the exceptional literary quality of the work itself and the translation, as well as the unconventionality of the subject matter and style. Almost all of the translated poets and authors in this book were guests at our workshops, where they participated in sessions with their translators and gave talks. We have included in our collection excerpts from these talks, which provide a glimpse into the writers' views on their lives, writing and translation, and which we hope will bring them closer to readers.

A few words about the Turkish literary tradition and recent trends in Turkish literature may help explain the CWTTL's dual focus on poetry and prose, and the sequencing of the poetry and prose selections in this book. While new writing in fiction has proliferated in subject matter, style and viewpoint much more visibly than in poetry, it is poetry that forms the backbone of Turkish literature, classical and modern. Hence, an awareness of the modern Turkish poetic tradition is important to understanding and appreciating the broader literature. Indeed, prose writers like those included here are often avid readers of poetry, and in many cases this shines through in their writing. In view of this symbiosis, the works and talks by various poets, and the fiction pieces, memoirs, essays and talks by prose writers have been interspersed to interrelate, sometimes thematically, at other times only suggestively, in a complementary arrangement. We believe that such an arrangement offers our readers much more than a strictly chronological sequence would, and hope that what at first appears as a maze of interrelated individual works when seen accumulatively will provide valuable insights into both individual and collective consciousnesses in modern Turkey—not only from Istanbul, but from central and southeastern Anatolia and the Aegean as well. The work of Murathan Mungan, for example, who participated in two of our workshops, straddles poetry, fiction and biographical essay, connecting the personal and the social, the rural and the urban. Similarly, the work of Hasan Ali Toptaş branches out from fiction into poetry, and that of Gülten Akın includes her artistic reflections on a forty-two-day prison hunger strike, represented here by four excerpts, two of which are prose poems.

As the *Vision/Versions* of our title suggests, the pieces in this collection reflect a viewpoint shared by the translators to envision and create distinctive versions of texts—a viewpoint that is as apparent in the work of promising new talents as in that of more established figures. Be they poet–translators, freelance literary translators, or scholars of literary and translation studies, all work together in Cunda as peers, practicing the art and craft of translation, their shared perspective nourished by this collaboration among themselves and with the guest poets and writers. The theme of versions is represented in the collection in some instances by multiple English versions of a Turkish poem, and in one instance by a translation into a third language as well. The collaborative nature of the workshop allows translators, who often feel they are laboring entirely on their own, to join a community of like spirits, and they are usually delighted to find that their work is enlivened by it. They also find that the individuality of their translations is not lost, for our work at Cunda has manifestly revealed that, even in collaborative translations, a distinctive voice and character is imparted by every translator to his or her text.

This brings us to an important point: a major aspect of translation that we emphasize at the Cunda workshop is the presence and visibility of the translator. Literary translators do not simply serve as a conduit through which a text is magically rendered in another language. Rather, they are vocal agents who exercise ownership over the texts they produce. By underscoring the role and voice of the translator, we aim for the book to speak to literary translators as much as to readers of literature in translation. In the collection, the translators are of course named with each of their translations. We have also included a list of all of the translators who have participated in the Cunda workshops, and biographies of those translators whose works appear in this volume. The biographies include the titles of most or all of the translators' published works, current and forthcoming, at the time of this book's publication. We provide these names and titles not only to credit the translators, but so that you can seek out their further works, which we strongly encourage you to do; for in them, you will find many riches of the kind we highlight here.

A brief survey of the poets and authors who have participated in the annual Cunda workshops provides a good introduction to the collection. During the first workshop, in 2006, we focused on the work of Gülten Akın, Zeynep Uzunbay, Murathan Mungan and Haydar Ergülen. Nurdan Gürbilek, one of Turkey's foremost literary and cultural critics, gave a talk at the workshop, and our collection very fittingly begins with an excerpt from this in which Gürbilek points to the need for a broader, more interconnected context for translations from Turkish in world literature—a necessity which holds true for literatures from other "peripheral" cultures as well. This is followed by a translation of part of "Bad Boy Turk," Gürbilek's essay on the novel *A Mind at Peace*, a modern classic by poet and author Ahmet Hamdi Tanpınar (1901–1962), and then by two excerpts from *A Mind at Peace*, which Erdağ Göknar presented for discussion at the workshop while still in the process of translating the work. By starting with Tanpınar, a cornerstone of Turkish literature, we lay the groundwork for a collection that takes readers through the rich gamut of Turkish literature from the mid-twentieth century onward.

As the doyenne of modern Turkish poetry, Gülten Akın holds a special place at Cunda, which she has visited on two occasions from her home nearby, and her poems figure very prominently throughout the volume. Akın was not only a primary breaker of the sex barrier in Turkish poetry, but also a lawyer and teacher who took an active role in social justice issues as she lived in different parts of Anatolia with her husband, a government administrator, and their children. As revealed by her talk excerpted here, Akın's poems are characterized by her deeply humanistic and spiritual concerns as well as her critical focus on womanhood. Aptly, the poetry of Zeynep Uzunbay, Gülten Akın's younger follower in writing personal poems that incorporate social justice issues and feminist themes, was also taken up by the poetry group. Four translators were especially fascinated by Uzunbay's poem "sesinle," which the poet explained was inspired by a special kind of coat that she and other female

5

students had to wear at boarding school. Three different versions of the poem are featured here.

Murathan Mungan is a prolific poet and writer in myriad forms of prose, much admired in Turkey, whose work is woefully underrepresented in English. It is therefore with great pleasure that we present in this volume not only some of his wide-ranging poetry, but also one of his best known essays, "The Money Djinns." A cutting slice of history, this autobiographical essay relates a very personal story of exile and displacement in the various meanings of the terms. Mungan is also represented by an excerpt from his short story "The Legs of Şahmeran," based on the mythical half-woman half-snake figure from southeastern Anatolia. Mungan visited the Cunda workshop again in 2010, so we could explore and translate more poems from his exceptionally rich oeuvre. Through these workshops and continuing projects, the poetry group has expanded its corpus of Mungan poetry translations and ultimately hopes to publish it as a separate volume. The work of the preeminent poet Haydar Ergülen typically has an intimate and beautifully idiosyncratic quality that almost defies critical discussion, a trait that is clearly evident in several of the poems included here. Ergülen's poetry at times takes on a mystical cast as he leads us through linguistic and imaginative mazes reminiscent of labyrinthine medieval gardens, suggesting a spiritual journey back to the primal self and a state of original purity and innocence. Since 2006, several members of the poetry group have continued to translate Ergülen's poems, and our corpus of his work as well may soon be substantial enough to be published as a collection.

In 2007, the Cunda team translated the works of Latife Tekin and Hasan Ali Toptaş, two of contemporary Turkish literature's most celebrated and most poetic authors. Here, you will find a taster of Latife Tekin's latest work, *Muinar*—an extravagant, satirical, feminist narrative, voiced by a wild, ageless, all-knowing woman in constant chatter, from prehistory to modern times. We also include an excerpt from Tekin's earlier, far more sober novel, *The Garden of Forgetting*. Set among a small community whose members fled the city to a presumably peaceful retreat in Bodrum but who find they are nevertheless driven by tension and conflict as they try to pursue an alternative way of life, this narrative is punctuated by ruminations on memory and its loss. Hasan Ali Toptaş's fiction writing is represented by translations of his short story "The Balcony" and an excerpt from his novel *The Shadowless*. Already rendered into many European languages and garnering much critical praise for Toptaş as "the Turkish Kafka," *The Shadowless* is an enigmatic, postmodern thriller of shifting viewpoints and settings between life in the Anatolian countryside and the city. The Cunda poetry group collaborated on translating excerpts from Toptaş's book *Lonelinesses*, a series of poetic meditations and childhood reminiscences, six sections of which are interspersed throughout this volume.

The 2008 workshop hosted Murat Gülsoy, an award-winning and innovative author, and upon his suggestion, we tackled what was then his most recent novel, *A Week of Kindness in Istanbul.* The novel, like much of Gülsoy's work, is visceral and experimental. It consists of forty-nine texts, written by seven narrators (who were conveniently paired with the seven translators in the prose group), and each narrator pens one text a day for seven days, in response to illustrations from Max Ernst's *A Week of Kindness* sent to them by a mysterious someone who has asked them to look at the illustrations and do "automatic writing." The result is a panorama of Istanbul characters, men and women, old and young, from various walks of life, each writing in a style all his or her own. We have included chapters "written" by two female characters, "Deniz" and "Ayşe," in completely different styles. We also feature the short story "The Forgotten," a highly challenging text by Oğuz Atay (1934–1977), a major writer of twentieth century Turkish literature who would become an influence on nearly every author after him, Murat Gülsoy included. Gökçenur Ç., our poet for 2007, was chosen on the advice of Haydar Ergülen, who had spoken enthusiastically of him as a leading figure in the younger generation of Turkish poets. Impressed by the highly original verse forms of Gökçenur Ç.'s poetry and its signature mordant wit, the poetry group finished the workshop with several versions of the same poems. Readers curious about the word choices translators make with the aim of making their translations more widely accessible to English readers may find of particular interest the two versions of a morbidly humorous poem by Gökçenur Ç. that takes as its theme the character and personality of Death itself. Gökçenur Ç. is distinguished from other writers who visited our workshop by his dual literary career as a poet and as a translator. So, along with his own poetry, we have included two of his translations, of poems by Haydar Ergülen and Gonca Özmen.

Behçet Çelik, a renowned short story writer, novelist and essayist, was our guest prose writer at the 2009 workshop. He had recently received the prestigious Sait Faik Short Story Award for his fifth short story collection, *Mid-Day Desire.* The two short stories that we have featured here, "My Big Brother" and "A Cold Fire," exhibit Çelik's mastery in depicting existential crises and confounding human relationships. We also took on excerpts from the novel *After Gliding Parallel To The Ground For A While* by Barış Bıçakçı. Because the novel has several different characters narrating their own chapters, interspersed, each translator chose a different character and chapter to work on. The narrators all reflect in some way upon another character who has committed suicide. It is a dark book; but, as is often the case in Bıçakçı's writing, even the darkest times may be penetrated by light. Our visiting poet that year was Gonca Özmen, who was also recommended to us by Haydar Ergülen, and who in her twenties had already published two books of poetry and won several literary awards. Özmen's sophisticated use of form and imagery, epitomized in the poems by her that we have included in this collection, reflects how strongly stylistic features came to function as an essential means for women poets to express their intensely personal experiences of carving out their niches in a traditionally male-dominated cultural milieu.

As was noted earlier, in 2010, the poetry group again took up the work of Murathan Mungan, this time concentrating on his body of poetic works. That year, the fiction group veered into new territory with guest author Hatice Meryem. Meryem's short story collection *May I Have a Fly-Sized Husband to Watch Over Me*, rife with insightful, acerbic wit, had been a surprise hit when published in 2002, and has proven enduringly popular. The narrator of the collection imagines herself as the wife of a plethora of different men, and the result is a poignant, often hilarious series of portraits, four of which are included in this book. We also translated some pieces by Sevgi Soysal (1936–1976), a pioneering writer of prose fiction and essays. Politically outspoken, Soysal wielded her pen courageously and ventured into unchartered territories, interweaving the personal and the political with a biting sense of humor, resulting in a style that would influence many writers, especially women, who came after her, including Meryem. You may discern threads of continuity between the two when you read Meryem's stories alongside translations of a chapter from Soysal's prison memoirs, "The Plan," and two short stories from *Tante Rosa*, Soysal's collection centered on the adventurous, and disastrous, life of an unrelentingly upbeat character named Rosa. Despite the pain so acutely evoked in *Tante Rosa*, it ultimately remains ebullient, enriched by touches of humor—a modern fairytale of odd incidents, oddly true to life.

The workshop welcomed in 2011 the short story writer Ahmet Büke, who had just received the Sait Faik Award for his fourth collection, *What the Pigeon Saw*. Büke's stories are layered, rich in images and metaphors, often marked by a sharp political edge; opaque at first, his texts frequently require multiple readings, and thus foster a uniquely intimate bond with the reader. Büke's stories may provoke you to think, laugh, cry or all of the above, but what they most certainly do not do is leave you unaffected. This is true for all of the stories by Büke featured here, but perhaps especially so for "Saturday Mother" and the closing piece of the collection, "Yellow Notebook of Dreams." The poetry group's focus in 2011 was the book-length poem *Yol* by Birhan Keskin, one of the most widely acclaimed voices in contemporary Turkish poetry. Tackling such a large project was a first for the group, and this two-part poem is itself one of a kind for the poet (as she confessed in her talk at the workshop), written in a fury of emotional turmoil over a short period of time. Yet it was just this quality that attracted us to the poem—its emotional intensity conveyed through brilliant imagery and a subtle interweaving of personal and spiritual experience, forming an extended rumination on a broken relationship. The poem became a profound challenge for its translators, from whose collaboration three versions emerged, excerpts of which we include here.

In 2012, Güven Turan, a well-established name in Turkish poetry, visited the workshop with his long-time translator Ruth Christie, and we have included a selection of his poems in the collection. Our fiction writer that year was the lauded novelist and short story writer Mine Söğüt. The prose group took a turn for the dark, tackling Söğüt's collection *Tales of Madwomen*. Translating these macabre tales, which chilled and horrified the translators, was a challenge to say the least, yet they persevered, quite successfully, we believe. Norwegian translator Venke Vik identified a rhythmic quality to İdil Aydoğan's English translation of Söğüt's story "Why I Killed Myself in This City," which she then sought to reproduce. Her resulting version, a rare translation of Turkish literature into New Norwegian, is presented in parallel with the English. We have included as well Söğüt's stories "Kurdish Cats and Gypsy Butterflies" and "Snake."

As you will soon see, in this translation collection, we have not only highlighted translated texts but we have tried to construct something of a context out of which these works gained their voice in another tongue. We are fortunate to have had a hand in shaping the Cunda workshop and sharing it with other translators, who have come from near and far to enrich our visions and generate the versions that are vital to our common task of launching the literature that we love out into the world, where it belongs, where it can be savored by a readership hungry for a greater diversity of voices than that commonly offered up by mainstream publishing.

Our hopes for this volume are twofold. The first is that by reading these translations you will gain a deeper appreciation of what Turkish literature is about today and come to share our belief that while it still remains largely unknown in Europe and the United States, it has experienced a recent flowering in both its poetry and prose that has put it on a par with literature being produced anywhere in the world. And the second is that by having a chance to read different versions of translations, you will gain an insight into the process of translation and a greater appreciation for the work of translators, who labor behind the scenes—too often overlooked and unsung—to provide a window into the ceaselessly rich lands and seas of the imagination. Finally, we wish you happy sailing on these rising Aeolian winds.

—Mel Kenne, Saliha Paker and Amy Spangler

Translated Texts from the Periphery

Excerpt from a Talk by Nurdan Gürbilek (2006)
Translated by Şehnaz Tahir Gürçağlar (2006)

. . . writers at the periphery have a different fate. They are read as a means of know-
ing more about a certain part or aspect of the world—a certain country, a religion,
the Muslim world, the East or something of that nature.

Although the list of works translated from Turkish into English is long, these texts are somehow lost. Lost in the sense that they don't have a context and seem to come out of nowhere. They are like free-floating stars without a galaxy, they do not make a constellation, either among themselves or among texts in other languages. They do not talk among themselves or with texts written in other languages. There is something missing there . . . I'm afraid that most of them become victim to the tendency to take them only as a localized color of the periphery, a different flavor, a different taste in world cuisine. If a text does not have a context, we know that it will have one only if the literary market can offer it.

* * *

Here in Turkey, even young students don't read Baudelaire or Proust to learn more about France, Dostoevksy to learn more about Russia, or Shakespeare to learn more about the history of England. We read them because they are classics of world literature, because they speak to us of the adventures of the human soul, of the existential problems of humankind. But writers at the periphery have a different fate. They are read as a means of knowing more about a certain part or aspect of the world—a certain country, a religion, the Muslim world, the East or something of that nature. Orhan Pamuk was fortunate enough to go a little beyond these limits. Still, it is no coincidence that in his interviews abroad, he is asked more questions about Turkey's membership in the European Union, Islam, human rights in Turkey, torture, the Kurdish problem, the Armenian problem, or almost anything other than Turkish literature or literature in general.

I don't want to be misunderstood here; every writer has the choice of becoming a political figure. But I think in Orhan Pamuk's case, his position has less to do with personal choice and more to do with the fact that he comes from a country in the periphery. A few days ago, I was talking to the novelist and short story writer Leylâ Erbil about her novel *Tuhaf Bir Kadın* (*A Strange Woman*), which was translated into German. She told me how disappointed she was when she learned that the best review of the novel focused on how women meet their doom in an underdeveloped Muslim country.

We know Frederic Jameson's notorious speculations on third world literature—that all third world texts, even those that are seemingly particular, are necessarily allegorical, and that they should be read as national allegories. This was fiercely debated in the 1990s, and it is not my intention to start the whole discussion all over again. In fact, I think that as a theory it has its strengths, especially in explaining some of the traumas related to the belated arrival of the modern Turkish novel. But I think his theory is also significant in showing us some traps that await us when one culture is translated to another. Actually, what Jameson was trying to do was to translate, to convey what he calls third world literature, to the western world. He was trying to draw attention to it, to remind western readers that there is a different literature out there—different, not primitive, naive or anachronistic, as western judgment tends to see it. He was exposing the limits of western judgment. He was saying that third world literature, with its national allegories, its political implications, always keeping in mind its particular social totality, can be a model for western writers, to remind them of their own repressed political consciences. As I said before, however, talking about cultural difference has its traps.

Bad Boy Turk I (Kötü Çocuk Türk I)

By Nurdan Gürbilek (2001)

Translated by Erdağ Göknar, Şehnaz Tahir Gürçağlar and Nilüfer Yeşil (2006)

One of the few abject heroes of Turkish literature appears in Ahmet Hamdi Tanpınar's *A Mind at Peace* as Suad, who is one of the major figures in the novel, if not the main character. Suad's character transforms the novel into one of *dis*ease, through his alienation and animosity, his foul smirk, his atheism and his insolence. His character, which is pathologically depraved, fundamentally destroys every possibility he might have for contentment. His dark soul disturbs everyone's peace by valorizing the material over the spiritual, nothingness over being and perverse pleasures over moderation. He dims the all-illuminating light of love, and reminds all who believe in culture and happiness that death is nothing but wretched decay. He believes that salvation from the cruel game of life occurs through yet another cruel act; that the way to discovering one's own treasure of goodness passes through murder.

Resenting the unfairness of his affliction, Suad has become the enemy of kindness, joy and health, as from his sickbed in the sanatorium he tries to poison everyone. This is not to say that denial is absent in his malevolence. Suad opposes the awareness and will that İhsan represents, as much as the love and aesthetic pleasure represented by Mümtaz. He confronts their ideals and dreams with all his vulgarity, brutality and defiance. Frustrated with social etiquette, he ridicules the mediocre ideas, moderate pleasures, measured compassions, trivial hopes and half-hearted anguish of the intellectuals around him. Onto the love story that we read he casts the shadow of destructive emotions unrepressed by culture—spite, anger, vengeance, misery, and malicious doubt. Tanpınar has chosen to describe him as a "dirty hand."[1] He enters everyone's lives "just like a dirty and sticky hand whose grimy fingers soil a cabinet full of clean laundry in the dark." He "turns everything into a disgusting sludge" and sucks everyone into this "black, sleazy, ash-colored mud." Suad is openly compared to shit: he contaminates everything he encounters with "the disgusting slime of his miserable personality," smearing everyone with this "runny mess." Sometimes

---

1. All quotations in this excerpt are from Ahmet Hamdi Tanpınar's *Huzur* (1949).

13

Mümtaz gets a whiff of "the worst kind of toilet stink" from him, repellent and nauseating. In all these aspects, Suad deserves to be considered one of the few pathetic as well as devilish heroes in Turkish literature.

It is obvious that Suad plays an essential role in the development of *A Mind at Peace*. Under his influence Mümtaz is overcome by "the merciless seduction of deadly thoughts," and Nuran feels revolted by love, by his existence as much as his suicide, with the awful grimace on his lifeless face. But again, it is Suad who succeeds in drawing Mümtaz's attention to the underworld of high culture, to the people whose lives he otherwise would not have known about, whose opinions remain unsolicited; to those who would never have appeared in this novel of ideas. It is only after Mümtaz has been overcome by Suad's influence that he momentarily averts his gaze from mosques, *yalı* seaside villas, and the beauties of the Bosphorus, seeing, if only out of the corner of his eye, things beyond aesthetic culture. He now notices streets where raw sewage flows, where people live in houses built of tin and mud bricks, where boys serve coffee-vendors and porters hunch under their burdens: "a humanity ready to leap over all culture or good breeding." Moreover, it is again Suad who brings nightmare into Tanpınar's "dream aesthetic," destroying the triangular theme of art, nature and love in the novel's second chapter, denying the representational terms (like "dream," "reign of the soul" and "chance") that contribute to the novel's philosophical depth, and violating Tanpınar's beloved notion of "civility." Clearly, Tanpınar tries to include the opposite of his own aesthetic viewpoint through Suad, and attempts to portray evil not just as an external enemy but as an inner force with its own appeal.

Herein lies the problem: despite his essential role in the novel, Suad is not a believable character. Furthermore, in many ways he appears to be an imitation; an excessively textual, representational and symbolic character planted in the novel only to represent evil. Although he enables us to distance ourselves from the aestheticism of Mümtaz, who sees life as a matter of taste, and saves the novel from becoming a procession of ideas and dreams, Suad cannot save himself from being a kind of pale copy or a foreign "concept." At best, he can only represent Mümtaz's morbid, solitary and exilic melancholy, his emptiness in the years following his parents' deaths, and his inner "deathly leaven": Suad is an externalized embodiment of Mümtaz's bleak consciousness. He seems to be placed in the novel simply to render meaningless Mümtaz's inner accumulation of culture, to smash its layers, and reveal the emptiness beneath; in short, to authenticate the "leading man"s melancholy rather than his own misery. Apart from this, Suad is a stranger, a foreigner, as made evident by his act of suicide to the accompaniment of Beethoven's violin concerto. In fact, critics have been preoccupied with this matter: Suad is artificial and awkward, an imitated—in other words, "translated"—character who seems to have emerged from a novel by Dostoevsky. In particular, Suad's suicide resembles too closely that of Stavrogin, the protagonist of *The Possessed*; Suad's suicide too is a "translated" one.

There are elements of truth in these criticisms. What Tanpınar writes elsewhere about Beyoğlu also applies to Suad. Just as everything in Beyoğlu has its "more authentic" counterpart abroad, everything about Suad also has a "more authentic" foreign counterpart. Indeed, Suad stands before us as a textual character, culled from European literature and philosophy, as a veritable Russian–French–German mix. Behind him, there is a pinch of Nietzsche, a pinch of Baudelaire, and a handful of Dostoevsky. His words parrot sentences we have read elsewhere, some of them from fascist Italian futurists. Suad desires "virgin *türkü* songs" and "celebration songs for the newborn." He rejects "any scraps from bygone days," believes in war as a form of cleansing, the only way to free humanity from decrepit models, and shrugs off the poetry of both Ronsard and Fuzûlî. This man who appears as though he has accidentally fallen into an environment of Turkish taverns, of Mevlevi rituals performed in the Ferahfeza mode, or of Rumelia türkü songs is truly a foreigner. In contrast to holy Kandil night-pastries, Ramazan rhymes, Kandilli's printed kerchiefs, Bursa's woven fabrics, in short, to "all the forms and shapes that we have created through our lives on this soil," Suad remains an *alla franca* evil assembled from foreign ideas, a low-life snob, and an excessively elegant bad boy.

From *A Mind at Peace* (*Huzur*)

By Ahmet Hamdi Tanpınar (1949)
Translated by Erdağ Göknar (2008)

From Part II, Chapter 12

Toward the end of September, the bluefish runs offered another excuse to savor the Bosphorus. Bluefish outings were among the most alluring amusements on the straits.

An illuminated diversion stretching out along both shores beginning from Beylerbeyi and Kabataş in the south, extending north to Telli Tabya and the Kavaklar near the Black Sea, and gathering around the confluence of currents, the bluefish catches gave rise, here and there, to waterborne fetes, especially on darkened nights of the new moon. In contrast to other excursions that developed as part of a venture demanding long outings, this carnival dance developed right then and there, together with everyone.

Since childhood, Nuran had adored the seas over which caique lanterns shimmered like brilliants swathed in black and purple velvets, the translucent darkness beginning where such radiance ceased, shattering a little further onward due to another cluster of anglers, the wake of a ferryboat, or small swells; she adored the rising of this luminous silhouette within a thousand prismatic refractions, the way it spread through the setting as if it might abduct her. In brief, she loved these nocturnal excursions for bluefish that conveyed a sense of occurring in a realm where reflection, glint and shocks of light alone appointed a highly polished, radiant palace accompanied by crescendos progressing from small melodies and musical measures to vast and idiosyncratic variations.

Before she'd married, and even when younger, her father, who considered his daughter and Tevfik his only like-minded cohorts in the house, would take them fishing for bluefish. When she reminisced about these nights with Mümtaz, he didn't miss the opportunity to take summer, which had been so wondrous, to a plane of higher pleasure.

* * *

Mümtaz adored this old-world philanderer, who, around the time of Mümtaz's birth, declared his love for the neighborhood ladies five times a day as if it were an inseparable part of the call to salvation sounded to the entire neighborhood from the minaret of the quaint mosque. Tevfik was possessed of a gentlemanly Epicureanism that found open expression only in the subdued air of satisfaction that collected in his eyes when he wiped his grayed mustache with the back of his hand.

A gentleman of rare experience, he greatly facilitated Nuran and Mümtaz's appreciation of Bosphorus bluefish outings and their understanding of the role of ardor in human experience. From the very first day, he'd taken Mümtaz under his wing, diminishing the atmosphere of animosity in the household created by Fatma's jealousy, which had found a most fertile ground under Yaşar's wardship. Mümtaz was quite cognizant of the part Tevfik's friendship played in his amicable acceptance by Nuran's mother at the Kandilli household. Even when most resistant to Mümtaz's visitations, she could not withstand her brother's enthusiasm and was oftentimes swayed by him.

The way this salty philanderer regarded their love so earnestly astounded Mümtaz. Tevfik's profligate life contained little that might naturally indicate his admiration for such passion. At first, Mümtaz assumed that Tevfik's mask of approval concealed expressions of mockery toward him and his inexperience, or that he took Mümtaz this seriously only due to respect for the feelings of his dearest beloved niece. Later, as Tevfik gradually entered Mümtaz's life, he realized that his rakish, extravagant and at times brutal existence obscured bewildering Pangs of Nostalgia. One day, Nuran's uncle casually confided to him that most ladies' men—objects of envy during a reckoning of one's life, or whilst one wallowed in depression after a missed opportunity for gratification due to a bankrupt phantasy—hadn't had the chance to love a woman fully or had lost this chance and had attempted to make up for it by chasing after contingencies, an ideal or an array of tired repetitions of the same experience . . . In short, men like Mümtaz who lived through a singular beloved were the objects of genuine envy.

From Part IV, Chapter 2

Mümtaz recognized the *türkü*. During the last war, while in Konya with his father, soldiers being transported by evening freight trains and peasants carting vegetables to town toward daybreak always sang this song in the station. It had a searing melody. The entire drama of Anatolia was contained in this türkü.

"How strange!" he said. "It's acceptable, even forgivable, for the masses to moan and complain. Just listen to türküs from the last war! What spectacular pieces! The older ones are that way too. Take that Crimean War türkü. But these songs aren't liked by intellectuals. So the people have no right to whine! That means *we* are responsible."

Nuri returned to the earlier topic: "And how d'you know that things won't run amok this time? Brought about by only one piece of straw, more or less."

Mümtaz completed his thought: "I'm not defending war. What makes you think that I am? For starters, can humanity even be divided into 'victorious' and 'vanquished'? This is absurd. This division is sufficient to bankrupt values and ethics and even what we're fighting for. Naturally, it's a mistake to expect good or great things to follow in the wake of every crisis. But what's to be done? You see, there are five of us here. Five friends. When we think independently, we find ourselves possessed of an array of strengths. But in the face of any crisis . . ."

His friends gazed at him intently as he continued: "Since morning I've been debating this on my own." Abruptly, then, he returned to the previous topic: "On the contrary, worse, much worse things could arise."

"What have you been deliberating since the morning?"

"This morning, near the Hekim Ali Pasha Mosque, girls were playing games and singing türküs. These songs have existed maybe since the time of the conquest of Istanbul. And the girls were singing them and playing. You see, I want these türküs to persist."

"That's a defensive struggle . . . That's different."

"Sometimes a defensive struggle can change its character. If there's a war, I'm not saying we'll rush into it at all costs. For nobody knows what the developments leading up to it will be. Sometimes, unexpectedly, a back door opens. You look to find an unforeseen opportunity! In that case, waging or refraining from war becomes a matter that's within your own control.

"When one contemplates it, it's confounding. The difference between those who controlled humanity's fate at the start of the last war and today's statesmen is immeasurable."

Mümtaz turned to İhsan in his thoughts as if to ask him something.

"Of course there are a lot of differences. Back then, humanity seemed to emerge out of a single mold. The values that were still regarded in high esteem. Not to mention that centuries-old diplomacy, its gentility and protocols . . . Today it's as if a lunatic has moved into the neighborhood. Europe as we know it has vanished. Half of Europe is in the hands of renegades bent on provoking the masses, on vengeance and on spinning new fables." The more he spoke, the more he assumed he was leaving fixed ideas and fabrications behind.

"Do you know when I gave up hope on the current predicament? The day they signed the Nazi–Soviet Nonaggression Pact."

"But the leftists quite applaud it. If you could just hear them rave! They're now all praising the Führer. As if the Reichstag Fire Trial had never happened." Nuri's face was yellow with wrath. "As if so much murder hadn't been committed."

"Of course they praise him. But only until the next news flash. You get my drift, don't you? Mind that one doesn't lose his sense of ethics and value judgments! Despite being opposed to war, I'm not afraid of it, and I'm waiting."

He spoke with unfamiliar certitude. From one of the neighboring coffeehouses a radio or gramophone cast another variety of turmoil into the evening hour. Eyyubi Bekir Ağa's version of the "Song in Mahur" lilted through the twilight, staggering Mümtaz on the spot. As he heard the melody, the version that Nuran's grandfather had composed, that ominous poem of love and death filled him. *Tomorrow she'll be leaving, and leaving full of resentment* . . . A fury, so vast as to be unbearable, rose within him. *Why did it have to happen this way? Why is everybody imposing on me like this?* She'd been talking about her general peace of mind. *So then, where's my own peace to be found? Don't I count? What to do in such solitude?* He was all but thinking through Nuran's words: *Peace, inner calm* . . .

"The entire matter hinges on this . . ." Orhan didn't complete his thought.

"Go on!"

"No, I've forgotten what I was going to say. Only you're right on one point. Two wrongs don't make a right. Each injustice condoned gives rise to greater injustice."

"There's another point: avoiding injustice while fighting injustice. This war, if it comes to pass, will be a bloodbath. But the torments suffered will all be in vain if we don't change our methods . . ."

I shouldn't be seeking peace through Nuran, but through myself. And this will only happen through sacrifice. He stood.

"I'm worried about İhsan," he said. "Please excuse me. And purge yourselves of these thoughts. Who knows, maybe there won't be any war! Maybe we won't get involved. We're a country that's lost so much blood, we've learned many lessons. The circumstances might just permit our neutrality."

As Mümtaz took leave of his friends, he realized that they hadn't discussed the stages of such a war, were it to happen. Inwardly, this pleased him.

Will it actually come to pass? The voice accompanying him said, "Don't worry about it," then added, "Well-spoken, you've put yourself at ease! That's all you need to do, nothing more!" He ran and hopped onto a streetcar, perhaps to escape the derisive voice of Suad.

Garden Vines (Bağlar)

By Gülten Akın (2007)

Translated by Saliha Paker and Mel Kenne (2012)

It was still the green almond time, we hadn't yet faded
you two little girls would come up
one with big blue-eyed comical looks
the other, quiet, passive

blue pretended to be the world
a breeze of Ulvi Uraz from places of no return
a joy that couldn't fit
into my big-sisterly shell
in the music room fugitive moments
at the window knee-high grass
the back yard

from those days to these
what have you carried over
what have I?

of course in those days too
a few things happened
but Afghan towns
weren't yet a legend
Iraqi children, their mothers . . .
Iraq in ashes, Iraq in ruins
the Middle East a world wound

As if day no longer exists now
the sky skips over it
nights fall fall into dreams
on the globe some place
a black stain that grows perpetually.

The stain harsh, hurting the onlooker
The one who sees the lesions
Which is why the media
created blindness first of all

from those days to these
what have you carried over
what have I?

Up against the Ziverbey mansion
a house, Istanbul
between roses and screams
I must've been blind, blinded I was then
Outside the sun shone past us

Once the hot frame cools down
it turns really cold
the mouth is shut fast
the eye is no longer an eye

from those days to these
what have you carried over
what have I?

At last the desert dust
Also rained on us
The seas withdrew, the rivers turned yellow
The earth lay to rot

what have you carried over
what have I?

An elderly poet points out root sources
church music, the little boy with the siren voice
wild violets, the Aleppo vines

poplars, olive trees, the wind
the gypsy girl picking wild chicory
The eagle owl
The water having to pass between heavy stones
While all these still exist here . . .

gülten is all I'm left with, a rose
if ever planted, stranger to any garden

Poetry, Ideology and Conscience

Excerpt from a Talk by Gülten Akın (2006)
Translated by Saliha Paker (2012)

If you ask me about the place of ideology in poetry, I can only say that it must never constrain the aesthetic quality of the poem. A poet's ideology is like the sap of a tree, which cannot be seen but only imagined.

For me, art in general arises out of the observation of the world, nature and human relationships. It consists of the recording of perceptions in memory and the arranging of them into some kind of order. This process applies to poetry, in particular, as the creation of something new expressed in writing. The poet selects both what to write about and the diction that fits the chosen theme. The syntax is no longer that which we use in spoken language.

The poet goes for a selection of extreme points taken from life's phenomena—from nature or human relationships. The main issue in poetry is to create a spell, to make magic, which can only be produced through tension. To create this tension, the poet picks out reference points and joins them together. That is, you take life or relationships as they are, but then you transform them as much as you want, and reflect that in your poem.

Poetry has to go deep into certain unknown domains of life and living relationships, or at least it has to make them felt. The poet draws her poem out of something like a labyrinth.

I also believe that the poet's diction is a means for reorganizing ordinary language in the same way that plain language organizes life and nature. This finer rearrangement of language improves communication between people in an age of tensions, where people and nations fail to understand one another as they engage in the mechanics of war, and of self-defense against aggression. All of which leads to a loss of conscience.

On both social and individual levels, poetry is an act of opposition. At the very least it is criticism. I'm a poet who takes criticism in some of my poems to the point of revolt, who writes in order to change life at a social or individual level. You can't write poetry just standing where you are. Poetry also responds to a need, a necessity. Some will object to this and say that I'm thinking in pragmatic terms. That's partly true. I'd like poetry to be a means of communication between people, in forming a universal—not a national—conscience, because, in my view, ordinary languages do not seem to be able to achieve this. Nor do ideologies which have now gone bankrupt yet may still hold some hope for the future. Poetry seems to me to represent some hope for those who are now struggling in emptiness, believing that everything they do is futile.

I think one of the tasks of the poet is to heal miscommunication. To use language with a view of making matters more penetrable, more deeply understood. Poetry possesses the fine quality of creating hope in many different ways. It helps in the forming of a conscience. This holds true not only for readers of poetry, who may find some respite in it, but also for those who write poetry.

I was born in a small town in Anatolia. After ten years of a happy childhood there, the winds of World War II and its aftermath of hardships drove us, with our families, to the big cities. It was traumatic for me to move away from wide spaces and try to fit in narrow ones, and to have to make do with less, to witness unfairness and injustice in human relationships. The feeling that everything was alien transformed me from an extroverted, cheerful, easygoing child into an introverted adolescent. That was when I felt literally in the underworld. Then I wrote a poem. And it was poetry that saved me. As Behçet Necatigil said, poetry creates a counterbalance to life's challenges and difficulties. That's how it was for me. I tried to write good poems. I don't know why, but the response I got satisfied me, I was happy.

At first, I was preoccupied with my own problems, which seemed to be at the center of everything I knew. I couldn't help it. The sudden encounter with new things in life and the difficulty in adapting led me to write introspectively about myself. Then, after a while, it was back to the provinces, back to my blurred Anatolian childhood. I became re-acquainted with the people, their language, their ways of life. We lived in many different towns, central or remote, in Anatolia, for short periods. We were appointed to some, on account of my husband's work, while we were sort of exiled to others. My husband was a government district administrator, somewhat headstrong, and I was writing poetry. As you know, poetry too makes people feel on edge.

As a result of the discomfort this kind of life produced, we never got to live anywhere for more than two years; we moved about a lot, which was all to my advantage. I worked as a teacher and sometimes also as a lawyer, making use of both jobs to get to know many different kinds of people and to acquire priceless tools for my poetry, which became imbued with real life as I experienced it with and among other people. I felt that I had the entire gamut of social themes at my disposal. As a result my poetry changed.

At first my poems embraced a wide field of references that were only indirectly connected. Then I started to write poems which I imagined as arrows that would make an impact with a direct hit. And that's how my poetry changed. In my most recent books, I've tried to bring in the indirectness, the multiple connotations of my earlier style to merge with a certain overall directness that has sunk in deeper. Now, I'm happier with myself.

If you ask me about the place of ideology in poetry, I can only say that it must never constrain the aesthetic quality of the poem. A poet's ideology is like the sap of a tree, which cannot be seen but only imagined. If it has to be integrated in poetry, that must be achieved without doing the slightest damage to the aesthetic quality.

My Sufi beliefs appear in some of my poems, as in "Two-Way Gypsy." They are also in my *Hymns* (*İlahîler*). For instance, two lines in "Hymn for Patience," ("A fret-saw in my heart / round and round I pace on a burning stone") show that life itself can become a "burning stone." For eight years I waited at the gates of a prisonhouse. This poem, like all the others in that collection, were written during those years and belong to a burning phase in my life. My son, who was only nineteen and had just started university, was inside, still a boy. He was released after eight years without a conviction. Can you imagine? All those years spent in vain? Later he won his case at the International Court of Human Rights and received compensation and all that. Such things didn't happen only to us, which is why I dread to dwell on it, but I felt I had to mention it now. Everybody's life was like that in those days in Turkey.

As I was saying, my Sufi beliefs are in my roots. Although I was born in the tenth year of the modern Turkish Republic and raised in an environment that desired a modern outlook but was accustomed to pursuing the traditional way of life, I was not divided by this double perception. On the contrary, they nurtured each other, and this was my greatest advantage. Knowing about modernity and benefiting from it, I was able to ingest the traditional. The Sufi tradition has always remained a fundamental part of me, and my poetry has nothing to do with what is now fashionable in literary and artistic trends.

From *Poems of 42 Days* (*42 Günün Şiirleri*)

By Gülten Akın (1986)
Translated by Saliha Paker and Mel Kenne (2009–2012)

19.

Dear God, may they who deny healing themselves not mend
Dear God, may these days be gone never more to return
And smother us before a swelling breeze can arise

20.
Blight

From the outskirts of Sansayama, the eastern city of many gates, and from villages far and near, they came. It wasn't the imprisonment of their sons, daughters or daughters-in-law that drew those thirteen mothers together. It may not have even been the hunger strike. Because the mothers didn't quite understand what had been happening. They couldn't have understood. The world had to penetrate so many layers of cloakings and taboos before it could reach them. They had always stayed silent, had always been weak, always submissive. Lords of the land, their overlords, fathers, husbands, sons . . . Could they have ever reached the world, have ever made it through all those layers? It was on that side of those folds and layers, in their partly visible dream-world of wood and wire fencing, that they had first opened their eyes. That's all they'd ever known. Nothing else.

The men, now . . . they'd go out. And they'd return bearing signs of the other world on their clothes, in their looks, in their manners and on their tongues—on their tongues especially. The women were left spellbound by the tales they told. Females came into those stories too, with their hair, their lips, their clothes, their money, their demands. With names and titles, and with men who bowed down to them, may God help us.

Then one day the alphabet, along with notebooks, pencils, schools, teachers and writing, reached them. Spanning those layers. If only for show, girls and boys stood side by side. On equal footing. The race was on. Lots of things started happening. Folds and layers started to fray, to wear through. To grow threadbare, beyond repair. Tattered, ready to fall to pieces.

The mothers felt uneasy. A brutal wind from outside was blowing through every rip and tear. They had no one but God to watch over and forgive them. He alone could be trusted. Lately, however, something had happened to him too. Couldn't he see or hear? Why wasn't he fixing the things that were falling apart? Couldn't the mothers go on living as they always had, snug in their sheltered nooks?

No, they couldn't.

The gale that had whisked their sons and daughters off to the prisons was raging too hard to be turned from and ignored. It swept them up. Bore them away to see how their sons, daughters and daughters-in-law were faring. They went each week or two. And they learned about orders, iron bars and force.

Their first link to the outside world was forged by guns, death and blood. That was their introduction. They were educated through pain.

For so many years, on so many occasions, they came to the city walls, entering through a gate in the wall. For so many years they squatted beside walls made of stone and cement, before the iron gates. So many times they came to line up with IDs in their hands. Their names were called out. From afar they saw their sons. They weren't so very different from the mothers of prisoners in other cities. But for one thing: how poor, how desperately poor, these mothers were. To find such poverty as this, we'd need to go back to an age before our age, and to one before that, before the times of worked leather, nylon and plastic, all the way back to the iron age and the stone age. Most of them walked barefoot. These feet had never met rawhide or plastic. Should I swear to this? How else to make you believe that their feet were naked?

As they deboarded the train from the east at the capital city's railway station, they were still bound to their poverty. The feet of two of them yet remained bare. Winter was turning toward spring. The others had at least managed to find some old shoes to wear. But the feet of these two were still totally exposed.

The prison in the eastern city was infamous. Even birds gave it a wide berth. Rumors spread. Were whispered from ear to ear. As the repression, torture, beatings and cruelty became unbearable, death fasts had begun. With each passing day the inmates weakened more. And were carried off to the hospital. Over the headboards of some perched death. An early death.

It was then that the mothers had united. Had taken their petitions in hand. Had somehow scraped up the means to board the train. Had got in touch with people they knew there. Friends who'd come to the station to meet them.

The mothers deboarded at the station of the capital city. And walked and walked and walked. Never once thinking about their heads, their backs or their feet. I can't say they were like "space" creatures, because we've been trained to imagine space people as wearing ultramodern outfits. No, they were more like creatures from the backwaters of time.

As they went on and on, the mute found their tongues, the voiceless found their voices. Those who'd never cried out in anger shouted loudly.

"Come and help us, our sons and daughters are dying."

Why did God stay silent? This was something he could never, ever let pass. He must be waiting for just the right time, one humans couldn't know of. But for the mothers, time had run out, none was left. God said nothing. The big doors stayed closed. Those with authority remained silent. The mothers were bounced like balls from door to door.

On the second day, already death announced itself by telegram. Death, may blight strike you and turn you black.

The sons and daughters-in-law of both barefoot women had died. Then others, more sons. Like crops still green. Yunus, the poet, saw into those whose hearts had been seared so.

The mothers left, taking back not only their bodies but their ashes. After rising up to cross over all those folds and layers, after finally reaching that fairy-tale world of dreams, they'd gotten more than they'd bargained for. They went back. And while they went, they left an offering behind them.

As they made their way along, they took rage, rancor and incalculable pain, mixed them together, and planted them all up and down the roadsides, right where the soil met the cement.

BLIGHT.

Will these structures with seeds of blight creeping into their foundations ever thrive?

The blight will rot them. There'll come a day.

22.
Opened and Reviewed

They knew those we desired
"Reviewed" all that we fancied, what we craved
Which mountains we smashed in our anger
Which rivers we gazed down on in grief
"Reviewed"
Our greetings and barbs

Deep inside us, deep
Down in the seas, in grief-stricken lakes
We bear a longing, we rub it
Each night we make it shine
Without a stamp without a sign

23.
In Passion

They've set him apart. In a place under siege. They've taken him inside walls within walls, filled with wire fences, iron bars and locks. Might he be three steps from the farthest wall? One day he'll prevail against all those windowless walls, those cement courtyards, those narrow corridors, the iron bars. He has no doubt about that. No matter how many years go by, he'll be up to it.

One thing he can't bear. A life without passion. Hunger, thirst, sleeplessness, these he can do without. He's proved it. But he can't exist without passion. That's the one problem he has with himself and still can't solve. If the other end of his passion has no life, he knows this end he's on will rot and fall apart. He has to be able to keep the other end alive too.

Passion was given to him. From outside. Once upon a time. This is the most precious gift, or more truly, the most vital one, he ever received. Do they want to take that away now? Do they want to withdraw that from him so he'll cool down? That's the one thing he won't stand for. Passion must be preserved. Even if it costs him his life.

Intuitively he sees destruction looming. He sees that what he can't touch, what he can't reach right off, is fading away. Nobody can help him. Only he himself can do that. How to stop the deluge descending on him? How to keep it from sweeping that most precious thing away? Passion, however, is looking for excuses to fade away. It wants to take away, one by one, all the loves he's stored up. His feelings for a close relation, a comrade-in-arms, a brother or sister, a friend. Such hopeless cases he can endure. He passes on his loves. He counts them for nothing. At first bit by bit, then the whole lot. He meticulously rubs out his mother and father. With great care erases his friends. He nourishes passion with all he's given up. But passion, just as gigantic, always wants more and more, lots more heads. Until there's only him left.

He agrees to all that. He sacrifices everything and is left with no bonds. The game isn't played in secret. It could never be played that way. He takes up all the painful sounds made by his close relations and friends and hands them over to passion. Passion screams out its triumph.

He doesn't want to see anyone. So he sees no one. He writes to no one. And he forbids anyone to write him. Just look at him there, all on his own. With no protection or defense. Face to face with passion, and one inside the other. At times passion reaches out to him from its outpost of retreat, only to complain, to ask for more, to broadcast signals of despair. Let it stay there. And be just enough not to disappear.

One day, left with nothing of interest or no other life to offer, he offers up his own soul. The soul neither eats nor drinks nor sleeps. Seared by tobacco. Thin, wasted.

On some days, passion doesn't broadcast its signals of hopelessness. Days when it shows its face in greetings or news. Once he's seized onto this lure, he doesn't drop it but runs with it for a long time. He scatters flowers along the roads he hopes he'll be passing down. It's this aspect of the game, this turning to face hope, and beholding it, that brings him back to life. Whether dying or undying, he's made it this far. He'll go even farther.

a (a)

By Zeynep Uzunbay (2006)

Translated by Ronald Tamplin and Saliha Paker (2006)

as mist the word rolls down
to your eyelash tip
tomorrow go once more
be pure be clear
the rose geranium tremble at your breast
rise the three day moon
curled in your soul

i cannot go the children will grow pale
flowers grow pale i cannot go
i wither then and rot

come now it's you who winds
love's kind clock
hush don't speak
don't speak write your name
on the moon's misted page
let it shine
you too shine

i give my word the children will blossom
flowers grow
what i foretell will come true i give my word
flown already to the clouds
the joker there stoops down to glimpse his gear
will keep putting on stripping off your life
no fear you will be shaken

my word is mist

to your finger's tip
tomorrow i'll go once more
may i be pure be clear
the rose geranium tremble at my breast
rise the three day moon
curled then in your soul

sesinle

By Zeynep Uzunbay (1995)

mor imgeli deli pardösümün altında
çıplağım, usulca açıyor sesin düğmelerimi
önce o öpüyor omuzlarımdan

adın kapatıyor dudaklarımı
içime eriyor gitmek

mor imgeli deli pardösüm düşüyor yere
çırılçıplak sarılıyor belime sesin
koşuyor koşuyor yetişemiyoruz ırmağa

* * *

Three Versions:

With Your Voice

Translated by Saliha Paker and Mel Kenne (2006)

under my spring coat's zany purple pattern lies
my nakedness, gently your voice opens unbuttons me
from my shoulders first kissing me

shutting my lips with your name
a letting go melts into me
my spring coat of zany purple designs drops
with your voice stripped naked clutching my waist
on and on we run, still no match for the river

* * *

voice
Translated by Ronald Tamplin and Saliha Paker (2006)

my swinging kaleidoscopic coat
is madder than purple i'm under there
naked, gently your voice unbuttons me
the first kiss is upon my shoulder

your name stops my lips
abandon suffusing in me

the coat kaleidoscopic purple
mad swings falls from me naked
so naked your voice tangles my waist
we run we run yet we cannot
make it to the flowing river

* * *

With Your Voice
Translated by Kurt Heinzelman and Saliha Paker (2006)

Under this blue-paned spring raincoat
I've nothing on, your voice is gentle
unbuttoning it, kissing me first on the shoulders
your name buttons my lips
a closing sweet as parting

my blue-paned spring raincoat slips from me
stark naked your voice embracing my waist
we run and run but cannot make it
                    as far as the river

Saturday Mother[1] (Mahur Beste)

By Ahmet Büke (2010)
Translated by Kenneth Dakan (2011)

—monday

"Ah, Mother."

I'd never said that. I'd said, "Mommy, Mom, Mother Sultan, Mullah Lady," but that was something I'd never known to say. It just spilled right out as she tossed in her sleep.

A patch of streetlight fell on her back first. The flowers on the quilt cover stitched by Zekiye the Tambourine Player from the neighborhood down the way, glowed yellow. Back then too, Mother's gaze would get caught on the ground. On the stray bits of gravel forgotten by the asphalt, on the shadows of cats scurrying by, on threadbare fates . . . Rubbing her bare toes on the carpet, she'd said, "Ah, Zekiye, seeing that you've got a skill like this, you should quit that other job." Pointing with a thimbled finger to the tambourine under the table, Zekiye had murmured, "Never mind, Sister. If I didn't play, how would life go by?" The quilt cover she'd had sewn that day was the one that slipped off her shoulders early this morning.

"Ah, Mother," I said.

People shudder. Then they get a chill. And do they dream the more they shiver? Icy winds are blowing over her in the desert. As she turns her face to the sun, a cold snowy mountain is building on her shoulders. She wants to turn back, but it's impossible, just impossible. Mother's feet are turning into roots, her back into a rugged cliff. An avalanche falls onto her back.

There, she's opened her eyes.

She pulled the end of the quilt up off the floor. She pulled back the curtain a bit more. She looked out at the street. A brush-tailed cat raced over to a garbage can, stretched and dropped inside.

"Water," said Ah-Mother.

---

1. The Saturday Mothers of Turkey is a group (consisting primarily of mothers) that has been gathering since 1995 in front of Galatasaray High School in Istanbul, to demand information on their children or other loved ones who have been disappeared.

Fresh water on a crocheted doily on the side table next to her bed. She moved over to the armchair. She looked at the clock.

"It's late. I must not have heard it," she said.

She said, but her own voice sounded strange to her. In a completely empty house before sunrise, and, what's more, the snow still trickling down from that mountain on her shoulders.

She stood up. Made the bed. Went to the bathroom. I heard the sounds she made. She performed her ablutions in a whisper.

She started praying at the same spot where she'd prayed with my aunt when I was a child a long time ago.

For me and my brother, spoiling prayers was a national sport.

We'd shoot glances at each other whenever my mother and my aunt turned side-by-side towards Mecca.

"Auntie . . . Auntie . . ."

Mom's face would instantly sour. My aunt would start gritting her teeth.

"Auntie, Mom made some pistachio *kadayıf*, two trays full, it's just great. Look, it's oozing flavor."

We'd begin smacking our lips at our imaginary kadayıf dessert.

The instant my big brother smacked me on the back with, "You greedy bear, don't eat the whole thing," my aunt would rock back on her heels and burst out laughing.

Mother chasing after us with a slipper snatched from the floor and cries of "little buggers . . .," we'd be out the door in no time flat.

Mother turned her head to the right, and to the left. She set her prayer beads on the hem of her prayer scarf. She went over to the sofa. She looked at the clock. Outside, the morning cool flowed up and over the rooftops, gently snuffing out the night lights. The morning brightness unfolded in pomegranate blossom. Cars stalled and wheezed. Sashed at the waist red and yellow, this side of the world started the day.

Mother looked down at the floor again. At the old carpet that runs from the foot of the table, the corner of her eye landing on a corner of the carpet, on a tiny motif she'd never noticed. Two tiny silhouettes. They rose up and embraced. Also rising up to the ceiling were memories mixed with pain, longing and nurturing, memories which had been hovering and circling for some time, incomprehensible to those who've never known what that is, invisible to those who've never seen it—those memories that take the form of a familiar scent bursting from pillows, of regrets, of if-only's, of the inability to forget anything at all, of loving more deeply the more you remember.

Ah.

Mother.

She nodded off as the day began.

"Let her sleep," I said. With the back of my hand, I scattered the particles of cold falling onto her shoulders. Because that much I could do.

—tuesday

Zekiye and Aunt Gülten came over this evening. They were going to poke their heads in and go. At mother's insistence they came inside.

"Tea, coffee?"

"Don't go to any trouble. We just came to check up on you."

Zekiye put her tambourine on the edge of the living room table. "Not just to check up, Gülten Hanım."

"Oh, that's right."

"Anything the matter?" mother asked.

It was the visitors who insisted this time.

You know how the grocer's grandson was going to get married, and at first the girl dug in her heels and said no, and then, when the boy said he'd changed his mind, she sobbed and had fits; well, the girl's mother paid a visit to the boy's mother, and said, Ayşen's going to cut her wrists, she's so feeble that yesterday when she was having some soup a noodle got stuck in her throat and she couldn't breathe until her father picked her up by the heels and shook her like a kilim; meanwhile, Ayşen was in the storage closet with her wedding things, in the dark and the smell of mothballs, sniffling and sniveling as she waited, phone in hand, for some good news from her mother, while, at that very moment, the boy was in the kitchen with his breakfast in front of him, busy flicking ash onto the eggshells and listening to what they were saying out in the hallway.

"Then what happened?" Mother said.

Completely forgetting about the tea, she waited at the door.

Zekiye smoothed her skirt and continued.

"Well, then the boy said okay."

When the girl got the phone call with the good news, she jumped up and down in the closet. Oh my God, it's an earthquake, her father cried, springing up from his nap and throwing himself out the door in his underwear.

"For goodness sake, Zekiye, stop being so silly," Aunt Gülten said.

So now they're going to the henna night. And Mother has to go too. But how can I? What business have I got there? No, you've got to come. How many more years will it be before we see a smile on your face? This is life, and it goes on. I made a promise to myself. Zekiye, I swear I'll go off and sulk. Look, you're my witness. That's right, sister, I swear I'll never speak to you again. Besides, we're all neighbors. We'll kick up our heels for a minute and clear out. I don't expect you to waggle your head and wiggle your hips or anything. My goodness, Zekiye, the way you shoot off your mouth. But it's the truth, isn't it? She should come, it'll clear her mind and cheer her up. Don't keep pushing me. I'm telling you, you're coming. We're all going to the party tonight, and that's that.

Toward midnight, on the way back home, Mother slipped her arm through Aunt Gülten's.

"I've made up my mind. I'm going to Istanbul this week."

Aunt Gülten gave Mother a sideways glance.

"If it'll do you good, go."

"It'll do me good," Mother said.

They said their goodbyes on the corner.

We walked along, Mother ahead, me trailing. A sheepdog stopped next to me, and growled. Through my teeth I went "hissss." The dog drooped its tail and fled to Mother.

—wednesday

"Here's your change, ma'am," said the man with the thin moustache.

Mother was lost in the picture frame in her hand.

Mom, is the *köfte* ready? Ah, my son the rascal. Where's your bag? It's starting to rain. You're sweaty. Look, don't go anywhere near that girl again. Come on, wake up, the service bus will be here soon. Why are these men asking about you? Who are these people at my door? What's going on? Hello? Metin, come help find that brother of yours. He hasn't been home for days. No no no no no no attorney petition why are these walls so gray my feet so cold open the door where is he where I'm here at the window all the time perched like a bird on the sofa my eye on the street day and night the patter of feet cars that sound just a cat ah the neighbors who are these men why do they look like they're going to kill me give him back to me give him back he's innocent no no he'll come I'm not going to sleep he'll come tonight . . .

"Ma'am . . ." the photographer repeated. I brushed Mother's shoulder. She snapped out of it.

"You forgot your change."

"Ah, thank you, thanks."

The frame, me and Ah-Mom went back home.

—thursday

Anxious and tense, my big brother is pacing around the middle of the room.

"Metin, could you sit down for a minute. I feel all dizzy."

Slumped into the armchair next to Mom's, my sister-in-law is toying with the tassels on the throw pillow. Mother is calm, and occupied with wiping her glasses.

"Mother, how are you going to get there?"

"There's a bus, son."

"That's not what I mean. You don't know the road, don't know the way. All alone . . ."

"I've taken care of that. Someone's meeting me."

"Ah, Mom, you've got high blood pressure."

"I've got my pills. I'll take two if I have to."

"Look, I'm the one that should be going, not you. Okay?"

"You've got things to do. Anyway, what do you mean by you, and not me."

"Look, Mother . . ."

"Metin. Son. Stop saying that. I told you I was going. Come on, I've cooked up some greens. Let's all eat together."

My big brother sank down onto the sofa next to the window. He looked at the hands of my sister-in-law. He felt like going over and holding those long, slender fingers in his.

They all sat down to dinner together. The news began on the TV.

—friday

That bus station smell of the road came and settled in our noses. Mother is fastening the buttons on her coat. Next to her is a small bag, and next to that a plastic bag standing upright and four-cornered. My big brother is chain-smoking. Arms crossed, my brother's wife is watching them.

"Mother, call us when you get there, okay? Your phone's working, isn't it? Have you got enough phone minutes and everything?"

"I've got everything, don't worry."

She took a slip of paper from her pocket and handed it to my brother's wife.

"Could you save this number on your phone, my girl? They're picking me up when I get off the bus."

While my sister-in-law was dealing with the phone number, my big brother tried to tuck some money into my mother's pocket. Mother isn't having it. She's practically beating him up with her eyes.

The bus.

Ah.

Ah.

Mother.

The next seat over is empty. Together, we look at fields rippling towards the moonlight. Rooms lit and unlit. Inside them, people; inside them, children, mothers.

Sleep is taking hold of the living.

—saturday

The thin, brown-haired girl who picked us up, points.

"Here we are, Auntie, that's Galatasaray High School."

Mother looked at the crowd that had gathered.

A woman came over to us. She rested her hands on Mother's shoulders and spoke. Mother didn't understand, and neither did I.

The girl smiled. "She says welcome. She asked how you were."

Mother smiled back.

"Thank you, nice to be here . . ."

She went and sat down on the pavement with the others. She opened the plastic bag and took out the picture frame.

As a pigeon with black markings flew by, the one next to me brushed my arm.

"Do you remember the day you had that photograph taken?" he said.

I thought about it.

"I think it's the photo taken for my driver's license."

He smiled.

"Good for you," he said. "I've been thinking and thinking, and I can't remember when mine was taken."

I looked at the photograph he was pointing to. He looked handsome in it.

"Who's holding it up," I asked. "Your mother?"

"No, my big sister. My mother's gotten old. She can't come here. What about yours?"

"My mother."

He smiled. We smiled at each other.

I looked at Mother. She was fumbling for a handkerchief. She checked her coat pocket. The woman sitting next to her offered her the one she held. Mother took it, and wiped her eyes.

Voices, smells and birds passed over us.

From *Lonelinesses* (*Yalnızlıklar*)

By Hasan Ali Toptaş (1993)

1.

Translated by Mel Kenne and Şehnaz Tahir Gürçağlar (2006)

Seen from any angle,
in each sentence there's a pair of eyes
and in every full stop a human being.
This someone who observes us and looks beyond us;
a someone who, if he peers behind his outfit of time
always
remains worried, hesitant and quiet;
and if in saying I've come there's a silence, or in saying
let's kiss, if in saying you haven't left yet or
in wanting to die there's a silence,
then silence has its own words
and every stance as well:
a look, a reaching out,
a smile . . .

But loneliness has no words.
This word composed of every other word.

2.

Translated by Ronald Tamplin and Şehnaz Tahir Gürçağlar (2006)

Where is lonely? It is the architect
of architectures. The story of the story
not the one on the paper, the way that poem
sounds, the color of the song,
the singer, the bone behind the glance
of a thousand years, always
each way we turn our eyes
stopping, standing there.
Each moment it finds other clothes
shelved in the past,
writes every sentence,
it is every word,
behind each page the mirrored silver,
the presenting eye.

Lonely writes: it reads.

The Plan (Şema)

By Sevgi Soysal (1976)

Translated by Amy Spangler (2010)

The latest big thing to happen in the ward is the arrival of the new captain. There are two things the captain is particularly fond of. One is talking, the other is asking questions.

These two characteristics of Captain Kemal have nothing to do with the people he addresses. Because when he speaks, he's not the least bit interested in the listeners or the questions they may have.

He does the talking, and he asks the questions. That's it.

He's our new prison director. Captain Kemal is the director of Yıldırım District only though, while Saldıraner is the head of the federation of military prisons, which includes Yıldırım District and Mamak.

Captain Kemal is determined to bring innovations in his capacity as a member of the federated administration of Yıldırım District. He wants us to be more prisoner-like and more soldier-like too.

This being the case, he expects everything, from eating to sleeping, to be strictly regimented in compliance with the dictates of military order and discipline, so that in the likely event of war, Yıldırım District prisoners will be capable of executing a flawless military response.

The Captain is doing everything in his power to make sure that when we are released from the prison, we leave as perfect little soldiers.

He frequently stops by to inspect the ward.

Before the Captain's inspection, we line up in front of our bunks for the headcount. First, a petty officer issues the command:

"Atteeeeen-tion!"

While we stand at attention in front of the bunks, the Captain poses his questions:

He points at the table we eat at everyday.

"What's this?"

"That's a table, sir."

He opens and closes the pantry containing the bread provided by the military.

"What's this?"

"That's a pantry, sir."

On the table are flowers brought by friends and family during visiting hours.

"What are these?"

"Those are flowers, sir."

"What are they doing here?"

"They're being flowers, sir."

While the Captain goes on and on asking such questions, we continue to stand at attention in front of the bunks. Our feet are killing us.

This time the Captain heads over to the corner where the girls' drawings are hung. He examines the drawings.

"What are these?"

"Those are drawings, sir."

Then he examines the bunks.

"Why are these bunks like this?"

"Those bunks are bunks, sir."

"Hmmm . . . No . . . No . . . That's not going to cut it."

When the Captain starts saying, "Hmm" and "no" and "not going to cut it," that means he's about to transition from the "question" to the "speech" part of his verbal salvo.

Standing at the head of the long table, he embarks upon his speech.

"The layout of this ward is not according to plan. This ward must be laid out according to plan. And then a plan must be made of the layout. The plan in question shall then be hung on the opposite wall! Everyone shall settle into her bunk according to the plan. The plan shall show the order of the bunks.

"1.a) Sevgi Soysal's bunk

"2.b) Olcay Altınay's bunk

"The bunk beds in the far right corner shall be written in the upper right corner, and the bunk beds in the far left corner shall be written in the upper left corner. Those who sleep on the right side shall be noted on the plan according to their places on the right side, and those on the left side shall take their places on the left side as indicated in the plan.

"The seating order for meals too shall be explicitly stated in the plan.

"Meals shall be eaten according to the plan.

"Those on the right side shall take their places on the right side of the table, according to the plan, and those on the left side shall take their places on the left side."

At Yıldırım District, "at ease" is one of the commands we like least of all. As if it were possible for us to be at ease here. But if the Captain wants to continue this travesty and say "at ease," I'll be more than happy to put myself "at ease." My hands, pressed tightly against my pants, are clammy with sweat.

I fix my eyes on Nina, who's standing just across from me. Nina bites her lip to keep from laughing. This is awful; if Nina starts laughing, I'll never be able to keep a straight face. And if I burst into laughter, well, that's it, I'll be in stitches.

But I don't laugh; there's nothing to laugh about.

The Captain carries on with his educational session.

"When you go to the mess hall, you shall get in line according to the list. A list shall be drawn up and hung on this wall. Mess shall be taken in order according to this list. You shall sit and eat according to the plan.

"There shall be no breach of the order dictated by the plan.

"The order for both taking mess and sleeping shall be in accordance with the plan."

I look away from Nina to keep myself from laughing. This time I look at Tülin. She's standing in line, in front of the bunk just across from me. It's much better looking into Tülin's eyes. There isn't the slightest sign of laughter in Tülin's big eyes with the long black lashes. As I look into Tülin's eyes, I sense that she's not well. She's definitely not well; her eyelids grow heavy. As she stands at attention, she seems to be swaying.

I turn to face the captain.

"Captain, our friend is not well."

The Captain doesn't hear me. During his speeches, he'll have nothing to do with his listeners.

He continues:

"The names of all items in the ward shall be written on them. A piece of paper with the name of the person to whom it belongs shall be attached to each of the bunks. And everyone's name shall be written on the table according to the seating order."

Tülin's really wobbly now and her face has turned yellow.

"The names of the owners shall be indicated on the suitcases on top of the wardrobe. The suitcases shall be lined up in accordance with the order valid for the bunks and mess."

* * *

Drops of sweat run down my back. It's like I've been nailed to the spot here in front of my bunk. A voice inside me tells me to run and fill a glass of water from the faucet and make Tülin drink it. But it's like my hands are handcuffed to my legs.

"There are to be no items in the ward other than the pieces of state property that belong here. There are to be no drawings or pictures attached to the walls other than the plans, lists and the codes of conduct. You are to exit to the yard in accordance with the order valid for sleeping and eating. The order for exiting to the yard is furthermore to be written on a piece of paper. Your spokesperson shall hand this piece of paper over to the police. Before exiting to the yard, you shall line up in order in accordance with the line-up for exiting to the yard. When the ward door is opened, you shall be in line according to the line-up for exiting to the yard. You shall march out in order in single file in accordance with the plan for exiting to the yard. The plan shall be hung to the right of the door. To the left side of the door the codes of conduct shall be hung . . ."

I'm afraid to look up at Tülin. She's swaying back and forth, only the whites of her eyes are visible; my hands are released from their cuffs, and I take a step towards Tülin. At that moment, the entire ward takes a step towards Tülin. But before her friends on either side of her are able to grab her, she collapses to the floor like an empty sack.

We don't know whether the Captain is still talking or not. All of us run to Tülin's side, gathering around her. Someone brings a glass of water.

The Captain turns the corner of the long table and approaches Tülin, who is lying on the floor.

He looks at her as if looking at some thing, at some item he'd never before seen in his life; he looks at her with some surprise.

Actually, a few moments before, one of the girls had put forth an explanation, saying, "Our friend's passed out." But the Captain must not have heard.

After examining the girl lying on the ground, he asks:

"What's this?"

"This is a passed out convict," I nearly say, but I can't. The Captain leaves the ward, his subordinates in tow.

From "The Return," Part V of *Secret Domain* (Dönüş, *Gizli Alanlar* V)

By Güven Turan (2010)

Translated by Ruth Christie (2012)

CCXIII.
To throw a fig whole
into the mouth

Between tongue and palate
to savor its texture
its smell
its sweetness

Association of the senses

All
are innocent

CCXIV.
A smell

Peppery
smoke

The child
comes out
from his hiding place

They're burning
fresh laurel branches
laurel leaves

Here is not

that shore

Where has the child gone

CCXV.
To track
the sleeping cat

Inertia
stops
at the end of its tail

Where does your inertia
end

How have you managed to hide the panic
in your eyes

CCXXIV.
To look inside
an emptied
coffee cup

In the morning
No coffee grounds
no signs to read
A slight stain
at the bottom
round the rim

Tarnish

Can't tell
my future or
the past

CCXXV.
The sky is blue

Is the word
appropriate

The sky is changeable

And there's one
who likes
the blue of hyacinths

CCXXVI.
To confront grief
with grief
The conflict
is in midsummer
In the sea

Exactly between two fathoms
while the arm is upraised

Easy
in autumn

San Gimignano (San Gimignano)

By Güven Turan (1999)
Translated by Ruth Christie (2012)

Not the towers
– your terrible fear of heights
you never tried the climb –
not the streets,
nor the squares
ringed by houses
with no windows
or doors

Three things:

A gaze from the wall
to the plain, right down to Volterra,
sun and shadows racing
under a sky that shifts
cloudy to clear

In the Piazza della Cisterna
as soon as the cafés
come alight
waves of darkness
spread through the sky
the rooks in flight

Strange smell,
an old library smell
of golden brown
–huge mushrooms,
rising

from the basket
gripped in the knees of an old woman

What more did you expect
from an Etruscan town.

The Poet's Share of Words

Excerpt from a Talk by Haydar Ergülen (2006)
Translated by Şehnaz Tahir Gürçağlar (2006)

Mother, child, pain, bird, rain . . .

The first poem of my first book is entitled "Mother." "Was it really you who gave birth to me, Mother / when roads, rivers and mid-mornings are all there / is a child born by a human / . . . / Mother, can a heart of stone take it / can a heart of birds, a heart of flowers, a heart of daytime take it / won't a violet bend and break in pain / . . . / this time let the mountains give birth to me mother / and you can become a warm raindrop / raining on my bleeding parts." This poem I wrote in 1980 is a poem written in pain to remember the destruction caused by the 12 September military coup and to pay tribute to my friends who were killed during that time. It aspires to raise a silent objection, if not resistance, to the inhuman practices of those days.

"Mother" is one of my most popular poems among readers, critics and poets. It can also be considered a summary of my poetry. As some critics have rightfully argued, the sound of my poetry has not changed much since those days and that particular poem. I can even maintain that it has not changed at all. The words and images I used have not changed much either: mother, child, pain, bird, rain . . . Throughout the years, I have added new words and images to these, but the new ones have not been that new or different, or as colorful. In a way, they are all colors that have a place in the same picture, images that can be thought of in the same framework. These are some of the words and themes: kindness, grief, love, home, brotherhood/sisterhood, nature, countryside, balcony, courtyard, garden, aspiration, word, letter, friendship, death, body, paper, memories and poetry.

I believe in *nasip* (one's allotment in life) even as I aspire to write poetry. Each poem, and each poet even, has her or his lot, or share, of words. That is why, even if I do not regard them as my own "property," I think that certain words are exclusive to certain poets. And that is why I believe that a poet should write with few words. I look for these words in the poems a poet has written (or even in the ones a poet has not written), for I think it is important for the poet to hold to his or her own cause. It is also necessary to avoid wasting the words or accumulations of other poets, if one is to be satisfied with one's lot.

Letter to God (Tanrıya Mektup)

By Haydar Ergülen (1999)
Translated by İpek Seyalıoğlu (2006)

1.
I just saw the clouds
start to pile up in the sky, God
and I saw that you're
writing a poem in secret

2.
I think of you sometimes
God, it grieves me.
Cats, birds, clouds,
trees, grass, fish,
girls, boys, children,
if only you were theirs alone,
not the God of the whole
great humankind!

3.
In civil war
God is killed first
then the good people
among us

4.
My God, so many trees
you've got here,
and so many people
who say "in this world
I don't even have
one tree planted
only for me"

If you ever decide
to create another tree,
please let it be
a Human Tree

5.
The clouds you've shown me,
God, an artist has seen them too
and thought you were an artist!

6.
Wise enough to stay in this world,
nomadic enough to risk life,
in search of a pearl and deep
enough to get lost in the self,
and intense enough to gush out
even after a brief allusion to water . . .

What are humans, if not
masters at waving goodbye
to everything before they lose it?

But God, I guess you'd
waved goodbye to us
even before we did

7.
When a village burns
the silence of the world dies
the whispering of kissing dies
when a forest burns up

when they burn down a hotel
the guestwork of poetry dies

the laughter of childhood dies
when a city burns down

Whoever sets life on fire,
God will set their hearts
in ice

8.
God, either forget you've created this world
or don't altogether forget me in this world!

We're Lonely, Brother Cemal
(Yalnızız Cemal Abi)

By Haydar Ergülen (1999)

Translated by Elizabeth Pallitto and Arzu Eker Roditakis (2012)

This *rakı*, Cemal brother
you know, drinking this rakı with you
was like going to Kars

In your poems, how we would drink rakı
for hours, you know, Cemal brother,
we would go to Kars for ages

You know, after you, Cemal my brother,
no poem goes to Kars
Kars is brief, rakı tasteless
in poetry, after you,
everything hits bottom
see how lonely we are

My Big Brother (Ağbim)

By Behçet Çelik (2002)
Translated by İdil Aydoğan (2009)

My brother called this afternoon; who would've thought. "We're coming over tonight," he said, without asking whether we'd be home or not. I didn't ask any questions; I could guess why he was coming. His voice was cold, he kept the greetings and so on short, and the harsh tone of his voice upset me. I had been planning to get through all the work piled up on my desk, but I just couldn't; I was glued to the spot. For some time I had been telling people that there was no one on this earth who could make me happy, and no one who could make me sad, and I kept complaining that people's words are nothing but lies. All of a sudden, I understood that despite everything, there's always someone, someone whose words speak to you, from deep down.

I went shopping after work. I bought *rakı*, meat for the *çiğköfte*, fruit and vegetables. I walked in one end of our neighborhood's street market (it was that day of the week) and out the other. But the parade of colors that always soothed me on my most agonizing days wasn't enough to lighten the heaviness of my heart. The closer I got to home, the more nervous I became. The house had been a living nightmare for the past three days as it was. I hoped to God my brother wouldn't make a big deal out of it. When I walked into the house, my wife still wore the same long face. I spoke my first sentence in three days.

"My brother's coming over."

She spoke her first sentence in three days.

"I know."

We worked in the kitchen without brushing against each other. My wife washed the onions, and as I chopped them up into tiny pieces, I was thinking that my brother would solve our problem. His visit alone would be enough, perhaps. Seeing as we had started cooking together before he'd even got here . . . For the past three days, we had practically been avoiding each other under the same roof, much less doing anything together.

At around eight, when my brother and sister-in-law arrived, I had just started kneading the çiğköfte. I had poured myself a glass of rakı, and was drinking it; the rakı glass was smudged with tomato puree and bulgur. My brother had a long face; I kept smiling. I wondered why on earth we didn't see each other more often, and I realized how much I missed him.

The three of them sat at the table; I was still in the kitchen, slowly kneading the köfte mix. Was I buying myself some time? Or maybe I was doing this so my brother would come into the kitchen and talk to me; that is, if he was going to. He didn't come. But his voice did; I heard him yelling from the living room:

"Where the hell are those köftes!"

"Go ahead and start, don't wait for me."

One summer, the two of us worked together at my father's kebab shop. As a child, I used to work there every summer, but that summer, my brother needed to behave. A relative of ours had whispered into my father's ear, "Your boy's drawing too much attention, it could spell trouble," so my father put him at the cash register to keep an eye on him. He was bored; he looked out the window onto the street all day. Startled by the slightest sound, he'd sit bolt upright, alert, as if he were about to make a run for it. He never drank in front of my father; he would run and hide in the kitchen, and I would be the one to hide his rakı and his cigarettes. I envied how he gulped down the rakı, and the moustache he had. The moustache he hasn't had for a few years now.

The night his best friend was shot, he told my father he was leaving. My father's eyes were ablaze. Unable to say a word, he just sank into the chair my brother had been sitting in for months. I was mad at my brother back then. Not long after that, two years later, when the classmate who sat next to me was shot the exact day after he had given me his worry beads, the only person I wanted to talk to was my brother. He was in prison. I was silent for days.

Here I was, silent again, for a totally different reason. Again I was convinced that the only person who could understand me was my brother. I was afraid, not that he would get mad at me and scold me, but that he wouldn't understand me. He sounded irritated on the phone. He would go on about what an irresponsible, ungrateful asshole I was. He would praise my wife, as if I didn't know . . .

Once I had finished placing the köftes on the plate, there was nothing left to keep me from joining them at the table.

As soon as I sat down I asked, "So, how's business going?"

He gave me a reproachful look, as if to say, "You really think now is the right time?"

"Not too bad," he said. I needed some time, and a few glasses of rakı.

"Were you affected by the downturn?" I asked.

This time his eyes were saying, "You'll never grow up."

"No, because we don't do business with Italy. Last year we almost did a deal with the Russians; thank God we didn't."

I told him about the company I worked for and how they were affected by the downturn, although he hadn't asked. Was he mad at me for not working for his company? I'd always wondered. We had never talked about it. He had never offered me a job, and I had never asked for one. After I decided to settle down in Istanbul, I started working for an old friend of his. I wouldn't have been given the job if it weren't for him. Whenever I got the sudden urge to run off and never look back, I would suppress it, to save my brother the shame it would cause him. If I had been working for my brother, nothing could have stopped me. When you decide to settle down somewhere, you want to cast your anchor into the deepest seas.

My wife and sister-in-law left the table and sat in front of the television. My brother raised his head and looked at me. He'd usually come home late, and as he ate the food our sister had prepared, he'd look up at me and wink; I thought he was going to give me that look again. But no, he wasn't smiling, wasn't showing his dimple, the dimple on his cheek that looked like a blade cut, that startled you when he was angry, and which you envied when he smiled.

I put my hand on his shoulder and squeezed tightly. He shook his head. It wasn't a gesture of sympathy or anger; it was a gesture addressing himself, not anyone else.

"It's not right, what you've done," he said. I didn't answer him. I looked him straight in the eye and stared.

"It's not right," he said again. He was the one to look away.

I looked at him. "I haven't done anything wrong." I wanted to say, "I still keep the secrets I was trusted with, like precious stones. I never told anyone about the secret safe where you kept your gun. And no one else but me knows about how you used to secretly meet up with Zeynep." There was a letter my brother sent me from prison. If I went digging for it, I'd find it somewhere. At the end of the letter he had written, "Say hello to her." He had never told me before that there was someone he loved, but he knew that I knew. Zeynep was a pretty girl. She had big black eyes. For days I waited outside her house, anxiously. One morning, I caught her on her own as she was going to the market and said "Hello." Her face lit up when she saw me. Once again, I was proud of being my brother's brother. I said, "My brother says hello." She blushed. "Tell him I say hello too," she said, and quickly walked away. I wonder where Zeynep is now.

The longer my brother remains silent, the more I sweat. Rakı always makes me sweat anyway.

"How's the spice in the köfte?"

"Good." A single word. A single word is worse than silence. You can guess that a person who is silent doesn't want to talk. But the meaning of a single word reply is obvious: "Shut up!"

The longer he was silent, the more drunk I became. "Please talk to me, brother," I begged him silently. "Say something. Hear my testimony. Scream and shout at me. I'm not going to lie to you; I couldn't. I lied to my wife because I didn't want to hurt her, to upset her. People nowadays are so strange, brother. Someone wasted no time telling her. I'd been seen with another woman. 'Who said so?' I asked. 'It doesn't matter,' she replied. The guy at the reception desk looked quite suspicious. Could it be him? Why on earth had I argued with him? How could I have guessed that the bastard would go and do this . . ."

I wish we had met, just the two of us, instead of him coming over with his wife. Then perhaps we wouldn't have fallen silent, but talked. About father, mother, Zeynep, the old days, today. I would tell him about my lover, and how much I still loved my wife. I would tell him about how my friends found this strange and said, "You can fool yourself, but you can't fool us," and about how I consoled myself, saying, "My brother would understand me, he and I share the same cells, the same strange genetic code."

"Say something, brother. Tell me, is your heart like mine? I toss and turn in bed at night; I think of one when I turn to the left, and the other when I turn to the right. When I'm with one, I miss the other. I know you're just like me. There's something about us, something excessive, or something lacking, in us . . . I don't know."

I'm sure my brother knows what's going on inside me. That night, he could hear what I said, but he remained silent, to punish me.

They stayed until midnight. My brother and I drank, we drank a lot, but we didn't talk. Even his face was tense. It was like he'd start crying if he just let go a little. He sat there with a stone-like face, and drank.

As they were leaving, "Family, family is what's important," he said. We were seeing them off at the door. Nervous, I reached out for my wife's hand, which I thought she would pull away; her hand was sweaty. My brother had silently solved our problems. His presence was enough. I was looking at my brother, my eyes full of gratitude. I didn't let go of my wife's hand; I was holding onto it tightly when I saw the look my sister-in-law gave my brother; there was resentment in her eyes; I ignored it. At that moment, I wanted to hold my brother tightly in my arms.

I may not have known how to be silent, how to comfort others in silence, the way he did, but I did know how to touch.

It didn't happen. He said, "Take care," and walked out the door.

A Cold Fire (Soğuk Bir Ateş)

By Behçet Çelik (2004)
Translated by Jonathan Ross (2009)

When they left the house, the sun was shining, but by the time they came to the last buildings on the edge of town, dark gray clouds had covered the sky, leaving room for not even a splash of blue. On their way there, they had agreed that they would sit outside and get some fresh air, but the first drops of rain scared them off, and they moved to the covered area. So it was through the grimy windows that they would be looking at the trees, the dirty green river, and the clouds descending gradually towards the horizon.

When they entered, they noticed that only one table was occupied; the couple sitting there were in their forties, or perhaps much older. They chose to sit at a table far away from them. While drinking his first beer, the man didn't pay any attention to the people at the other table. They talked about the past. Around the time that he had bought his first car, he and his family had often come to this part of the world. Back then, his son, who was just clinking glasses with him, was still in primary school. They chatted about those days too. About how the area they were sitting in now used to be a popular picnic spot, before it filled up with tea gardens, then beerhouses and so on.

Having finished their first beers, the father and son hardly said a word to one another. Something was bothering the father. Maybe it was the couple at the other table. For some reason or other, the father had the idea that they were having an affair. The man at that table seemed fairly well-off; it was clear that he could afford to go to much higher-class establishments. Like the window glass, the tables in this joint, which was difficult to define—was it a scruffy tea garden or a pub?—were dirty, and the place itself was enough to bring out the gloomy side of the most cheerful person in no time at all. The man thought that the couple had gone there so as to avoid running into anyone they knew. There were times when he didn't want to be seen by anyone either, though not because he was involved in any kind of affair. Whenever an acquaintance happened to ask him, "What are you doing here all on your own?," it was more difficult to give a sincere answer than to come up with an excuse. He wasn't sure whether the problem was with the size of the small town he lived in or with its inhabitants, or whether he was a coward; whatever the reason, he chose to keep himself locked away at home.

Did his son like wandering around town on his own? He could think of nothing that might help him find a definitive answer to this question. And he felt really ashamed, as if he had committed a great sin. For twenty years they had been living together under the same roof, and on the face of it, he and his wife had raised this boy together, but the truth was he wouldn't be able to answer even the simplest question about his son. There were questions that he wanted to ask him but hadn't been able to. At breakfast that morning, when his wife mentioned that she was expecting visitors in the afternoon, he suggested to his son that they go out somewhere together. He had hoped he'd have a chance to ask all those questions he hadn't asked yet so was happy when his son replied, "Good idea, Dad, let's go!," and he suggested that they go to the lakeside. Now, though, his son wasn't saying a word, and he realized he wouldn't be able to ask about those things that sometimes preyed on his mind. It would seem forced. His son might think that he'd been brought here for interrogation. Perhaps there were things that he wanted to say and he was just waiting for his father to ask, but having downed that first beer, his father started to feel that he'd missed the boat long ago.

Every now and then, the father's eyes fixed on the people at the other table. Maybe it was their sullen demeanor that made him feel he'd missed the boat. Although he avoided looking at them too blatantly, he still followed them out of the corner of his eye. The man was clearly affluent; the woman didn't really appear to be in the same league. Given the time they had chosen to meet, it was clear that this was not a relationship the man was paying for. Still, it was an illicit love, one that would remain so forever, illicit and hopeless . . .

And then the father wished he could have a relationship like that, a fling only possible in out-of-the-way beer halls. A relationship in which there was no touching—someone might spot them—and no talking either—what was there to talk about? Perhaps sometimes, in a dirty hotel room, a fire would be extinguished—a cold fire extinguished in cold weather.

All of a sudden he felt ashamed that, with his son sitting right opposite him, he had started fantasizing about being with a woman other than his wife. What he should have been doing was discussing his son's dreams. Next year his son was going to finish university. He wondered what he wanted to do then. He'd never asked him about things like that. Most of the time it turned out that he didn't need to ask; his son made up his mind on his own. It was only after his son had submitted his university application that he found out which schools he'd chosen to apply to. He was a bit hurt by this. Not because his son hadn't asked him or told him anything, but because he'd always had this idea that his son would go and study in Istanbul or Ankara. His son, however, placed their local university at the top of the list and managed to get in. At first, the father thought that his son had done this to avoid being a financial burden on the family, which upset him. After all, he'd set aside some money for his son's education. He was angry with himself that he hadn't made this clear when the time was right. But a while later he understood why his son had made this choice: he had no passion, no ideals. No desire to go to the big city, to discover new worlds. Sometimes he reckoned that, if he said to his son, "Forget about university; just get a job and start working," his son would take this advice, without being upset or getting into a huff.

He thought about how he had been in his youth. He'd talked about it umpteen times with his wife, and even more with himself. "There was nothing I wouldn't do," he said, "to get out of this town. Even when I was in middle school I realized that you couldn't get anywhere in this town." His wife's answer was always the same—that this town wasn't the same as the one they had grown up in; it had developed and was now a proper city. Well, he'd been living here for fifty years, and as far as he was concerned, it had nothing to offer. His wife listed the cinemas, shops and shopping malls that had opened up, and couldn't understand what her husband felt was missing.

The son obviously took after his mother. His father had never been able to explain to his mother what exactly was missing in the town, so how could he be expected to explain it to his son? Some things were missing for sure, but he couldn't spell out what they were. The moment he tried to explain, the sentences he formed struck him as meaningless. He could only convey this feeling to someone who knew it themselves, but such a person didn't exist. He had a few good friends who likewise weren't so keen on the town and who were forever lamenting the fact that they hadn't moved elsewhere when they had the chance. But their expectations were different. What riled them was that they weren't able to do enough business, to lead the more luxurious kind of life they saw on television. What really got to him was that his wife saw herself as belonging to this category. He wanted to say, "No, we're not like them," but because he couldn't put into words what they *were* like, he remained silent.

Whenever a new play or concert came to town, he and his wife would quarrel. His wife would get angry, saying, "You're the one who likes stuff like that; I just don't get why you don't want to go and watch." He couldn't bring himself to say that the mere thought of sitting together in an auditorium with everyone he didn't want to see or to be seen by simply suffocated him. It made him sick that while he was trying to be invisible, all those people around him were jumping through hoops to get noticed. This was why, when he went to the cinema with his wife, it was for the weekday matinees rather than at the weekend. So many times he watched a film together with his wife which he had already watched on his own, just so the poor woman wouldn't get upset! On the other hand, for years he had fantasized about bumping into his son when he went to watch a film on the sly, his son having bunked off school on his own or together with friends. But their paths never did cross, not once, in this town where there was such a strong likelihood of running into absolutely anyone at any time and place.

If he'd had the opportunity to speak with his son about such matters, he would have asked him what he saw in this town. He would have asked him why he had chosen not to go elsewhere, even though he had the possibility. He'd failed in bringing up a child. The more he looked at his son, the stronger he felt this. Being a father wasn't about sending one's child to a good school, being generous with pocket money, decking out a wardrobe; it was about sharing one's passion, passing it on. He hadn't passed his on. And yet the son was quite content with the father. He would always speak with great pride about how, when his family sat down and discussed things, his father never imposed anything on him. Whenever his friends at secondary school talked about their fathers, they always complained about how much they meddled in their lives. The clothes they wore, the music they listened to—these were always a problem. In fact, the son had once declared, "I'm lucky." That evening, his father had been really pleased, had felt so proud. Now, though, he was wondering where he had gone wrong. He knew that he'd made fewer mistakes than the others, but this didn't change the fact that he and his son had been sitting there for an hour without really saying anything. He couldn't ask about those things that were nagging at his mind. Clearly, in his effort not to interfere, he'd allowed his son to slip from his hands.

If things went on the way they were, the son wouldn't turn out disgruntled like his father. When he reached his father's age, he wouldn't find regret and self-reproach gnawing away at him. But what would become of him? "That's his problem," the father thought to himself, "Why the hell am I being so gloomy?" He'd always been a loner. At the time of their marriage, he and his wife had been head over heels in love, but even when he held her he felt alone. As he did when he was out drinking with his friends. It never changed. Had he believed that, once he grew up, his son would fill the vacuum inside him? Was this what he resented?

Looking at his son's gelled hair brought a smile to his face. Was he trying to imitate those foreign pop stars? When the father was young, one of his biggest dreams had been to travel abroad, to get to know foreign places and people. But the way he saw it, his son had accomplished all this without budging an inch, by emulating those foreigners. All the same, he couldn't figure out why his son was so apathetic. Or was he really? This at least he wanted to know.

Once again, his attention shifted to the couple at the other table. They weren't speaking. Not an ounce of emotion could be traced in the man's eyes. Didn't the father recognize the way the man was looking? Not his eyes, but the way he was looking? Just when he was thinking that, if he had a lover, he would probably look at her just the same, the man and woman clasped hands above the table. He could feel the woman's cold fingers in his own palm. He shivered. But he guessed that, in a while, those cold fingers would be roaming across the body of that man, whose look he knew so well. When that happened, would the man go on looking at the woman in the same way? And the woman, when they made love, would she squeeze her eyes shut or would she gaze wide-eyed at this man, who had made such a late arrival in her life? The father was happy for both the man and the woman. Obviously, they hadn't seen him as a threat, which pleased him and made him look over to his son, smiling. The way his son slouched in his seat, his eyebrows and his eyes—they reminded him so much of himself. Maybe at that moment his son was thinking about a girlfriend. At least the father had been able to work that out. His wife had told him that their son was seeing a pretty little thing at school. At first he'd been offended that his son had chosen to confide in his wife rather than him. As if he'd provided the opportunity for his son to tell him but his son hadn't said anything out of sheer stubbornness! Hoping to catch the train he had missed by hopping on at the next stop, he said, "Son, do you mind if I ask you something?"

"No, go ahead."

"What are you thinking of doing when you finish school?"

"Dunno. S'ppose I'll do my military service. Want to get it out of the way. Then I'll find a job."

And there you have it. That was that! The next stop would be to get married. That pretty little girlfriend of his was bound to be as indifferent as the boy's mother. Of course, in no time there'd be a kid; for some reason, the man presumed it would be a boy. Would he take after his grandpa? He started laughing at himself. What was he doing, counting chickens before they'd hatched?

"Is that it?" he asked rather pushily.

"What else can I say?"

Our kids' dreams have been stolen and we haven't been able to do anything to stop it, he thought to himself. The system was to blame, the people who rule this planet . . . "No, no," came a voice inside him. "It's not right to put all the blame on the system and the people at the top." The fault lay within him. The model that the son saw was his father. It was true that someone had stolen somebody's dreams, but the dreams that had been stolen were his own. To stop them being stolen, he'd kept them hidden, but he'd evidently kept them hidden too well. If a passion existed but no one knew about it, could you still call it a passion?

This late in the day, when his son was about to finish university, there was no point in him digging around in the past and unearthing old passions. The moment the sentence "When I was your age I wanted to go abroad" came to his mind, he sent it right back. It was far too late for that. There was no point. The best thing to do was not even articulate that sentence. At least then his son would one day say, "My dad never uttered sentences beginning with 'When I was your age.'" That he could be proud of; it would be good enough for him. The father took a deep breath and looked out through the dirty windows at the trees in the tea garden. His mind drifted back to the old days.

"When we used to come here, we played football together, remember?" he asked. By the time it dawned on him that he had asked the very same question when they took the first sips of their beers, it was too late. His son started laughing.

"Are you going senile, dad, or are you drunk?" he asked. They both laughed, together.

Poem of the Girl Who Died Alone
(Yalnız Ölen Kızın Şiiri)

By Gülten Akın (1998)
Translated by Mel Kenne and Arzu Eker (2007)

why does it come back to me now,
that girl, her black hair
sleepless as nights without end
in a hospital room
and why was it I whom they placed beside her?

she had hepatitis and a special someone
named Joan
after the letters and phone calls reached her
Salonica, Piraeus, Athens
with the other long sunk into her eternal rest, Joan came

helpless to hold her for a few hours more
in this world, I was embarrassed
they'd closed her eyelids, that deed accomplished
their touch couldn't reach her tears
those Joan kissed

Being the Mirror Boy and the Son of Scheherazade

Excerpt from a Talk by Hasan Ali Toptaş (2007)
Translated by Şehnaz Tahir Gürçağlar (2007)

. . . I believe that there was a god of literature helping me.

I was born in a little Aegean town and am the child of a semi-nomadic family. We would go up to the high plains in the summer and stay there for four or five months. My father kept goats, and we would climb the mountain accompanied by horses and donkeys. I remember my uncles wearing rifles on their shoulders, and I remember the sounds of the bells and the jingling of the copper pots that we brought along with us.

I know the gap between being a child of a nomadic family and the art of the novel. There was also a great gap between our town and the world. We had no electricity, no running water. We lived in a two-room mud-brick house. My family of four lived in one room. In the other room, our donkey, cow and sheep slept, and we would all enter through the same door. The atmosphere was dark and dusty, and it wasn't truly related to the world. When I tell about it, it sounds like a medieval image, or at least some place in eastern Anatolia, but this was a town in the Aegean.

My mother couldn't read or write. Only my father was literate. There were no books, no newspapers, not even a Qur'an, which hangs up high on the walls of many homes. So you may wonder what really pushed me into the world of words. Many writers mention why they started writing, but I don't believe the reasons they give are genuine ones. I think it is impossible to know exactly why one starts to write.

When I was eight years old, a sore developed on the back of my head. The women in the town tried to cure it with home remedies. They later admitted that they fed me porcupine meat, and perhaps even snake meat. Then they mixed garlic with soot and applied it to the wound. They boiled herbs. They read verses from the Qur'an, made amulets, and so, as it happened, they made a simple sore that would have eventually healed worse.

So then, as a last resort, they took me to a hospital in the city. This was the first time I had visited a city. I stayed in the hospital for two weeks, and when I returned to the town, the wound had healed but no hair grew in its place. It was during those years that students in Anatolia kept their hair trimmed short with clippers to guard against lice. I wondered how that hairless spot looked, so I looked at it by using two mirrors. It looked like a round pocket mirror.

Only the men would carry mirrors in their pockets, but not just to groom themselves. In part because of the social structure in Anatolia at that time, reflecting a pocket mirror on a girl's face was the language of love, a means of communicating. As I walked around the town and went to school, I imagined that the reflection coming from the mirror-like spot on the back of my head shone on the mud-brick walls. I imagined that it shone on the faces and in the eyes of passersby. I felt embarrassed and began to walk around town like a faded, quiet shadow.

It turns out that I was not the only person who thought the spot on my head was like a mirror. One day, as I walked toward my friends, a tactless child with a strong imagination blurted out, "Look there, the mirror boy is coming."

I think it was that sentence which changed my whole destiny. I don't remember who said it, and I don't believe he was aware of saying anything that would change my destiny. That sentence resonated through the town, and throughout my entire world. Everyone heard it, and after that day, apart from my mother, no one called me Hasan Ali. Everyone, children and adults alike, started calling me "Mirror Boy."

I became extremely unhappy. I wanted to leave the town, but where would a nine- or ten-year-old boy go? I hated people. I didn't want to go outside. I never went out to play during breaks at the school. I was a very unhappy child, and I believe that there was a god of literature helping me. He did me a great favor by sending someone to the town. I'm sure he sent him especially for me.

This man, to whom I paid tribute many years later in the first pages of *Sonsuzluğa Nokta* (*Full Stop to Eternity*), was a postman. He worked in Aydın, Izmir and Manisa, and came to our town as a retired postman. But as soon as he settled in, he set up an interesting business. He started bringing in pastries, soft drinks and small books from the city to sell to us.

If you believe that books are letters sent to readers by writers, then even though this fellow had left his job as a postman, he had not really retired from being one. He continued to work as a postman, bringing books and encouraging us to buy them. So I bought my first book from him, a book called *Konuşan Katır* (*The Talking Mule*).

I was terrified when I read the book, because it was a tale from *A Thousand and One Nights* told by Scheherazade. It was an oriental story. There were caravanserais, markets, cities, palaces and citadels. Evil witches turned Hasan, the protagonist, into a mule. Hasan was struggling inside a mule's body. He tried to tell everyone that he was human, but no one listened.

So Hasan was watching the world from inside a mule's body. I identified with him because we had the same name. And we had something else in common too. Just as he was imprisoned inside a mule's body, so the townspeople had imprisoned me inside the Mirror Boy name. My mule was the Mirror Boy, and I could not become Hasan Ali. This was the role through which I had to view the world.

As I lived among evil witches dressed up as townspeople, I got my first taste of literature through that book. I discovered that the world was far more than our town, and that to escape I did not need to leave the town. I could escape into the world of words. So I became a very good reader. Four years after reading that first book, I had already started to read Balzac, Hemingway, Tolstoy and Dostoevsky.

I don't know why, maybe it's because I started with Scheherazade, but I also view myself as a storyteller. When I began wondering where I got this side of myself, I realized that it's my mother who is Scheherazade. I am actually the son of Scheherazade, who lives in the Aegean and is known by the alias Hatice. My mom knows nothing about storytelling techniques. She doesn't even know what the word "technique" means, but she is a great storyteller. I visit her every year. When I go to see her, she starts telling me about something, her trip to my uncle's house, for instance, which is twenty meters away. And it takes her three days to tell of this journey.

How to slow down a story, how to create suspense, how to create poetic language through repetition, how to turn daily language into a melodious language: you can find all of these in my mom's three-day story. They are all there. I listen to her with awe, and sometimes I get bored and ask, "So, Mom, what happened next? Did you ever get there?" She says, "Wait." She talks about the whiteness of a stone in the courtyard—how strange that seemed to her—and creates a flashback to ten years ago. She jumps between different times. She is a terrific storyteller, and she is married to Beckett. My father is just like Beckett. I am the son of Scheherazade married to Beckett. I truly believe this, because of his facial features, the blue of his eyes, his silence, the wrinkles on his face, the way he says nothing to anyone, the way he takes his jacket and leaves. Because of all this my father is exactly like Beckett. I don't think this is a coincidence.

I think I later found writing to be another form of escape, just as I had lost myself in reading as a way to escape. When I was thirteen, I tried to write a novel. I had to pay for the publication of my first two books, both short story collections, because I couldn't find a publisher.

After my two books were published without a single leaf being stirred, I turned bitter. I was expecting that even my first book would shake the world. It didn't. So after my second book I decided to stop writing. I had a strange job, at any rate, working for twenty-five years as a debt enforcement officer. With my small salary I had no intention of paying to get my books published. I thought it best to stop writing and continue to be only a reader of literature.

However, I couldn't do that because I saw writing as my only remedy. I know of no other lifestyle. So, being unable to stop, I went on writing. The god of literature continued to do small favors for me. I started winning prizes. Literary prizes are always controversial in our country, but none of my books would have been published if they had not won awards.

The Balcony (Balkon)

By Hasan Ali Toptaş (2001)

Translated by Amy Spangler and Nilgün Dungan (2007)

It was not yet noon, and we were sitting out on the balcony. You were dressed in blue, your long hair tousled by the gentle breeze. You kept looking at my face, perhaps in search of the origins that had seeped into my skin; your eyes sought the shape of my hands, the curve of my lashes.

As for me, I had closed my eyes, fearing that they would grow wide, for it was as if I too would grow with them; that the ancestral shiver of handcuffs would begin to glow on my wrists, that the chained dog spirit of my soul would grow wilder with each clink of the chain, that searing notes would rise from the pipe of my nomadic past, that the desert eyes of my granny, grown barren in the shadow of men, would look through my own, and that my voice would speak the silence of the steppe in my heart.

That day, the most difficult puzzle God posed to himself was you, and I was happy, as if it befell me to solve it. Your hands were too beautiful to get lost among the red oleaster peels and the crack-cracking of the sunflower seed shells, your fingers were a scattering of questions, and you were too exquisite to adorn yourself with small affectations.

The kettle on the small gas bottle had begun to bubble quietly when the sound of trumpets and rumbling tanks rose from the avenue below. You must remember how we later heard the boom of the drums and, with that rattling beneath our ribs, dreamt of the broad, dancing figures of the Aegean *zeybek* who dare to defy life. Along with the sounds that filled our ears came a fluttering of images, a reel of visions playing out beneath our eyelids. Billowing clusters of people frequently changed colors as they watched from windows, balconies and terraces. Following the band were horses, their tails tied with red ribbon, their manes beaded. Sluggish, with large, horizonless eyes, they looked nothing like those that reared up out of our history books to gallantly transport our childhood from one battlefield to the next. The white-bearded veterans on them were stooped, either from the weight of their medals or the fatigue of their memories. Going through the motions of greeting, by now slack from repetition, wearing calpacs bereft of the smell of gunpowder and bearing mottled mausers, their lifeless parade trampled over the glorious image of the National Forces.

When I opened my eyes, you were still there next to me, an utterly complex puzzle, undoubtedly basking in your own beauty. By now the sound of trumpets below had receded into a distant fairytale. Tanks squashed emotions, rolling over murder, escape, love, oppression, pressing forward to the printing houses with their cowering entryways so fearful of tax clerks and police officers, before finally mixing with the blood of lead letters and entering the pages of books. Still, they left in their wake indelible remnants of images that no cleaning boy could erase. From now on, under the shadows of those remnants, shirts would be sewn, shoemakers' foreheads would wrinkle much too soon, faces of chiselers would grow paler than ever, and barbers' hands would begin to tremble before their time. Perhaps after that day, the rumble of the tanks dangling in the air would spoil a few notes in every song, and the roll of the metal treads would smudge architects' sketches of stairways.

Our tea had brewed and you were pouring it into the glasses. The rising steam veiled your hands. Just then, birds passed through the shiny silver tea tray, spilling half of their songs on our balcony, half on the tanks. The sky embraced everything, turning an intense blue, pouring down onto the surrounding apartment buildings, avenues, hands and shoulders, filling the crates of the trucks, the canteens without lids, the mouths of the trumpets and the barrels of the rifles.

Our being together on the balcony surely fed our being apart, and we were silent. Getting lost in thought, our melting smiles flowing into one another, the lowering of eyelashes and the raising of eyebrows were ever more meaningful than words. Perhaps we were performing worship without ritual, surrendering ourselves to the primitive intoxication of our few remaining cells still in touch with distant ages. Or we were whirling like dervishes, whirling so fast that to a third pair of eyes, we would have appeared motionless. Who knows, if we really wanted to, perhaps you and I could have escaped the confines of time. For just then, time was entangled in the treads of tanks, welled up in the eye sockets of veterans, ripening on the nipples of girls hanging over balconies, and growling in the stomachs of people applauding on the sidewalks. Perhaps time was the blink of a trumpeting soldier who had fantasies beyond the firing range and who marched not with his friends but with his dreams. He didn't know it, but in his own eyes, he was flesh and blood; he was to return to the steppes some day, lean his ears upon the rustling of the grass and the barking of dogs and maybe he'd even miss his trumpet. And when he did, he'd love other things instead without ever knowing why. The crowing of roosters, for instance, the neighing of horses, or the droning of the wind . . .

I can't recall if we had our tea that day. I stood up a few minutes, hours, days or years later. I was leaving, feeling distressed at having failed to solve the puzzle. I no longer remember walking from the balcony to the living room, to the hallway, to the door, to the stairs. Maybe I did not; maybe I, alone, flew off the balcony, just like a bird. You may have watched me as I vanished into the blue of the sky. Who knows, maybe you even wondered where I had gone, as you placed my tea glass, surreal in my absence, back on the tray.

It was not just the balcony but the city that I left that day, a city held captive to the Independence Day parades, deafened by the noise of motorcycles, blinded by greed for money, muted by technology. You remember the trumpeting soldier? It just so happens I am now in his dreams, on those endless steppes. At times, I tell people about the rumble of the tanks in my ears, the chill of the trumpet on my lips, the weight of the boots sinking into my footsteps, the absence of letters that clouds up my eyes, but I never tell them about you and that morning. Even so, there are times I drop a couple of balconies into my tea.

That morning, it just sits there in the photo that hangs on my wall. Up front once more, the flock of tanks with their squeaking treads and barrels that resemble rearing erections, rolling toward everyone who looks at the photo. Behind the tanks is the band, their uniforms fading with each passing year. The sound of the band, which once roared throughout the city, is now faint in my ear. Horses follow. No one is riding them, for the white-bearded veterans are now dead. As their names were announced on the radio, they got off their horses one by one, tottered to the edge of the photograph, brushed the applause off their calpacs with the back of their hands, and vanished. From now on, I suppose everyone must place imaginary veterans on those riderless horses.

Behind the tanks, the band and the horses, all the apartment buildings appear intact. Only the owners and the colors have changed. People very much like their grandparents, fathers and mothers now hang out the windows.

And also from the balconies.

There you are on one of those balconies. Still pouring tea in glasses, paying no heed to the applause that has gradually become a matter of routine, drowning out the growling of the guts in the avenue. The rising steam has obscured your hands from the eyes of time.

As for me, I am blowing my trumpet in the second row of the band, staring up at you.

Night Moods (gece halleri)

By Zeynep Uzunbay (2003)
Translated by Ruth Christie (2006)

we'd be born to the heart of night
trains would leave, poems run
our kids would ask for an earthquake
we would sweet-talk, be rose-hushed
the star was drenched in the waters of sleep
Berenice's hair would flow over our faces

when we were wrapped in night's heart
we'd forget names and addresses
and even who we were
our kids would want stories
funny or fearsome
we'd tell tales of our shadows growing white

all passing through night's heart
were at ease and spacious, we were never troubled
the kids would ask for our childhood
trains would arrive, poems alight
drowsy words in their arms
we ready to love tenderly again

must forget must forget must forget
must first send waiting to sleep
no one comes at this hour

Carry Us Across! (Bizi Karşıya Geçir)

By Haydar Ergülen (1995)
Translated by İpek Seyalıoğlu and Mel Kenne (2006)

they pity us a lot here
we're so naked even our wound
is healed in an other, in vain we hide
in the relief the fallen find in us
wherever we go, a city, to whomever
we go a distance remains within

cast off your lines into our abyss
look how our borders merge as if
like our scents they change   who the apple
who the dreadfully ill   and who
tossed in his own boat from one shore
to another of his mind

so right through the middle my
mind a split apple: face to face
its gardens, in one hard, soft in the other
O my mind don't come out even if I say apple!
O the nakedness that pacifies the suns
above, half as I am far from my mind's
scent still in your gardens
I should've been you, to be more,
to pay off your debt to the future,
cast off my lines, let my mind
unfurl its sail, the wind is within me,
cast off my lines, the more
we drift away from each other, the more
we are bound together,
cast off my lines!

your boat has time yet to ply onward,
its load not the old wine, not the black olive
not the fig jealous of the tasty lie
fallen from illusion into our garden
to your boat that heavy apple's a burden

carry us across, filled with words
you called for your boat we arrived, filled with pleasure
you uprooted your garden we arrived, filled without shelter
you betrayed your tongue we arrived, filled with traces
whitenesses covet your dreams

carry us across
this is an apple gone out of its mind
whose garden is uprooted
don't take us into your boat,
carry us across you!

From *The Shadowless* (*Gölgesizler*)

By Hasan Ali Toptaş (1995)
Translated by Saliha Paker and Mel Kenne (2008)

1.

"Step right in, sir," said the barber, gently raising the tip of his scissors, like a toast in my honor.

The barber's boy may have repeated this but no one heard him. He only opened and closed his lips as, observing his master's movements, he circled the barber's chair with mincing steps. He appeared to be lost in a dance to an unknown tune struck up by the clicking scissors. The boy sometimes rolled his eyes to one side as he watched the customers sitting over in the corner. Everyone there, in fact, was a spectator, each quietly waiting, eyeing the boy's movements, their ears and hearts reaching out toward the snick-snicking of the scissors.

Then the snipping stopped. The man just done hefted himself out of the chair, like a mound of flesh and bones left behind at the end of the game, and slipped into his jacket. As he tipped the boy, he said to the barber, "My heart's still feeling all tight. See? It's still . . ."

Without uttering a word, the barber looked long and hard at the man stepping out of the shop before he turned back to the other customers. The one fiddling with a string of dungeon-black prayer beads shifted in his seat as if to say his turn had now come round. The barber missed the signal, however, or if he didn't, he mistook it. "You can step right up," he bade the goateed man sitting beside me, as if he were trying to underline the fact that no games were permitted here other than those he conducted.

"Thus begins a new game," I thought as the goatee got up quietly and walked toward the chair where the barber's boy stood at the ready, holding out his towel. The barber himself stood bent over the counter, attempting to select a razor from a row of blades while simultaneously glancing in the mirror to watch the approach of the goatee. The miniscule eyes of an executioner had now grown within the barber's eyes.

"This has all the marks of a bloody game," I heard my inner voice say. Then the dungeon-black beads started up clicking, each one trembling hard on the other, clacking along with the ire of a man who has just lost his turn to another. The music appeared to have changed as well, with the irately clicking prayer beads setting just the right tone for a bloody game; in fact, everything now seemed exquisitely suited to it. The goatee had plopped himself into the chair like a mute victim. The barber had picked out a razor and placed it to one side. And the boy had fastened a white cloth to the man's neck, pulling the ends down to shroud his knees (from spurting blood, who knew?).

Amidst all this a deep silence descended.

"Don't you want to say something, sir?" the barber inquired.

"What's to be said?" I replied, with the anxiety of one preparing himself for a bout of bloodletting.

"Say anything you like," he said, "just tell us something . . ."

This was rather like a preliminary interrogation. He was trying to pry something out of me before leading me up to the chair. I looked at them, those minuscule executioner's eyes that from time to time glinted deep within his own.

"For example, are you still writing novels? Why not tell us about that?"

"I am," I replied, my voice dry. Then, raising my eyes above the mirror, I looked at the drawing made by the barber: a sketch in black pencil of a large pigeon. By now, it had become dog-eared and was stained yellow by cigarette smoke.

"What's the title?"

Our eyes met in the mirror.

"The novel's . . ." I said in a distant voice, "I don't know, really."

Suddenly the clicking of the dungeon-black beads stopped. The barber put down the brush in his hand and peered out at the street, the executioner's eyes growing ever larger within his own. His gaze seemed to reach out past all the city's streets, to focus on some place far away, lying somewhere behind the mountains. More of him may have been way out there than could ever stay confined in this place. He may have been in a village, sitting in a shop like this one, dressed up like a barber, from time to time turning his head to gaze over here.

2.

Then he turned his gaze to the *muhtar*, who was walking across the village square. They greeted each other from afar with a wave. "Now, in a way, you too belong to this village," the muhtar said, smiling to himself. All the way home, his smile made him feel happy and light, so that he forgot how exhausted he'd been left by the election. When he stepped through the double-winged gates of the courtyard, his wife was just sprinkling olives over the lettuce.

"Did you win?" she asked, forgetting the hand she still held aloft.

The muhtar took off his hat and tossed it towards the doorway.

"So I did," he replied. "Head man once more!"

He then took the stairway to the rooftop and sat at the base of the chimney with his legs crossed. On the tray before him lay a whole chicken roasted in tomato sauce, its legs pointed skyward, along with green pepper pickles, a salt shaker, some thin layers of pastry folded in fours, and a bottle of *rakı*. Every four years he would have this meal prepared for him so that he could celebrate his victory in solitude. With eyes asquint, he would sit watching the village lying under the shade of the cliffs until, one by one, the earthen rooftops were swallowed up by darkness, as all the while his mustache was kept moist by rakı. Though, as the years passed, instead of turning green and lush, his mustache only grew grayer.

During those times, he would think of how this village was the one farthest away from both God and Government. With each tilt of his glass upward, his eye would catch the cliffs sinking more deeply into darkness, and he would long to climb up to their peak and see what lay beyond the forests, highlands and pastures. But he knew he would never do so. Then, turning to the plain, he would gaze for a long time at the horizon that appeared to stretch far beyond the human imagination. But then his mind would fall prey to absurd thoughts, such as pulling down those mountains so that God could have a view of his village, or so that Government would deign to turn and take a peek at it, if only for an instant. Then at once he would repent, fearing that he had shown God contempt, and he would start murmuring the names of all the prophets he knew, one by one, from the merchants to the ironsmiths, from the wrestlers to the healers. And it was possible that he didn't really have to drink so much, because one of these days Government would turn up anyway, without waiting for an invitation, to plant its staff right out there in the middle of the plain. It would say, "Somewhere around here there has to be a village that keeps waving my flag to affirm my existence and fulfill it." And so Government would finally show up at the doorstep of the head man. Without a doubt, the village's white-bearded elders would be most astounded by this miracle, for way back in their childhood they'd heard talk of the construction of irrigation canals, and they themselves had been going on about it for years. Rumor even had it that the plain had once been toured by a few deputies from the national assembly, in heaven knows what pre-election time, to plan out where exactly to dig the canals. In all probability the locations had been fixed with wooden posts and tapes. No one from the village had actually seen the guests visiting the plain, however. There was no way they could have, for in the time the villagers needed to walk the distance to meet them, the deputies would have already sped off and arrived back at the capital.

As he quickly tipped back his glass and stroked his mustache, the muhtar felt as he had before that he was about to choke, and found he was getting cold. So he buttoned up his jacket and sat for a while shrinking into it. Then, for some reason, he undid the buttons and tried again to sit up straight.

But then a moment later he found himself at the top of the stairs, in the arms of his wife and son. His wife stayed silent, but his son grumbled and from time to time shook his head. Unable to make sense of the words, the muhtar would straighten his back at every two steps and peer into his son's face. By the time they finally made it down the stairs, he was unable even to do that, as his head dropped to his chest and his breathing stopped. And he'd been laid out on his bed for no longer than a second when he started throwing up, bellowing through it all. From his throat came tomato slices, and ragged bits of lettuce were left dangling from his lips. His eyes had grown wide as a calf's as he hugged his belly with one hand and reached out blindly with the other. As his head dropped to the pillow, he took a deep breath and imagined that he'd been drinking rakı all night long on the rooftop.

"Don't wake me up before evening," he grunted.

3.

Standing at the window, the barber continued to look at the village square through the eyes of the executioner inside his own.

Other than a few words spoken out of necessity, he'd hardly said a thing since he'd come here. Even if he'd wanted to, he could find nothing at all to say. Not a trace of the past was left in his memory. He remembered only that he'd come from very far away to an even more distant place. But where was that? Was it he who had wanted to come to this village? And for what reason? He had no idea. He had come up with hundreds of possible answers to those questions, but in the end had killed them all off. "I may have been living in a city," he said one day. "For instance, I had a home, a balcony, looking out on the garden, I had a sweet dream of a wife, I had kids. And if I was a barber, I had a shop, of course. On a busy street, right on the corner. Then, too, I had customers. Some young, some old, some chatty, some quiet . . . And I had my troubles. All the troubles of my customers too. Couldn't get this, couldn't sell that, couldn't do one thing, couldn't say another, couldn't go . . ."

"Could it be that I've had my fill of that?" he asked himself. So had he then fled from the grip of the city to deliver himself up to the mountains? One evening, after night had fallen, had he loaded up his suitcase with the equipment he needed from his barber shop and hit the road? Had he journeyed through nights as if in a trance, crossing over mountains, through plains, without a clue where he was going? Had he descended the mountains into the head man's office, sensing that Cıngıl Nuri, this village's one and only barber, had abandoned his profession?

He had no answers.

Perhaps he was still in a city, was in his shop now, with his back turned from the scent of soaps and creams, looking out upon the street outside, or on a place very distant, never seen even by the goatee sitting in the chair.

4.

Upon opening his eyes the next the morning the muhtar saw his wife bending over the bed. "Get up, get up," she said. "Reşit wants to see you."

As if in a dream, a long-tailed brown cat with eyes like fiery pits weaved itself about his wife's feet.

"So let him wait," the muhtar replied. "I'm on my way."

He remembered having seen that cat, those eyes that burned like glowing embers, some time before now. "But when?" he asked himself as, cradling his forehead in his hands, he straightened up. No answer was forthcoming. He followed his wife and the cat with his eyes as they left the room, stroking his mustache again and again, as if he could wipe away the odor of aniseed that hung beneath his nostrils.

Then, recalling when he had last seen the cat's fiery eyes, he froze.

It was sixteen years ago, on the day after he was first elected head man, that he had opened his eyes and seen his wife—hardly his wife, really, just a shadow that grew fainter and fainter—as she leaned over the bed and said, "Get up, get up." Exactly as she had just done. "Cıngıl Nuri's wife wants to see you."

At that time the muhtar hadn't said, "So let her wait." On the contrary, he had quickly leapt to his feet and dressed, brimming over with excitement about his new position. No sooner had he entered the courtyard when his hands were grabbed by Cıngıl Nuri's wife, and he stood transfixed by the fearful stares of her three children.

At first the muhtar became confused and didn't know what to do with his hands. Then it occurred to him that the last person in the village who should be confused by local goings-on was the head man. So, veiling his confusion in a cloud of cigarette smoke, he beamed a smile at the kids.

The woman was dishevelled and a fountain of tears, her knees flattened from being beaten in lament. She explained that her husband had walked out the night before. "I'm feeling all tight in my soul," he had said before leaving. Meanwhile, the muhtar was inspecting the kids lined up on both sides of their mother. He thought they looked like four prayer beads in search of the big one that was their leader.

Next, the woman had let him know what her husband had eaten the day before, what he'd talked about, how he'd looked up at flying birds as he walked home from the shop, why he'd slapped his little daughter on the doorstep, and what kind of shirt he was wearing when he'd sighed and said, "I'm feeling all tight in my soul." She'd asked the muhtar where in the world he could have gone—if he'd been killed and thrown in a creek or left for the vultures to scavenge, if he'd plummeted from the cliffs or had just mysteriously vanished.

The muhtar had listened to her patiently, considering each of her words as though he'd been head man for a thousand years, right at home in the cloud of smoke from the cigarettes he chain-smoked. He found it incredible that these villagers, who usually could find no way to disappear except to the grave, could wipe themselves right off the face of the earth. Surely, Nuri had gotten held up somehow, in a drinking bout, perhaps, had passed out, and would be back home by noon, if he wasn't already there, to open the shop and start shaving customers. Still, on that very day he had strolled between the heaps of dried cowdung on his rooftop, as if he could somehow catch a glimpse of Nuri emerging from behind cliffs that echoed with eagles' cries, or standing alone at the far end of the plain opening out like the sadness of a saffron-toned lament. And upon descending from the rooftop, he had absentmindedly patted his calf on the brow, and then gone out to find Cıngıl Nuri's wife, wondering where *he* would have gone if he had been Nuri and *his* soul had felt drawn as taut as a needle's eye, leaving behind his wife and three kids. The thought frightened him and left him feeling hollow. It was then that he understood how deeply his very soul, not to mention his eyes, his skin and his ears, had grown attached to the stone and the soil of this village where he'd been living for forty-two years—to the dog sounds, the smell of cowshit, even the sharp winds and the crackle of grass—and how he would never go anywhere else, no matter how much he might long to do so. Only then did he give up on being Nuri and settle into his own body, which assumed his wrinkly old forehead, eyes and sleepy features before it came to a dead stop in front of Cıngıl Nuri's wife.

"Where do you think he might have gone?"

The woman had taken a long look at the sky, like she was passing on the muhtar's inquiry to God, but no answer came, or if one did, she couldn't hear it. At that very instant, the muhtar had glimpsed a deep hollowness in the woman's eyes. As the years passed by, he remembered it often and came to believe that in every woman's eyes there was such an abyss into which a man could vanish. He had even peered at the eyes of girls with breasts no bigger than the halves of an apple to see if that emptiness was a kind of birthright.

The search for Nuri that day had been comprehensive, with all questioned, and without the tiniest clue brought to light. His existence was nil, like he had never lived, and no one known by his name had served as the village barber for so many years. Suddenly, his face too was forgotten. What about his nose? Did he have eyes that could see? Did he have a mouth that he used for eating and drinking? No one remembered. The shop therefore remained the sole proof that he'd ever existed, but now that too was crumbling deep into dust. Observed through the window, it had grown invisible; scissors, razorblades, towels, even the scents of lotions and soaps, as well as the mirrors, were no longer in the shop but only in the memories of those still able to remember.

A full-lipped gypsy woman and her companions who roamed about at the time knocking on all the village doors, had toted Nuri's disappearance in their bundles to other villages. Someone had even ventured, "If he's ever going to be found, it'll take one of them to do it." Who, though, had said that? That remains unknown to this day. It may have been one of the villagers or it may have been one of the gypsies. Or it may have been somebody never known or seen by anyone. That somebody apparently had a hairy mole on one cheek—a man who gazed far, far away, as though his soul were in some other place. Yet the women had held that the somebody was a woman. And how could she have been gazing so far away when anyone could see that her eyes had been fixed on the ground when she'd said, "If he's ever going to be found, it'll take one of the gypsy women to do it."

Consequently, when the gypsies came clattering back in their horse carts, everyone, women and kids included, rushed hopefully toward the black tents being pitched in the meadows fringing the village. Women whispered to other women, and the gypsy gentlemen, caps tilted to one side as they twirled their mustaches, were led to the coffeehouse or to the courtyards where tables had been set for drinking. Many earthenware jars of wine had been drunk, many red-combed cocks and hennaed lambs slaughtered and cooked. In only a few days, the gypsy men's mustaches had thickened and spread out like ram's horns and the women, who had left their tents to scatter out through the village, had made their way into the courtyards, then into homes, into kitchens even, and shady corners where bridal chests were kept. And, still, not one of them had reported any news of Nuri.

When the tinsmith arrived, the villagers once again became hopeful. Every summer, the man came sauntering along behind his scabby donkey, sporting a sprig of crocus behind his ear, to set up his workbench in the village square. Even before he could unload his donkey, they had begun to inquire if he'd got wind of anything concerning Nuri as he'd journeyed through the mountains, highlands and those villages where refugees had settled. The tinsmith had maintained a pitchblack silence, perhaps thinking that doing so would balance out the glorious glow of the products that came from his hands. And after he'd bestowed a royal dazzle on hundreds of pots, plates, spoons and chain-handled copper water bowls, he had packed up his workbench and left. Yet he'd appeared sad—had even sighed on feeling some agony at his helplessness in the face of a disappearance with which he had besmudged himself, however lightly. "I'm striking out for the place where I live," he had confided to the guard as he was leaving. But before the meaning of what he'd said struck the guard, the tinsmith had already crossed the stream by the mill.

"It seems that the fellow lives in more than one place," the guard had muttered to himself.

A week or so after the tinsmith had left, from over by the mill, the wooldyer had come into sight with his tophat and gray-brown donkey. The pair was heading toward the village, growing first smaller and then larger in the bright sunlight. In the shimmering heat, after a while, the wooldyer looked like his donkey and twitched his long ears as he dropped down to the stream, until, when they reached level ground, the gray-brown donkey, now looking like the wooldyer, sported a tophat and puffed out cigarette smoke. After proceeding for a while in this manner, they finally arrived at the village, dead on their feet. There, beneath the plane tree in the square, they again became separate; wooldyer became wooldyer and donkey donkey. The men who were lounging in front of the coffeehouse quickly offered the man a seat; the donkey, loaded down with two dyeing cauldrons, with donkey-like instinct, ambled over to the mulberry tree beneath which they set up shop every year. There, he stopped stone-still and let his ears flop down.

The wooldyer had no sooner taken a seat than he had asked after Cıngıl Nuri. Hoping for news, everyone had drawn closer and faced their chairs toward him. All the wooldyer had said was, "I only heard he was missing," for he knew nothing else. But apart from the fact that it wasn't his duty to know anything, the villagers had still stared long and hard at him. And when he was building a fire for his cauldrons, Nuri's wife and three kids had appeared before him and stood there for a long while, waiting. And so it happened that all winter long, the spindle-spun wool had come out in the hues of Nuri's absence, even though the man supposed that he was dyeing them flag-red, paradise-green, bead-blue or dungeon-black.

And so the muhtar had finally announced, "I'll go and report to Government about Nuri. Then they can make a record of it and arrange a police or military search." After the muhtar had ridden his horse to the county seat, Nuri's disappearance had grown deeper and his barber shop dustier. For many days the villagers awaited the muhtar's return, from morning to night holding vigil on the rooftops. And to herself, Nuri's wife pictured the muhtar riding over the mountains, through the plains, highlands and villages. Then she went over and sat on a pile of rocks in front of his house, her eyes fixed on the flag fluttering above his roof. She saw Government doors, huge ones that were the same color as the flag, and became flustered. Was she scared or pleased? She didn't know; if she was joyful, it was a fearful kind of joy she felt; if scared, it was joy mixed with fear.

When after a thousand years he had returned from town, the muhtar said to the woman, in a voice that was as tired as his horse, "It's all right. Everything's all right."

He had reported everything to everyone; had rapped on every Government door; had had Nuri's name inscribed on official stationery with notes on top of notes; had even called at every coffeehouse in town, and all the eateries, inns and hamams. He had duly reported the incident, and now everyone knew everything there was to know. All had been gathered by Nuri's absence into its embrace. Nothing was left to be done but to wait patiently, and one day some red-winged happy tidings were bound to come sailing in.

Nuri's wife, on hearing this, had been left jubilant; she felt as good as though her husband had been found. She wept and wept, hovering over her children and hugging them with a hundred kisses. Still, every day she would trudge over to the muhtar's house and look at the flag on the rooftop while she sat on the pile of rocks. In her eyes now, the Government doors that were painted the same color as the flag took on a greater prominence. Sometimes she would jump to her feet in a flurry, feeling that she was sitting in the very shadow of those doors; she even stretched out her neck to have a peek at what was going on behind them. Inside lay a big hall bathed in twilight. Long-faced scribes were gathered around a long table, copying down her husband's name. Their hands, flashing with each movement, held very long pens resembling the rods used by shepherds. Finally the papers were stamped with a gigantic seal, many times larger than the muhtar's, something resembling the grandfather of all seals, so big was it—bigger than any shadow anybody could ever cast.

Then the papers were stuffed into envelopes, and pointy-faced messengers who waited beside the door grabbed the envelopes and put them in their pockets. However, they forgot to take one of them, which still lay there right in the middle of the hall amid the rustling wings of the messengers. Nuri's wife was upset by this. She was afraid that the writing inside that forgotten envelope might be Nuri himself. Then, taking a few steps forward, she would come face to face with the muhtar, who was just now leaving his house.

The muhtar trusted that one of these days Nuri *would* surely turn up.

The door swung slowly open once more, and there stood the cat licking itself, its tongue unfurling like a red handkerchief.

"Reşit's still waiting," said the muhtar's wife. "Aren't you coming?"

The muhtar pulled off his vest that was spattered with dried vomit and flung it down beside the wall.

"I'm on my way," he said gruffly. "Let him wait!"

5.

With the same executioner's glint in his eyes, the barber shifted his gaze from the street to the goatee.

"It appears that you're a total mess," he said in a voice that veiled his look.

The goatee gave no answer but just sat in his seat with his eyes closed as if he was afraid to view himself in the mirror. As if he weren't in fact the very same untidy man—as if one half that no one knew about was alive somewhere and the other half had gone to sleep here in the barber's chair. But no sooner had he awakened than he heard the snip-snip of the scissors.

"Just trim the mustache ends that keep getting stuck in my mouth," he said, turning his eyes to the black-pencilled pigeon above the mirror. "Did *you* draw that?"

"Yes, *I* did, and I told you that before," replied the barber. "Everytime you come in here you ask me the same question."

Like a scolded child, the goatee clamped his lips shut and shifted his eyes to the mirror. Meanwhile, the barber's boy started sweeping up the hair on the floor with a long-handled brush he had pulled out from behind the curtained-off partition.

"Quit doing that," the goatee said. "Stop it."

Frozen stock-still, the boy stared with popped-out eyes at the man who had gotten out of the chair. Whom the goatee was addressing remained unclear as he hurried over to the door, turning back only once before plunging into the city mob.

"No money!" he shouted back at the barber. "Nothing out there but carcasses!"

Shaking his head, the barber watched forlornly as the goatee loped along the pavement. His eyes never left the man until he had crossed the street, zigzagging between cars, and disappeared around a corner. The barber seemed shrunken by the man's exit..

"Who was that?" I timidly ventured to ask.

"His name's Nuri," the barber answered. "But where he calls home and what he does is a mystery to me, too."

Flour Soup, Cherry Raki, a Pinch of Time
(Un Çorbası, Kiraz Rakısı, Biraz Zaman)

By Gökçenur Ç. (2001)

Translated by Mel Kenne and Suat Karantay (2008)

I'm all right here
under eucalyptus leaves, banana trees
amidst splitting pomegranates, here
we lunch on noon at night
drink oleander *rakı*, chew the fat with fishermen
coming home from cutting cane, they say this river
can see why all things contain the essence of rain
these rivers, say I, stressing each syllable, these   rivers!
the locals don't know there are twin rivers flowing by, sharing one bed:
parallel to the sun, that look from a distance like two snakes mating

I'm just fine here,
here, in this viceroyalty of mosquitoes
they've given me a room with a view of the river
flour soup, cherry rakı, a pinch of time
"humans," I told the doctor, didn't think in words in the old days,
while in the sky the sun stood like a stripped fishbone,
the endless possibility of thinking in images got to be too much
for them, that's why they conceived a limited lexicon
the doctor, jotting down notes, points out that when I say "humans"
I exclude myself, the doctor
doesn't believe that time has the essence of rain

like an eel Time slides through our separation,
here we whitewash trees, patch up the pier,
we toil over the tongues of shadows lengthening and shortening
yesterday we ran into a couple of beekeepers coming home
from a fire lookout, they said this forest

may be its own best explanation for being
I said these forests, these   forests!
the locals aren't aware that inside the forest rises another forest:
another forest that, seen from afar, appears as rain

I'm doing okay here,
days I stare out at the mountain, nights I secretly write
they say writing plunges one more deeply into isolation
I think not

Nothing in Nature Says Anything
(Doğada Hiçbir Şey Konuşmaz)

By Gökçenur Ç. (2002)

Translated by Mel Kenne and Deniz Perin (2008)

I keep quiet, so you can detect me
if you trace the footprints of silence
if you can't you'll still find the meaning
people find meanings everywhere, that's obvious

I keep quiet, clouds gather to gaze down on your hair
the river dawdles before the pier where you dip your feet in the water
we loved watching the hazelnut shells flame up
with you, there were fine days too

(I keep quiet, for in nature nothing says anything
a stone never doubts its need to be stone-like, nor does a tree,
birds aren't like that, they heed their own voices, because the island's sky is a
                                                                  stable
for night's unshod horses and can't be estranged from the sea's sky, only a human
thus speaks, and speaks relentlessly, the result of unconfirmed suspicions)

I keep quiet, the island's crows recite
passages from *Habits Change Too*
I've got to write twelve letters saying I miss you
bear them like a frozen tulip bulb on your chest, don't forget

(I keep quiet, because nothing in nature says anything
the storm's grasses adore how the wind murmurs a pure idiom of non-
                                                        understanding,
the bee racing the river doesn't try to understand life, rain
has no language other than water's, I want to say
that while on the one hand we try to speak to nature whose serenity we desire,

on the other hand, by believing that nature speaks back to us,
we project our own restless characters onto it)

I keep quiet, this is meaningless,
my going without leaving even a one-line note,
dropping my manuscript on your pillow
you'll find some significance in this too
because humans find a meaning in everything
from the moment they hear themselves speak

The Lakeshadow (Göl/ge)

By Ahmet Büke (2006)
Translated by Mark Wyers (2011)

A bird took flight from the neighborhood. It traced an arc, half in shadow. Shaking the morning dew from its wings, it circled on rising currents of warm air. It first cleft the void in two. Then, patiently, it glided in and out. It rent the air, like starlight. If its feathers had been dabbled in phosphorus, everyone who looked up would have seen the firmament aflame with dazzling explosions like the fizzling of popcandy fireworks.

Since birds, especially those plump palm-sized ones, tire quickly, it perched on a branch of the poplar. Paying no heed to its own stature, it upended the hourglass of time; it landed, clutching the edge of the rolling steel shutters of the Cougher's Cornershop. Frightened by the sound, the smoke-colored cat and her kittens fled and cowered under tomato crates. The first scent of tea from the teapot which had long been brewing beaded into steam and trickled down the windows of the Youth Cafe.

I awoke.

I am a dolorous sleeper. That bed, into which I fall after recoiling in terror from the fracas and fray raised in my struggle against sleep, is itself a battle wound. Maned horsemen at full gallop charge through my window, which I never close, and thunder around the walls. I pull the wool blanket around me as if it were a suit of scale armor. Once again the Trojan horses within me burst open their gates. Undoubtedly, the stones from catapults pounding the castle walls, the battering rams splintering the gates and the stench of gunpowder from the mines exploding beneath me will finish me off. If not for this half-death of sleep, life would be beautiful.

"Mutaf, Allah damn you a thousand times over. Morning, day and night . . ."

That's Yeter, the puppetmaster's wife. She is an attractive woman. Even if she does constantly flap her jaw, when she walks, swaying her alluring hips, all her faults just fall away. She never wears a slip. Every time she goes out, everyone wants to see her against the rays of the sun. I know it's a disgrace, but I also cock an eyebrow, and look.

"You stole my youth, you bastard . . ."

When he becomes irate, Mutaf, my master, calls her a "cabaret puss." Supposedly he had rescued her from the seedy clubs of Basmane district. Everyone knows it's a lie. At least, I don't believe it. Because Mutaf has never had it in him to save anyone. How could he, when he can't even save himself.

Their love is like a sword duel. One draws, then the other. They bicker all day, and as soon as night falls—well, I know the rest. They light candles and play the tambourine. Colored smoke wafts from their single window. It is hard to figure out the shadow plays on the wall, but I can understand them.

The man on the tired donkey ascends the two hills, one by one. He rests on the first. On the summit. There, he guzzles from the white spring. Then he slides down the hill. And climbs the next. This is the nature of thirst, could it ever be so easily quenched? He arrives at the other summit, his steps growing weary. He breaks the seal with his lips. Pours the most shameful, unmentionable liquid down his throat. And lets himself go. Down. The slope becomes less and less steep. Warms his heels like velvet. The nap of the thick fabric wears thin.

The path enters a hollow. Like a parched oasis. The wellspring has sunk. At the cusp, the man with the donkey heaves a deep sigh. He empties his goat-leather waterskin into the dry well. As though water may draw water. As though the spring may remember it is a spring. He prays. Strews wheat on the ground. Implores Allah to look after His creatures, and take pity on man. Perhaps He will see that His subjects have nourished all flying, and even slithering, beings. Weeping, the man slaps his hands against the soil which has forgotten its moisture. This is a wisdom known by all. He hears everyone, He is aware of all. Pushes the clouds with His fingers. They all gather together. Below, the man and his donkey. Below, a massive dark mourning.

"Ah, sir donkey, the most difficult thing to do in this world is wait . . ."

Allah never waits, but makes us wait. Are two palms enough? He wants all hands to open in supplication. May all souls that have fallen into sin learn contrition. Let everyone open their coffers, and spread across the sand the filthiest sins that they have committed since birth. May they weep for each of them. Then fold them, put them back. And take them out again. Lament again. But below there is the man with the indolent donkey. That's all. No matter how you look at it, there are two creatures. But don't count one of them. Don't count the donkey. It goes mad from thirst. Rattles its horseshoes on the sand. Insane donkey. Slips out of its halter and escapes. Runs between the two hills. Disappears into the valley where the two hills begin their ascent.

Does the man stay? Alone. Utterly isolated. The donkeyless wanderer resembles a dead tree. Beneath the clouds his shadow remains. The shadow disappears. Should he weep? What's the use. Should he curse?

"Ah, ancient soul, I shall complain to your father of you. May your lord's lips be sealed."

Allah strikes the clouds together. Becomes enraged. If He desires, sets the world ablaze. But He wants to hurt the man, not kill him. He says, let him suffer to his very core. Strikes the clouds together, but doesn't let one drop fall, as a lesson. He is almighty. Back there, there is the lone, donkeyless man. The well comprises the entire world. It is the driest of dry wells. What if he returns to the hills? Places his lips to those florid springs? Drinks of the snow-white water? But his knees cannot carry him. The wanderer who lost his donkey should die in this world. Does the old man have regrets? Donkeyless wanderer.

This, too, is fury. A sublime presence difficult to appease. Even the golden thrones on the peaks of rugged mountains could not contain its rage. It sends mad lightning storms. Billows forth even drier barbed winds from the driest of deserts. But it's not enough. Is it enough to appease this smoldering fury?

Then hyena-headed birds of prey descend. They whirl beneath the infertile clouds. Below, the donkeyless man. Regretting he was ever born. They dive and attack. Dive and swoop upon him. Swarm upon the old man's rib cage. Not a drop falls. The soft skin becoming a desert. Drawn tight. The cracks grow. Grow, and seek to swallow all that flutters above, all the donkeyless wanderers.

He crawls. Let him crawl, he is not even worthy of rain. He should forget water. He should not even remember what moisture is. Wetness is a thing of the past, it should remain buried in the depths of memory.

The wanderer claws a path with his fingernails. Crawls, inch by inch. The spring is far behind. No matter, that well has long been parched, drained, dried out.

He climbs a small mount. Farther ahead, down below, there lies a joy whose name it seemed he had forgotten. He rubs his eyes, stares hard. Had his bad luck finally turned? It seemed that in the distance, or perhaps nearby, but in any case somewhere over there, flaxen reeds swayed—short, petite, coquettish stalks. It was as if the breeze were on his side once again. No matter if it were just a mirage, it was still enchanting. Even dying for the sake of a drop of water, a droplet of dew or the clammy damp of a snake's skin, even if illusory, would be a thing of beauty.

"Have you forgiven me, and my imprudence? Or, would you have me in the grave before my time is up?"

Trembling, he rises. His bones clatter.

"This is the lake. I recognize the reeds. Behind that curtain of reeds, there is water and the bubbles on the surface, catfish, snakes and mole crickets."

The old man runs. Donkeyless wanderer. Ah, if only his donkey were there too. If it had not gone mad from desperation.

Then the puppetmaster runs the man towards the lake. The shadows grow larger and larger on the wall. The reeds slow him. Flaxen reeds. The moisture laps at his bare heels. From where I am, I can feel it. Through the window. The wanderer's rapture fills me. Butterflies ripple through my stomach. The shadows tremble. Rise to their feet. Yeter flutters with her hills, dry spring and lake, and that long stretch of desolation. She takes Mutaf by his arms. Pulls him over her. Yeter is the most naked shadow in the world. Mutaf, master of shadows, midget Mutaf, starts a new shadow play.

Sleep comes with difficulty. At the ledge of the window across from mine, just an arm's length away, I am defeated. Every morning, on my most decrepit of castle towers, my head is lopped off by the horsemen of dawn.

A bird takes flight from the neighborhood. Mutaf closes his eyes. I open mine. The whole of my palms ache with the agony of the shadows. My shame swells.

The Land of Mulberry (Dutluk)

By Gonca Özmen (2008)
Translated by Ruth Christie (2009)

Come to the land of mulberry
To the remoteness of dwellings

I'll teach you quiet
And the branches' concern

I'll kiss where you're waning
Where nature wanes

Cross the plain
Come to the land of mulberry
Into the grasses

I'll make you listen to the storm
To the scream of the storm-god

A long while later
I'll wait for you again
Beyond a stream

Cross the field
Come closer come
To the mulberry scent

I'll show you the ants

Autumn Chills (Sonbahar Üşümeleri)

By Gonca Özmen (2000)
Translated by Ronald Tamplin and Cemal Demircioğlu (2009)

My childhood strewn with mudmade toys
Gleanings starved of water
Always etched on my face in pain the steppe
Crisis in my hands, desolation in my voice

Nobody heard the bellflower
Seed unknown to the soil's fire
The river, blazing in its red breath,
Meandered through unexclaiming lives

The curve of night ceased in a wilderness of grief

Because of this, harsh history on my white skin,
(the white skin of women, only, is remembered)
Much loneliness, few windows, because of this
Autumnal chills sheltered me, and hidden dens

The Forgotten (Unutulan)

By Oğuz Atay (1975)
Translated by İdil Aydoğan (2008)

"I'm in the attic darling!" she called down the hole. "Old books are really worth something nowadays. I want to have a look." Did he hear what I just said? "It must be pitch-dark up there. Here, take this torch." Fine. A quiet day. A certain someone used to tell me that for all my life I had constantly been seeking attention. If only there was a mirror to show I was smiling, and some light. "You'll hurt yourself in the dark." Through the hole a torch appeared, illuminating a corner. She stroked the hand. It disappeared. I wonder what he is thinking. She smiled: Is he thinking again?

She hadn't been up in this dusty spider's web of darkness for years. A few bugs fled, disturbed by the light. She was afraid. But the idea that she had a purpose gave her strength. Perhaps I'd better just keep quiet and get this over and done with. He is not expecting anything in return. Is this really helping him? I don't know. Sometimes I get confused; especially when I have this buzzing in my head. I wish I could think like him. He's trying not to let on but he's watching me. He hesitates. So I should hurry. She held the torch close; pictures of her mother and father, an old shoe sack between them, a few broken lamps. Why didn't they ever love each other? I was terrified, back then, thinking that they'd die on me. She went through the sack: I wore these at the first ball I went to wearing an evening gown. I'd go out with someone different every night, to dance. Oh God! How could I do that? She wiped off the dust on her hands, onto the dress. She looked at her purple shoes: they were wrinkled and moldy. She put the left one on: I'm still the same size. She felt ashamed but just couldn't take it off. Limping, she took a few steps and went to the pictures, knelt down, and placed them side by side. With her elbow she wiped off the dust on the pictures. They didn't understand me or themselves. How I had cried. Do I have room for them downstairs? In the corridor, in the lumber room . . . I'm being stupid. I haven't forgotten them, I haven't. There was a proud sulk on her father's face. I can't put them on the same wall. She whizzed through the layout of the house in her mind. They wouldn't want to be side by side, even in the grave. She put the torch on the floor and picked up one of the pictures. Not knowing which picture she was holding, she put it somewhere fairly high. A bit flustered, she hit her knee on a wooden plank, stumbled and fell to the floor; a gentle fall. Not having the courage to stand up, she crawled on the floor to get the torch. Another sack. She emptied it: old photographs! She was erring away from her purpose. I mustn't think that he is putting pressure on me. Even if I tell him to his face, I mustn't believe it myself. She spread the photographs out on the floor in a hurry, and shined the torch over the dusty figures in the dark. I could have moved to some other place, could have left all this to someone who I would never see again. She went through the pictures: Oh wow, I've had a lot of pictures of myself taken, haven't I! And in most of them I look horrible. She smiled; skirts back then were terribly long. I look ridiculous. God knows what movie this is from. I turn my back, and it looks as if I'm walking away, and then suddenly I turn my head around to look at the camera. I wonder who I was looking at. Another picture with the same dress on. There is someone next to me in this one. The picture is awfully dusty. Even in a dusty picture, one can always recognize oneself. She wet her finger. First the dust turned muddy and then . . . she saw the smiling face of her first husband at the tip of her finger. Oh God! Once, I was married, and then . . . and then I was married again. Oh well, you can't always get there on the first go. Get where? We were both so unhappy because of feelings I couldn't define, couldn't explain. She knelt down and picked up a handful of pictures. Before this picture was taken, I had made such a big deal out of nothing and then just walked away. And then what happened? And then . . . here you are . . . in this house. So then nothing much happened with him. Nothing bad, nothing good: so nothing. But I didn't sense it; the changes were so imperceptible . . . No, your thoughts were jumbled; or rather your words . . . What's that got to do with it? But I . . . how on earth could I turn around and have this picture taken when running from him? Is this how I always posed in pictures? She sat somewhere up high, put her head in her hands and started thinking. God knows how *his* face looked. It must have been my fault; not at the moment the picture was taken . . . at the time, maybe I was right, I must have been right. Long before that . . . long before.

   She wanted to get to the books as soon as possible, for this endless journey backwards in time to end. She tried to get her old ballroom shoe off. And then couldn't find her soft slippers. She staggered to where she had left the torch.

The chest of books should be in the corner ahead. But all she could see were dark bulges, nothing that looked like a chest of books. She held the torch up to this strange bulk. She stepped back in fear: there was someone there, someone sitting right there. Clinging to the torch, with all her might she wanted to run down the hole, but she couldn't move. Despite her fear, she moved closer, holding the torch steady. All her life, everything she had done, she had done in spite of her fear. Otherwise she would have been long lost. She shined the torch on his face: Oh God! Her ex-boyfriend was lying on the floor. Dusty, covered in cobwebs, like everything in the attic. Like an ancient statue, held fast to the chest of books and drawing boards by cobwebs. His right arm resting on the edge of a table, hanging down in the air; his fingers bent, as if holding a pen. Her knees quaked, her teeth chattered, the floorboard slid from under her, and as she slipped, the drawing board fell, hitting her leg. His arm was still in the air; it was held fast to the ceiling by cobwebs. What was he trying to do with his right hand? Was he trying to write something? What a shame, I'll never find out. His left hand was on the floor, holding a gun. Oh my God! Had he killed himself? That's impossible! I would have known if he had; he used to tell me everything. That was what we promised. He wouldn't have left me all alone.

Then she remembered: one day, after a fierce argument they'd had, her ex had gone up into the attic. A day on which they'd both announced that they just couldn't take it anymore. She was digging for the details: maybe it wasn't such a fierce row after all. They were, presumably, a bit at odds. She smiled: how he hated the word "bit." She had left him in the attic and run out into the street, with the feeling that she was going to die. Well, but why? She didn't know; all she could remember was the intensity of the feeling. Then she saw "him" on the street; and despite her misery, how frail she felt, her desire to die, for some reason, she had noticed the sympathy in "his" eyes, the alterity that swept one away. Of course, she went home on her own that day. And after that, how many more numerous days I went home alone. If he were to speak right now before me, he'd exclaim, You can't say "how many more numerous." She bent down on her shaking knees, held the torch up to his face: his eyes were open, and alive. She couldn't look, and turned her head to face the dark. Then she looked once again, again drawing on the strength that never left her in matters of life and death. Hasn't deteriorated one bit; maybe this wouldn't have happened if I hadn't been late. She was saddened. But he hasn't changed at all; just like the last time I saw him, even his eyes are open. Only, there's a strange alterity in the spark of his eyes: a look that shows he can't be moved, even though he knows everything there is to be known. Don't be deceived by how I look on the outside, on the inside, I'm dead, he'd say, and frighten me. I never believed him. Although he was dead, he'd come up with the strangest things. Perhaps he's watching me again. He has changed his position. I used to upset him by telling him that he didn't pay attention to me. No, he's not looking at me. Perhaps he's thinking. He'd start talking all of a sudden. When do you do all that thinking? I'd ask him. Somehow I just can't tell when he's thinking. No, he isn't really dead; because I wouldn't have been able to live if he was. He knew so. I hadn't known he was this close to me, but I'd told him that I'd only be able to live knowing he existed somewhere on earth. No matter *how* you are, knowing that you still breathe will do for me, I had said. I had said this long before the row, but he knew that our fights wouldn't change a thing. Then, although I hadn't wanted to see him for a while, although I'd known he was right there, although I just couldn't go up in the attic, he knew that I thought of him, and that I just couldn't live without him. Then, why didn't I search for him? I just didn't get the chance; although he was constantly on my mind, something always got in the way. He didn't come down for some time probably because he heard strange voices and noises. Although he knew that no stranger mattered between us; we had discussed all that. And I must have been waiting for *him* to come down. At first, I thought he wasn't coming down just to upset me. And then . . . somehow it just didn't happen . . . I couldn't go up. Visitors, making ends meet, the cooking, the washing, the cleaning, taking care of him (just like a kid, he didn't know how to take care of himself), the death of my mom and dad, the flurry of life, the things that needed to be done that kept piling up in front of me. I eventually forgot he was in the attic. (Of course, I didn't forget *him*.) I don't know, there were people who were much more desperate; I was dealing with them. I probably didn't think he'd stay in the attic this long. I thought he'd find a way out. Perhaps when I wasn't in . . . Yes, that's certainly what I thought. What else could I have thought? For me to live, he needed to exist every second. If I had felt any differently, I would be dead by now. Besides, how many times did I imagine going up in the attic? Above all, if I had heard that he had killed himself, I would definitely have gone up. Never mind our being out of sorts or anything.

Or had I heard a noise? I think there was a racket upstairs once; I had thought it was the wind slamming the door shut. But how come? I had heard that noise days after he went up into the attic. And I was curled up in a corner for days. I didn't leave the house. So, he had fired a gun. Into his heart . . . Shivering, she bent down: I must check his heart. The left side of his shirt had rotted; it disintegrated with her touch. Cockroaches scurried out from inside him and spread all over the place. I didn't see to his needs, I never mended his clothes; perhaps the cockroaches had gotten in through a loose stitch I hadn't mended and starting feasting on him. And the hole got bigger. She searched underneath him with her hand. Well, at least they hadn't gotten through his underwear. His skin is untouched. His skin isn't so warm but his heart is probably still here. I'm afraid she touched the left side of his chest: here it is, I knew it. I wouldn't have been able to live otherwise. (Otherwise should be at the beginning of the sentence; he's going to have a go at me now. Yes, I lived every moment of my life thinking of his words, thinking what he would say in certain circumstances.) Only a bit has decomposed. Good. Now, how can I convince him that for all this time I have been living with him? That I was always thinking of him when pretending to have forgotten him? He wouldn't understand, he'd get stuck on how things looked, he wouldn't understand. Just because I came across someone else, he'd think that this new relationship made me forget everything. Whereas I remember everything; even these clothes he was wearing that day he went up in the attic. She moved the torch over the dead body; behind the cobwebs, it looked all so hazy. Only the place where I reached through the cobwebs and touched his heart is dark. It's like a dream picture. We never had a picture taken together. Like a lot of things we didn't do, it just never happened. The constant rush of life, a constant struggle . . . Why were we running, what was our hurry? Until the day he went up in the attic, we did one thing after another, non-stop, without repeating a single course of action. And then, I was in my corner for days; I didn't eat, I didn't think. I just smoked constantly. I finally managed to make the house an unbearable place to live in. An end-of-war chaos spread everywhere. I struggled anxiously amid filth and dirt, even though I quite like to live in a well-organized and tidy way. Maybe that's how I punished myself. I wanted to fall into a deadly pit of hopelessness so that I could run out into the street, and go to "him." Who knows? Perhaps I'm saying all this because you might be pleased to hear me thinking such terrible things for myself. But I never thought that you would die, that you would kill yourself. I imagined that you would be leading at least a seemingly quiet life, out there somewhere.

She noticed a cockroach trying to run from the light, and came to her senses. She followed the bug holding the torch up to it: the ugly beast was trying to climb up on him using the cobwebs as steps. She was afraid the bug would ruin his clothes. It had been years; they probably wouldn't be able to bear even the gentlest touch. There, it climbed up his neck and then staggered a little on his cheek; his beard has grown, that's why; he never liked shaving every day anyway. The bug crawled up his cheek and disappeared at his temple. Should I hold the torch up to it? No. She was afraid; but in the half-dark she saw the bullet hole. Just as she drew back, the cockroach came out of the same hole, carrying a small, rough piece of something. In horror, she shined the torch into the hole; the rays bounced off the inner walls of his skull. Oh shit! The bugs had eaten his brain, his softest part. That cockroach might be carrying away the final particle. She couldn't hold back any longer: "Have you been lonely, darling?" From below, through another hole, she heard her lover's voice:

"What, dear?"

"Nothing," she answered instantly, hurriedly sticking her hand in the book chest. "I was just talking to myself."

Eastern Mountain (Doğu Dağı)

By Murathan Mungan (2007)
Translated by Mel Kenne and Ruth Christie (2010)

Some mountains are made from landscape stone
Some from philosophy's stone
Some from the East alone

What those who take to the mountain remember best
From a childhood reared to nature

You know,
That rekindling light is the East
From fire and blood it greens
It yellows
Into three colors
The saga scatters on your anvil
An old necessity
From the way the East was created

Some mountains are born blacksmiths
Anvil and hammer
Scythe and mace
They've got the know-how

The kite rips, the landmine stirs
A person grows

The Translator's Voice and Halal Magic

Excerpt from a Talk by Murathan Mungan (2010)
Translated by Şehnaz Tahir Gürçağlar (2010)

Good translators can transform anything they touch.

No matter what our sexual identities are, as writers and as translators we need to be careful about freeing our language of sexism, in both perception and expression. As far as I know, Gabriel Garcia Marquez is heterosexual, and the language of Adnan Benk's translation of Marquez from French has a quality of machismo. That made me wonder whether Marquez's language really *does* have such a macho ring to it. İnci Kut's translation, on the other hand, is more neutral. Specifically, at least, it does not contain machismo. When I say this, I'm not referring to fertile layers of meaning that have been translated from Spanish, its original. I'm only referring to the gender of the language. And this is why, when I turn back again and again to Adnan Benk's translation, I see that he didn't translate into Turkish; he translated into his own language. He made the text talk like a man. Slightly aggressive, slightly condescending. This is a language that I recognize. I bring up this example because it typifies how a translator may fall into the trap of letting one's own voice guide the translation. In my own work there is room for such traps.

We have another, similar problem when we have so many distinguished poets who have translated the work of international poets. When one translates both Raymond Carver and Pavese, for instance, all of a sudden we have these two international poets who speak alike, or have the same voice in Turkish. Does this mean that the poems have been translated? Or does it mean that only the content of those poems has been conveyed? Especially when they translate poetry, translators need to have resolved issues concerning their own voice, and they need to choose the poets and writers they will translate carefully.

At this point I would like to talk about my own poetry. As I mentioned previously, I write poetry that contains different egos, and I don't write the same kind of poems all the time. This causes problems for the way people perceive my poems, because they aren't easy to label or categorize. When I look at those international poets whom I love or enjoy reading in Turkish, such as Joseph Brodsky, Anna Akhmatova, Andrei Voznesensky, Raymond Carver and Philip Larkin, I see that their poems are largely narrative ones; they are poems that tell stories. Some of my poems are narratives too, and as with the work of those poets, they lend themselves more easily to translation. However, translating poems in which I play with the internal logic of language or grammar, or those that include many cultural allusions, could be quite challenging. That's why when it comes to translations of my own poems, I'm still a few steps behind—more of my prose than my poetry has been translated into other languages.

In Ottoman poetry, there's this thing called *sihr-i helal*, that is, "halal" magic. It is based on the relation of the final word of a line to the preceding line and the line that follows it. In other words, the middle line unites the meaning of both the preceding and the following lines, which makes it a visual rather than a sound poem. When reading it aloud or translating it, you have to make a choice. I use this sihr-i helal in my poetry, which I think is an additional challenge for translators.

I think literary translators should have a preference. If you aren't interested in, or if you haven't grasped Marguerite Yourcenar, for instance, it's pointless to attempt to translate her. I believe professionalism has limits too. Just like the movies we watch or the books we read, we have individual preferences. Ideally, translators should choose their own poet or writer and find *that* writer's voice as they perform the task of conveying the text from language to language. Yet I am careful to go outside of myself time to time. Otherwise, we get sucked into a whirlpool in which women writers are translated by women, or heterosexual writers are translated by heterosexual translators. This can be another form of blockage. It is, of course, beneficial to be well-equipped with empathy or a cultural similarity. While we were translating *Lal Masallar* (*Tales of Lal*) into Greek, we had some difficulty when I tried to produce something like muteness in the text from the word "lal" that means both color and muteness. Here, if the translator doesn't have a sense of the culture, if he or she isn't concerned about conveying such meanings, if he or she has no word or world-view based on the recognition of different cultures, the flattening, or smoothing out, begins. I was lucky in that I met many writers and translators when I was going to school. I witnessed their pains. I believe translators should choose for themselves. They should be able to figure out on their own what sort of translator they are. It all depends on that. Once they do that, they can convey the play of sounds and differences. In crime fiction as well as in major works of literature, I've seen how good translators are able to transform anything they touch.

Appropriation (Temellük)

By Murathan Mungan (2007)
Translated by Arzu Eker Roditakis and Ruth Christie (2010)

For the roads of the East that are not oriental
there are no passages in the West, with its confusion of parts: the History
                                                    atlas, emblems
of the soul, inaccurate scales, broken compass, blind lighthouse, difference in
                                                    mentality
points of view, chain of continuity, units of currency, kinds of measuring,
                                                    wounded
consciousness, eclipse of reason, Plato's cave, Gazali's mirror,
an empire of signs and images
whatever you care to enumerate—
Go tell it on the mountain
The name of a book that just came to mind.
Surely it might have been the name of a youthful time when parts passed for
                                                    the whole,
when images worked instead of concepts. I had long hair then, it touched my
                                                    shoulders.
My youth, passing rapidly from flares to parkas could not pass for my life.

A first novel: Go Tell it on the Mountain.
While the West, of which we know all,
knows nothing of us
What we've written on the world
is the sole irreplaceable
silk road

The Money Djinns (Paranın Cinleri)

By Murathan Mungan (1997)

Translated by Ruth Christie, Angela Roome, Jean Carpenter Efe and
Jonathan Ross (2006)

When I was very young I was enamored of a deer.

I can't be quite sure, but I must have been three or four when my father heard
me raving for days about a deer. He eventually lost patience, had a deer captured
and brought down from the heights of Mazıdağ to the plain and on to Mardin.

At the time we were living in a house high up near the castle. It had a long
steep stairway that led from the courtyard to the top floor. We converted the
space under the rounded arch of the stairs into a cage to house the deer, and
from there its forked antlers gleamed as if polished, and its slanting green eyes
looked at us, baleful and desperate. I was very happy. Every morning I'd get
up early to watch, and never tired of standing in front of the cage. Infatuated
by the deer, I'd gaze at it for days. Later, in secret, they sent the homesick deer
back to its homeland, and put a stuffed one in its place. I'm told I never realized
the change, but would stand there as before and watch it for hours.

And perhaps what remains in me as a deep, painful, indelible mark, is that
first love of mine for the deer. For love so blinded my eyes I couldn't tell the
difference between the living and the dead. But then if love weren't so blind,
could it truly be love?

* * *

A friend of mine who was brought up in a big city, after a business trip to
Mardin, told me, "It was only when I went there that I understood your work,
especially your plays."

At first, I felt misunderstood. His words seemed to confine me to a narrow
geographical locality, but when he explained, I realized what he really meant,
and it became clear that he had understood what I was trying to say. After all,
isn't art essentially the art of "trying to express"?

They set out at daybreak, and at one point along the edge of the endless steppe, they saw a villager harvesting with a sickle. Behind the man, the sun was slowly rising on the enchanted landscape of a cool, rosy-fingered summer dawn. My friend was greatly moved by the phantom sight, almost a hallucination, of the man standing all alone on the desolate steppe. That evening as they passed by the same way, there was the same villager in the same place, doing the same job, his sickle still suspended in the air. This time the sun was sinking behind him, just as it had risen in the morning. And they were returning again to the same place. On that vast plain was nothing but time and infinity. "It was then that I understood what you're doing, what you're trying to do," he said.

* * *

Mardin, located in the southeast of Turkey, is one of the country's oldest cities, a city of stone built on slopes below a castle that towers to the sky.

I was born there. I grew up there. I died there.

What followed was a long, inward journey. Cavafy, my distant kindred spirit, understands me well when he says: *You'll always end up in this city/ Don't hope for things elsewhere:/ there's no ship for you, there's no road./ Now that you've wasted your life here, in this small corner,/ you've destroyed it everywhere in the world.*[1] Some poets, some writers always make us think of their "native land." I have always associated the golden age of writing with the golden age of childhood. Of course I can't understand a human life in its entirety or explain it by just describing childhood, but I think where one was first swaddled and rocked in a cradle has special significance. I am indebted to Mardin for my understanding of the lands of others, of Lorca's Granada, for example, or Pavese's Piedmonte. Mardin is a city I love with a passion. I have always been an outsider there. Always the other. Yet I was so much a native of Mardin that I've remained an outsider in these "modern times." Years later when a friend told me I was a "westernized Mardin man," I was as pleased as a child. In my eyes this meant uniting two worlds, east and west, and creating a style from two cultures.

Mardin is not a city whose importance I understood only later, after I'd learned from books what to think of it. Mine was not at all a nostalgic love.

---

1. "The City," *A Bilingual Collection of Poems by C.P. Cavafy*. Translated by Edmund Keeley and Philip Sherrard. Loizou Publications, 1995.

I knew from the start in what kind of place I exist and what kind of place I inhabit.

I think that what excites me most in Mardin is the way history can become tangible, how the city's fabric and architecture hint at a mystery, then conceal it. The labyrinthine nature of the city, which is like a maze both historically and physically, gives you the chance to hold time in your hand and touch it. I believe this may be why I read Borges with so much pleasure and feel a little more privileged than others. This is a game I know. I have played with stone, light and history.

Mardin, for me, evokes pain. A deep nostalgia. My childhood, my youth, my first love, the first shocks of adolescence and confrontations with the world, fragments of lost time, missed opportunities, stumbling steps of inexperience.

On the other hand, Mardin is some "thing" I can't write about at all, although I'm always writing about it. A "literary" object.

Later, much later, it was the place I kept returning to, to settle my accounts. But every time I went back, I wasn't in the place I'd gone back to.

Beginning from that unknowable fragment of a moment when he promises himself to write, the writer grapples with profoundly problematic questions: *How shall I write it? How to tell the story? How to describe it? How to make it come alive for someone else in such a way that it reflects reality?* And how acutely the writer struggles with these questions when it comes to place, when it comes to rooms, halls, windows, gardens, streets, with houses, stones, courtyards and the play of light, and with the infinite forms of the relationship between time and place. Since childhood, I have suffered many labor pains trying to give birth to Mardin in language.

Over time, the place you intend to write about gradually encompasses you almost imperceptibly; you yourself are usually unaware that it has happened. The place takes you captive, yet without giving you any assurance in return as to what you have written, or your capability to write about it at all.

Now, once more I ask for some assurance, for this story.

For this story which is to be translated into another language, another culture.[2]

---

2. I was asked by a German review to write an autobiographical piece on Mardin for a special issue on Turkey. It so happened I had already written three pieces on more or less the same subject. Their combined excerpts came to be known as "Paranın Cinleri" ("The Money Djinns"). It was not published in Germany, and I laid it aside. But in 1990, it was published in *Argos*, where it met with considerable interest and acclaim. Eventually, by complementing it with several other pieces, I came to write a complete book.

* * *

I was born into one of the oldest families in Mardin.

Our family tree goes back to 1647. My grandfather was one of the descendants of an Arab emir in the Deyrizor region, which is now within the Syrian border. As early as the time of Murat IV, he was exiled to Mardin for fear that his authority in the region might increase. My grandfather was brought up as a true nobleman. I never met him; he was in his grave long before I was born. All that remains of him is a portrait, later color-tinted, from which, melancholic and dignified, he looks out at the world as if unable to fathom what's going on. Slim, tall in stature, he was known as a man with a taste for life. Knowledgeable about horses, silver, silks, tobacco and carpets. His greatest passion was chess. They say no rival could stand up to him for long. At that time, employees from the German firm contracted to build the railway would come all the way from the border to be received in my grandfather's mansion. There they would wait in lines of twenty or thirty to challenge him at chess, only to return defeated every time. In Mardin they still boast that he never lost a game of chess in his life.

Of the stories told about my father's ancestors at the traditional *taziye* gathering organized at his death, this was the one that attracted the most interest among the children of today. I think it may have induced them to review their opinions about the east and the past.

My grandfather married at seventeen. The entire retinue, together with the nursemaids and tutors who had raised them, made the hajj to Mecca and back before the wedding. Thus his wedding was blessed.

My grandmother was known as a Kurdish "sultan," from one of the first Kurdish principalities to give up nomadic life and settle down. Today their descendants still live in Gercüş in the district of Mardin. Her grandfather Hacı Osman Agha fought against the French in the War of Independence. He was said to be a very good marksman for he shot down airplanes with his rifles and freed Turkish pashas captured by the French. As a reward, he would later be held exempt from exile.

I was only seven years old when my grandmother died. Her name was Pevruze. She had shadowy, deep-set, dark green eyes, in a lovely face with firm, keen contours that enhanced its expressiveness. I can still picture this staunch icon of my childhood, always dressed in black. She spoke in a husky voice, distanced herself, and was measured in her treatment of everyone. She forgave but never forgot. She'd tell wonderful stories as she pulled tobacco from her tobacco tin and rolled it with her long slender fingers. She knew all the various dialects of Arabic, and knew Kurdish, even its rarer dialects of Zaza and Bothi. She'd recite Persian lyrics and quatrains. They say she bore no fewer than sixteen children. They died at various ages; only six children survived.

We're told their lands were vast, their properties immense. They owned entire villages, bazaars, shops, hamams and caravanserais in the cities. From Aleppo and Mosul their caravans brought goods. They possessed wealth of the sort found in fairytales.

They lived in Mardin in a grand residence with four separate gateways opening into four separate neighborhoods. The building in Mardin's Deir quarter, named after those exiled from Deyirizor, was erected by my grandfather's grandfather Hacı Abdülgani, and still looks southward in all its glory. The mansion has a mysterious appearance. One wall, for example, has no windows, only a single door which opens to stairs leading directly up—without access to intermediate stories—to the courtyard at the very top. Reminded of an enchanted journey in my childhood, I made this door and staircase part of the castle in *Taziye* (*Sympathies*), a play I wrote years later.

The rest of the family history reads like a nineteenth-century novel:

Violence breaks out in the east following the Sheik Sait uprising. Exile. Mandatory residence, then resettlement. In 1925, the Law for the Maintenance of Order is passed. First the men are sent into exile, then the women. The family finds itself in complete chaos. Lands are overrun and property seized wherever a power vacuum appears. Those peasants who are cunning enough lay claim to any abandoned lands and proclaim themselves aghas. The landlords typified in our novels and stories are based mostly on those aghas who emerged in these tempestuous years when land and money changed hands. This is the reason why their past cannot be traced any further back than three generations. They do not possess a "culture" which they inherited from the past or could pass on.

The men sent into exile are first taken to Diyarbakır, then sent to various parts of Turkey. My grandfather is exiled to the Niğde Prison in Central Anatolia. Knowing not a single word of Turkish, his is a life-and-death struggle, and little by little he loses his psychological balance. Later, the exiled women find themselves in Adana. Pevruze Sultan arrives there with her six surviving children, three boys and three girls: İbrahim, Lütfüye, İsmail, Zekiye, Sadiye and Abdülkadir. Meanwhile, my grandfather tears up the money sent by my grandmother, who had sold her gold. He hides the shredded notes among the apples. Asked why, he replies that he has imprisoned all the djinns hidden in the money.

After all, they were people of an era when money was not everything.

The family spends two more years in Adana after my grandfather's two-year exile in Niğde. People who had never worked before in their lives now attempt to start a business and fail. They then legally take over the assets of my grandfather who has thoughtlessly begun to sell off everything he has. My father becomes a boarding student at the Adana Lycée for Boys.

Back in Mardin, they find the whole area dominated by chaos and violence. Pevruze Sultan—shedding her black *çarşaf* and veil—tries to win back control of the village, but intense conflict ensues. With moral values topsy-turvy, positions have changed hands. Relatives turn on one another; looting, plunder and slaughter rule. In yet another feud over land rights, my elder uncle İbrahim shoots the village headman Uso and lands in prison. At the cost of hunger at home, only the finest cuisine is taken to the prison for İbrahim, the grandson of Hacı Faris Çelebi, one-time governor of Mardin. Nobility preserves its honor.

When İsmail finishes his studies at the Adana Lycée, my grandmother moves to Istanbul with all her children. They rent an Armenian's house and settle in Büyükdere, which in those years was home mainly to Armenian and Greek families. Having sold everything they managed to salvage, the hardship they nevertheless face had made life in Mardin unbearable. As changing conditions are no longer possible to ignore, their one remaining hope is a good education for my father. Then my father wins a place in the Faculty of Law in Istanbul.

With no more possessions left to sell, no more gold to exchange, everyone must find a job. Once cared for by nursemaids and tutors, the girls who had worn golden coins in every braid of their hair, are all suddenly thrown into a different culture. Now they wear clogs and work for the tobacco monopoly or in factories producing matches. In the years of World War II, Turkey remains neutral but is in the grip of a severe economic crisis. Everything is rationed. Their identity in fragments, the family suffers loss after loss. Zekiye dies in a sanatorium for tubercular patients. Hoping to escape and start a new life of his own, my younger uncle Abdülkadir runs away from home. My father leaves university for political reasons and flees to Syria.

After three years in Istanbul, my grandfather goes back to Mardin and sets off for Syria where he hopes to collect old debts from a Syrian merchant and build a new life there. But the money djinns dislike him. No one repays their debts, and on his way back to Mardin a frustrated man, my grandfather is arrested by Syrian border troops who take him for a Turkish spy and release him only after harsh torture. His fear of uniforms and the State that had haunted him ever since his experience in Niğde Prison grows worse, and he is sent to the Mardin State Hospital. There, a woman cleaner who had once worked in his family home recognizes him and informs his relatives of his death. They pick up the body for burial, but do not fail to subtract the funeral expenses from the money they later send to Istanbul after they sell off the family's poplar grove in Savur. The money djinns have claimed their last rights.

While waiting for her fugitives to return, my grandmother learns Greek and Armenian from her Istanbul neighbors. My father is back to complete his interrupted education, my younger uncle comes home in disappointment having failed to make a life of his own, and my elder uncle is finally released from prison after fifteen years.

"Now at last we can go back home," says my grandmother.

When she returned, and till the day she died, my grandmother never spoke a single word of Turkish. She didn't know it, or had refused to learn it.

* * *

My father was a very good lawyer, who soon rose to great heights in his profession but made local enemies in the process, and so tended not to leave us—my mother and me—on our own. When he went on business trips to villages, towns or cities near and far, he would take us with him. We traveled along rough roads, past deep chasms, precipitous rocks and bare mountains. Even as a child, I grasped the feelings of loneliness and harshness that untamed nature can evoke. We had a 1958 model Ford, and I set off on a world tour seated in our so-called "taxi." I came face to face at an early age with human relationships and unforgiving customs that bore all the marks of nature's pitiless laws. I saw great poverty, pain and tears. But there were also unspoiled beauties and uncorrupted values. There were always a few books in the "taxi" as we traveled from one village to another. One day I'm going to write about all this, I kept saying. These trips never made me happy. They were the landscapes of a world I wasn't ready for. I came up against honor killings, blood feuds, land disputes, kidnappings, revenge killings, vows of revenge, concepts by which people lived their lives, for which they died or were killed. Even as a child seduced by films, always dreaming of being elsewhere, I always stayed where I was, understanding much more than I wanted to understand.

School performances introduced me to the magic of theater. I was entranced. In the third year of primary school, I decided to write a play based on what I had seen and heard in the villages. In a diary my uncle had given me as a New Year's present I began to write my first play. But I gave up on the very first page where I was describing the décor, because of my difficulty in describing the kind of low, backless wicker chair peculiar to the area. In this part of the world, people called it *Kürsiyye*, but what would I call it in Turkish? I was up against the problem of translating between different cultures that live in the same country.

At one time in Mardin, it was forbidden to speak any language except Turkish. In the shops and the market, council officials would fine people for speaking Arabic or Kurdish. When my father became a boarding student at one of the newly established lycées of the Republic and spoke Turkish with a broken accent, his friends mocked him; he was humiliated and made to feel small. Foreseeing the future of the Republic, my father forbade me to speak any language except Turkish, and everyone who spoke to me had to speak Turkish. Well, I faintly remember I had a nursemaid whose name was Fasla. She was a Kurdish woman from a village near Mardin. She wore bright clothes and colorful headscarves and as she didn't know Turkish, she couldn't speak to me. Since I hadn't been allowed to learn Kurdish, there existed a powerful bond between us, secure in its intensity and depth, a bond that only those without language can develop. Years later, I tried to repay the heartfelt debt I owed her by naming one of the characters Fasla in *Taziye*, the play which brought me fame as a playwright.

This is how I first encountered the problems of foreignness and communication.

Today I believe I am a writer who uses Turkish well, and who is able to show his appreciation of the power and possibilities of the language. Perhaps this stems from a desire to speak on behalf of my grandfather, my grandmother, my nursemaid, all those whose tongues had been stamped with a heavy seal. There must be a reason why I haven't been able to learn any language other than Turkish for so many years, why I've been locked in. According to the Jungian school of thought, this represents a sort of hidden stutter. I don't know, I'm just quoting.

As I write these lines, the three dumb characters from *Lal Masallar* (*Mute Fairytales*) are smiling behind my back.

* * *

In some of the villages near Mardin there live the Yezidî. Greek writers of the second century AD mention one of the tribes known locally as the Marde who lived on Mazıdağ and worshipped the devil. They are said to be the ancestors of the Yezidî.

On one of my father's business trips, I witnessed a passing scene through his car window, which stayed with me for years. A man was being stoned continuously by a great crowd but was unable to step out of the circle drawn around him. He was said to be a Yezidî from a minority community who worshipped the devil and believed that peacocks and circles were holy, and I learned that unless someone erased this circle, those inside could not get out.

Much later, I realized that those who ridiculed this idea were themselves in invisible circles from which they were unable to escape. Just as later, when I emerged into a wider world, I understood that everywhere on earth, every kind of minority is subjected to a hail of stones.

Perhaps years later, when I was writing my first play, *Mahmud ile Yezida* (*Mahmud and Yezida*), I found the essential metaphor for the dramatic arts. The circle was a comedy for the one who drew it. He was outside the circle. Using as a weapon what he thought was an absurd belief, he could force the believer to surrender. This gave him power of authority. For the one inside the circle it was drama. Taken captive, his fate was abandoned to the mercy of the Other.

And suppose a person drew a circle around himself with his own hands? Well, this was a tragedy. He would have to suffer the end he had chosen.

* * *

Mardin, that city which simultaneously sheltered different cultures, different tongues and different beliefs, taught me the world's variety and the importance of difference. I believe that this is how, in my own way, I acquired a feeling of democracy in its fundamental sense; that its mosaic texture has instilled in me an appreciation of the benefits to be derived from diverse layers of labor and riches. I loved both the Syriac churches and the Artuk mosques. It was in Mardin that I learned there could be, in fact there should be, people like the Şemsî, a very ancient sect in Mardin, who worshipped the sun, or the Yezidî, who worshipped the *Tavus-u Azam*, or Peacock King. I listened to haunting examples of the Arabic *ezan*, the call to prayer, at the same time as chants in Latin. I heard Kurdish laments and ballads in the depths of my heart. Long-legged, slender youths, their faces somber and shadowed by grief or passion and revenge, leapt into the saddle, gun in hand, rode off into the horizon and back in a cloud of dust; in them I saw swift grace and the poetry of fingers rolling tobacco leaves.

As a child, the house I most enjoyed visiting was Polin and Yvon's. They were much older than me. I still keep in all its unspoiled freshness the memory of how I used to contemplate their icons and their candles that burned day and night in little niches, and the way they went to church wearing their snow-white collars. Later, like so many other Syriac Christians unable to withstand the oppression, they left Mardin for some other place—perhaps Belgium or Argentina—and we never heard word of them again.

Are you still alive? Can you hear me?

* * *

On my way to primary school there were two buildings which stood side by side, the Courthouse and the Prison. In rows along the walls of these two buildings would be Kurdish women, dressed in black, weeping and holding their heads in their hands, wailing their shrill, touching laments. The juxtaposition of these two buildings became for me one of the profound mysteries of life. From this I carried into my life both an intense sense of justice and an anger against injustice. The link between them also became one of the fundamental images in Faris's relationship with his childhood, set in the first story "Suret Masalı" ("The Figure Story") in my book *Kaf Dağının Önü* (*This Side of Mount Qaf*).

I would listen to the *Rubaiyyat* of Khayyam in the great salons whose walls were adorned with silver swords and inscribed with calligraphic texts from the Qur'an. I realized the power of poetry to deepen and enhance the evenings. I recall the symbols of a lost golden age, the bitter taste of the thick Arabic coffee we called *mırra*, the soft light from lamps as big as watermelons that played with shadows on the walls, the smell of musk from the far east, of ambergris and frankincense wafting through the halls and the vaulted inner balconies, and watching the sun set over the vast steppe as we listened to the sound of water growing louder as it bubbled in the upper courtyards.

On searing summer afternoons, the coolest, most protected spaces of the big mansions were the storerooms, and the back rooms where cotton mattresses, pure white sheets and coverlets smelling of soap, were spread. At the head of these were placed copper mugs and jugs of *ayran* in which floated large pieces of ice. Everyone, every house, everywhere, the whole city sank into a deep sleep until the cool of evening. Then we would emerge into the coolness, and wash the house with water drawn from the well in the courtyard. Heat steamed from the stones. As I grew up, this seamless sleep gave place to troubled dreams. Never again did I awake from such an abyss of sleep.

In Mardin I learned to understand the language of stones. The nearness of the sky and its infinity. Its vagaries, its secret ways, its peaks, its loneliness. On long summer nights, we lay on our beds side by side outside in the courtyard and fell asleep counting the stars. As our eyes closed in the whispering coolness, our fingers remained fixed on the stars. Never again were the stars so bright.

* * *

In Mardin the use made of stone is very important.

The streets are connected by dark tunnels called *abbara*, most of which pass under the houses. For a few meters you walk in the dark, cut off from the light; above you rooms, halls and courtyards . . . When you leave the abbara, the street does not end. A little further on, another abbara is planted in front of you. The daylight reflected in the window of the house above looks like a sticker pasted on the abbara by mistake. The darkness at the mouth of the tunnel with the sunlight laughing at you from the window is a joke played by architecture. In the heat of summer, the coolness strolling through the abbara like a corsair, caresses your skin as though wishing to ease the burden of the steep hilly stairways.

The many cultures that have passed through Mardin have all left something in their wake, as if the city has grown by accretion. Its architecture, which has thus far preserved its integrity, is gradually deteriorating . . . For example, in addition to the new buildings built to replace those in ruin on the edge of the city, where the cemeteries must not be destroyed, houses are being erected on four concrete pillars, like those built to protect an African tribe from floods. Houses over streets, cemeteries under houses—the joke continues.

I think something that prepared me for the wide vista that extends from Osman Hamdi to the Flemish painters, were the tones and shadows created by the light which filters at different angles into rooms at certain hours of the day, for the windows overlooking the street are higher than a person, while those looking onto the courtyard are lower. Some feudal restriction must be responsible for the fact that in classic Mardin architecture no window ever confronts any other; the wall of another house is all that can be seen. The house interiors and the lives of others are concealed from one another. I have seen this inward withdrawal turn into an endless sigh in those stay-at-home girls who have never married and set up their own house. From them I learned the meaning of these windows and doors. Through them I witnessed the pain when, reaching a certain age, all hope abandoned, they finally become carers of their brothers' children, and must take gifts to newlyweds from their own dowry, treasured in chests inlaid with mother-of-pearl. Purposeless lives sacrificed to others!

I must have acquired not only utopian strength but impossible intensity too from the harsh climate, from the profile of this steep city, and from the powerful language of its solid stone.

* * *

The first time I saw the Şahmeran's image was on the wall of a house belonging to a friend from primary school. It was an old Mardin house, whitewashed, with a high dome and wide courtyard where little sun slipped through deep-set inner windows. The Şahmeran motif and the sad story of this twofold creature with a human head and serpent's form, its body of bright red scales, bewitched me both visually and emotionally. Though I found it easiest to dismiss as a religious superstition that for some reason remained incomprehensible to me, I was enthralled, and formed a secret bond with it. Yet I tried to keep it and its influence at bay. But how could I help it, when I breathed the same air, and shared the same environment and climate as this myth? Years later, when I was writing "Şahmeran'ın Bacakları" ("The Legs of Şahmeran"), that whitewashed wall came between me and my past. Or perhaps it had always been there.

Where I saw it as a symbol of both back and front.

The face that aroused my curiosity most throughout my childhood, and that always appeared veiled in nearly every religious picture on the walls of every house in Mardin, was the face of the Prophet Mohammed. I believe that everything I've written and all my stories have been based on removing that veil (and all veils). What could be more understandable, living as we do in a world of images?

We had a servant called Halise. I was eight and she was about fourteen. We had a relationship that was based on secrecy. When no one else was in the house we barred the door and caressed each other. Eventually she told me her secret: she belonged to a mysterious order, whose sheikh lived in Syria. She told me that the members of that order acquired supernatural powers, so that at night they could fly invisibly from one edge of the world to the other in the twinkling of an eye. She asked me to keep all this to myself. I was so spellbound by this black magic that I begged to become a member of her secret order. She was a girl of fertile imagination and told me amazing, colorful stories. At night she roamed the world. Istanbul, the deserts of Arabia, the glittering nights of Baghdad and capital cities we had seen in European films . . .

In that stone city, in that parched silence where the only horizon was a steppe, people used to sit in the cool vaulted spaces that opened onto the courtyards of houses neighboring the sun. They would listen to stories, and they believed the stories they told each other. In the heat of those scorching afternoons when nothing moved, not even time, on nights full of stars, the stories whispered from beds spread next to each other on rooftops or courtyards brought the faraway near and made all dreams real.

I really believed Halise's tales. All my life I have always believed in the marvelous. However, day by day, the conditions for my entering this religious order grew more and more demanding, and so the date of my initiation ceremony was constantly postponed. It was a ceremony to be performed with me alone before secret powers and invisible people from the order. My insistence must have been unbearable, for one day, when no one else was at home, she told me to get in the bath and perform the ritual ablutions. I obeyed and she added a few more details that she claimed were necessary for the ceremony. I carried out those too. Meanwhile, trying to frighten me in the hopes that I might be driven to second thoughts, she spoke of the ghastly trials that awaited me. For example, she told me of painful rituals and other forms of torture in store for me. But I swore I could endure them all. Nothing would defeat me. My determination to become part of the sect scared her. We had reached the end—or the threshold—of the story. She had realized that when she ran out of stories her power over me would be lost. Finally she said, "Soon a black serpent will appear, a Şahmeran. Winding itself around your body, it will bite your navel and your flesh will burn. You will feel great pain, but you mustn't be afraid and you mustn't scream! But after that, if you're not afraid and you don't scream, no snake will ever be able to poison you!"

The snake story scared me and I gave in. Halise was delighted and made her feelings more than clear. Perhaps she imagined her lies could not be discovered and that she could maintain her hold over me. But, at that moment, I suddenly understood everything. For me the spell was broken and from that day onwards, I believed nothing Halise told me, which made her very unhappy.

Now after so long, in trying to find a place for myself among the stories of our time, perhaps I am still telling Halise's stories.

Today Let It Be Like This
(Bugün de Böyle Olsun)

By Murathan Mungan (2007)

Translated by Elizabeth Pallitto and İdil Karacadağ (2010)

Today let the book stay put
Let the mountain be silent,
Let the star be silent,
Let the distance not call.
There are forty-one caves inside me
Let them be lost, my ropes and strings
Let forty-one of them be blind
The world is too much, the world is too little—
The world is narrow.
If I were in the village now, I'd climb the mountain
until it stops.
Let it be night, let the wolf and bird become one.
If I had a mother, I'd lie down in her lap.
Today let it be like this.

Railway Storytellers—A Dream
(Demiryolu Hikâyecileri—Bir Rüya)

By Oğuz Atay (1975)

Translated by İdil Aydoğan and Amy Spangler (2007–2012)

We were three storytellers who worked at a railway station, in a remote corner of the country, far away from the big cities. We had three huts all in a row, right next to the station building. The young Jew, the young woman, and me. We were story peddlers. Business wasn't too great because trains very rarely stopped at our station. And you could hardly say business was good on the days when only the mail trains came in. For the mail trains that stopped by in the afternoon, it was apples, *ayran* and garlic sausage sandwiches that sold the most. During those hours, we, the storytellers, would usually be asleep. And that way we would be rested for the night; because all our hopes depended on the one and only express that came in after midnight. The other peddlers usually couldn't drag themselves out of bed at that hour. There were times when we (the storytellers) too would oversleep and miss the night express. Yet we were on good terms with the stationmaster; still for some reason, he, the station's only civil servant, usually neglected to wake us. We couldn't really blame him, in a way; he was the switchman, he answered the telegraphs, controlled all the signals, and what with selling the train tickets, opening and closing the gates . . . All this work was on a single man. We'd often give him stories for free, just to win his favor, but even then he'd still forget to wake us sometimes. Most of the time, we had to wake up on our own. And considering that we spent the whole day writing stories, obviously this wasn't such an easy task. Yes, we'd sleep in the afternoons; but our inspiration would usually arrive around sundown and wouldn't leave us be until the late hours of the night. The stationmaster would make fun of the whole "leave us be" bit; and at such moments, forgetting that he worked alone and couldn't possibly cope with everything, we'd criticize him severely. Was it really too much to ask him to stop by our huts, which were right next to the stationmaster's room anyway, as the express pulled in? We could all be considered civil servants working at the same post, in a way. What's more, on some nights, we'd type out our stories in the stationmaster's room, on the only typewriter there was. The stories we had written by hand, getting so carried away we'd even forget to eat. Because I was the first one to start the storytelling business, my friends would let me go first when typing out our work. But I usually let the young Jew have my turn. I was really fond of that skinny, sickly young Jew.

Yes, in a sense, we could be considered civil servants of the railway administration. And our huts were built on the grounds of the station building; what's more, they were identical, with the same architectural characteristics as the station building. The stationmaster would laugh and call us "civil storytellers." And then the never-ending debate would ensue: no, we could not be classified as civil servants; for one, we were paid at piece rate. Besides, it was the express passengers who paid us, so the money we earned could hardly be considered an official salary. The stationmaster would tell us that we were merchant storytellers. Truth is, I didn't want to be identified as a civil servant or merchant; we were artists. Our position should have been a privileged one. However, on those nights when the ayran, apple and garlic sausage sandwich peddlers were awake, and we'd be pushing and shoving each other as we tried to hawk our goods, you could hardly say our position was "privileged." And we yelled out just as loudly as the other peddlers. Of course, the young Jew's feeble voice was barely audible, and the young woman would get squished between the food peddlers and the passengers trying to get off the train. And we didn't have many goods to sell anyway. We were only able to turn out a copy or two of each story on the stationmaster's old typewriter. And the final copies always came out rather faint; we had a hard time finding buyers for those. If the stories weren't sold within a couple of days, they'd get old and it would become nearly impossible to find buyers. Because we wrote stories dealing with current events, when we handed the passengers outmoded stories that were a day or two old, they would frown and say, "We already know these, don't you have anything new?" and throw our stale stories in our faces. Then we'd lose our turns to the apple and ayran sellers.

And we had other difficulties to deal with too: the train didn't always stop outside our huts. The stationmaster would usually have the freight trains pull up to the first platform. So the express had to pull over to the second and sometimes even the third platform (if these could be called "platforms"). Having prior knowledge of this, the food peddlers would be right there, waiting for the train to pull in. Because we always woke up at the last minute, we'd usually rush out and crash into the freight wagons, still drowsy with sleep. Then we'd have to make our way around the wagons and carefully over the tracks in the darkness of the night. And there wasn't proper lighting where the train stopped either. This, above all, was the most important thing for us. Our stories, which were in small straw baskets rolled up into scrolls, wouldn't sell right away. Each passenger would unroll the scrolls (often quite roughly), and at least glance at the pages. But the darkness made our job difficult. They'd hand them back to us after a perfunctory look, because they couldn't see the lines of words clearly.

Sales were low. It was the war years. Even bread was expensive. Besides, there were frequent blackouts; the dim lights of the station left our works of art completely in the dark. And so on nights like that it seemed pointless to work. Behind our windows, our black curtains drawn firmly closed, in the pale light of the lamps that we wrapped up in blue paper, we tried to write our short stories, uncertain whether they'd sell or not. Thank God we had the sleeping car passengers, who would scramble for our goods without properly inspecting them, and they'd even pay twice the price. *They* had their dinner in the dining car, so they wouldn't pay any attention to our filthy ayran, apple and garlic sausage sandwich sellers (especially them). And because this was the only station in the country where stories were sold fresh, they had heard of our fame. We'd always save the first copy for them; they were discriminating customers. However, it wasn't easy for them to get out of their comfy beds, to wake up after midnight just to buy a story. And yet we had found an easy way around it: we'd give the sleeping carriage conductors a bit of change and get them to wake up the passengers at our station. (Besides, each time, they'd all get a free story. I doubt they ever read them. They probably just sold them secondhand.) If it hadn't been for the sleeping carriage passengers, we would have perished. And we had made friends with a few of them. They knew the pitiful state we were in, and so they'd sometimes give us food, like the cakes and cookies their friends had brought them when seeing them off. Because we usually worked at night, we'd get really hungry. We'd write the stories at night, copy them out at night, and try to sell them at night. Once the express had moved on, we'd return to the station building, exhausted. In the waiting room, we'd eat the cookies the sleeping carriage passengers had given us. Sometimes the other peddlers would join us too. The ayran peddler would offer us some of the ayran he hadn't been able to sell; it would be sour by morning anyway. I think they felt a bit sorry for us. And the apple peddler would peel an apple for us—though not always. We couldn't give them the stories we hadn't been able to sell; none of them knew how to read or write. The garlic sausage sandwich peddler would sometimes ask us for a story—didn't matter whose—on the condition that it was one of the last copies; because the paper was thin, he'd roll cigarettes in our stories.

Sometimes, when I was in a cheerful mood, meaning when sales were good, I'd read my stories to the food peddlers. (The young woman was opposed to this.) The garlic sausage sandwich peddler and the apple peddler would start dozing off after the first few lines, but would remain in the waiting room until the very end. (And they'd wake up towards the end of the story.) The ayran peddler would listen to me attentively; I enjoyed this attention. While reading, I'd do my best to act out the dialogues of the characters in the stories. Finally, the garlic sausage sandwich peddler would shake his head and say with a sigh, "These are hard times we live in." And the apple peddler would say, "These things, the things we witness in life, they happen." And I had also written narratives that told the sad stories of the peddlers. Even the ayran peddler would doze off when listening to those.

The stationmaster couldn't care less about our writing either; but for some reason, he never failed to attain a copy of each story we wrote, and these he would carefully file away in their own separate cabinet. That's what the regulations stipulate, he'd say. Because we wrote on the railway management's territory, our status was covered under article 248. I couldn't help but lose my temper whenever legal articles were mentioned. Weren't there any laws that would help improve our status, that would grant us too an honorable place within the station grounds? I was always against the mentality that considered us equal to the garlic sausage sandwich laws. And then another long quarrel would ensue: The stationmaster would take down from a cabinet one of the black books and assert that, regarding food sellers, the Health Protection Laws applied.

It seemed to me that things were getting worse. The young Jew kept growing weaker. I think he had some hidden disease. We didn't have the money to get him treated. And the railway hospital wouldn't admit us either. I'd rage at the stationmaster. They sure knew how to take the stories right out of our hands, almost by force, claiming that our status fell under article 248. Couldn't they find an article that would get the young Jew treated? Everyone knew that business was bad. And there were rumors going around that a railway was going to be built that wouldn't stop at our station, in order to provide a shorter route. From then on, only mail trains would stop here.

I was downhearted, and what's more, I had fallen in love. I had fallen in love with the young woman who lived in the third hut, of course. One night, a sleeping carriage conductor who didn't know us had shoved her out the carriage door. Peddlers were forbidden to board the sleeping carriage. The young woman had fallen to the dusty ground, and her basket and stories had scattered all over the place. I consoled her, stroking her hair, telling her not to cry. There was no one on the platform but the two of us. The other peddlers had sold their goods quickly and then left the station right away. We hadn't been getting along with them lately; they wanted to sell fizzy drinks in sealed bottles, manufactured according to Health Protection Law regulations, garlic sausage sandwiches wrapped in translucent paper, stuff like that. And they'd struck up a deal with the sleeping carriage conductor too. Lord, why did each new day have to bring all these new problems? And after all the food they'd have in the dining car—who knows what they ate there—those voracious sleeping carriage passengers would be hungry again after midnight. Luckily, we'd found an interim regulation, and so they didn't dare go anywhere near the sleeping carriages. But this impudent rule would be lifted in a month. Shivering in the cold night, the two of us—the young woman and I—had embraced. What wind had blown us to this town? What terrible conditions we were working in. We couldn't practice our art properly, we were so busy dealing with the food peddlers, the train conductors, hunger and poverty. To begin with, we didn't even have any proper books. Under these circumstances, what could possibly be expected of us? The more I thought about it, the better I grasped the hopelessness and oddness of our condition: The railway management hadn't really done us a favor by giving us rooms the size of coffins right next to the station building. We were never able to sleep during the day because of all the noisy trains that passed by blowing their whistles. And no one knew the value of our writing. One night, a young and clean-cut sleeping carriage passenger said that he had shown some of the stories we had sold him to a renowned critic and that this famous writer too had found the stories old-fashioned and banal. It was drizzling, and the outer pages of the stories in the basket were getting wet. It was autumn. I was shivering inside my thin, tattered old sweater. How on earth could I possibly write better under these conditions? I grew furious at the young sleeping carriage passenger all of a sudden and, turning to him, I said in a stone-cold voice, Just return the stories and take back your money, if you like. Truth was, I was lying: I didn't have a cent in my pocket.

I was preoccupied, thinking about all that had happened. I was unaware of my surroundings. The train had moved on. I suddenly noticed the young woman in my arms. She was snuggled up against me, her head resting on my chest. I kissed her. Carrying our story baskets on my arm, I walked towards our station, its lights visible in the distance. That night, the young woman and I made love, in a torrent of feelings born of hopelessness and loneliness. And now, as I write these lines, I am afraid of having been carried away by the cheap sensibility of the daily stories I write, here in my hut stuck between the other peddlers, the sullen stationmaster and the rails. Yes, I loved the young woman and frequently visited her hut. The young Jew's room was in the middle, so I had to pass by his hut to visit the young woman, and this made me feel uncomfortable. And his illness had gotten worse. He could no longer go out every night to sell his stories like he used to; and he had fewer stories with each passing day. Lately, I had begun writing his stories too. He was so weak that he couldn't even object to my helping him. Whenever he was feeling better he'd sit at the table and write very short stories. The stationmaster found them insufficient and maintained that, according to an article number I can no longer recall, we had to write more to cover the rent for the huts. He had begun to interfere with what we wrote about, and even the style of our writing.

It was around then that I started writing love stories. Claiming that they would lead to gossip, the stationmaster tried to put a stop to those too. We succumbed to his every whim whether we liked it or not. If we were to get thrown out of here, where could we possibly find another station like this with storywriting huts? My lover did the stationmaster's cooking and mended the seams in his clothes so that he wouldn't cause us trouble. The stationmaster despised us; in fact, if I'm not mistaken, he always had. And now he wanted us to write stories only about the railway since, he asserted, we had it to thank for our livelihood. He offered himself as an example: Was the stationmaster ever seen doing work outside the railway? I tried in vain to explain to him the difficulty of finding new things about the railway to write every day. Truth was, he knew that there was no way we would agree to this. Just to create a new source of distress in our lives, which we tried so hard to maintain under difficult conditions, he threatened to report us to the authorities. We had fallen out with the other peddlers too. In our tiny community, which consisted of only a few people, in this desolate and distant corner of the country, we just could not manage to live in peace.

I felt tired inside. Sleep disrupted every midnight, train whistles, the obligation to find new stories for a herd of inconsiderate and ignorant or carefree and arrogant customers, the young Jew whose condition kept getting worse, and the stationmaster who kept getting more and more peevish . . . I just couldn't cope. My lover too was worn out and fed up; I had to help with her stories too.

I had the feeling that my mind was blurring. My relationship with the world outside the station was gradually growing weaker. I could no longer keep track of how the days passed. I'd lost the ability to find current events to write about, and to weave characters and adventures together. Most of the time, I wasn't even able to find out about important things that went on. Okay, I knew about some of them. The war was over. Trains passed by, full of soldiers surging back from the war fronts. For a while, I pieced together war stories from the scraps of information that I gathered from them. But then there were a lot of things I just couldn't remember: Had the war happened in our country? Or had the battles taken place in distant deserts? Had our territories expanded, or contracted? The young Jew answered me with his weary smile: Seeing as our station always stayed in the same place, did any of this really matter? Seeing as we hadn't heard cannonballs firing, the war had never come anywhere near our station.

Later, from the looks on the faces of the sleeping carriage passengers who sullenly skimmed through my stories, I understood that the war had ended a long time ago. And then one day, a passenger even told me that I had started making noticeable mistakes in the names of the cities. I confused the names of our managers too, or forgot them altogether. This was perfectly normal since I hadn't said people's names out loud in years. In our station community, we hadn't called each other by our names in years. We'd never felt the need to. Even the name of the station, written only on the white wash of a side wall, had faded away and been forgotten. We didn't even have a dictionary to look up words when we needed to. And I doubted I remembered any words other than those in the stories I had to write every day. We weren't talking to the food peddlers. And the stationmaster now expressed his discontent only through his actions. The young Jew was now too ill to speak. He'd motion with his head to indicate what he wanted. The young woman and I made love in silence. It was only a brief amount of time before I got used to this situation.

The truth is, I wasn't quite able to judge for sure the briefness of the amount of time that passed, either. I had no other choice but to get used to this situation. I was no longer very young. And storywriting was the only job I knew. I could no longer go to the city, I could no longer make a new life for myself. And, naturally, as time went by, we were losing contact with the world outside the station. Because newspapers became more expensive and began to be transported by means other than trains, we first severed all relations with current events. Then the new railway route opened and the express began to stop once a week. And that was fine by me. I no longer wanted to write short stories that ended in a rush and made me chase after them anxiously.

I wrote all day long, without leaving my room. Only the noise coming from the shoemaker next door distracted me. Because the young Jew was no more; he had died a while ago. Actually, I wanted the young woman to move in next door to me. Alas, before I got the chance to announce this desire, the stationmaster, one day—a while ago—turned up with the shoemaker. And the man moved in straight away. Here, in the middle of nowhere, his business was hardly any better than ours. I was thinking of asking the shoemaker to move into the young woman's hut. I think I dwelt on this thought too for some time. Because, one day, when I went to his hut to make this offer of mine . . . Never mind, I'm a little confused now. This is what happened, however: Well, the young woman had left a while ago. Yes, her hut was empty. It was on a night when I had just finished writing one of my long stories and fallen asleep that she had gotten on a train and left. Back then, my mind was even more confused. For some reason these long stories did not sell. And since I was only selling one story a week, I may have been asking too much for them. And actually, it couldn't be said that the stories were very coherent anyway. I was barely surviving. One day—I mean some time later—a passenger before—some time ago—harshly criticized the story I sold to him. The page numbers were mixed up too. And I told him I had hardly eaten anything for a week. No, I didn't tell him. I said this to another—some time later. I tried to explain to the passenger from some time ago that I had done everything knowingly. I kept forgetting things. However, I was sensitive to criticism. At times like these, and at times when I was especially anxious, I managed to regain my former vitality. Then I lost it—some time later. For example, I grew anxious when the stationmaster told me that he was going to throw me out and that I was of no use anymore. Nevertheless, even though I didn't have many customers, I felt that I was writing better stories. The shoe-maker informed me about what was going on in the world too. I don't think I quite remember the things that he said. But he told me of a world that was complicated and beyond my understanding. And he didn't even listen to the stories I tried to read to him. However, on the one hand, I believed they were getting more and more difficult to express, and on the other, I felt they pos-sessed more and more value. I couldn't explain this to the shoemaker. Because he had left, he had abandoned me. After we last spoke—some time later—he had left the station.

This is one of the last stories I've written. I have plenty more like it. All of them are in my head. I remember them all very well. I may not have written all of them yet. Now, on some nights, out of an old habit, I wake up in the middle of the night and carefully place these new stories in my basket—or in the young woman's basket, or in the basket of the young Jew who is now dead—and go out on the railway tracks. Trains no longer pass through here. Lately, I no longer see the stationmaster around either. I think he is on leave—because he hadn't been on vacation for years. I now wear his clothes too. When he left he must have left me in his place. For some reason, the trains don't stop by either. Never mind, these are insignificant details.

I'm scared. Because I want to leave this place. The shopkeeper still lets me shop on credit. But this can't go on for much longer. I couldn't ask the shop-keeper because I was ashamed, but once upon a time—some time ago—because of the same reservations, I couldn't ask the shoemaker either; I wanted to write a letter but I didn't have an address. I mean, I didn't know any addresses. I was embarrassed because no one would believe this. Could you please give me an address, any address? I couldn't bring myself to ask. Yet any address would've done. Back then, there was another problem. There still is—I mean, even though it's been some time. The question of having to write my own address on this letter has got me thinking too. Now that the express or the mail train doesn't pass by—perhaps only for a while—even if this story does find its way to my readers—I have no customers left—how do I explain where I am? This question has me thinking too. But still I want to write to her, to him, to always write, to keep explaining, and to let you know where I am.

I'm here, my dear reader; where are you, I wonder.

Baroque (Barok)

By Gülten Akın (1991)
Translated by Cemal Demircioğlu, Arzu Eker, Mel Kenne and Sidney Wade (2007)

Inside every refugee grows a rose tree
Withstanding heat and drought
To have no country is to bestride all countries
Withstanding limitlessness and infinity

It wasn't yearning, no, not sorrow
But resisting yearning and sorrow
As if flung out suddenly with no reason
No law, no code, withstanding innocence

On this baroque body the refugee can place,
With the same elegance, the dreams and the birds,
On one end Vivaldi, on the other Borges
Withstanding crazed masses and sly loneliness

A rose tree grows inside every refugee

Stain (Leke)

By Gülten Akın (2007)

Translated by Cemal Demircioğlu, Arzu Eker, Mel Kenne and Sidney Wade (2007)

Here we stand at the messiest point of our time

someone should write us, if we don't
who will

the more silence kept, the duller became
the fine knife we used
to carve out raw day

where are they, the flashing miracle
and the shining magic in every motion

one more day unseen
one more day passed withering the grass

so we learn it was blind, as if there were
no alley no passerby
no one to record the passerby

they said
lock them up, leave the key in its old place

but the truth is
it's a shameful thing, as Camus says
to be happy on your own

voices and other voices, where are the world's voices

the stain invaded the tissue
saying nothing saying nothing

From *The Garden of Forgetting* (*Unutma Bahçesi*)

By Latife Tekin (2004)

Translated by Saliha Paker (2008)

If I were emptied of all memory, I'd be in favor of forgetting. But memories multiply as we forget.

"We can't grow any lighter without memories," I said to Şeref. "You can't just forget and fly like a bird."

"True, you can't fly like birds, but in the depth of memories you can fly like fish," he replied.

Şeref predicts that the garden which is our home, including the mountain that's just behind us, will turn into an island as glaciers melt and seas rise. "I can even tell you where they're going to moor the boats," he says. "Just look around you and think how it feels to be living on future's island."

He predicts that the entire valley will be flooded, all the way up to the plane tree on the border of the lower field.

In the early days, I used to dream that the creatures moving about there, down in the valley, were fish. The thought occasionally comes back, more in the mornings, leaving me in a daze for the rest of the day.

Olgun has scanned the landscape from the sea to the mountains and drawn up a map of the future of the region. "I thought you'd be upset if I wiped them off, so I let the black spots stay," he says. "Today's islands will all be gone, sunk in the sea."

What really upsets me, though, is something else. Our place doesn't look like an island on Olgun's map. There's a thin strip connecting it to the mainland.

Part One

I'd made up my mind not to read any of Ferah's writings, but she scribbled down a few words, impressed, so she said, by what I told her one day about how stories begin. About Ferah, who's been living here with us for some time,

I'll tell you later. "If I publish this, I'll dedicate it to you. Perhaps you can take a look," she said, thrusting a sheet of paper in my hand. I felt angry when I read it. She has turned my idea on its head and made it sound as if I worry about what I've forgotten.

This is the wind of forgetting that breeds memories. As I listen to its howling, my heart aches because of all that I've been through . . .

I never grieve that way, knowing that if I do, I'll drop my guard and be sucked in by the past. The idea of the wind belongs to me, not her. Before we had our discussion, Ferah believed that forgetting had to do with death, her magic word, always. She mentions death as casually as she touches up her lipstick. It's her makeup, how she makes herself pretty, expecting death's mystery to sink in her face. *I* told her that forgetting is a quickening wind, and she adopted the idea. Soon she'll forget and start thinking it was her very own.

Olgun came to live with us at the end of last summer. He used to be an accountant, working in his uncle's warehouse for pharmaceutical products. He has a sleeping problem which a friend of his identified as "an artist's ailment." Interested in drawing and computers, Olgun believes his friend. At times, you hear from him an unpredictable, soul-splitting cry which, he says, is to defy death. We pretend not to hear it. He's told Giray that he couldn't accept his mother's death. The first time I heard the scream I thought a rock had fallen on somebody in the garden. A bleak, orphaned, crushing cry, it had sent every one of us running to his side. Olgun was on his knees, breathing heavily, trying to collect himself.

At times, equally unpredictably, Olgun can strike up a tune. Some keep their distance from him, scared off by the way he behaves. His taste in music doesn't quite fit his appearance. We can hear the sound of hymns rising from his room at night. He wants to learn to play the *ney*, a wish he keeps repeating so often that sometimes it becomes worrisome. There's no space left to walk in his room from all the reeds and canes he has brought back from his walks. I was anxious for a while, wondering if he was thinking of making a ney from the reeds. His voice and speech sound so moving to me that I don't often question him, but one day I sounded him out to see if he was really thinking of building a shack for himself with the reeds. "No," he said, "nothing like that. I just . . . cut them and hold them in my hand, like looking at them. I like canes, they make fine sounds . . ." I felt relieved. "What I really like are horses," he went on, "these tasselled reeds remind me of them."

On the day he arrived, Olgun informed us that, back in the city, road drills and car alarms had kept waking him from his restless sleep. As those endless sounds continued to shatter his ears, his desire for escape became a decision.

Most of the people who come here tell us similar stories about the moment they made up their minds. In the old days, I used to find it disturbing to listen to them. Picturing them about to leave, never to return, always brought to my mind the sound of something cracking open, the whish of separation which, one day, quite suddenly and intuitively, was replaced by the image of a creature tearing into the world at the time of birth. I began thinking that those people were telling us memories of how they were born, without really knowing it. This is what I still imagine when listening to their stories, though I haven't told anyone about it.

I think Olgun came here to forget his mother. He spends most of his time in front of the computer where he designed our website, www.gardenofforgetting.org. Currently he is working on a new image for us. Assuming that each one of us here stands for a plastic bottle, he has done many drawings of colored and plain ones, some standing upright, some crushed under foot, and others scattered about on a different page. When he asked for my opinion I told him I hated plastic bottles, their production had to be banned. But it has taken him months to design the site, so I didn't want to demoralize him. "It's smart," I said, "very smart, but . . . these rows of bottles, lidded mouths, just stop my breath, otherwise it's fine . . . A bit like the website of a pharmaceutical company . . . but I guess it's okay, so don't bother with designing a new one."

"I agree they mean pollution but I also like how they look," he said defensively. "They'll self-destruct in time, that's inevitable, they've got a lifespan too, you know, no matter how long they hold out. Not unlike us, eh? What we've achieved will also be wiped out in time."

I haven't exactly figured out his meaning. My conclusion is that we are plastic bottles in his eyes.

Before I had time to shake off my irritation with the bottles, Olgun asked me if I'd ever paid any attention to the crawling of black beetles. I must have, but couldn't picture them. "They seem to be rowing on the earth as they creep around," he said. "Take a good look . . . I've designed a rowboat for future time just watching them. Would you care to see it? The earth under them must feel just like water . . . I'm sure of it . . . Certain. Don't forget to watch how they row."

"I will," I said, "if I remember, that is. I'm feeling absentminded these days— gaps in my memory."

I didn't tell Olgun but, at the time, I was forgetting about three or four years in a chunk, even five, all at once, like falling down a precipice, without a spark of memory.

I slept and woke in a huge emptiness. Events of the day wore out as if they spread into pools of forgotten time to be deleted instantly.

I've got to admit it's still a bit the same now. So I'll be keeping my story light enough for you to easily forget. I mean, it won't weigh you down, that's what I'm trying to say.

"What one remembers doesn't add up to a millionth of what one forgets," says Şeref.

I can't think and talk like Şeref in terms of numbers. A slight twitch of the mind triggers images one after the other in an empty space before my eyes. I watch them and say what crosses my mind, often in a murmur. I wasn't even aware of this at first. But Şeref gets angry with the way I speak, though I've never had any disagreements or problems with anyone else because of this.

Mine was just a comparison: "It flashes on and off," I'd said to Şeref, "like there's a fire we can't comprehend, sparked by a light, a sound . . . a smell, and what we remember is the smoke from that fire." Hearing that, Şeref had kept away from me for several days.

I used to worry that he mistook as disagreement my words, which were in fact meant to show that I agreed with him. Then I noticed that what really angered him was something else. That's why I don't bother anymore to explain myself as I used to.

"I don't understand you," says Şeref. "Are you saying what you're saying, in the belief that you've actually thought about something?" I wouldn't have minded his words so much if he'd spoken out when we were on our own.

The others didn't really have to know that Şeref was incapable of figuring out my speech, but frankly I don't feel like warning him. For years, I'd been speaking to him as I did to others. But then I began to have my doubts, which grieved me: what if I didn't make sense to anyone? Finally those doubts entered my dreams: there I was sitting quietly with my head down, apparently having altogether forgotten how to communicate . . . in a crowded meeting where everybody else was in conversation.

I told Olgun about my dream. Worried that he couldn't get along with anyone, I wanted to make him feel he wasn't alone, but as always, it was a mistake to try to sympathize with him. If you mention anything that might have some impact on him, Olgun will twist it, believing that he experienced that very same thing himself. I wasn't surprised when he appeared later and told me back my dream as I'd predicted. But what I also resent is how people here say nothing to Olgun when they have a similar experience with him. I don't like to see them pretending that he's just joking. So each time this sort of thing happens between us, I raise my voice, I just can't help it. There are times when I take him far too seriously and get angry with him, which, in fact, is upsetting in itself because Olgun never loses his temper with anyone, nor does he realize it when somebody flares up against him. He has completely forgotten anger.

"Olgun, that's *my* dream," I repeated. But he said, "I had the same dream too, and long before you did. I didn't tell you before because you were thinking it was *your* dream. Anyway, there's no such thing as *my* dream." Dreams travel from one person to another, that's what he believes. If you ask me, he's confused by the books he's reading. I gather this when he says, "at this very moment we are migrating towards each other." I drift into him as he drifts into me. We're in movement. Nobody is who he is or who she was.

One of us is definitely wrong about the reason we're here. If you keep your perspective wide enough to identify everything as the same, how can you tell the difference between what to keep inside yourself and what to throw out? What I mean is, you can't help wondering how Olgun made up his mind to forget about certain things. Once, I meant to ask him about this but was afraid he might say something to upset me. While it's true that everyone keeps talking to each other about what it means to be here, you have to think twice before you put your question or say anything to anyone. You might end up confused.

In all these discussions, I don't feel we have yet touched on any matters of substance, so I'm beginning to fall out with those who propose regular morning meetings to exchange ideas. They're anxious that precious words uttered during the day might be scattered away by the wind. Quite honestly, I've been careful from the start not to get dragged into ongoing discussions among us. Perceptions differ and there's no point in hearing upsetting words. When voices mix, I just move away.

Despite the constant disagreement between us, I only trust Şeref's opinions. Şeref is the only one among us who knows why he's here and what he's trying to do.

The first week of each month he publishes sections from his writings, each in a different graphic design, on our website. I prefer reading his pieces where ideas transform into stories, like "The Princess and the Fish," which I enjoyed very much. His narrative on liberation, as told from a buffalo's viewpoint, is also good.

. . . A rifle bursts into fire in that silence, the buffalo begin running in every direction, then suddenly they all . . .

* * *

I Heard the Sound of the Hunt

If we could just forget everything and dissolve into imaginaries!

This is what I was absentmindedly longing for, which had nothing to do with the awaited man at the bus terminal, the gardener we had hired before meeting him in person. It was just beginning to grow light when we set out. Gazing sleepily at the hillsides and the valley, you realize how the natural world can actually rest in comfort.

Such feelings are not against our goals, our way of thinking, but in Şeref's opinion, I've become far too indulgent. He sounds out a warning even at the slightest drift of an eye, certain that I'm trying again to delete a memory or something. We shouldn't inadvertently abuse our power to forget, but instead hold on to it so that we won't disintegrate: "*That* is in harmony with the way nature operates," he says. Apparently, even stones resist crumbling away.

Lately, Şeref has been overcome by a feeling that my desire to forget is growing out of proportion. "What can I do?" I say, trying to put on a smile not to make him worry. "Words just pour out of my mouth . . . Think of it as raving." He replies that the harder we try breaking rocks, the harder they get. I don't quite believe that's true.

"There's nothing incomprehensible about it," I blurt out. "Humans are first and foremost creatures who sleep. We give ourselves over to it regularly, every day. Just look around you, all living beings lie in the lap of emptiness for hours, months . . . for whole seasons."

"All right, make your excuses, let the void grow and lose yourself in it," he retorts.

As night turns into day, an animal silence creeps over the garden where we live. We hear hidden insects scratching and stirring the earth and foxes seem to have just bolted out of sight while we prepare to set out on our journey to the bus terminal to meet countless newcomers. Some of them arrive in such a state that even twilight intuitions can prove to be useless.

"Only the voice is mine, the words belong to life . . ." That's what I said to Şeref at last when I couldn't put up with him anymore.

"You're engaging in metaphysics," he said. "We can't be in favor of people letting go, fading away."

I shut up each time to cut the argument short, though I'm not sure if he wants to have even a single person around him, despite the fact that he *does* have a life-affirming attitude—but that's another matter.

I sneaked to a corner in the bus terminal as the time of our gardener's arrival drew near. When meeting someone for the first time, I make a point of taking a secret look without giving myself away. I shall explain why, of course, but just let me tell you I was deeply shaken by the sight of this man when I first saw him.

Never before had I felt so defenseless. As if, at that very moment, I was blown away to a far off, empty place . . . to a silent, snowy forest.

We keep experiencing unimaginable things here. Now, we happened to be facing that morning's liveliest traveler, the one readiest for duty. Our gardener had just stepped off the bus in a hunter's outfit!

Struck by the strong mountain sun where I seemed to have drifted in my mind, I began watching the man in a different light, but without condescension. Here, far too many of us seem to observe things from the heights of high ideals.

I watch all newcomers from my hiding corner but there's still something I haven't been able to figure out yet: they arrive here with absolutely no idea of what they're going to experience, then start a story which is impossible to stop. There's nothing you can do about it. But I'll tell you what I saw this time, as it sent a deep, distracting shiver down my spine.

In moments of fear I can feel absurdly good about people. Looking at the gardener in a hunter's costume, I thought, "God only knows but maybe the man had nothing else to wear."

Of course! That morning I had woken to the song of the blackbirds. They're fair game here. What's more, they can be so easily spotted, their yellow beaks showing against their black feathers! Shame that when they're scared, they flutter off to the echoes of their own song—if you could only hear them!—warning the nestlings against danger, of course, but at the same time giving themselves away as they hop about!

Şeref is foremost in my mind whenever I go to the bus terminal, because he never comes with us. "Those who want to come here, can find their own way," he says, "and those who can't, aren't wanted here anyhow." I remember Şeref not because I think he's right, but quite the opposite, because I don't want to get upset and cross with the newcomers I haven't met yet. Such words make you regret from the start what you'll be doing for those people. So, once more, I was overcome by sadness and guilt as I hid in my corner, watching the gardener. The man was full of enthusiasm for work. Fortunately, I'd figured that out soon enough.

It was also a fact that we had hired the man through a company on the internet. A few weeks before his arrival I had looked at his photo, slowly enlarging it on our computer screen. I followed a flashing arrow and discovered that his home had been destroyed in the earthquake, that he'd lost everything.

I didn't approve of the decision to employ him. It seemed to me there was no difference between looking for a gardener on the internet and calling spirits—but no point in remembering all those arguments. Here, we're living so close to each other that anyone's proposal seems to call for everyone's support. Whatever the issue, you just can't keep out, even when you're entirely against it.

Taken in by curiosity, I tried to figure out the gardener's character from his photo. If I saw *myself* on the screen like that, let alone someone else, I'd feel dead and buried in glass. Not even able to make the slightest move, I don't think I could make the journey back from light years away.

Never again do I want to see anyone like that before meeting them in person. I tried not to look at the photo, but couldn't possibly guard myself against the reflection riddled by the glitter on the screen. The man looked strangely worn out. "As if he's been beamed to the future and aged there," I remember saying. And that's how he stayed in my mind. But I should've kept those impressions to myself to prevent the others from reminding me of them all the time. I hope they won't tell him.

So when the man materialized full of life before us at the bus terminal, I felt a twinge of disappointment. I'm telling you this because you might think it strange that I'm looking for hidden meanings in his words and scrutinizing his behavior. He's only a gardener after all, you'll say.

A story doesn't begin with every newcomer. If you feel it has indeed already begun, you become uneasy, almost regretful. This is a great mystery— something that instantly fades you out.

Stepping back, you begin watching that person with an interest that'll appear strange to others.

Whenever I find someone intimidating at first sight, I feel a draining in my heart, but then my soul turns to that person with a sense of acceptance, urging me to adopt the stranger. But there's no point in dwelling on this mystery, for I've discovered that I can't solve it.

Because at that point I'd have already surrendered to the story.

Here, you can only talk to Olgun about such things. And with him you can get carried far, far away and find yourself all alone in the world. Maybe you can talk with Şeref, too, if you find a good moment . . .

But there *is*, of course, a way of telling who is concealing what inside them.

And it's foolproof. If it weren't for those people among us who simply can't stand being outwitted by anyone quick enough to grasp and speak out those secret truths that will thrill us all, I wouldn't mind revealing it. But this time, even if they'll take my words lightly as usual, I've got to sound out a warning to everyone, above all, to Şeref.

I believe in the power of the first look. Just for once, a person's soul will light up for you down to its most intimate details in a way that you'll never be able to forget.

The moment our gardener greeted us with a smile, a lone mountaintop light flashed in his face and in that light I foresaw the evil that would befall.

I make a wish for the blackbirds always flying about fearlessly over the firethorns in our garden! A story is bound to begin if you want to forget about something unforgettable that you've seen.

I refused to marvel at the man's outfit, as if to dispel the sense of looming evil. That was all I could possibly do. When my heart skipped a beat, I suddenly thought this was precisely the kind of feeling that that would rub Şeref the wrong way. Even if I *do* tell him about the gardener's arrival, I'll probably keep that bit to myself, for he'll start saying things like "the heart makes up for the mind's shortcomings." Once, when I happened to confide in him, complaining how I'd get caught up in innocent but unforgettable thoughts, mostly in the mornings, and how those silly notions would hover about in my head for the rest of the day, Şeref had given me a flash summary of the history of thought from the classical philosophers to the present day. I'm, therefore, more cautious now when I speak to him and just hope he'll get on with the new man so the garden won't be a problem for us anymore. Because this is our fourth gardener. Truth is, I don't entirely blame Şeref, for he doesn't seem to expect all that much, just a little bit of attention to keep the herbs from getting mixed up with the wild bushes. The previous gardener had uprooted all our lemon balm and burned it up before we knew what was happening.

Let it howl, the wind of forgetting . . . How else can I survive, with everything I've been through? I wouldn't be able to bear their heavy silence. If only I could tell now . . . is the wind blowing towards the future?

Kuzguncuk Hotel (Kuzguncuk Oteli)

By Haydar Ergülen (1995)
Translated by Mel Kenne (2006–2012)

I cheated on my home for a street upon me
a moon in this town's silver quarter the street's
third flight up, that's me, facing the sea

hey lay off me moon lady, at this Kuzguncuk hotel
go up to a virtuous floor, to your weighty guests
I'm a life being spent waiting on memory

this is my soul's very first hotel stay
in the same room, same bed, same mirror
for the first time we see each other, no more goodbyes
I'm having to sleep with a stranger over me

don't move your skiff away from this soul's quarter moon lady
I'm not ready for you I lie facing you on your side
whoever moves in I can't leave my home inside

this Kuzguncuk hotel of such many-storied goodness
like stars flying always up and away hey moon lady,
this child from some place you remember
this child from some place I have to forget

Lost Brother (Kayıp Kardeş)

By Haydar Ergülen (2005)

Translated by Arzu Eker Roditakis and Elizabeth Pallitto (2012)

To Şahin Şencan

O my god, my landlord, let me
live in your house a little longer
within me the brother I carry is alone
once I give birth to him, I won't stay here

O my brother, my street, let me
carry you within me a little longer
once you set out on your own,
I'll be all alone in the world

O my lifetime, my little room, let me
seek a path in poetry a little longer
if soul coincides, may I find the many
lost brothers I have on this path

Ghazal of Idylls (İdiller Gazeli)

By Haydar Ergülen (2007)

Translated by Gökçenur Ç. (2010)

your eyes just left the rain
as child as, as big as, as warm as

you must be town or a pomegranate
may be granada, may be september, may be red

your body is the summer night of your soul or what else
very idyll, very sea, very windy

you fell in love again like a child
as if to me, as if ah!, as if it can be

even love cannot fill the emptiness of some lovers
so that praise, so that to you, so that june

if desire is asleep, soul wanders all naked
ghazal about this, sorrow about this, secret about this

your eyes just left the town
as full as, as timid as, as loquacious as

go on! destroy new towns for our hearts from this love

The Worm in the Apple (Elmadaki Kurt)

By Ahmet Büke (2006)

Translated by Amy Spangler (2011)

The long shadows of the trees had reached our toes as the sun keeled over in the direction from which the bus would arrive. We were sitting on the old wooden bench at the stop. Me and Seyhan. I caught the scent coming from beneath her hair, which flowed down her long neck, over her delicate shoulders.

"Gimme a smoke."

My hand went for the backpack planted between my feet. I was loosening the drawstring when I stopped.

"No. You shouldn't be smoking anymore."

I must have smiled. She covered her mouth with her fingers, stifling her laughter.

"Oh, Mom! She told you, didn't she?"

Together we looked at the spot revealed by the clingy beige T-shirt that had climbed up her belly. She read my thoughts immediately.

"I'm only two months along, for God's sake!"

I gathered my feet together and stretched out onto her legs. My ear on her belly. "I wish I could stay," I thought.

"I wish you'd stayed longer."

I looked at the asphalt before us, bathed in what was perhaps the last sun of the summer. Mom appeared at the top of the hill leading down to the main road, carrying her small net bag.

"She was going to make you cookies. She left it till the last minute, as usual. She'll never change, that woman."

A pair of wasps in their yellow, poisonous colors, circled above our heads. They abandoned their turn mid-revolution, disappearing one behind the other into one of the concrete cracks peering from the bus stop.

"Do you really love that girl?"

"Who?"

"Mom showed me the picture of the two of you together. You were standing arm in arm, in front of the Clock Tower."

For a moment I struggled to gather my thoughts.

"What are you talking about? What's Mom doing with my pictures?"

I was a little peeved. I made to raise myself from her knees, but she pulled my hair, stopping me.

"You know how she came over to clean your place at the beginning of summer, sweets. Well, that's when she saw it. She said you two study together. That she made coffee for Mom."

"Oh, right, now I remember . . ."

This time, I righted myself. My hand went for my bag. At that moment, I desperately craved a cigarette.

"I'm never letting Mom into my place again. I can't believe she had the nerve to go snooping through my photos."

As she gathered her hair up, the weight of her scent pressed heavily against my body.

"What's wrong with that, sweets. The woman wants you to be happy. But that girl, she seemed a little ugly to me."

I'm looking at her face. She'd plucked her eyebrows, shaping them into bow-like arches. Whenever she squints her eyes and smiles like she's doing right now, the scar on her forehead becomes even more apparent. That day, too, Mom had made cookies, I think. Yes, definitely, I still recall the smell. Dad's leather suitcase was stretched out on the windowsill like a dead animal. He came and kissed us. He gathered Seyhan's hair, which had come loose, took her hand in his own and smelled it. And then he leaned over to my ear. What was he going to say, I wonder? Mom was grating apples, her back turned to us. The scent of those meaty fruits being violently shred into pieces mingled with the basil on the berm separating the kitchen from the living room, and hung suspended in the air.

When my father shut the garden gate and disappeared, Seyhan began screaming at the top of her lungs. My mother continued her apple grating. The palms of my hands meanwhile had become damp with sweat. I wanted to go over and hug her. But it was as if someone had poured concrete over my ankles. Seyhan's screams made the windows shake. Mom had put all the weight of her shoulders into the task at hand. I felt like covering my ears with my hands but the dampness didn't allow it. I was disgusted by my palms.

Mom whipped around just like that and chucked the red grater straight at us.

I recall that, as the grater approached us, summersaulting through the air in slow motion, a suddenly darkening cloud descended upon me.

When I opened my eyes, Seyhan and I were stretched out next to each other on the divan in the garden. She took my hand and placed it on her forehead. Yellowish antiseptic stains were visible beneath the white gauze wound around her head. Squinting, again she laughed. I embraced her, crying. A plate of cookies lay next to us. Apple cookies.

My mother finally appeared on the hill. Her face was red from her rushed steps. Breathless, she came up to us. She released a deep "oh" of relief, and then sat down between us.

"Your cookies have arrived, sir."

She was trying to stuff the bag filled with napkins into my bag, making the limp string strain, arrested by the eyelets.

"Mom, who asked you for cookies anyway? You didn't need to go to the trouble, all that last-minute rushing about."

Seyhan smiled and took the cigarette, which was almost finished, from my fingers. Her delicate coolness remained on my wrists for a moment. She took a few drags under the forked gaze of my mother and then threw the butt out onto the road.

Together we looked in the direction from which the bus would come. A calico cat darted into the middle of the street. It stopped. Then, lowering its tail it retraced its path, walking backwards.

"Ferhat called just as I was leaving. I told him we were sending Seyhun off. He'll be here to pick you up in a little bit. He says you're having guests this evening."

Seyhan remained silent. She ran her hand over her belly. Then she crossed her arms and with her fingers touched the scar on her forehead.

"It's best you don't go wearing yourself out these days. You want me to come help you?"

"No, I don't."

I was sure as sure could be that she was craving another cigarette. If it weren't for Mother, we would have had one last cigarette together.

A black car appeared out of the direction from which the bus was to arrive. It drove right up to us at full speed, a cloud of dust in its wake. It stopped with a screeching slam on the brakes. The gravel rolled down the belly of the hill and disappeared. The words "Akın Appliances Limited," spread across the side doors in gilded letters, gleamed beneath the sun.

Ferhat lowered the window. He took off his sunglasses and waved at us. My mother sat up straight and called out, "Hello, my child."

I turned to look at Seyhan. She pushed the hair that had fallen in front of her face behind her ear. Her earring, a tiny dot, was revealed. We embraced. She ran her fingers over the back of my neck again. She gently pulled on my hair.

"I wish you weren't leaving. You'll come back before the birth, won't you?"

I shook my head. She walked towards the car. Ferhat and Mom waved at each other. Once again the gravel on the road was flung in all directions.

My mom and me. We were alone now. At the stop.

"Gimme a smoke."

I shook the pack. I caught one of the dangling cigarettes between my lips and pulled it out. My mom took the other one. I lit mine. I flicked the lid closed and handed the lighter to her. Before lighting her own she looked at me. The pupils of her green eyes had narrowed into slits. These were the actions of people incapable of loving one another. Like when she barged into the room where Seyhan and I slept together years ago. It was as if her heart were beating in the swollen veins of her neck.

"You're grown up now. You need to have separate rooms," she had said.

A flood of rage had seized me, casting me out of the room. For the first time, my socks, my underwear, my Galatasaray posters hanging on the wall and I were being cast into a world apart from Seyhan. The dark room in the back was prepared. When I lay down on the bed with its squeaky springs, I was alone with the last thing remaining from my father (my mother had gotten nearly all new stuff when my father left), that huge clock on the wall, its pendulum lying coiled up like a dead snake. My mother was reading my insides, I think. My door would be double-locked from the outside, two turns of the key, at night.

Her eyes distanced themselves from me. She looked at the ash falling at her feet.

"You finishing school this year?"

"So it seems."

"You probably won't be coming back to these parts. Back here, to us, I mean?"

" . . ."

"You should come more often. Once a year, at least."

The cloud of dust rising into the air out of the expected direction of the road must have belonged to the bus. I got up. I walked towards the road.

"Definitely come for your sister's delivery."

"Alright."

The yackety sound of the air horn echoed from the hills opposite. My face was bathed by the sun leaning into the trees, while my back had turned to ice.

The bus approached, hissing. The gravel's song ceased. And at precisely that moment, my mother latched on to the bag on my back like a cold paw. Her breath drew close to my ear.

"How much longer will you bear this sin? Let her go already."

I threw myself onto the bus. There was a gushing wound on the back of my neck. As the bus took off, I quickly reached into my bag and opened one of the side windows. I threw the apple cookies at my mother's feet.

Swaying in the dust that filled the inside of the bus, I sat down. I pulled the curtain shut. Outside, olive trees, plowed fields, thorny gardens and telephone poles flowed by. I knew that. Shedding tears would do me no good, that too I knew. Still, all along the way, like a child stuffed into the back room, I cried and cried and cried.

Blemish (Leke)

By Gonca Özmen (2005)
Translated by Gökçenur Ç. (2009)

I.
The valley revealed its secret to me
I found you on a vast plain
When the leaf dropped, the fig fell silent

One side of me was scorched
And I placed you there

Take those sweet waters, those heady scents
What was distant comes closer
Surely a woman pours a river into you

Stay on the other side of touch
Embrace the absence that you imagine me

— Wind that blows through us
                    is picking up leaves somehow

II.
I thought everything fell silent with you
Time tells its secret to screens
A path winds through my body
I was those unending words
The expectant wood

I used to think the heavens descended with you
A squirrel zips into your lap
Takes me, leads me to a blemish
So I thought

You were those tireless waters
Those living sounds

I, you see, used to fill you ceaselessly

III.
You started, so let everything pass
Let the geranium in me bloom, the sea recede

Let me have a dream full of seeds inside
Let rivers pass through me, wild figs

Because morning has flurried lips
There are sanctuaries! Darknesses

If time stops let's put on silence
Let the light of your eyes know no return

Let the body's ache unwind in words
Let my face no more fade in photographs

You began, so let everything pass
Quiet, said the ant, let time march on

Shadows (Gölgeler)

By Gonca Özmen (2009)
Translated by Deniz Perin and Arzu Eker (2009)

A person looks at a yellow patience sometimes
However human a yellow patience may be

A person sometimes goes to olive trees
Feeds the horses, touches the curtains

Sometimes, too, a language dies
Or an ant smiles

A word goes and finds another
A walnut retreats into its shell
An insect suddenly forgets its voice

The evening, secretly, in the garden
In the garden secretly
A forever grows

The world belongs not to us, but to shadows

Start Again (Bana Beklet)

By Gonca Özmen (2008)

Translated by Arzu Eker and Deniz Perin (2009)

Save me the statue of your feet
Save me that shy flower in your pot

I, who am oppressed by the whiteness of a page
The solitude of mute houses on my face

Wherever I look, this garden's mess
If only I could pass through you
My sorrow's carriage, its limping pace

Save me the awareness
Of this wound, our mortality

I, who am the birds' migration time
The vicious snake you've been feeding

Oh, the spacious calm of unknowing

The wind brought fear
Set it between us, just like that

Break through the silent and start again

Why I Killed Myself in This City
Kvifor eg drap meg sjølv i byen
(Kendimi Neden Bu Şehirde Öldürdüm)

By Mine Söğüt (2011)

Translated into English by İdil Aydoğan with poetic prologue translated by Alev Ersan (2012)
Translated from English into New Norwegian by Venke Vik (2012)

*Sanninga er at verdet mitt berre er
kåt lyst
Safta mellom beina.
Ikkje meir . . . ikkje mindre
Slepp meg
Lat meg elske det eg lystar og døy der
eg vil.*

*The truth is, I am only as much as the
ache in my groins
the damp between my legs.
No more . . . no less
Let me be . . .
Let me love as much as I want and die
where I will.*

Kvifor eg drap meg sjølv i byen

Du kjenner til desse heilage byane
i fjerne land som folk dreg til
slik at dei kan døy?
Du veit korleis dei legg seg ned
på skitne puter i falleferdige tempel
som ligg nær innsjøar
og alvorstung, ventar på døden?

Nett som dei, kom eg til denne byen
frå eit land langt borte,
for å gjere det slutt . . .
for å ta livet av meg sjølv.

Eg kunne rett og slett døydd
i den byen eg vart født,

Why I Killed Myself in This City

You know those holy cities
in faraway lands to which people
travel so as to die?
You know how people lie down
on filthy cushions in ruined temples
situated near lakes
and gravely await death?

Like them, I came to this city
from a faraway land,
to end it . . .
to kill myself.

In fact, if they had let me,
I could very well have died

når tida var inne,
som noko sjølvsagt
om dei hadde late meg vere i fred.

Men livet pirka i meg
med ein roten kjepp.
Det sa, kom deg opp,
hald fram , følg etter galskapen,
følg etter likesæla,
følg etter ambisjonane,
følg etter tvilen,
hald fram og far til den byen,
streif rundt i gatene,
elsk i løynde krokar,
drep på åsane og døy i avgrunnane.

Frå første dagen eg kom til denne
                                    byen,
gjekk eg inn i kvar ham som helst og
                                    kasta meg
inn i den eine faren etter den andre.
I det stillaste nabolaget,
i ein ordinær bustad
i ein heilt ordinær leigegard,
med min ordinære ektemann
og ordinære born.

Sjølv om eg verkeleg førte eit ekte
ordinært liv, fall det raude, blonde,
                                    svarte,
brune håret mitt ut av vindauga og
faren klatra opp etter håret mitt.

Den eine dagen vert eg
knivstukken i hjarta av sjalusi,

in the town where I was born.
When the time came,
as a matter of course.

But life prodded me
with a rotten stick.
It said, get up,
tag along behind insanity,
behind mindlessness,
behind ambition; tag along
behind disbelief; get up
and go to that city,
roam its streets,
make love in its every corner;
kill on its hills and die in its pits.

From the first day I arrived in this
                                    city,
I've been in every guise,
                                    choosing
one danger over another.
In the quietest neighborhood,
in an ordinary apartment
in a most ordinary building,
with my ordinary husband
and ordinary children.

Even if I did lead a truly ordinary
                                    life,
my red, blonde, black, brown hair
would dangle down the window
and danger would climb up my hair.

One day I am stabbed in
the heart with jealousy,

den andre dagen knivstikk eg
mannen min i hjarta.
Alltid ein svartskjefta kniv
i kjøkenet mitt.
Armoda er dømt til å lukte død.

Eg føder den eine ungen etter
den andre. Nokre tek eg meg av,
andre får greie seg på gata.
Brannar bryt ut i huset mitt.
Nokre gonger kastar eg meg
i flammane for å berge borna,
nokre gonger vert eg spinngalen
av å tenke på dei som åt opp.

Det har hendt nokre gonger, når
eg og ungane vart drepne
av osen frå ein lek gass-sylinder,
eller av røyk som siva at
vi låg samakrulla i senga.

Nokre gonger er eg ei ung jente
som arbeider i ein frisørsalong.
Eg steller hendene eller føtene til kvinner
som har kjolar eg aldri får bære,
som har menn eg aldri får elske,
som har sorger eg aldri får dele,
og pressar dei mot dei tynne
skjelvande knea mine.
Og med saks, neglefil,
neglelakk, neglelakkfjernar,
såpe, krem, glede, smerte
og forakt i hendene mine, med
korte rosa fingerneglar,
får eg eit nervøst samanbrot.

the next day I stab my
husband in the heart.
Always a black-handled knife
in my kitchen.
Poverty is deemed to smell of death.

I give birth to children one after
the other. Some I raise, others
I let out onto the streets.
Fires break out in my house.
Sometimes I fling myself
into the flames to save my children;
sometimes I get delirious thinking of
the ones swallowed up by the flames.

There have been a few occasions
when my children and I were killed
from the fumes of a leaking gas cylinder,
or from smoke coming in from the chimney,
cuddled up together in bed.

Sometimes I am a young girl
who works at a hair salon.
I take the hands or feet of the women
with whom I will never wear
the same dresses, love the same men,
grieve over the same things,
and place them against
my skinny, trembling knees.
And with scissors, nail files,
nail polish, nail polish remover,
soap, cream, pleasure, pain,
and spite in my short pink
finger-nailed hands,
I have a nervous breakdown.

Den maniske demonen min
går til åtak på meg og taus
lyttar *ho* til endelause samtalar.
Ein dag kjem *ho* til å flykte
frå innsida mi og drepe deg,
meg eller alle saman, ein etter ein
Det ønsker eg å seie dei. Eg tagnar.

Når togna vert omforma
til eit mektig rop, er eg langt, langt
                        borte.
Frå alle i slekta, frå alle eg kjenner,
frå draumane mine, frå pasjonane . . .
Så langt . . . Lat oss seie eit hotellrom
                        i Beyoğlu.
Eg står framfor spegelen og
stirer på det bleike andletet mitt.
Med rennande sminke og små pupillar.
Farginga på dei kløyvde hårendane
                        bleika,
er bleika og den visne hjartesjela sliten.
Eg gjev meg sjølv eit nytt namn kvar dag.
Og dei er alle blomenamn.
Eit nytt namn for kvar mann.
Eg er Rose, eg er Violet,

eg er Daffodil, eg er Jasmine,
eg er Forgløymmegei . . .
og nokre gongar Calendula.

Til tider streifar eg
i gatene heile natta.
Med spritflaska i handa
søv eg på fortaua.
Stundom lener eg meg mot veggen,

My manic demon turns
against me and, silenced, she listens
to their ceaseless conversations.
One day she will escape
from inside me and kill you,
me or all of us one by one,
I want to tell them. I fall silent.

When my silence transforms
into a huge cry, I am far, far away.
From all my relatives, everyone I
                        know,
from my dreams, my passions . . .
So far . . . Let's say in a hotel room
                        in Beyoğlu.
I stand in front of the mirror
and stare at my pale face.
My makeup smudged, my pupils
                        tiny.
The dye of my frayed hair faded,
my faded soul's heart torn.
I give myself a new name every day.
And they'll all be flower names.
A different name for every man.
I am Rose, I am Violet,

I am Daffodil, I am Jasmine
I am Forget Me Not
And sometimes Calendula.

There are times when I
roam the streets all night.
A liquor bottle in my hand,
I sleep on the sidewalks.
Sometimes I lean against walls,

krøker meg ned på steinar,
set meg i bilar til framande.
Du ser meg i lastebilar
med ein røyk i neven
og full av bannskap,
det er heile tida sterk vind
over hovudet mitt som
bles lagnaden min omkring.

Eg ser ut av vindauga i lastebilen.
Ei lita jente som på fortauet får
fanga blikket mitt. Ho er kledd
i skitne filler, berrføtt, med snørrnase.
Eg veit mora er
nokon stad i nærleiken.

Samankrøka, nær rota av treet
vaktar ho på henne i løynd.
Jenta løftar hovudet og ser tomt
på dei som går forbi.
Med dei små, usynlege hendene,
klenger ho seg til leggane
til dei ho maktar
fange blikket til.
«Pengar,» seier ho,
«gje meg pengar»

Nokre gongar væter ho seg.
Pisset hennar renn som
ei lita elv nedetter vegen.

Eg fødde ein skokk med ungar
som drukna i den elva.

Stundom er eg ei seksten års

crouch down on stones,
get into strangers' cars.
You see me in trucks,
with a smoke in my hand
and a cursing tongue;
there is always
a violent wind above my head,
blasting my fate around.

I look out of the truck window.
A little girl sitting on the pavement
catches my eye. Dressed in filthy rags,
barefoot, with a snotty nose.
I know that her mother
is somewhere nearby.

Crouched down near the bottom of a tree,
she watches her secretly.
The girl lifts her head up
and stares blankly at passersby.
With her tiny, invisible hands
she clings to the legs of those
with whom she manages
to make eye contact:
"Money," she says,
"give me money."

Sometimes she wets herself.
Her piss runs like
a tiny river down the road.

I gave birth to numerous children
who drowned in that river.

Sometimes in this city,

gravid jente i denne byen.
Eg ligg i sovesofaen heime,
eller sit ved bordet og gret.
Kva om mannen min ikkje kjem heim?
Kva om mannen min bankar meg i
           kveld igjen?

Kjem barnet eg ber på døy?
Vil barnet eg ber på drepe
meg også når det døyr?
Om eg drog heim til far min,
Om eg ba han om å berge meg,
ville han åpne døra?
Ville dei sikte på meg med våpna,
ville dei steine meg i hel?

Og så ville eg føde barnet
heime, åleine.
Som ein katt ville eg
kutte navlestrengen med tennene.
Det ville skrike i eitt kjøyr i tre dagar.
Di meir ungen skreik, di meir
ville mannen min dundre i veggen.
Til slutt ville han trive ungen i
           genseren
og kaste han ut av vindauga.
Kva kan ei mor, som har fått ungen
sin drepen, gjere åleine i denne digre
           byen?

Eg er ho som stel damevesker på
           gatene
og ligg under framande i heslege senger.
Dei løynde lommane i *şalvaren* min er
fulle av pillar. For hundrevis av år sidan,

I am a sixteen-year-old pregnant girl.
I lie down on the sofa bed at home,
or sit at the table, and cry.
What if my husband doesn't come home?
What if my husband beats me again
           tonight?

Will the child inside me die?
Will the child inside me
kill me too when it dies?
If I were to go to my father,
if I were to ask to be saved,
would he open the door for me?
Would guns be pointed,
would they stone me to death?

And then I'd give birth
to the child at home, alone.
Like a cat, I'd tear
the umbilical cord with my teeth.
It would cry nonstop for three days.
The more the baby would cry
the more my husband would punch the walls.
Finally, he'd grab hold of it by its
           cardigan
and fling it out the window.
A mother whose baby has been killed;
what would she do all alone in this huge
           city?

I'm the one who steals women's
           handbags
on the streets and who lays under
           strangers
in foul beds. The hidden pockets on my

kom eg til denne byen frå eit land
            langt borte.

Alt som er å sjå er mørket gjennom
vindauga i det einaste rommet
eg eig. Det er grunnen til at eg
ikkje kan sjå fortida eller framtida mi.
Eit bekmørkt liv er både folksamt og
            einsamt.
Om du nokon gong spurte meg,
kunne eg fortelje deg at
eg faktisk likar denne byen.
Han er diger, fargerik og lokkande.
Han synast vere full av lovnader.
Men det er berre narrespel.
Det er grunnen til at eg kjenner meg ustø,
eg mistar taket, kjærleiken
og galskapen min er begge illusorisk.

Eg er dømt i fengsla hans.
Bomber dekker heile kroppen min
og med revolver i lomma, drøymer eg.
Kva om eg sprengde denne byen
eg ikkje var i stand til å overvinne?
Kva om eg splintra mannfolka
eg aldri har sove med?
Kva om eg stakk ned borna
            eg enno
ikkje har født, rett i hjarta.
Kva om eg møtte i retten og song
songane frå fjella eg kom frå.
Kven er sterkast, byen eller eg?

Stundom brasar eg inn
i dei mørke nabolaga i byen.

şalvar are full of pills. Centuries ago,
I came to this city from a faraway land.

All that can be seen is darkness
through the window in the only room
that belongs to me. That is why I can't see
my past or my future.
In a pitch-dark life it is both crowded
            and lonely.
If you were to ask me, I'd tell you
I actually like this city.
It is huge, colorful and alluring.
It seems to be filled with promises.
But that is just a delusion.
That is why I feel dizzy,
I black out; my love
and my insanity are both
            illusory.

I am sentenced to its prisons.
Bombs covering my whole body
and a gun in my pocket, I dream.
What if I were to blow up this city
that I was unable to defeat?
If I were to shatter into pieces
the men I haven't slept with.
If I were to stab the children
I hadn't yet given birth to right in
            their hearts.
If I were to appear in court singing
the songs of the mountains I came from.
Who is mightier, the city or me?

Sometimes I barge into
the dark neighborhoods of the city.

Kvinnene er kolsvarte.
Eg tumlar midt i ei himmelsk løgn
medan eg vitjar alle gravene, ei etter ei
Alle bønene eg kan vert til regnet
som strøymer ned over meg.

Nett då trur eg på alt . . .
Og for det meste på helvete, på
lidinga i grava og at eg aldri vil kunne
riste synda bort
frå akslene mine, korkje
i denne verda eller i neste . . .
At eg sjølv er ei kjødeleg synd.

Kva om eg kunne halde denne
byen i handflata mi og
skrubbe, gnu og pusse han
med ein klut, kunne eg då rense
byen frå alle hot?
Ville då dei hundre- og
tusenvis av kvinneliv til
slutt famne om ein ny lagnad?

Denne byen har vore mann i hundrevis av år og veit ikkje korleis elske
ei kvinne.
Det er grunnen til at eg drep meg sjølv,
i denne byen, gong på gong, kvar dag.

Eg eksploderer som ei bombe;
kastar meg ut fra tårna, frå bruene.
Med kniven i handa kuttar
eg meg over heile kroppen.
Frå taka heng alle løkkene så
eg kan henge meg sjølv.

The women are black as coal.
Tumbling inside a celestial lie
one by one I visit all the graves
All the prayers I know become the rain
and pour down on me.

At that moment, I believe in everything . . .
And mostly in hell, in the sufferings of
the grave,
and that I will never shrug
my sins off my shoulders, not in
this world nor in the next . . .
That I myself am the embodiment of sin.

If I were to hold the city
in the palm of my hand and,
if I were to scrub, rub and
polish it with a cloth, would the city
be cleansed of menace?
Would the hundreds and thousands
of forms of womanhood finally
embrace a new fate?

This city has been a man for centuries
and doesn't know how to love women.
That is why, in this city,
I kill myself over and over again each
day.

I explode like a bomb;
jump off its towers, its bridges.
A knife in my hand,
I slit my body all over.
All the ropes on the ceilings dangle
down so I may hang myself.

Bilane køyrer så eg kan
kaste meg framfor dei.

Min namnlause kropp er i
sjøen, i kloakken, i søppelhaugane.
Mitt grenselause mot vil finne rom
i den trongaste glipa
på gravplassen til dei ukjente.

Cars cruise so I can
jump in front of them.

My unidentified body in its sea,
its sewers, its rubbish dumps.
My colossal courage would fit
into the narrowest pits
in the cemetery of the nameless.

From *Lonelinesses* (*Yalnızlıklar*)

By Hasan Ali Toptaş (1993)

3.

Translated by Şehnaz Tahir Gürçağlar (2006)

A table naked, on its own, implies a chair for us
black implies white, white black.
A child has pointed a finger and implies a distance;
and distance implies the child.
The grass that sways along the bottom of the rock implies the wind;
the wind that falls
implies the grass.
The timidity of your steps,
implies the path you take;
the bird implies the sky,
it is the sky that implies the bird.
Whatever may cover up
whatever
with whatever what,
this thing, that thing:

Each thing is loneliness.

4.

Translated by Erdağ Göknar (2006)

Loneliness up and takes us,
a mute horse, its mane flickering endlessly
across our sight, the hoof-thuds through our body.
That's why the distance throbs
in fetlocks
and we in the distance.
Whatever else, lonely is the distant in our midst;
should noise fail to strike it, I wonder
is it still noise,
are lines still lines, people people,
throngs throngs?
Even fountains gush it in my gran's voice
before I reach my hand out to the flow.
Gran with her chestnut-scented voice then
fades within the mountains;
and in the place called Baklan,
so that a voice does not chill another voice,
shepherds who wrap their wounds in goat paths
sleep with the searing sound of a shepherd's pipe.

Loneliness is a shepherd
lone in shepherds' eyes
goading time.

Tradition and Innovation, *Ghost Ship* Adventures, and Writing for Effect

Excerpt from a Talk by Murat Gülsoy (2008)
Translated by Nilgün Dungan (2012)

Not many writers have the opportunity to participate in a translation workshop focusing on their own books, where they meet and discuss their work with the transla-tors. This is a very special experience in regard to writing.

I have always been intrigued by any experience that involves the writing process. Today, I plan to talk about not just *İstanbul'da Bir Merhamet Haftası* (*A Week of Kindness in Istanbul*), but about myself and my literary work, and how I posi-tion myself in relation to this work.

You can imagine how hard a task this must be. While preparing this talk, I did a little self-analysis. It's been said that when you take the boring stuff out of life, what remains is the drama. In other words, that's when the story emerges. There's this sort of relationship between life and the story. When someone tries to express himself or herself, he or she actually sets up a story. I, too, thought about setting up this story, and I reviewed my life up to the present day. Consequently, I noticed two things. The first is that during my talk you'll get to know me. And the other is that I constantly experience tension between two opposing poles: working as an engineer and academic on the one hand, and continuing my life as a writer on the other.

These two poles create tension; I mean, science and art involve different methods, indeed, even contrasting methods from time to time. Science is a field where certain questions are already posited, and which is based on your dealing with these problems, offering solutions and putting forward new questions. It has a method that evolves like an expanding globe—in a direct, measurable field. There's no such thing in art. Art doesn't have voids, and in reality you're not needed there. No writer, musician, sculptor or any artist is expected to write, compose or create a certain way, since in art there's no void. There's nothing like "Come on, let's invent a new genre like detective fiction." Art is not something that develops this way or expands with added knowledge. In art a different process is at work, one in which the artist's personal experience remains at the forefront, and through which the artist shares his or her experience with others. It's between these two poles of tension that I stand.

A second point of tension is something I can express by looking from a literary perspective. My adventures initially in reading and then later in writing have been a constant course running between tradition and innovation; a reckoning, in a sense, and a quest. This tension between tradition and innovation is surely nurturing; however, the two poles of tension—science and art, tradition and innovation—may fail to nurture a person as well. No rules exist per se, but I say "What doesn't kill you makes you stronger," and in this way something emerges.

*　*　*

I wondered how *A Week of Kindness in Istanbul* came about. I liked my idea inspired by a book by Max Ernst, and I wrote with vigor. As I thought about what I have done up to now, this book seemed like a meaningful summary, because I had experimented with alluding to other writers, even rewriting some of their texts in my stories or novels. But for the first time, I based a novel on another book. Why did Ernst excite me as much as he did? Why has he been on my agenda for years? When I think about it, I remember the first time I came across him. It was on the cover of a magazine we published, called *Hayalet Gemi* (*Ghost Ship*). This magazine was a construct that involved my entire writing and publishing career, which is why I need to talk a little bit about *Hayalet Gemi* in order to offer an insight into my approach to literature and art.

I was a successful student and enrolled in the Electrical Engineering Department at Boğaziçi University. Everything was fine, and I was interested in literature too. I could've been regarded as a good reader, and I also wrote little, romantic pieces, until I read Oğuz Atay during my freshman year, that is. I was immensely impressed by Atay's texts, since he was an engineer and I was going to become an engineer, too. He was also a major literary figure, and I thought to myself that I could become a writer too, although I wouldn't make writing my career. What he wrote was witty, different, childish, playful, sad and new for me. It didn't look like anything I'd read in Turkish literature up until then. When you aspire to be a writer, you feel after a while that you'll continue in the same tradition as what's been written at home. I thought that you could only exist once you're included, sooner or later, in that tradition. Or else I thought that only works in this style would emerge from this culture, this land, and I read them with pleasure. Yet I never felt really close to any of them until I got to know Atay. The transforming effect that had on me! I repeated out loud to myself: I can become a writer and I should. I should write, and that should be one of my life goals. It was just as in my dealings with science, yet the excitement even surpassed the one afforded by science. After reading Atay, I went on to write.

I finished my engineering education and decided to pursue a graduate degree in psychology. I got involved in my studies, interested in topics such as consciousness, cognition and perception. As I neared the end of my studies, I realized that whether I pursued a PhD or not, I'd start to work soon. Of course, I wasn't alone; I had many friends involved in writing. However, we'd all go off in different directions and our cultural and intellectual production would end. So we decided to publish a magazine, just as the previous generation had done.

It was 1992 and the Internet was not yet available, but advances were being made in desktop publishing. Then one day, when I was in the psychology lab and using my Macintosh for an entirely different purpose, I got involved in trying to help my girlfriend of the time with a book she was translating. The publisher had given her a page design program on a floppy disk to aid her with proofreading, and I was helping her figure out how to use the program. As I noticed how simple the program was and how user-friendly the Macintosh was, it occurred to me how easily a newspaper or magazine could be published with this page design. Right away, we designed a one-page newspaper about the funny incidents happening in the lab those days. Then, like so many others in our generation, we thought we had to use this technology to publish a magazine of our own. Since photocopying was widely available and desktop publishing was so simple, everyone at that time had started publishing fanzines.

Gathering around the magazine as a group much as older generations had done, we brought *Hayalet Gemi* to life. Later on, the Internet would become widespread, and instead of gathering around a table, people would continue in more personalized spaces, such as blogs and Facebook. We were familiar with the magazines published by earlier generations, and frankly, I regarded most of these as having dark, boring and uninspiring designs. We thought it necessary to express novel ideas in novel forms. Besides, we felt we needed to say new things, things that didn't declare the obvious. But then again, we wanted a magazine in which we could say our piece without coming up with a grand manifesto claiming that everything would be totally different now that this magazine was being published. You know the famous legend of the Flying Dutchman and the ghost ship? Borrowing from that legend, we decided to name our magazine *Hayalet Gemi* (*Ghost Ship*), because in the legend, unable to find love, the captain is cursed and destined to roam the open seas in a ghost ship. He goes ashore every seven years, looks for love, can't find it, and returns to the seas. And the ship never sinks, which is actually a curse. We thought to ourselves that if we named it as such, the magazine would not go under, unlike many other magazines published around that time did. Indeed, we managed to keep it in print for ten years, which in magazine publishing is actually a long time.

As for the contents, in addition to literature, the magazine included articles about philosophy, sociology, architecture, physics and mathematics too. What brought these pieces together was a theme. We thought we'd design each issue as a ship's voyage, with visits to ports, and with each contributor exploring the ports by using his or her own tools and perspective. In addition, we included authors who were not widely translated at the time. Our friends had translated many texts by sociologists and historians. Thus, the magazine quickly established its own authors and its own readership. We were trying to do something different as well through our awareness of the fact that when a text appeared juxtaposed with another text, it created a different impression than it would have on its own. We were particularly fussy about the covers too. We worked with expert artists and designers, so that the covers fit the themes of the issues. A picture by Max Ernst was used on one of the covers. Our designer intertwined a collage by Ernst with other elements relevant to our theme, resulting in a collage covering another collage, so that I was tempted to study it more deeply. Later on, the book that picture came from became an indispensible source for me. Whenever I needed inspiration I would stare at it.

It took me a while to get published, but once I did, I didn't part ways with *Hayalet Gemi* but rather continued with it through radio programs and the Internet. Preparing those radio programs was a valuable experience for me in that it not only allowed me to become more familiar with Turkish authors but also to gain story analysis experience through close reading of texts during the selection process. In addition, out of curiosity, I read up on literary theory and narratology. I discovered that reading theoretical texts could be inspiring too. Combining these theoretical readings with story analyses done by the *Hayalet Gemi* team on the radio, we started up a creative writing workshop in 2003. Within the scope of the workshop, I put together a book that offered formulas and included story analyses. In addition, it took a critical approach and had a theoretical framework. What we did in the workshop helped me with my studies in collective literature, a need I had otherwise been unable to fulfill after *Hayalet Gemi* ran its course.

Just as we had themes for the issues of *Hayalet Gemi*, each week at the workshop we tried to assign provocative and inspiring tasks. My friends thought these assignments were very similar to what the fictional writer in *A Week of Kindness in Istanbul* did. My friends who knew about my interest and involvement in creative writing said that the source of my inspiration for the book was the workshop. For five years I had been giving assignments to people, compelling them to write and observing what they paid attention to, what kind of relationships they established with the topic and the text, and how they expressed themselves. In the book, I tried in a sense to simulate all this.

After a long while, my books began to be published, and people reproached me for being postmodern and laughed up their sleeves. A group of writers, young ones especially, who aspired to be traditional, didn't take *Hayalet Gemi* seriously. They were particularly surprised that my books were published by Can Publishing, a well-known publisher of traditional literature. I had no idea why they published them, but I am a writer who sees art as based on effect. I mean, when you write a story or a novel, your goal is to create some effect on the reader. I'm always open to this effect too. If a book doesn't grip me in some way, I don't continue with that relationship; instead I try to deepen my relationship with writers who take hold of me. When my book *Bu Kitabı Çalın* (*Steal This Book*) came out, my previous critics mocked the title. But when it was awarded the Sait Faik Short Story Award, which is an award for traditional literature, my relationship with tradition became more profound. On the other hand, metafiction, that is, a text which constantly refers to itself, reminding the reader that it's fiction, dealing with the process of writing the text, is something that has always been present in my writing.

All of the innovations provided by the Internet were of course exciting, but what I found the most exciting was my realization that it entailed possibilities for hypertexts, different narration and plot construction techniques. The Internet motivated me to pursue more experimental products and drew me to more modernist writers of the past. With its visuals and music, it's the medium that enabled me to do the things I couldn't do in a printed book. For instance, using the axis of time is not something you could easily think of in a regular text. Let me give an example of what we did. I designed a text that changed a little each day. When you accessed the text, it did not appear to be very different from the one that was there the day before. I mean, when you compared the text to the previous or the following one, it didn't seem very distinctive, but when you looked at it ten days later, it was quite different. I came up with this idea while pondering life; every day resembles another in terms of our psychology or thoughts, but as time goes on, we're not the same person anymore, and in fact we've gone through quite a lot. I found doing such playful things on the Internet exciting, while at the same time I was excited about writing novels and trying novel ideas in my fiction.

Bu Filmin Kötü Adamı Benim (*I'm the Bad Guy in This Movie*) was some sort of a metafiction. Since the structure was somewhat complicated and it ended in a way that provided no sense of relief for the reader—a way that made everything blurry rather than clarifying things—I didn't think the book would be received well. Also, the protagonist was an unsympathetic antihero. But for this novel too, I won an award, this time the Yunus Nadir Novel Award, which again had a very traditionally-minded jury. After that a few critics said some nice things, but now whenever anything's written about me, I'm labeled as postmodern. This upsets me, but in my opinion whenever something is seen as new or different, it's called postmodern, since even modern, let alone postmodern, literature isn't understood well enough. But I don't dwell too much on that, because what makes me write is the effect, and the excitement created by that effect—can I do something new, can I say different things, does it allow me to gain experience? The most important thing in the writing process is to have that experience and to know that someone will read this, but how? That's something I'm very curious about. The main indicator of my curiosity is this: you know I told you I kept looking and looking at Ernst's book and didn't get it; well, I still don't. But then I thought to myself "What would others think if they looked at this book?" For instance, what would your significant other, your child, your uncle or your teacher think? I wrote *A Week of Kindness in Istanbul* with just such a curiosity.

When I write a story or a novel, I give it to someone to read whose opinion I'm curious about. If the person next to me is reading, I follow the sentences and imagine how it comes to life in his or her mind. If I give someone a book to read at home, I imagine how that person is reading it. In other words, I enjoy imagining someone else's perspective on the experience of reading.

I also consider characterization in literature very important, and I become very happy and am quite impressed when I find a flesh-and-blood character in a book I'm reading, especially if the character is situated in an unordinary structure or as an experiment. Consequently, I wondered whether I could create seven characters, seven life stories, seven perspectives, seven styles in this book. Of primary importance is the style, as it is something you see right away, but the life stories are held by the author, like an iceberg, of course. The fact that during the writing process, the book allowed such experiments excited me. It was great fun to create seven characters; it was important for me to do something about the pictures I'd been looking at for at least seven years. There were both male qand female perspectives in the book. The second thing was this: how will the reader read this? Of course, it could be read in different ways. Some readers could think that this task was actually given to seven people and written by them, and there's no reason why they shouldn't feel that way. I mean, nowhere in the book do I tell the reader that I didn't really give this assignment to seven people. Of course, I gave the fictional writer a life story of his own, in order to distance myself from him. But only a person who knows me would know I'm not that writer. In the second place, I thought that if the reader was really engrossed in the book, he would inevitably wonder about what he thinks of the picture himself, which brought a sort of interactivity to the book. I mean, it was like the interactive things I tried to do on the Internet. I even thought about putting a few blank pages so that the reader would ask herself what she thought and then write it down on those pages. There were some people, of course, who did just that and sent me their responses—some very nice ones actually. I wish those could be added to the book too.

From *A Week of Kindness in Istanbul*
(*İstanbul'da Bir Merhamet Haftası*)

By Murat Gülsoy (2007)

I.
[Sunday]

Welcome to the City [Deniz] (Burası Bir Şehir [Deniz])
Translated by İdil Aydoğan (2008)

THREE CLOSED WINDOWS IN THE BACKGROUND A TREE
RIGHT BENEATH IT THREE ORBS THREE MEN ONE WITH
A LION'S HEAD SWOLLEN BELLY LIKE A BALLOON A SUN-
FLOWER IN THE MIDDLE THE ONLY THING THAT LOOKS
STRAIGHT AT US IT HAS A TAIL TOO THEY'RE ALL ON THE
SIDEWALK TWO ARE WATCHING WELCOME TO THE CITY

Welcome to the City.

Where it is easy to get lost or thought to be so but you can't when you want to
quite the opposite on the contrary all the roads lead home leave home and lead
back home on the roads on the roads are shops supermarkets drugstores patisse-
ries agencies bottled water bottled gas banks newsstands banks bakeries banks and
rushing up and down up and down that road over and over again no time to stop
and look to take a breather in this jungle called the city is it possible to breathe
to take a deep breath or not without questioning taking a deep breath real deep
but swelling like a balloon taking in all that air and swelling and perhaps then the
daisy on your chest will grow and grow and grow and turn into a sunflower shining like the sun it becomes a sunflower a lion's mouth with mane with mast a wind
is then inhaled and that's when people stop and look get all curious wondering
who this woman sorry this man in the picture is but then no one wonders where
this woman who keeps writing these words down automatically is and would the
project writer reading these lines accidentally think what have I done how cruel
to make projects out of real people making them pieces of a project puzzle she
couldn't make out swinging her hips her skirts swaying as a nameless faceless city
woman a project puzzle piece now she's really some piece hasn't slept with anyone for ages but she's still wet soaked sweaty and in love and when he throws her
on the back of his saddle and rides his horse towards the loud cries from afar she
cries and rides endlessly but still when she goes out into the street she breathes
she sighs she takes it in she takes it in her mouth it comes in her mouth all the
air all the water all the dust and the whole city is fuel concrete tulips meadows

rocks rocks she's like a rock eternal and tough but still you can't satisfy the city it always goes chasing another who is younger another who is firmer a fresher fish with redder gills a fresh fish hooked in season the shopping the secretarial work the waiters the cleaning the fax ask her no reply it's five o'clock time to clock out behind closed windows dirt piles piles up filth filth is everywhere the duster the sponge the vaccuum sucks up the dirt the dust and swells and swells and swells but no one wonders what this is a balloon a woman a child is she pregnant won't the project writer ask who this is he likes to play he likes proper writing you need language grammar spelling commas compound words single words so that so the masculine world the man's world preserves its order but the woman's world but children come first it all starts with education but grammar and spelling and signs words bleat blah blah blah language falls apart holding a duster her bra's hook cuts her back itches misused but who speaks who listens two men look one man swells in front of the tree a tree in the city a gentleman city tree with epaulets and in uniform waits for the three orbs arms branches held up in prayer in a language not castrated writers swallow all god gives them and it makes them ill makes them belch makes them bloat makes them fart you have to crave food you have to embrace your fears soft sounding letters come together to whisper her name saying city woman come come to me and then she runs and then it's all loneliness waiting behind closed windows no fax no phone cables quiet stupid electrons not transferring information she must put a full stop somewhere so the project writer doesn't freak out thinking she's raving bullshit so he loves it so he goes on loving it so that love like a snail crawls on her window over her leaving its trace so it dries so it's not forgotten so it's not as if nothing ever happened no one should be should die for a project oh lord don't let the sun set on them don't let the moon obstruct them overshadow the bottom of the tree whoever left them there should come and get them should speak to him stop him swelling stop blowing him up you're a man as tough as a lion go earn your money just because you have a flower pinned to your chest so what if it's a sunflower so what if it's pinned to his chest he shouldn't be begging for attention no one cares about anyone no one knows anyone plus what is this place what kind of a city is this what kind of a woman is this writing all this while the child sleeps inside the big grown man sleeps inside the child is asleep big bad husband is asleep this is the city of sleep.

Welcome to the city.

The Power of the Predator [Ayşe] (Yırtıcının İktidarı [Ayşe])
Translated by Nilgün Dungan (2008)

The middle-aged professor who had pledged to contribute to the project of a student who had formerly taken one of her classes began immediately to write after quickly glancing at the picture sent to her. She did not question her student's purpose. She had acted naturally as if she had been expecting such a proposal. Nonetheless, this could not be considered an ordinary case. Initially she liked being a part of her student's project. She was so accustomed to the lack of enthusiasm, curiosity and knowledge, as well as the laziness and desperation of those masses filling up the classroom, listening to lectures with sleepy eyes, that when one of them made such a proposal—for any purpose whatsoever—she became excited. Of course, she guessed a few things on her own. She thought that her student might be working on his thesis. As a participant, she believed that she had already been given all the information she needed about the research, so she dutifully began to perform the task she had been assigned. She was expected to look at the picture and write down whatever came to her mind. She intended to do that now, but she began, already in the first paragraph, to stumble. She was writing in a cold and dry style. She referred to herself in the third person singular, thus trying to distance herself from her writing. She was used to recording what she had in her mind only in this way. Fortunately, there were no restrictions in terms of the writing style.

She had seen these kinds of drawings, etchings and lithographs many times. She knew the drawing was by Max Ernst, and she also remembered that the drawing was part of a series. And that Ernst was a surrealist painter. Even though she could somehow relate to their childish enthusiasm, she believed that surrealists, culturally and historically speaking, belonged to an entirely different world. As could be seen in the example of this drawing, she had a hard time establishing relationships. She could not bring herself to think of them as just any three men, but only as representations drawn with a particular artistic understanding of a certain historical period. The drawing was so very European. Observing from here, it seemed impossible for one to access what the drawing was expressing without somehow alienating oneself from it. Some sort of similiarity could be found in the indifference of the two men standing in front as onlookers. The man with a balloon-like body, i.e., the man being watched, was in the center of the drawing. Had those two other men not been drawn, she would be able to interpret it more freely. On the other hand, the depiction was of a moment of observation. It was a moment difficult to describe. The attempt to depict what cannot be described was the basic point of departure for surrealism, so this was not at all surprising.

Despite all this, the drawing has a clear and easy aspect to it. In between the eye that is doing the viewing and the figure that begs to be viewed stand two men, which, in the universe of the drawing, calls for "normalcy." The claim of a passive stance inherent in the act of viewing appears to be prevalent enough to be the main motif of this drawing. On the other hand, against the rationalism of the viewer, there is a ballooning body that mockingly expands beyond reality. Moreover, the expansion beyond reality is depicted as the body expanding fully into reality. A surrealist existence that claims a space for itself within reality and the silent witnesses of this existence. A giant figure of a daisy attached to the surrealist element expanding into ordinary life once again makes an ironic contribution to the story. A natural object attached to the supranatural!

The naiveté of the surreal masks what lies behind. The fact that the surreal invades the space only conceals the predator's power, represented by the lion figure behind him. Even though he looks like a balloon that could pop any minute, and is made somewhat ridiculous with the attached daisy, the figure retains its function: it conceals what lies behind, and reveals as it conceals.

If this drawing were to be named, it could be called the *Power of the Predator*. The fearlessness of the ones watching this entity with their hands in their pockets, indifferently, both reinforces the power of the predator and appears to undermine that power. This dual function also points to the nature of the act of observation. To watch, to look and to see, without intervention, is nothing but a mechanism of indirect approval. The way the postmodern world exploits the media is based precisely on this dual function. Malice can cause harm only to the extent that it remains concealed. Unacknowledged malice belongs only to its holder. Malice initially becomes possible through the possession of power; however, this kind of power depends upon its being sustained. Malice can have no other strategy than to expand towards eternity. Hence, the predator has to make its power observable one way or another. Once the power becomes observable, it receives the approval of the observers. Approval is not a voluntary act. Rather, it is a psychological transformation experienced by the observer the instant they realize their weakness and impotence. This process is completed when that which is malicious is transformed into something powerful and legitimate. The only way out of disapproval is to create a counterforce. The moment the observers realize that they do not have the strength to do this, they feel that they are on the verge of being sucked into the current of approving the malice. Observers have to find a coping strategy/an explanation to preserve their psychological integrity. Thus the power of the predator is legitimized in the mind of the observer. In other words, first comes the approval, then the explanation. This is the primary function of observation.

The second function, albeit not as strongly determinant as the first, is also significant. To watch and to witness create the effect of undermining the predator's power. This results from assuming that malice will be eliminated once it is expressed/declared. That one day the malice will be punished in the hands of the majority is an archaic belief, although it still retains its novelty. Modern life has long disclaimed such an understanding of justice. Having been pruned, it is no longer operational. Lynching is illegal; nonetheless, the anticipation of it at any given time remains fresh. It is always a last hope, just like the naive belief that the power of the predator will be overthrown one day. Now, the second (or secondary) function of observation is based upon the exploitation of these archaic beliefs. This creates the impression that "if malice is exposed, then its end is imminent" ; therefore, it looks AS IF it undermines power. Yet, the sole loser here is the observer; the one who is observed always wins.

II.
[Monday]

Do Teardrops Cover Three-Quarters of This Earth? [Deniz]
(Gözyaşı mı Bu Dünyanın Dörtte Üçü? [Deniz])
Translated by İdil Aydoğan (2008)

BED DEEP DARK EMBRACE QUILT SHEETS WHITE WOMAN
ASLEEP MAN WATCHING SHIPWRECK SURVIVORS CASUAL-
TIES DREAMS EVERYWHERE

Dreams everywhere sunk in water how she lies how she sleeps the man wonders
and looks looks and thinks man thinks woman asleep arms folded under her head
comfy a woman saying come caress me come hold me a city woman a woman of
fancy rooms of tulle beds of lacework of engravings of embroidery all glittery a
woman should sleep peacefully a stupefying life this is going from bed to bed from
man to no man being a woman in a city you can't check in stag playing checkers
trusting in the wisdom of elderly men is how grand a grand delusion a destruction the woman now in her own time is nothing but ashes and as she strives to
rise from her ashes by writing by writing this and as she strives on the one hand
she breastfeeds the child on the other she breastfeeds the husband striving to
write striving to rise striving forever but whenever the man looks at her a sleeping
woman is all he sees puzzled the project writer would wonder what kind of life
she is leading quote is this the woman or in other words is this that girl I once
knew I once sat next to at open-air cinemas that I built fires with on starry nights
is this that young girl as a woman now is this really her unquote would he think
reading her writing as a woman I mean now before going to sleep before midnight before twelve o'clock the writing must stop or else her pen will morph into a
dagger the writing must stop as soon as possible or the dagger will slash the flesh
open will split it in two will stab one from behind parted legs arms and now that
she is a woman she must diverge dissolve fall apart each fragment flying away like
thirty thousand birds in every possible direction in the eyes of the project writer a
woman falls apart falls from grace to the floor the floor is the sea the floor is deep
how a woman has to fall apart open up give herself always unlike a girl on those
summer nights seasides seastars illuminated by nightstars a girl must always be a
sealed box not fondled not touched a sealed box with tightly closed legs shoulders
drooped hunchbacked a spot at the tip of her nose an embryo star a starlet why

does the project writer give this girl he knows from summer places this chance to write perhaps he remembers her carrying around books by adalet ağaoğlu sevgi soysal nazlı eray selim ileri pınar kür into the outdoor café on the seashore on the beach on the porch atilla ilhan turgut uyar can yücel she reads wherever she goes that is how he knows that she secretly writes secretly lives in poems in lines in words deep down inside she has a heart craving for love gone crazy for love no doubt mistaking the most unlikely things for the least likely people no matter the big spouse sleeping next to her she dreams of sailors men natives caressing her had her hands turned manly clutching it as if clutching a pen pulling it apart tearing it into pieces obscenely she writes whatever comes to mind automatically freely ashamed nighttimes are times to be freely ashamed would the project writer scrape his nails in a flash non-stop all in one breath the woman senses something weird about this picture just like the one yesterday and still she writes and still she looks she is now a looker-writer who can't go on without seizing receipts and when making complaints she is most profound she grabs hold of her pen sharpened by years spent secretly writing poems sluggish on the paper like a slut the paper quivers the tip of her piercing pen quakes perspiring ink at its tip the woman sighs and begins writing to consumer rights columnists to columnists whoever she comes across like a bulldozer she writes and writes and writes and is almost nearly relieved when it is handed in to the post her poisonous pain is drained and only quote sediments unquote remain yet the project writer had now reminded her of the past by asking her to join in to write automatically whatever comes to mind look at the picture depict and write scribble in a flash he had said but he hadn't even asked who this woman was what she was like was she happy unhappy without even asking her how she had been for all these years everyone is in a flurry everyone wants to dream someone else's dream but just can't after all a dream is a dream fluid it streams the man holding his chin head heavy with anxiety a photo of a writer of the intelligentsia looks but just can't see through the woman in bedrooms of lacework huddled in covers a hidden heart a clot is all he sees and when she snaps out of her daydream going in out in out in out in a sea of clichés in sweat blood and tears why do you think the sea is salty do teardrops cover three-quarters of this earth is the remaining quarter laughter echoing in rigid mountains but I can cry when I'm laughing well you can't really call it crying but tears still stream down my cheeks salty like the mighty sea salty cool wet.

Factor of Solitude and Ego Fusion [Ayşe]
(Yalnızlık Faktörü ve Benlik Kanaşması [Ayşe])

Translated by Nilgün Dungan (2008)

The professor who contributed to her former student's project had a good night's sleep, the most peaceful one she had had in a long while. She went to bed with the sweet fatigue of someone who has worked, toiled and, in return, deserved to sleep, and she woke up feeling content in the morning. This was worth analyzing on its own.

Probable reasons:

1. To think and to put her thoughts in writing
    a. To think without feeling academic responsibility
    b. To write without the anxiety of making a mistake
2. The side effects of letting herself go into the free flow of thought
    a. To witness the emergence of new thoughts
    b. The pleasure felt during the proliferation of thought

This is an experience she has long forgotten for she has not felt this way in a while. Remembering brings pain as well, since it characterizes what loss is. Losing makes reality even more real. Losing reinforces the thought that what is lost was once real. What is not yet lost, what is still at hand, always remains in some sort of suspicious existence.

CASE STUDY: Ayşe is a young woman of thirty-two. She has been married for six years and has a four-year-old daughter. On the night of the case in question, her daughter is asleep; her husband, who is a professor like herself, is in the study. It is one of those nights, very similar to the others in recent years. Right then, Ayşe is overcome by an odd feeling. In the beginning, the feeling is like a game, almost fun. What if she were to just slip out the door secretly . . . when would her husband notice her absence? For a grown woman—especially for a professor—this question which stuck in her mind is certainly not an agreeable one, which is why she tries to put it in scientific research format, trying to make light of it.

Noticing/being noticed was the basic parameter of measurement, one minute being the unit of measurement. She even found a fancy name for this elapse of time to notice/be noticed: **factor of solitude**. The purpose of the study was to measure the solitude of couples living under the same roof. This study had to be conducted on couples of different socio-economic status. The length of marriage had to be one of the variables, too. Hypotheses began to emerge in her mind:

– There must be a positive relationship between the length of marriage and the time it takes to notice **(factor of solitude)**. The longer the marriage, the longer it would take to notice.

– As the socioeconomic status increases, the time to notice **(factor of solitude)** could increase proportionately. This could be said to be an inevitable consequence of the fact that low income groups tend to live in relatively smaller houses. Or, it could be assumed that the couple's sensitivity to the presence of one another may have increased. Perhaps, in order for this variable not to affect the measurement, the time to take notice could be normalized (e.g., in order to eliminate the deviation caused by the socioeconomic status, the duration could be divided into the square footage of the house in which the subjects lived).

She had an intense desire to set this imaginary research into action. However, she could not be both the subject and the object of this study at the same time. Who would measure the time if she were to leave the house? Then she had a bright idea: to hide in the closet! And that night, the thirty-two-year-old sociologist Ayşe with a promising future hid in the closet. As they were going through their divorce five years later, she would not remember this night, which is why she would feel more exasperated than expected while trying to justify this separation to friends and family.

As much as failure to notice what is nearby, oversensitivity to it could be another potential cause for concern. The definition of closeness in interpersonal relationships could be contingent upon many different variables. One of these is the presence of an effect labeled **ego fusion**. **Ego fusion** means that an ego absorbs another one, makes it its own, letting it dissolve in itself. This condition, observed among couples who have been together for a long time, is the reversal of the mirror phase in childhood. The child realizes, at an early stage of development, that s/he is an entity apart from her/his mother. The boundaries of the world begin to gain definition as this realization takes place. **Ego fusion** is the reversal of this phase at one level when an adult integrates other egos into his/her own. **Ego fusion** becoming collective in nature is the mechanism that underlies the process of becoming a community. In a couple's relationship, the most striking examples of **ego fusion** are seen in marriage. In long-term marriages, the **ego fusion** effect will emerge as the loss of the ability to see the spouse as another entity, and the fallacy of seeing the spouse as an indispensible part of one's self. Accordingly, the spouse who disappears in the house will not be noticed, for as long as the individual perceives her/himself, s/he assumes that the spouse is there as well. The **phantom-spouse** feeling which follows the death of a spouse is an extension of this feeling, although it does not last long. The middle-aged professor put forth this thought model while she was suffering from post-divorce blues: during one night when she realized that the variable she described as the **factor of solitude** was based on an entirely inaccurate model . . .

Now, looking at the second Ernst drawing sent to her for the project to which she is contributing, she thinks that in the drawing, the look in the man's eyes corresponds to the pre-**ego fusion** period. The look is depicted as representing curiosity. Curiosity is the innocent first name of doubt; hence, the person who is here doing the looking has doubts. The person who is looked upon seems to be aware that she is being watched even though she appears to be asleep. The position of her arms signifies a feminine presentation of herself. Furthermore, the design of the fabric which surrounds the bed gives it the appearance of a stage. The woman who is being watched seems to be aware that she is the center of a show. However, the fact that she's asleep—i.e., unconscious—suggests that her awareness is not conscious. A situation that is on the threshold of sexist discourse. It could be discussed separately . . .

The male figures in relation to the woman's provocative position are depicted on two levels. One is extremely self-confident, curiously watching the woman's desirous invitation. As for the two other male figures, they are sinking in the water covering the room's floor. The masts sticking out of the water indicate the presence of a boat, or a craft, underneath, which means that—before the desire of the woman took shape—she was swimming with the others in the craft. But a storm capsized everything and sank the craft. The "craft" (etymologically speaking, craft is a word derived from the Greek *tekhnologia*) is capsized here to symbolize the male culture's instrumentalization of the world through reason.

The desire of the woman threatens the culture of reason; the male culture (here it should be noted that the figures in the sinking craft are naked), seduced by the desire of the woman, is collapsing. It is being pushed under the water. Water, which is a feminine symbol in many cultures, symbolizes life and the soul at the same time. The idea of "underwater" points to the subconscious or the dark and irrational chaos of the unconscious. The male figures who are about to drown have fallen outside the circle of the rational. However, above and beyond all this chaos stands another male figure who manages to stay put in the drawing. The male standing in this depiction with the posture of an expert (the phallic grace of his posture is another noteworthy detail) owes his strength to this expert posture which transforms his desire into an object to be examined. The male figures who are drowning in the storm of desire are holding onto their own phalluses, which are symbolized by the masts of the craft; however, the standing figure appears to have successfully resisted desire by metamorphosing into the phallic symbol itself, rather than holding onto his own phallus.

The middle-aged woman now reads her thoughts, which she has freed, through a different lens.

First, she wrote that she experienced a temporary period of happiness after having materialized the first step of the project. As she was listing the probable reasons, her anxiety at the loss of happiness triggered the memory of the long forgotten case study. Perhaps it is an attempt at confrontation undertaken with the strength powered by happiness. She tried to probe into her psychological state of mind as she put forth the **factor of solitude** and **ego fusion** models. However, the *desire-of-the-woman* motif that she noticed as she was "reading" the second drawing now stresses once again the inadequacy of these models. What is lacking, forgotten—of course, suppressed—in her approach to the case study—in two different periods—is the problematic of desire. The thoughts she posits as she is "reading" the drawing are focused on the destructiveness in male culture of the desire of the female. Desire and destructiveness. She doubts whether she is ready to question how she brought together these two notions in the above-mentioned case study, for the only thing that was destroyed by the desire to be noticed felt by the woman who disappeared (erased herself) in the house (in life) was her own ego. Burning with the desire to become whole again after a long time, the crumbled ego developed the **ego fusion** model. Now she realizes that all this is nothing but the struggle of a woman who is suffering because of her desire to clear her name by using her mental faculties. Nonetheless, the impossibility of satisfying desire, filling the void, comprehending the unconsious: these are all concepts that she has known for a long time. To know?

Done with the City (Kent Bitti)

By Gülten Akın (1995)

Translated by Mel Kenne, Arzu Eker and Cemal Demircioğlu (2006)

Voices closeby gone
nights have changed hands, demolitions
not even mentioned, left tongues
disintegration on the agenda

no one can unite
with the metallic discourse of antennas and satellites
do those who encounter each other
in the midst of foreign names traffic signs alarm bells
really meet? they can't
this is more like a collision
crashing crashing all day crashing
in the city's heavy waters
everyone wounded

men
pricking into their blood alcohol splinters
men being born out of their madness
women
shutting themselves up in their wombs
playing with their secrets

done
with the city

Rubai for the Saints (Azizler Rübaisi)

By Murathan Mungan (1978)
Translated by Ronald Tamplin and Cemal Demircioğlu (2010)

at night our voices slip off their maleness
always something of the woman's there, her time to enter upon the streets,
and the romance begins long and dark the smoke from cigarettes
each morning we are shipwrecked stained with blood

Write, and You'll Really Be Up Shit Creek
(Yaz da Gör Ebenin Şeyini)

By Ahmet Büke (2008)

Translated by Jonathan Ross (2011)

"ASTRONAUTS SPEND EIGHT HOURS WORKING OUTSIDE SHIP"

"Rıza Abi, I'm talking to you."

Rıza is dozing away, a bottle in his lap. He's really miserable this evening. Couldn't sell his book. "That bastard of a publisher," he mumbles to himself on and off. And the fish aren't biting. All we've caught are two condoms and three garbage bags.

I turn the newspaper towards the pressure lamp. On the back page are the usual pictures of decent family girls. The rowboat rocks gently. Opposite us, the lights from the shore at İnciraltı. What's going on in this or that house, I wonder.

"Bet you're thinking, who's giving it to whom doggy-style?"

"For God's sake, Rıza Abi, are you listening to me?"

"That bastard of a publisher. He didn't get them to put my books on the front shelf."

In the distance, a passenger ship drifts by. Its glimmer shatters the mirror of the sea.

In an instant, I grab hold of Rıza Abi's legs and tip him into the water. He's a good swimmer. If he can splash around for a bit, he'll come to his senses. Otherwise, he'll drive me nuts until the morning. So he couldn't sell his book—who the hell would read those shitty stories of yours anyway!

"Ahmet, when we get to the shore, you're fucked."

"Don't worry, abi, I'll fix us some *rakı* and a bite to eat. I'll even get some ice."

"Ahmeeet!"

In the darkness, we slide smoothly through the sea, my soul captivated by this moonless night.

I should have a go at this writing lark too. There's the story of Işıl from the girls' dormitory, for example. The story of how, one night, she jumped over the wall and came to our room. Of how she undressed silently. Of how she didn't know where to hide that tool of hers. Of the money she had saved to get rid of it. Of how Rıza Abi collected money for her from his friends.

Get real, Ahmet. If you wrote, who would read you?

That bastard of a life.

The pebbles are easier to make out now. I'm getting closer to hell.

The Spokesperson of Words
(Sözcüklerin Sözcüsü)

By Gökçenur Ç. (2005)

Translated by Kurt Heinzelman and Saliha Paker (2008)

With greetings to Wallace Stevens and Enis Batur

My dear editor,
I've received your letter reproaching me
for turning down the proposal for an interview.
You may recall we experienced a crisis like this before
when you wished to publish my picture with my poetry.
This is the jasmine leaf's resistance, you said then, *to the reality*
of autumn. A noble gesture but in vain. You'll damn well get wet . . .
This time you say, *We don't know your actual name, your real*
surname or gender, where you come from or when
you might deign to tell us.
The reality of my name is no redder than the redness of autumn;
best, therefore, to name me as I sign the poems—Gökçenur.
The gender of salutation (Mr/Ms)—what does it matter?
I hoped you might see (a careful editor like yourself
and the kind of good reader one doesn't meet with often)
that I don't like adjectives. *The poet*
who would gather words like large wrasses
into a net woven of invisible cordage
between objects and their names must throw back
into the sea such qualifiers, as if they were
accidental starfish. Are these not
your very words, in the article "The Spokesperson of Words:
Portrait of a Poet Who Turned Down the National Academy Prize"?
I felt humbled. Even coming from you, a longtime
and loyal reader, such an extensive analysis of my work . . . Well, my sails

billowed. And now perhaps I should add this.
Some of your statements are astonishing.
Not many people know this about me. Many of my poems
I know by heart. It's not because
I find them so important or so I can be doubly impressive
when I speak them at readings. In part it's just because
I memorize as I write, and that's in part because
I know no other way for a poet to avoid repeating herself.
Writing of poems I'd composed years apart,
you compared them to *railroad tracks beside a river*
and I saw at once how my lines ran parallel
to each other as surely as the sun's rays do. I was
gobsmacked, you might say. I felt
the critique in your words the way a fly
feels the wall after the whack of a newspaper
folded up eight times. So, not even memory,
which we try to keep cool and upright
like a pear tree shading the sun-scorched field of the mind,
is enough to stop us authors from repeating ourselves.
Enough, then. And yet there are issues
where we don't agree. It is not a contradiction—
certainly not—for poems dedicated to understanding life
to be as incomprehensible as mine. Besides,
I did not turn down that Prize for the reasons
you insinuated. I would have preferred
that you not mention any of this. Once, I would have taken offense,
would have stopped sending my stuff to your journal for years.
In time, the sea subsides, the sky calms, after all
life's contradictions, everything which proves
how opposite things partake of one,
all these incomprehensible things together
put on, in time, the raiments of the rain.
One day, as I was waking from an afternoon nap
all at once I understood the importance of trees in the garden;
the freshness of the oak leaves, not so much

as oak leaves but for the way they looked.
To think away the sun, to think away the grass, the clouds,
but not to transform them into things other than themselves:
that was my sole aim.
I was never driven by fame. For me,
it was not important that the poems survive.
What was important was this: that they should,
within the poverty of their half-comprehended words,
contribute a being to the world of which they were a part.
I didn't create this vale of mist.
Believe it or not,
everything started when my first and last names
wouldn't fit together on the title page
of the journal where my work was first published.
Many add to their surname the initial only of their first name.
I did the opposite. Surely you know
Frost's famous verses: *Two roads diverged before me*
and sorry I could not travel both and be
one traveler, I took the one less traveled by
and that has made all the difference.
Two roads diverged before me and I took off to the fields.
Adding to the happenstance of having no surname,
nor could my gender be guessed from my given name.
I liked that my poems diverged from my personhood.
How old I am, where I was born—
why does the reader care?
In the 1996 Poetry Annual my birth date's given as 1967,
in the Annual of 1999 it's 1968,
one anthology gives '71, another '78.
In all of these I am "a young poet."
I have never myself put a birth date on any of my poems.
Let me tell you, however, this much:
a hummingbird hovered in a horse chestnut as I was about to be born,
a pistachio-green Murat 124, license plate 34ZN063, turned
from Jasmine into Linden Street, counting the crows on the phone lines

while crossing the street, the grocer's boy, taken by surprise,
started cursing, the wind changed direction, someone was thinking
how hard a winter this year's had been when a large walnut
dislodged and crashed on a dumpster, the cat who was rummaging
amidst the rubbish leapt in fear, a woman's shopping bag
fell open, scattering lemons and eggplants all over the street,
and a man watching from the window was cutting out
Installment 137 of *Memed, My Hawk* from the newspaper
whose headline read "War Is On Our Doorstep" and also
"Our Army Is On Alert"—oh, and if you ask my aunt
the stars changed places at the moment of my birth.
I think so many clues sufficient.
I leave it to the curiosity of scholars to fix the actual date.
For what it's worth, of course . . .

A Monument to the Impossibility of Utterance
(Anlatmanın Olanaksızlığına Anıt)

By Gökçenur Ç. (2007)

Translated by Mel Kenne and Cemal Demircioğlu (2008)

two facing windows left open for circulation
on my sweaty belly *The Short Summer of Anarchy*
like a redbud's crumpled branch you lie beside me
so beautiful, so broken, so like Istanbul

as the curtains lift on the wind
the bird that just flew in
sails out through the other window

what can't be held in mind—a moment's pure beauty
it lengthens in language, as it lengthens dims
happiness and the void it leaves behind
miracle's need of a beholder
ah! impossible to express

the burden of being sole witness
to the moment that will never return

From *After Gliding Parallel to the Ground for a While* (*Bir Süre Yere Parelel Gittikten Sonra*)

By Barış Bıçakcı (2008)

Equilateral Hell (Eşkenar Cehennem)
Translated by Ruth Whitehouse (2009)

Mom and I were clearing up in the kitchen after dinner. She raised the subject yet again, saying, "At least the poor woman's old mother would . . ."

"No, Mom!" I shouted. This nonsense had to stop. "No, I tell you, no!" I threw the sponge as hard as I could at the African violet on the windowsill, covering the poor plant with foam. "There you go again, acting like some angel of goodness!"

My right hand clutched at my throat while the other dripped soapsuds onto the floor.

"I don't want to be 'kind,' don't you understand, Mom!" I said, taking my hand from my throat and pounding at my temple with a clenched my fist. "Do you understand that? If she's dead, she's dead! It means she's free! If only I could die and be free!"

Mom pointed anxiously towards the sitting room, tapping her lips with a finger to indicate that I should keep my voice down. As if they cared. Pointing to Father and making silent gestures like that had become a real habit of hers. Then, pulling herself together, she shoved me aside and retrieved the sponge from behind the flowerpot. As if nothing at all had happened, she took over wiping down the sink. I could see the redness of her hands gradually spreading to her arms and shoulders, climbing its way up to her face.

Not knowing what to do, I just stood there watching as Mom held the sponge under the tap with one hand and swilled running water around the sink with the other. I walked out of the kitchen and, as I did so, I heard her say, "So rude, so obnoxious!" She said some other things too, but they got mixed up with the noise of the refrigerator and television.

In fact, everything gets mixed up in this house. It makes me sick. Mom takes an interest in the problems of others, as if everything in our life is a bed of roses. She's blind to the misery that exists in this house, where every corner and crevice is occupied by demons. Her main concern is cleanliness. She wipes the doorstep twice a day and wants us to roll up the bottoms of our trousers whenever we enter the house. But the demons remain.

My father and big brother communicate silently with each other through a secret code of winks and smiles. The only time anyone communicates with me is to ask whether I am doing any work for my university entrance exams. They've been asking me this for years. No, I'm not studying, and the idea of talking to some woman I don't even know and pretending to be her granddaughter drives me mad. What's more, the granddaughter's dead!

There was no way I'd let Mom bring the matter up again. We went back to our usual arguments. Who do I talk to for so long on the phone every evening? Why do I keep going out on to the balcony? Am I going out there for a cigarette? Why don't I help her with the cleaning? Why aren't I studying? Life returned to the normal hateful routine in which I felt like a spider crawling to and fro between home and classroom. The spider's web is supposed to be a wonder of nature. I see it as a trap.

Then one day, I met her, the woman whose daughter had committed suicide. She was in our house, sitting on the sofa in front of the window. Sunlight streamed in behind her and appeared to pass through her short curly hair into some deserted space. At least, that's how it seemed to me.

"Canan, my pet, this is your Aunt Türkan," said Mom, in her good angel voice. The voice that made me feel sick. The lady smiled at me. She recognized me, but I couldn't remember her.

"Of course, it's been a long time," she said, still smiling. Her eyes seemed to have shrunk. No, not shrunk, it was as though they had escaped and gone into hiding.

"We used to see each other more often," explained Mom. "But after the incident . . . Well, we lost touch," she said, and fell silent.

She didn't know how to continue. As for me, I couldn't take my eyes off Aunt Türkan. She looked shriveled. Not thin, but shriveled. Seeing her like that, I instantly understood the reason for her strange request. For one last time, she wanted to squeeze a final drop of life from her shriveled being into the parched earth of her aged mother's existence. The old woman knew nothing about her granddaughter's death and Aunt Türkan wanted to make sure it stayed that way.

I indicated with my head that I wanted Mom to come out to the kitchen. "Tell Aunt Türkan that I'll phone her mother," I said. To avoid seeing Mom's pleasure, I went straight to my room and buried my head in my pillow. I wanted to cry, but I managed to control myself. A bit later, Mom called me out to me.

As I entered the sitting room, I heard her saying, "We too have a boy and a girl. Canan's a marvelous impersonator. In fact, she wants to be an actress." I instantly regretted my decision and wanted to storm out and slam the door. But it was too late. I'd caught the look in Aunt Türkan's eyes.

"My mother's hearing isn't very good," explained Aunt Türkan.

The grandmother had been told that Başak had gone to America to do a PhD. Aunt Türkan told me all about her family and Başak, who I hardly knew. Başak had graduated from university in art and gone on to do a master's degree. Her older brother was a mechanical engineer. Their father and Aunt Türkan had separated years ago. If the grandmother asked where I was in America, which was possible since her husband had previously worked there, I was to say I was in Detroit, at Michigan University. Aunt Türkan explained all this in an easygoing, cheerful voice, so as not to scare me. To make me think it was all just a game and nothing to do with death. I understood.

"When Başak was a baby, she couldn't say 'Grandma' and always said 'Nana,'" said Aunt Türkan, "Even we call her Nana." She stopped for a moment, and then repeated, "Nan-na." As she did this, her eyes retreated even further.

Like a primary school child, I repeated "Nan-na," nodding my head in time.

That evening, I looked up the time difference with America on a calendar Father had brought home from work. I made up sentences to myself: "Nana, I've missed you so much. Dearest Nana, how is your health? Take care of yourself, dear Nana."

The next day in class, I blurted out everything to my friend Ebru.

"Did you know this girl?" she asked excitedly. "Why did she commit suicide? Was it over a man?"

"Yes, we were very close," I said, lying for some reason. "We don't know why she committed suicide."

Ebru advised me to cover the telephone receiver with a paper towel or hand-kerchief. She also suggested that if I had nothing to talk about, I should say, "I must hang up now. Telephone calls are very expensive here."

"I seem to remember a film like that, with someone making calls and pre-tending to be someone else," said Ebru, staring out of the classroom window for a long time as she tried, without success, to remember the name of the film.

The first time I called Nana, I didn't object to Mom standing next to me. I wasn't nervous at all. As soon as I'd finished, Mom took the phone from me and called Aunt Türkan.

"My daughter sounded exactly like . . ." she stopped and shivered for a moment, perhaps thinking, "God forbid that it should happen to us." She swal-lowed and continued, " . . . yes, exactly like Başak. They spoke for a full five minutes and . . . Yes, yes, Türkan dear, your poor mother was very happy."

The old lady had indeed been very happy, but Mom exaggerated as usual. The conversation had lasted no more than two minutes and the woman had been crying at least half the time.

Mom started going on again to Aunt Türkan about my impersonation skills, but I interrupted, "That's enough, put the phone down!" My teeth were clenched so hard that my words came out in a sort of hiss. Like a snake trying to bite a stupid good angel. "That's the first and last time," I said to myself.

I knew it wasn't the last time.

The next day, I met Erhan after class and, as we walked hand in hand towards the metro station, I told him what had happened.

"How could you agree to do such a thing!" said Erhan. "How could you do that to me!"

He spoke as if he'd been wronged, as if I'd deceived him or betrayed him. He let go of my hand. Oh, so what. It was all stupid and pointless anyway.

About a week later, Mom looked at Father over dinner and said, "I was at Türkan's today. She kept telling me how grateful she is to Canan."

"I don't suppose that woman's still involved with the lefties at her age," said Father, glancing at me and adding, "Don't let this go on for too long!"

"Why on earth did the girl throw herself over anyway?" asked my brother, stifling a laugh as he slurped his soup. He winked at Father.

I jumped up from the table, leaving the plate Father was holding up for a helping of green beans suspended in mid-air. Served him right.

I called Nana. I called because I was upset. As soon as she heard my voice, she began to cry and ask when I was coming back.

"Dear Nana, I've told you," I said crossly, "I'll be back at the beginning of summer." I enjoyed getting cross like this. It was more realistic, more credible.

Nana fell silent. Then she sniffed and said in a polite voice, "Darling, I'd like you to listen to a song."

"A song?" I was astonished. I heard her put the receiver down, then the sound of her slippers shuffling away and some crackling sounds, followed by a song. It was a song I knew, one that was always being played on the radio. As well as the song, I could hear snatches of Nana laughing. Without bothering whether she could hear me or not, I said, "My phone card's running out, Nana. I have to hang up." The palms of my hands were sweaty.

Before going to bed, I said to Mom, "I called Aunt Türkan's mother this evening." I didn't look at Mom. I didn't want to see her face.

A few days later, I called again.

"It's raining here," said Nana. "Have you got an umbrella?" she asked, as if it was raining in America too. "It was always raining when we were in Boston."

I stopped myself from saying I wasn't in Boston.

"Yes, I have a raincoat," I said. "The weather's turned awfully cold here. It's really freezing in the mornings."

"I hope you've got some thick woolen socks," said Nana. "What do you eat over there? Their eating habits are very different from ours."

And so on, and so on. I've grown used to her and to our trivial conversations. I now call her any time I want.

"When you were little, you used to think cherry jam had living creatures in it," she says, and we both laugh. I get her to tell me about the latest TV shows. I listen to her complaining about the doorman and gossiping about her visitors. She's even told me about the foreign cash she keeps hidden under her mattress.

In exchange, I tell her about my dreams and my hopes for the future. Naturally, I can't mention anything about acting, but it doesn't matter. Nana just listens, muttering a response occasionally.

Sometimes she sighs and says, "Wait there, just let me turn the TV off." Other times, she just says, "Of course, dear, of course." And the more she says it, the better I feel.

Someday, I think I'll be able to explain everything to her. About this hell we're all in together, this misery, this suicide.

Someday, I even think that I'll tell her I committed suicide.

"She's Nana," I say to myself. "She understands. She's bound to understand."

Give Me Your Mother (Bana Anneni Ver)

Translated by Selhan Savcıgil Endres and Clifford Endres (2009)

I did what I had to do as soon as I heard that Başak had committed suicide. I kept my eyes on my mother. I didn't take my eyes off her. I was afraid she might lose control and hurt herself.

My mother didn't lose control. She didn't pull her hair out. She didn't repeat an absurd sentence over and over, like "What should I cook this evening?" or "The balcony is so dirty, I should clean it." The only thing was that her movements slowed down. And something appeared in her eyes. They became smaller, without a doubt, like they'd been nabbed while trying to escape into hiding.

Pointing to the phone, she said, "Your father has to be told." She always constructed this kind of short, practical sentence whenever my father was involved.

The living room was crowded. I wanted to be in my room alone when I spoke with him. "Başak is dead," I said. "Suicide . . ."

My father did not say a word. He remained silent, completely silent for some time. Then, "Alright," he said. "Give me your mother."

From the living room door I called to my mother and gestured toward my room. "He's asking for you."

For the first time in all those years, they talked.

"Tomorrow," said my mother. She was cold and distant. She listened to my father for a while. She listened as if he had no right to talk. She shook her head from side to side. "No, nothing like that is going to happen." "No, we're not going to do that." She was getting angry, it was clear.

"The dead belong to their *immediate* family." Her voice was trembling.

I put my hand on her shoulder. I squeezed gently. Her flesh was both yielding and unyielding. Her strapped dress was embellished with a pattern of faded flowers. I felt a sense of age and fatigue. Stay calm, mother, calm.

She hung up. I thought she would cry or curse my father. She didn't. She took a tissue and dabbed the sweat that had broken out on her neck and under her arms. She was calm. She went back to the living room and the friends trying to console her. She sat wordlessly on an armchair baking in the sun. Under her dress her small sagging breasts appeared to be pointing in two different directions.

She looked at me.

My mother was carrying an old hell inside her, stumbling before a god in whom my father believed, yet forging ahead, fearlessly.

An Older Woman (Yaşlıca Bir Kadın)

Translated by Bengisu Rona (2009)

The city buses kept going past all full; they didn't even slow down. The drivers just threw their hands up in the air in a way that people waiting at the bus stops could see. On the buses, some passengers had to stand right down on the steps with their backs leaning against the doors. The people waiting at the bus stops were furious. Some stood in the middle of the road as if they were trying to stop the buses. And some pointed at the empty spaces on the buses and complained about people who forgot about those left by the roadside as soon as they got on the bus themselves. Some even swore at the mayor.

Finally, somehow a bus did stop, and they managed to squeeze themselves on board. Then a white-haired man started shouting:

"We've been waiting here for an hour!"

He seemed to be shouting not just at the driver but at everyone on the bus. "I'm fifty-three years old. Honestly, I'm not myself anymore! Every morning all my nerves are on edge. I quarrel with everyone because of these buses. I even screamed and shouted at this lady here."

The people around him first looked at the band-aid on the man's forehead and then at the woman he motioned at with his head. She was an older woman with short curly hair that had gone white here and there. She was clutching a brown leather briefcase to her chest—in the crush it was impossible to carry it by the handle. A man in a suit sitting in the front row got up and gave up his seat to her. She was confused. She hadn't noticed that anyone had shouted at her, and in her confusion she sat down in the seat the man had offered her. Then she raised her head and said "Thank you." She settled her briefcase in her lap on her faded dark blue skirt. She looked at the young woman next to her who was sleeping with her head against the window. Rubbing her sweaty palms together she placed her hands on her briefcase.

The white-haired man had calmed down and started to share his woes with the driver and the people around him. Once the bus got on to the Istanbul road, everyone seemed to calm down. They were going at a steady speed without being held up by traffic, and at this time of the morning everyone welcomed the speed. "You think I'm happy! With all this driving I can't even go to the toilet," complained the driver. Those near the front fully agreed with him with all the sincerity of well-meaning folk.

And the woman had also calmed down. She stretched her legs out and settled herself properly in her seat. A little later she opened her briefcase and pulled out a book from among a bundle of papers. Her hand instinctively went up to her chest. When she realized that her glasses were not around her neck, she felt in the front pocket of her briefcase, pulled them out and put them on. She opened the book and chose a story short enough for her to finish reading during the journey.

The young man, the hero of the story, was nervous. He had to spend a weekend by a lake away from the city with a crowd of people from his workplace; an outing organized so that they could get to know each other, so that they could bond and increase productivity. The young man spent most of Saturday traveling with a group of colleagues who became childish as soon as they left the work environment. They didn't miss a single opportunity to have a laugh, and even if they did, they still laughed. They sang songs, they clapped their hands, they danced dances. The young man took part in none of it. He seemed to be carrying a heavy burden on his shoulders. The woman looked up from her book and glanced around her. They were at Batıkent Junction. When they reached the guesthouse where they were going to stay, it turned out that there'd been a mistake with the booking, and there weren't enough rooms. The young man was almost in tears. Not having a room to himself and the possibility of spending the night with someone from his workplace had totally exasperated him and frozen him rigid. The guesthouse staff said they'd find a solution to the problem before dinner that evening. The group lost none of their glee. After leaving their belongings where they were told to, they decided to go for a walk around the lake. The young man walked behind the group all by himself. The woman jolted forward as the bus braked suddenly. Without letting go of the book, she supported herself by pressing the backs of her hands against the bar over the seat in front of her. The driver and the passengers sitting at the front swore at a car that swerved into the path of the bus. The woman tried to see what was happening outside and then settled herself back into her seat. The young man was walking and watching the soothing autumn landscape, but somehow couldn't let himself go. They sat on the benches by the shores of the lake and ate the flatbread provided by the people at the guesthouse. They returned to the guesthouse as it was beginning to get dark. It became clear that the room problem had still not been resolved. In the end a sharing scheme was devised under the direction of a couple of people who were trying to have a go at leadership on this bonding outing, even though they'd never done such a thing in the workplace. They'd get extra beds put in some of the rooms, couples would have their own rooms and the rest would share with men and women in separate rooms. Chance and mathematics conspired to increase the young man's unhappiness: when it became impossible to work things out, it was decided that an older woman who worked the switchboard at the workplace would share a room with the young man. This morally repellent idea, this "safe solution," based as it was on the assumption that young men would not pester older or ugly women, outraged the young man. He wanted to make grand statements and shout in protest at their hypocrisy. When the woman noticed that the bus had slowed down, she looked out of the window. They had passed the Çiftlik Junction and were proceeding slowly in the congested traffic towards Yenimahalle Bridge. After dinner, when everyone went to their rooms, the young man lingered in the lobby for a while so that the woman would not feel uncomfortable. Then he knocked on the door and went in. The woman was in the bed by the window; she was lying curled up with her back to the door. The young man went to bed without turning the light on and without taking off his clothes. His anger kept him awake. He got up and approached the older woman's bed. He put his hand gently under the covers looking for the woman's flesh to stroke. The woman looked up abruptly and snapped the book shut. Her face was flushed. She took off her glasses and put them into the briefcase with her book.

Suddenly she thought of upbraiding the white-haired man who'd said he'd shouted at her. She looked around her, but couldn't see him. She noticed the man in the suit who'd given her his seat. Now she felt furious at him.

At Gençlik Park, the bus turned towards Sıhhiye. The woman got off at the Adliye bus stop, along with almost everyone else. Just as she was getting off, a girl suddenly appeared beside her and said, "Good morning, Türkan Hanım!" Before the woman had a chance to turn around and look at her, the girl leapt off the steps of the bus onto the pavement in one go. The woman watched the girl darting off, but could not work out who she was.

The woman started walking towards Kızılay. Everyone seemed more cheerful and faster than she was. The whole city was cheerful.

Whereas she had a ghastly feeling of defeat within her.

Metaphors for Rent (Kiralık Metaforlar)

By Murathan Mungan (2009)
Translated by Elizabeth Pallitto and İdil Karacadağ (2010)

Hey buddy, do you need to rent some metaphors?
Image, symbol, irony, simile: take them all now, the whole lot, priced cheap
                                        to go fast—
we have Icarus for wings, Prometheus for fire, Narcissus for stars,
Pandora's boxes for every cursed thing—
made to order, when you want it, on demand.
If you want, we can make postmodern wigs out of Medusa's snakes for your
                                        loved ones.

On Saturday and Sunday, you don't need a passport on the bridge of metaphors
that binds East to West. Customs is open, and
if you want to go a little bit Oriental,
we have the latest Şahmerans—just in now, trust me—
newly minted, bright and shiny, newly scaled with sequins.

We have phoenixes: a wealth of choices, shapes and sizes,
and we can give you the ashes in a jar if you want them.
In our shops, you can find Salamanders resistant to any fire and to all the ravages
                                        of time.

We will give thirty birds to anyone who has enough sky,
and if you wish, we'll build the Van Lake Monster for you—
we can even make it look a bit older in essence and image;
we can give it an ID card in the old language
so as not to let on that it's new.
Believe me, we don't make much of a profit from all this;
our only desire is to promote Mount Qaf tourism.
Anyway, come back soon, and don't forget to recommend us to your loved
                                        ones!

Every profound poem needs rented metaphors these days.

On the edge of the century, the dark ritual opens up a storefront skeptical smile . . .

Network ID (Şebeke)

By Murathan Mungan (1991)
Translated by Nilgün Dungan (2010)

I looked in your mirror.
The one with a picture of you tucked in its frame
I thought your face looked good on mine
I used your looks, your toothbrush, wore your underwear
Read all your letters,
your books, notebooks,
copied your memories up to my fingerprints
I ransacked your past, looted your den, you're finished.
Now I have your ID on me
and it's time to exchange your skin with mine.

Tanaba Tanaba Entububa
(Tanaba Tanaba Entububa)

By Ahmet Büke (2006)

Translated by İdil Aydoğan (2011)

Let me tell you from the very start that this is a story about a dog with a red coat and black nose. The author first saw him on the last hot day of September, lazing about with his long ears resting in the warm sand, and wanted to recount a story of a few minutes, through his eyes. Of course he never got to find out if the dog really experienced the feelings here to be described. Did he really need to? And what exactly was the point in his writing this strange introduction?

According to the author, the source of all this was an ancient malady. When he first came to possess this rupturing feeling inside, which consisted of slight anxiety, a shudder akin to fear and shame, he had only just started primary school. The windy season had again arrived. The nearby thorny plot of land, cleared of electric wires, rang with laughter. High above, up above in the sky, dozens of delicate, frivolous kites flickered in a swirl of rainbow colors.

The author followed the swaying of the strings and the paper that smelled of flour paste, as he did every kite-flying season, with damp eyes. Wasn't it the worst thing ever to want something so badly and not have the courage to do it? In his dreams he'd watch his fingers, his fingers that were unable to fix the spar in the hexagon, his fingers that kept letting the cellophane paper slip. He simply couldn't center the spars or fix the tail on his hideous creation that looked like a ragged bundle. Even when he did manage to finish it, not even the rat-footed kid of the neighborhood, who nobody would go near because of his bald spots, would hold the reel and help him launch his kite, which resembled a dead spider.

And these nightmares were replaced with that strange muddle of feelings during the day: slight anxiety and a shudder akin to fear . . .

Back then, because the author couldn't fully comprehend this feeling, he gave it a name: TANABA.

Tanaba followed him about like a lame monkey wherever he went, sometimes its tail wrapped around his neck, sometimes clinging to his legs. But he'd become more mischievous in the kite-flying season. He would bounce around him and squeeze his nose with hairy fingers.

Then, on one of those cursed festive days, unable to bear her son's misery any longer, the author's mother paid one of the craftiest kids and commissioned him to make a kite. How could she have known the author would be so hurt by the arrival of this yellow and navy kite with frilly edges, made of shiny paper for two and a half liras?

The boy walked out into the open land in front of the eyes of the whole neighborhood. People mumbled among themselves, pointing at him: "Look, that's the kid who paid someone to make him a kite." The whole world curled up and spun around him. God, how shameful it was.

Yes, shame. Now his feelings were joined by another. And he found a name for this one too: ENTUBUBA.

Tanaba was the lame monkey and Entububa its paper hat. Have you ever had friends like these that you've carried around with you for thirty-five years?

He did. He had his Tanaba Entububa. And never in his life did they leave his side.

And so, as soon as our dear author began writing this story and saw Tanaba Entububa right by his side again, he knew he had to recount all this. Why? Probably because he thought he would fail in describing the dog and what he was feeling.

The dog with the red coat and black nose opened its languid, sleepy eyes and looked out onto the beach sadly. Summer was almost over. No more kids chasing him around with sticks in their hands, no more ice cream wrappers to lick. He could smell the approach of a long, hungry winter. He yawned. Beside a broken sun bed which had been tipped over, he spotted a bare-chested man sunbathing. Wearily, he got up and ambled along. The man opened his eyes and looked at the dog now crouching down beside him. Together they watched a ship gliding into the distance. The dog with the red coat and black nose lifted his leg and peed on the one-inch gap between the man's socks and his trousers. He turned around and stared at the author who looked back at him in astonishment. Then, moving away a couple of steps, he lay down. "It's going to be a tough winter," he thought.

Poetry, Pleasure, and the Im/Possibility of Being Correct

Excerpt from a Talk by Gökçenur Ç. (2008)
Translated by Şehnaz Tahir Gürçağlar (2008)

It's a small miracle that so many people have come together around a table for poetry, literature and translation. I'm very happy to take part in this miracle.

Translation really feeds my poetry. I read somewhere that there are two kinds of writers and poets in the world: those who write at night and those who write during the day. Unfortunately, I can only write during the day. After dark, it stops for me. However, if you're working at a regular daytime job, it's very difficult to write during the day. During those times when I work all day, translating in the evenings keeps me in touch with poetry.

I enjoy translating poetry very much, but for me translation is like . . . well, I read something in English, I like that poem, but I can't like it as much as I would if I were reading it in Turkish. If I like a poem, I try to turn it into a good poem in Turkish. For example, in my translations of Paul Auster's poems that have now been published, first of all I liked the poems. I liked those poems very much, and after I had translated them into Turkish I was able to read them again as someone else's poems. So the first reason I translate poems is to have the pleasure of reading them in Turkish. Other people want to read translations too, so, since I like to share, I translate for them as well. However, I'm sure that all those poems could have been translated in another way. If you ask me if they are correct translations, I can't say that I'm very sure.

And by "correct," I mean the exact meaning, and also whether I have correctly understood the different meanings a poem may have. In the preface to my Paul Auster translations I said that in poetry, and especially in the work of Paul Auster, you have three or four meanings for each word. If you choose one meaning as the primary one, and another meaning as the secondary one, and so on, the poem makes one sort of sense. But if you order the meanings differently, the poem makes another sort of sense. If you have a chance to contact Mr. Auster and ask him, he might say he meant all of them or maybe only one of them. Maybe I came up with a wrong combination, or maybe I got it right. I don't know. And even if there is a very powerful meaning in one word, a common word that you always use in English, and it has other connotations, some of which might work better in Turkish poetry, I sometimes choose one of those because it makes the translation better in Turkish. I don't think we're able to know what exactly is meant in any given case. Therefore I just try to make good poems in Turkish. Sometimes they contain mistakes, sometimes they don't. But I didn't study translation. I just started doing it on my own because I enjoy doing it. When people said they wanted to publish my translations, at first I had doubts, but I don't any longer.

Ölüm, Yıldızları Gecenin Kabuk Tutmuş Yaraları Sanıyor

By Gökçenur Ç. (2006)

Ölüm, kapalı çarşı fesçiler sokağında dükkan işletiyor

Ölüm, arada ingilizce kelimeler kullanmanın çok havalı olduğunu düşünüyor,

Ölüm, bembeyaz zebraların varlığını herkesten gizlemeye çalışıyor,

Ölüm, zamanla hesabına tavla oynuyor,

Ölüm, güzelliğin tanımını bir atın kulağına fısıldıyor,

Ölüm, çok korkuyor çünkü gerçek adını bilmiyor,

Ölüm, gri gözlü, bir zamanlar mavi gözlü olduğunu hatırlamıyor,

Ölüm, kuşlarla konuşuyor, tek dostu kuşlar, onları anlamıyor,

Ölüm, yasemin bahçelerinin küçük orospusu yosadhara'yı sidharta'dan çok
seviyor,

Ölüm, 5800 ödenmiş prim gününü bağkurluluğuyla birleştirip emekli olmayı
düşlüyor,

Ölüm, sarı ateş böceği, dokunduğu herkesten birşeyler öğreniyor,

Ölüm, taşraya yerleşme fikrine sıcak bakmıyor,

Ölüm, cüneyt'e babanı gördüm diyor, o iyi gözlerinden öpüyor,

Ölüm, günlük tutuyor ama tarih atmıyor,

Ölüm, ölünün yakınlarına unutkanlık pelerinleri armağan ediyor

Ölüm, her akşam içmezse uyuyamıyor, tekirdağ'ı yeşil efe'den çok seviyor,

Ölüm, alışkanlıklarına çok bağlı, dişlerini tuzla fırçalıyor,

Ölüm, kredi kartı borcunu kapatmak için tüketici kredisi alıyor,

Ölüm, sevmediği bir işte çalışıyor,

Ölüm, van kalesi kartpostalları biriktiriyor,

Ölüm, yıldızları gecenin kabuk tutmuş yaraları sanıyor,

Ölüm, allaha küs, yine de uyumadan üç kulluvallah bir elham okumayı ihmal
etmiyor,

Ölüm, sevdiği dizelerin altını çiziyor,

Ölüm, en çok "neden ben?" diye soranlara kızıyor,

Ölüm, artık ağlamaktan utanmıyor,

Ölüm, aramıza karışmış, bizden biri gibi geçinip gidiyor.

259

Two Versions:

Death Imagines Stars as the Night's Scabbed-Over Wounds
Translated by Mel Kenne and Deniz Perin (2008)

Death   runs a shop on the street of fez makers in the grand bazaar
Death   thinks the occasional use of English words is really cool
Death   tries to keep everyone from seeing the reality of stark white zebras
Death   wagers with time in a game of backgammon
Death   whispers the meaning of beauty into a horse's ear
Death   lacking knowledge of his true name, is terrified
Death   being gray-eyed now, has no memory of having once been blue-eyed
Death   consults with birds, has only birds as friends, can't grasp their meaning
Death   prefers that little whore of the jasmine gardens, yosadhara, to siddhartha
Death   hopes to retire by amalgamating 5800 days of paid-up premiums
                          with his social security

Death   a yellow firefly, learns something from everyone he touches
Death   doesn't care at all for the idea of settling down in the country
Death   says to naive cüneyt i met with your father, he's doing fine, he sends
                          you his kisses

Death   keeps a diary with undated entries
Death   offers mantles of forgetting to the kin of the dead
Death   can't get to sleep without drinking every night, fancies tekirdağ rakı
                          over yeşil efe

Death   is firmly set in his habits, he brushes his teeth with salt
Death   takes out a consumer loan to manage his credit card debt
Death   labors hard at a job he dislikes
Death   collects postcards from the castle at van
Death   imagines stars as the night's scabbed-over wounds
Death   is pissed off at god, but still dutifully recites three *kulluvallah* and one
                          elham before going to bed

Death   underlines sentences and phrases he likes
Death   is annoyed by the ones who say "why me?"
Death   isn't ashamed anymore to cry
Death   is our neighbor, like us, gets by

Death Thinks the Stars Are Night's Scabbed-Over Wounds
Translated by Kurt Heinzelman and Deniz Perin (2008)

Death   runs a shop in the Grand Bazaar on Fesçiler Street
Death   thinks using foreign words from time to time very cool
Death   tries to hide the existence of stripeless zebras from everyone else
Death   bets with Time on Fantasy Football
Death   whispers the meaning of beauty into a horse's ear
Death   is scared to death because he doesn't know his real name
Death   is gray-eyed but does not remember he was blue-eyed once
Death   talks to the birds, his only friends, whom he doesn't understand
Death   likes the little whore in the Jardin des Plantes more than the one in
                                                                    the Tuileries
Death   dreams of cashing in his term life and retiring on Social Security
Death   learns something, yellow firefly that he is, from everyone he touches
Death   does not relish the idea of settling down in the country
Death   says to his neighbor, I saw your father, he sends his love
Death   keeps a diary, one without dates
Death   donates overcoats of forgetfulness to the relatives of the dead
Death   can't sleep if he doesn't drink every night, he prefers Jack Daniels to
                                                                    Old Grandad
Death   is a creature of habit and brushes his teeth with salt
Death   takes out a consumer loan to pay off credit-card debt
Death   works at a job he doesn't like
Death   collects picture postcards of Corfe Castle
Death   mistakes the stars for scabs
Death   is angry with god but faithfully recites 3 *kulluvallah* and 1 *fatiha*
                                                                    before sleeping
Death   underlines his favorite passages
Death   gets angriest when people ask "why me?"
Death   is no longer ashamed to cry
Death   lives among us and is just getting by, just like us

Thrashing Life (Dirim Dolu Çırpınma)

By Gökçenur Ç. (2006)

Translated by Mel Kenne and Selhan Savcıgil Endres (2008)

I saw you as a rusty tackle box in the Salvation Apartments in Kadıköy,
The door was ajar, under that fresh-scrubbed stairway amid soapy wafts we kissed.

I saw you as a lead sinker snagged in the rock jetty, a gardener from Buldan
Who held in one hand a rose like a broken mirror angled to catch the sun.

I saw you as a spinner, as long as you spun there would never be snags.
Sleep, a pair of socks, everything I could or could never write.

I saw you as a snarled fishing line, snapped in four places, knotted in five.
I was on my way to serve as a witness at a divorce hearing.

I saw you as a red plastic float, a tea kettle, as umbrellas, as a can opener.
You bore no resemblance to any of the usual things I felt close to.

I saw you as a fishing line's fly, smiling over something you'd read,
Your smile: a feathery whiteness concealing the hook.

At the tip of the tightly stretched, invisible line, I'm the thrashing.

The Perforated Amulet (Delikli Nazarlık)

By Sevgi Soysal (1976)
Translated by Ruth Whitehouse (2010)

It was *Saban*, the eighth month of the Islamic calendar, and a saintly cherubic son was born to my esteemed master İzzet Efendi, originally from Salonika. The boy was a beautiful, tender little thing. The midwife told İzzet Efendi that the darling boy should be named Necip, so they called the darling boy Necip. A succession of grandmothers, wet nurses, great-grandmothers tut-tutted as they generously pinned gold pieces to Necip's pillow. Why didn't the poor child have an amulet? Very well, very well, the father said, and he went to Istavro the jeweler in Rıhtım Street, where he bought an amulet of the purest gold. He went home and pinned it to the pillow of darling Necip, to the applause of the great-grandmothers, wet nurses and grandmothers.

Ah, ah, who will inherit the farms? They will go to Necip. Who else should own the products of Pisona Farm, the cattle, hens, eggs, chicks, broilers, the steaming milk, cream, honey, oh, and the traitorous Bulgarians' finest yogurt, the goose livers, lamb livers, chicken breasts, and the breasts of all the women with their abundance of milk? Necip, of course Necip. They all belonged to Necip, didn't they? Had they not all been waiting for the birth of Necip? The magic of the amulet would multiply all that ten times over, no, a thousand times over for Necip. Why not? Had not everything just been waiting for the birth of Necip? The amulet would ward against the evil eye. Its magic would create peaches, melons and pears that were even sweeter and juicier.

Necip urinated, oh, how he urinated. Necip defecated, oh, how he defecated. Nappies, nappies and yet more nappies were washed, washed and washed again with busy hands, wagging tongues and much swearing by scullions, orphaned servant girls and Greek nannies. Hey, you scullions, hey, you servants, put Necip on your backs, carry Necip downstairs, carry Necip upstairs. Giddy up, scullions, giddy up servant girls, giddy up, giddy up. With a clip to the ear, a slap on the butt. As Necip's hands grew bigger, he was able to clip and slap for himself with his own dear little hands.

He pulled people's hair. First his mother's, then his wet nurse's, his great-grandmother's, his grandmother's, his grandfather's and the servant girls' too. He threw the amulet at their heads and jabbed its pin into their backsides over and over again. But they knew the amulet wasn't to blame. It was God protecting him, ensuring that the evil eye would seek out other children. He shouted "Donkey!" first at his mother, then at his father, his wet nurse, his great-grandmother, his grandfather and the bald servant girl too. Oh, bless his little mouth, he was so cute when he said the word donkey. What a gorgeous rosebud mouth, what a sweet little tongue. He cried "Shit!" How delicious, but oh my, this dear little boy shouldn't speak like that to his mother, father, grandfather, great-grandfather and grandmother!

Or to the servant girl, scullions or the Greek nanny. Oh, oh.

Ten exhausting years passed and he was still being breastfed. Continually urinating, feeding, shouting donkey, saying shit, hitting scullions and everyone else, jumping on people's backs, spurring them like horses, downstairs and upstairs. However, those years were so constructive that by the end of his tenth year, Necip abandoned his mother's shriveled breast and started sucking on the fresh young breasts of the servant girls, young scullions and widows living under the family's protection. The evil eye would never touch him because the amulet was always there, ha, ha.

He sucked and he beat, he sucked and he cursed. As he cursed, sucked and beat, he grew and he grew until eventually he became a man. All thanks to the team of scullions, servant girls and the other parasites!

İzzet Efendi's son Necip, that gentleman, that gentleman of gentlemen, that hero of heroes, that pasha of pashas for whom no sacrifice was too great, wanted all hearts to beat for him, all virgin creatures to be at his disposal. First, he mounted the dogs, then the donkeys, then the horses. Yes, he can chase away all before him on horseback! Yes, he can scare away all before him with a whip! How else was he to become a man? Anything else missing in his life? Indeed there was. His father bought him a rifle from a Bulgarian revolutionary. And what a good thing he did. Necip became a real man, a lion of lions. If he didn't, who would? First, he took aim at empty oil drums, then at melons in the field, peaches and pears in the trees, grapes on the vines, the gardener's hat, and then he'd shoot at whatever took his fancy. What a young lion! Run for your lives, all you hens, dogs, cats, calves and servant girls. Oh, what a lion! Of course you should be scared! Of course you should run away! Scatter like chicks! The lionheart is here! And he has the amulet to protect him from the evil eye.

The weather was hot. All the animals were dozing, and a wasp landed on Necip's shoulder for a sleep. How could it know it had landed on the shoulder of such a lion? As Necip was aiming his rifle, perhaps at another wasp, it took fright and stung him on the shoulder. Necip felt a pain. He scratched and his hand touched the amulet. The amulet had been unstitched and stitched, unstitched and stitched, unstitched from dirty shirts and stitched on to clean shirts by mothers, grandmothers, great-grandmothers, wet nurses and Greek nannies, all of whom had one common purpose in life. Necip was delighted to find this tiny target. He placed it on a distant spot and pulled the trigger again and again. That lion of lions, that sturdiest of men, that valiant young thing shot at the charm until it was perforated all over like a colander. Yes, he kept on shooting and he entered the world of pashas and gentlemen.

At Pisona Farm, hens were regularly garrotted, cows regularly gave birth and servant girls were regularly fired. One day a pregnant servant girl was fired. She was either fired because she was pregnant, or made pregnant because she was a servant girl.

Servant girls were sent packing with only a small bundle, a special bundle for sacked servant girls. Those bundles would be inspected by the maternal grandmother, paternal grandmother or mother, yet, after her departure, they would still complain about how much the servant girl had managed to stash away in her small bundle. They would accuse her of making off with an impossible number of things. Lost something? The gypsy put it in her bundle when she left. And this, and that, and those. However, it is true that, before she left the house, the servant girl picked up the perforated golden amulet, which she had found in the garden, and put it in her bundle. She sought refuge with a distant relative. Oh, who would take her in? Why should anyone take her in? Why should anyone heed her calls? Why did those men and women who couldn't bear to be alone in their villas welcome her to their beds so easily? Coming and going, window cleaning, dusting, five cents here, five cents there. Oh, alright, she'd stay. As soon as the poor unfortunate girl was settled, she gave birth. She bore not a stone, not a dog, but a son. If only I'd given birth to a stone or a dog instead of you. The distant relatives cried out: Who is to take care of the boy? Who'll sing him lullabies? Who'll clean up his wee, his shit? Who'll take him in their arms? He came into this world, but so what? Why did he come into this world? What awaits him? All that work, but for what? What did she have to offer him? She had some sort of amulet. Oh, you wretch, oh, you scum, oh, you bitch, oh, you whore, oh, god damn you, you godforsaken piece of filth!

She cried and she was beaten. Her milk dried up and she was beaten. She threw up and she was beaten, she had diarrhea and she was beaten. She had a stomach ache and she was beaten. How could she avoid it? Beatings were her destiny, were they not?

Every day was laundry day at the house of the distant relatives and the wretch was always around under their feet. Oh, the poor unfortunate girl. She only went and upset the washing cauldron! She only went and scalded herself with the boiling water! She only went and died from her burns!

Later, the distant relatives and neighbors all talked about how the boy had been affected by the evil eye. The poor boy had been touched by the evil eye, the evil, evil eye that had penetrated through the perforations in the amulet, as if through a colander. Yes, he had indeed been touched.

Borges Slum (Borges Varoşu)

By Murathan Mungan (2003)
Translated by İdil Karacadağ and Mel Kenne (2010)

Inside me the old neighborhood of the knife
go where I may, my heart winds up
at the same dead end
that one I'd tried to uproot from the past
impossible memory of having died
forged from the same metal as the night
knife I use to hone my words
like a river, innocent and blind
flowing muddy between my legs
as I come near to where, in the deep
isolation of a library, those who
can't appraise their own way end up
the spit of the blade glinting
as if it had struck
on the lines of the secret that forgot to hide

most of us die sleeping
with those we would like to be
in the yet unread slums of Borges

literature can unspeak for itself
thus do maps tell of blood

this many words that much blood
from the slum of a page
seeps into us

Old Dream (Eski Hayal)

By Murathan Mungan (2004)
Translated by David Connolly and Arzu Eker Roditakis (2010)

There would be five women on stage.
Their voices thick and dusky, piercing the heart
All five of them
With hooks, needles in their hands, as if mending nets, they would be weaving
an earth-colored sea with words, silences and sighs on a stage slowly undulating
under a softness,
as if covering everything.
A sea of sackcloth.
Only their heads, necks, arms, hands would be visible in the sea's blackness that
they would be wearing.

In their eyes would be the depth of women who have long gazed at the horizon.
A distant lighthouse, lime white. Sometimes in turns, sometimes interrupting
each other with lines hopping from one to the other like waves they would be
reciting on the stage of the Istanbul Municipal Theatre Yannis Ritsos's Old
Women and the Sea, which I was reading at the time.
I don't know why, years later, this old dream visited me; on a sunny winter's day,
fresh as a Monday start, when I was thinking of my life's unfulfilled dreams. As
if there were women still waiting for me at a rehearsal somewhere.

On the last days of a year and of an age in which I've come to the threshold of
long gazing at the past.

Glass Summer (Cam Yaz)

By Murathan Mungan (1989–1991)
Translated by Ruth Christie and dedicated to Saliha Paker (2012)

Cipher in search of its name
Make me a summer of Septembers
In a world of only an acre
My poetry's a cleansing zone
Make me a summer of Septembers
A childhood of only an acre
That I put in glass bottles
a rainbow   a kite
a landmine   a cork   utopia
I wrote poems unlike one another
like fake jewels
then facing the ocean I wept.
Look, the moon mingles with evening
They were novice seasons
For years under the name of love
I played football with one goalpost
Glass blew my poems
Sunken rainbow, exploded mine,
torn kite,
before September utopia in my baggage
I bought myself separation by rail.
Look, the moon mingles with my forehead
Cipher in search of its name
keep this cork
Then read this poem
tear it up and throw it away

Kurdish Cats and Gypsy Butterflies
(Kürt Kediler Çingene Kelebekler)

By Mine Söğüt (2011)
Translated by Bengisu Rona (2012)
Poetic prologue translated by Alev Ersan (2012)

A single eye will spin round and round in its socket
A single pair of thin, thick, white, pink, purple lips will part and pour out words
smoked, moldy, estranged.
Pick them up.
Dig a deep pit. Chuck them in.
All of it . . . all of it . . . all of it.
Chuck them all in.

Two butterflies landed on my window. One of them was a Kurd, the other a Gypsy. Yesterday two sparrows came, one a Kurd, the other a Gypsy. Planes pass overhead: now you see them, now they disappear behind the clouds. Some of them are Kurds, some Gypsies. It's that kind of place, our part of town: Kurds everywhere, Gypsies everywhere. Just because I'm old, they think I'm blind. They think I'm deaf. The old woman's about to die, so they think.

Yesterday someone stole some of the wood in my shed. "It was the Gypsies that stole your wood," say the Kurds. The Gypsies say, "The Kurds stole it." But once, in the dead of night . . . when we old folk can't get to sleep, I was sitting all alone by the window. My eyes were closed, but I was all ears. The night was silent. The night was dark. I began to remember what things were like a very long time ago: The times when people like me, people they'd address as "Madame," used to live around here. I remembered even earlier times, when I was called "Mademoiselle," the times when my father was addressed as "Monsieur." I recalled the religious festivals, milk pudding with mastic, torch-light processions, children's songs I'd sing in my mother tongue. I was thinking of the really old times; just then I heard sounds coming from the woodshed.

Gypsies. Children of a tribe that can never keep quiet. Born thieves, they'll die thieves. I've only got a few old bits of wood: they'll steal those too and make me die of cold. When I'm dead they'll pull the house apart. First they'll break down that lovely door, the one Yorgos the carpenter carved so intricately. Then they'll smash up the wooden shutters on the windows. They'll kick down the walls which lean a bit more every time it rains or the wind blows. My house will just collapse. The Gypsies will steal my house bit by bit. They'll burn it in the stoves in their one-room hovels, and they'll dance in the light from its flames.

I put a glass over one of the Gypsy butterflies. It struggled and thrashed around inside screaming. I pulled the wing off one of the Gypsy flies. It struggled and struggled trying to fly. Then it fell on the floor. I stepped on it. It died. A yellow fluid oozed out of it.

Last night, just as the Gypsies were stealing my wood, I was watching them surreptitiously from behind the curtain. They thought I was in my clapped-out old bed half asleep, half dead and gone, out of it, in limbo . . . Just when they'd stuffed the wood into their big basket and were about to leave, the Kurds went into my woodshed.

Scene: The woodshed. Three Gypsy cats, seven Kurdish cats. They arched their backs at each other.

The walls hissed: "Everyone can speak their own language among themselves, but you must speak to each other in Turkish!"

"You—drop that wood!" said a pitch-black Kurdish cat.

"And if we don't?" challenged a deep ginger Gypsy cat.

The Kurdish cats bared their teeth. The Gypsy cats pulled their knives on the Kurdish cats. The Kurds and the Gypsies are going to kill each other, for my wood, in my woodshed! The Gypsies may have knives, but the Kurds have a gun. Just three shots: bang bang bang.

The corpses of the Gypsy cats lie on the ground. One yellow, one red, one brown, three Gypsy cats. Killed in my woodshed by the Kurds, whilst stealing my wood.

The Kurdish cats turned into Kurdish angels. These angels with black wings chucked the dead Gypsies into three holes they just dug there and then. The three thieving Gypsy cats that had stolen my wood from my woodshed were put in the ground by the seven Kurdish killer cats. Earth was thrown over their bodies. The Kurds went off with my wood from my woodshed.

Tomorrow night, the women will be ululating, lit by the glow from my burning wood, and the men will be cleaning their guns. And Kurdish babies will be sleeping soundly, warmed by the heat from my wood. In their dreams they'll see the flickering of my fire, the fire that was stolen from me.

It's cold. The Gypsy women tiptoe right up to my bedside, gingerly bending over me, checking if I've died of the cold. I haven't got any wood left now, but I do have my house. When I'm dead, they'll steal my house and burn it in their stoves.

The Gypsy women leave, and Kurdish women come into the room. Brazenly, noisily they march up to the side of my bed, clomping their heels on the floor. They bend over and peer at me: am I dead, or am I still alive? Then they mutter to each other in their own language. They glance back at me once more as they leave. They smile. They have gold teeth just like the Gypsy women. Just like golden butterflies with gold teeth. The Kurdish and the Gypsy women fly above my bed, fluttering to and fro. Their wings—what a riot of color.

There aren't any houses round here where there isn't a funeral or a wedding going on. Whenever there's a wedding, the Gypsy merry-making drowns out the din of the Kurdish ululating. When there's a funeral, the Gypsy mourning comes across as more subdued than the Kurdish lamentations.

The Gypsies have come to fear the Kurds.

I fear both the Gypsies and the Kurds.

The Kurds fear nothing.

The other day a Gypsy girl came and sat by my bed for a long while. As she talked and talked, her green eyes darted right and left, her pupils like black beads. When her full lips smiled, they spread sensuously to both sides of her small face, and her gold tooth appeared and then disappeared like an extraordinary jewel.

She was wearing a headscarf of indeterminate color that kept slipping down her long greasy hair, and she'd keep her dirty hands busy rearranging it. And while she talked, she'd throw her head back time and again, as if trying to make the headscarf slip down. She stared right into my eyes. Underneath the layers and layers of blouses, jumpers, baggy pants and skirts she was wearing, she had a very slim body. Her breath smelled like an animal's—that's why her voice was savage. Perhaps she was a fox, or a wild cat.

"You know, Madame," she said, "as soon as their babies are born, the Kurds slash their skulls with a razor, to make them rebellious, brave and fearless. They drain out fluid from the brain, mix it with blood and get the baby to drink it."

Then she got up from the chair she was sitting on and opened the cracked door of the walnut wardrobe. She took out my old green two-piece suit and held it against her body. She looked in the mirror.

"Why don't you give me this, Madame?"

I wanted to scream "Help, thief!" at the top of my lungs from where I was lying. But if I did, all the lizards in the neighborhood would crowd into my house. The worms would get into my wardrobe. The snails would gnaw at my hats, the leeches would trail over my scarves. And the Gypsy vultures and the Kurdish crows would swoop down and gouge out my eyes.

What kind of a world is this? Where's everyone gone? Isn't there anyone left who speaks my language?

Now I'm going to get out of bed. I'm going to put on all my clothes, all on top of each other. I'll put on all my hats. I'll drape all my scarves around my neck. I'll put my bracelets on my wrists and my rings on my fingers. I'll put on blue-green-violet eyeshadow, I'll paint my lips with red-purple-maroon lipstick, and I'll put the hooks of all my earrings through the one hole in my earlobe, making it bleed.

Then I shall light a match.

All the stuff on me will catch fire.

Everyone will scream in their own language.

"Bibezîn, mala Madam dişewite."

"C'mon, hurry, Madame's house is going up in flames."

Two-Way Gypsy (Ters Çingene)

By Gülten Akın (1991)

Translated by Ruth Christie and İpek Seyalıoğlu (2006)

I'm the silver fox of a long chase
I ran through rivers, I ran in snow
I gave up killing lives are holy
I turned and hunted myself

The lines were ready, gave life to the seeker
They were ready I just retaled the tale

I'm the sun's two-way gypsy, I followed only him
The ways bled with longing, hills rang with my name
I became a tree, my fruit was shaken down, I'm content
My feet walked to my core

I am Hallâc, I am Nesimî, I so believed
I walked out of my skin

I Cut My Black Black Hair
(Kestim Kara Saçlarımı)

By Gülten Akın (1960)

Translated by Saliha Paker and Mel Kenne (2006)

It was far away   turn
                    it was close   turn
                        it was all around   turn
Taboo
        law
                custom   turn
Inside
        outside
                    beside you   I'm not
Inside me   shame
                    Outside me   work
                            My left side   love

How could this   be life turn

Couldn't do without them
                    had to carry
                            to use them

Enslaved and stuck-up
                    —how funny—
Eyes growing
                wider
                    harder to bear
Inside me
        a churning
                a sickening

Forth and back   my black black hair   I found it so

I cut my black black hair
                                    now what
Not a thing
                        —try it, please—
I'm day
          light
                    loony
                            breeze-borne

Good morning   wind swaying the apricot tree

Good morning   reborn one   set free

Now I wonder   at a pin's round head

That some weigh out   as a lifetime

Forth and back   from my black black hair   I cut myself free.

Translating the Silence of the Poor

Excerpt from a Talk by Latife Tekin (2007)
Translated by Nilgün Dungan (2012)

I'm a translator of the silence, of the muteness of the poor, into some kind of a language. There was a time when I described myself as a translator, not a writer . . .

I believe I'm a translator too, which is why I feel close to translators. I'm a translator of the silence, of the muteness of the poor, into some kind of a language. There was a time when I described myself as a translator, not a writer, and I think that was a revolt, a resistance against an aristocratic understanding of literature. So I considered myself to be non-literary, or outside of literature at large, trying to write literature while I maintained my poverty. I wanted to write about adventures of the poor in cities because only a few of them who migrated from rural areas were able to find regular jobs. The great majority had to seek out money each and every day. I wanted to tell the story of the poor in factories and shanty towns, and how the poor go about pursuing money in cities. And I wanted to do this as a translator. I mean, the leftists don't know much about these people, but I do and I'm actually a sort of translator between the leftists and the people I grew up with.

As I walked around the shanty towns, I began to collect sentences in my mind so that I could tell the story of the poor. I drew from my experience of becoming part of a political movement, but it's strange, I wouldn't use that language. I wouldn't use that language in my writing but the one of the poor. I was like the Other, both in the world of the poor and in the other world. Being young and a woman, and having lost my sense of location after migrating to the city, I felt even poorer. So I'd be speaking from an angle that was three times harder to understand. As I collected my sentences, I began to feel quite decisively about certain things concerning the nature of language itself. I began to develop a grammar and a linguistic sensitivity.

When we migrated from a rural to an urban area, I was nine, an age when you're vulnerable to trauma. You can't forget about past experiences, but you can't understand what's new right away, either. You're forced to learn a language, the language of the city—which you learn quickly—but deep down there's still pain. There's something I felt very strongly about when I was growing up in the city as a young woman of no means, about how it might *seem* as though all life's opportunities were there for the poor too. You know how they ask kids what they're going to be when they grow up. Well, they'd ask the poor kids what they were *not* going to be. This, of course, is a kind of knowledge that arises from poverty, and you internalize it. It goes something like this: you're poor and you won't be able to do a lot of things in life; your family or others tell you this in an unhurtful way; they say you should live without disturbing anyone, that you should bear your poverty gracefully and not mess with anybody. On the other hand, they say if you're poor but gutsy, smart and trainable, if you run fast enough, you can close the gap. So I thought if I ran fast, I could catch up. I mean, I'm confident about my brains, but there's something that holds a person back. I intuitively understood this had to do with language—perhaps because I wrote poetry.

Others use language differently than we poor people do, who only murmur. I mean, the poor have been using language this way for a thousand years. They aren't aware that life is constructed through language. Language, for us, is like water, something that's part of life. We only drink it because we have to stay alive. It somehow came to me that we're defeated by others, in some bizarre way, through language. So here I am, I'm going to write these books, but what kind of language will I use? Who are the people I'll be depicting? I'm thinking about poverty, but also about language. And all of a sudden, I noticed something. I saw that the language we speak features a process that was formed long ago, before there were words, when language was nothing but cries. Suddenly I felt as if I had moved back to a time before language and noticed some things about the nature of words and how language worked. I refer to this experience as that of "language appearing before me." The language people have constructed is a way they've found to redeem themselves. When we read language accurately and in depth, I mean as it was first constructed, in every case we see fear and passivity. Language, by its nature, is only concerned with people's survival and redemption. If feelings and thoughts were to move outside people, if they came and went, I could make a sentence as follows: I saw love on the street; it was talking to loneliness. I can say such a thing because such a perception as that exists. All things reside outside us, and as they fill us up or drain us, we display vitality. That is to say, at each moment we reconstruct ourselves. We're a part of that eternal flow. Of course, if everything is outside us, that means we're in the middle of everything.

It was when I observed *from within language* the poor and others who used language as a means of power that I thought about creating a different kind of fiction. It was impossible for me to write novels that had a beginning, a middle and an end. I'd have to strike a deal with the reader, as if I were saying, look, I'm going to tell you something but it will be a lot different from what you want to hear. I'm going to relate something to you from the wrong angle. This produced a tension in me because for me the system had collapsed. Western thought, in a political sense, had collapsed too. I couldn't accept the idea of progress now, and my thoughts regarding communism also evolved. My sense of time, or perception of time, changed because cyclical time interferes with linear time. Given all this, I couldn't create a hierarchical fiction. It became obvious that I wouldn't write like Orhan Pamuk. So how will this be read, where do I start, what will I tell? That's why whenever I start to write I feel tense.

We assume the poor are always visible because they walk around in their tattered clothes. But it's just the opposite; it's actually others who are visible because of the poor who are watching them intently. The poor cast their beady eyes on the world of those holding the power, while the latter remain unaware of this. I wrote *Swords of Ice* (*Buzdan Kılıçlar*) from such a perspective. I told the story of the poor seeking money by means of constructing a language. I described the murmuring of the poor as a state of innocence. Innocence gained tremendous importance for me. As I discovered all this, I was losing my own innocence. Starting from innocence, I turned to nature, and arrived at *Muinar*. In *Muinar*, a ten thousand-year-old hag tells from the perspective of the Other how we arrived at the present day. An old hag awakens within me and tells us a story in her own language. I found a place for myself by looking at that language. A place of opposition, but an odd one.

Chapter One of *Muinar* (*Muinar*)

By Latife Tekin (2006)
Translated by Güneli Gün (2007)

Nights, as my sleep deepens, someone seems to be clapping over my head; the sound of applause in my ear is like hearing the rain in my sleep; my chest opens, revealing my heart; I'm just dreaming: there's no fear in my mind; I've heard about chills from old wives whispering about uncanny seizures like this; a tree made of fire is growing out of my breast . . .

All these many months I've been shivering in my bed, waiting to wake up under a tent of light. This morning, before daybreak, I opened my eyes, the sound of drums banging in the stillness inside me; because I'm a woman no horse has been sent to take me up to heaven; I'm to pull myself up grasping the branches of the tree of fire.

I was slipping through at last, the drumming growing fainter . . .

A smoke-blue shadow broke loose and rose out of my chest, cursing. "MISBEGOTTEN MISCREANTS! MAY YOUR BONES TURN TO DUST! CORPORATE BASTARDS! YOU'VE THROWN THE EARTH TO JACKALS!"

I began humming the song of the fire that burns higher than the clouds. Sleep-fairies were supposed to take me by the hand and a latent loophole was to open in the ceiling. I must not give into fear. I struggled against the creature that had me in her power, blocking my ascent to heaven and using my voice to scream at pot-bellied hucksters, making me gasp under her rash curses. My head crashed back into the pillow . . .

"MAY YOUR BONES RUST, YOU CURS SPORTING ANTLERS! NAILED TO THE CROSS OF FINANCE CAPITAL . . ."

The shadow attempted to cast a spell in the air, but, seeming to fail, cringed and began to fall apart.

"LATİFE, GET UP! TAKE SEVEN DEEP BREATHS AND RISE! WOULD IT KILL YOU TO KEEP A DROP OF COGNAC AROUND?"

My heart beat in deep thuds, the ache in my chest was like a shot of vaccine. I closed my eyes in a state of confusion, keeping quiet and listening until it was almost mid-spring.

"I'M STUCK IN THE AGE OF POISON! GET UP!"

* * *

"Once, we weren't left to our own devices like you are, all alone in this world with your bitter voices. Courage brings joy, so don't avert your eyes, listen with a pure heart. Once, fairy maids and fairy retainers constantly hovered around us; I had my own private deity who answered my every call, not failing me until the hour of my death; when my mouth was stopped and my voice lost, my deity Siyutu was raised up above that has no above, melting into those who no longer must suffer being reborn. Siyutu . . . !

"All ideas, old and new, shall founder because life on this earth is at an end. Take my word for it, time is already buried in the past. Listen to me, and you shall be transported into the next age."

you gotta go when you gotta go (Gitmekse Gitmek)

By Zeynep Uzunbay (1998)
Translated by Ronald Tamplin and Saliha Paker (2006)

to drown in the narrowest of words
in the blackest abyss wasn't that how it was
to go within me and straight off be lost wasn't that love
in legs tired of life
like knotted veins the pain now
tops spinning spinning tops
how could it be like that, how like that
in one swoop of time that's how i was made

crooked needle straight lie
it was knitting it used to say the truth
two swelling floods in my legs
burning upwards from the feet
fire in the flooding waters
lights gone out work gone
so let it go let it be I said to the sea
one more chance, the walnut split from the fig
let the empty brackets close and fill

how many times unraveled
my belly that raised children my lap
everything knit one purl one the sickening mix
water writhing in ash
i'm tired of shivering
cover me the cloth a shadow the wave-top phosphor
look my coat is cut compassion wrong-side out
i say that water is death
and knowing all there is as well as I know

pretending to have forgotten it fed my thirst
if a star should touch my shoulder it would shrivel up
my tongue tobacco dry will moisten
i'll flick away my last ash

"you gotta go when you gotta go"

wet (ıslak)

By Zeynep Uzunbay (1995)
Translated by Arzu Eker Roditakis and Elizabeth Pallitto (2012)

broken,
i kissed the rain
became an exile to my heart

for loves that could not unfold
i undressed layer by layer
i made mad love
became a wanderer to the alphabet

where else
my dream, where
have i arrived
at the flushed skin of feeling
now i am wet even at the wind's touch

From "The Legs of Şahmeran" (Şahmeran'ın Bacakları)

By Murathan Mungan (1986)

Translated by Abigail Bowman (2010–2012)

2.

I drew up a small stool and sat at his knee.

My master said:

"Just think for a moment, what is Şahmeran? Who is it?

"What has its picture revealed throughout the centuries, migrant and magnificent, reaching from the adobe walls of village cafes to coffeehouses in all the rural provinces? What does Şahmeran say to these people, embroidered on their throw pillows and bed skirts?

"Think of how many Şahmeran-makers live in these lands; each year they create hundreds of Şahmeran pictures and plaques, and sell them. The people who buy these pictures to hang on their walls—what do they see in them? They keep some memory safe there, but a memory of what?

"What venom is hidden in the breast of the Şahmeran story? A venom that tastes of fairytales, spreading from one mouth to the next for a thousand years. Snake and human have been old, old friends (or enemies, one could say), since the time of the garden and the apple.

"In the climes of this tale, the snake is noble and the human deceitful.

"What was it Şahmeran said to Camsap: 'I told you, Camsap, humankind betrays.'

"Let's start from the beginning; to return yet again, yet again to the truth left behind by the forty legs of Şahmeran:

* * *

A long time ago—that is, a time whose date we do not know or do not wish to make known—there was a sage named Danyal. He was the kind of man who was never satisfied with what was given to him—this Danyal—always searching for something more, more than this, a man who dug at what lay behind the visible. He did not restrict himself to what he knew or content himself with what he could do. The visible facet of the world—or what people thought was visible—wasn't enough for him; he wanted more, always more. He tried to reach a deeper and more fundamental truth, a truth that he believed lay hidden. Knowing and learning became his passion. He had devoted his life (and his death) to being a scholar, a sage, and so others had great difficulty understanding him. Yet Danyal had long since accepted this loneliness. After all, those who take the risk of knowing must also risk loneliness and damnation. Do they not?

For many long years he occupied himself with research in numerous fields ranging from medicine to philosophy; he uncovered interesting results and cultivated various ideas. Although he was undertaking studies one might consider ahead of his time, he was also researching subjects popular with every sage of every era. For one, he had fallen into the pursuit of the secret of immortality; he was searching for the magical power to stay young forever, strong forever. Everything lay hidden in nature's bosom. (And could we have even known all that nature offered us? Did we truly discern all that we saw, observed and touched? Did we know what all they held secret in their cores?) He made useful ointments from medicinal herbs; these ointments could quickly heal the deepest wounds, relieve the sharpest pains. As he witnessed more and more of these small miracles, Danyal believed that someday he would be able to achieve immortality as well.

But Danyal's lifetime was not enough. He didn't live long enough to live forever.

Knowing, learning and researching may be endless, but a human life always comes to an end. The life nature offers us is limited. When he grew near to death, he called his wife to his side. On the bedside table lay a black book in which he had written everything he had learned until that day. He had spent his entire life on these pages, crammed his entire lifetime into a journal. When his wife came to his side, he picked up the book. He was holding his entire life in his hands.

He said: I was not enough; let my son carry on where I left off.

He said: My life was not enough; let my son carry on where my life left off.

He said: Human life is short, and there is no value in the things we learn, the things we know, the things we obtain, unless they are completed by someone else, by the life of someone else. Everything returns to the earth with us when we are buried. I am entrusting this journal to my son, and my son to this journal.

He gave the book to his wife, committing his life into her hands, and closed his eyes as if he never meant to open them again.

His son—Danyal's son—was still very small.

Danyal died.

His son was left behind.

* * *

His son was a misbehaved, mischievous and curious child . . . He grew up so fast. When the time came, his mother sent Camsap to school. Camsap, the rascal, only liked to play. He didn't study. His mother's thoughts always lay with the black book in the bottom of the chest. Camsap would master the alphabet, he would learn to read, and when the day came his mother would give him the black book; he would carry on where his father left off, carry on his father's legacy.

But as she saw her son going to school and then not going to school, escaping from school and home and life to spend all his days in the trees and water pools, the river banks and forest nooks, she understood that it was all a dream. Little by little, as time passed, she forgot about the black book lying abandoned in the bottom of the chest. She had to forget.

With nothing else to do, she took her son out of school and put him to work. He got himself a donkey and headed off to the forest. There, Camsap began to work as a woodcutter with his friends. Every day with an axe on his back, a whistle on his lips, and a donkey beneath him, he would go to the forest to chop and deliver wood; in this way they managed to make ends meet. In time his mother grew used to her son. Camsap was not the Camsap that Danyal had considered, or imagined. If Danyal had lived, he might have been that Camsap—or maybe he still wouldn't have—but such thoughts were of no use to anyone now. Besides, sons are not their fathers' shadows. Fathers can't keep seeing their sons as disciples, carrying on wherever they left off. A son is not a disciple; a son is a son.

Camsap was Camsap. There was nothing to do but accept him as he was. He was a grown man. An individual with his own fate.

Camsap and his friends spent their days enjoying themselves, not a care in the world. They'd turned their work into a game. Woodcutting was nothing but a pleasant outing for them. They were at the age where everything seemed like a game; they had not yet faced the fundamental difficulties of life. They lived straightforward lives, unaware of what choices, problems and excruciating pain existed in the world; they thought their lives would be like this forever. They were blinded by the zeal of youth. They lacked basic knowledge of the world and of life; they still did not know themselves or people in general. They had not gauged their own strength or stretched their limits; they had not put themselves or others to the test. Life was all just a spontaneous adventure for them, and they lived accordingly. They were healthy, strong, active, cheerful and full of life. They had not yet learned betrayal.

On a day just the same as any other, they headed for the forest hills, straight towards the sharp-edged cliffs, spreading out among the impregnable trunks of the old and noble trees that had parched and dried up in the sun, trunks no axe could cut. Their eyes were full of greed. They were trying to clear away these great trees so as to leave nothing for any woodcutters but themselves. They must have thought they could finish off the whole forest. Passion has no sense of accounting; humans must train their passion in this, for only then can they control it.

Just after they arrived at the foot of the steep cliffs of the summit, clouds heavy with rain closed in from all sides and began to pour, followed by thunderstorms without end . . . Camsap caught sight of a small cave hidden among the dark branches, its mouth veiled by dense vegetation. Pushing aside the predatory branches, he entered the cave. His friends dashed into the cave a step behind him. During the long hours they spent there (the rain didn't stop for some time), Camsap picked up a stick to dig around in the cave, and eventually struck a marble surface. He cleared away the surrounding dirt to reveal a marble lid. Calling his friends over, the group of them heaved together to lift the lid, and discovered beneath it a great well of honey.

And from that day forward the well became the source of all their income. They abandoned woodcutting and took up the honey trade. Again and again, they would get on their donkeys and ride to the tall cliffs of the forest, enter the cave and open the marble lid of the well. Then, they would sell the honey in tins at the market.

This well of honey they had found was their secret, shared by all of them, and all of them promised each other that they would never speak of the well to anyone, vowed that they would keep it a secret until their deaths.

The days ran into weeks, the weeks into months, until one day they glimpsed the bottom of the well they had thought to be bottomless.

The mist of a fairytale was gathering then, there in the mouth of the emptying well . . .

For one last time, Camsap climbed down the rope—hand over fist, as he always did—to extract the last few tins of honey left from the bottom of the well. He filled the last of the tins, sent them up to his friends, and prepared to climb. But they gathered up the rope they'd sent down, closed the marble lid of the well and left Camsap behind, abandoning him to his fate . . .

We should pause here now and catch our breath. Why did his friends leave Camsap at the bottom of the well? One story says that they did it to take Camsap's share. But this seems unlikely, as his share of the last few tins would not be enough for anyone. Especially considering the number of his friends—which is never directly stated in any account or written source, but the use of "friends" leads us to picture at least several people—it is doubtful that Camsap's share would be so coveted, a share that would crumble apart if divided between a few people.

Well then, what could be the reason?

Think for a moment . . .

First of all, we could say that the flow of the narrative demanded it.

Then we could say that from the time of the Prophet Yusuf until now—and for just as long again before him—people have betrayed those whom they lowered into wells.

After that, we could say that these young men's age of betrayal had come. We could say that it's hard to sustain a common secret, watch after it, protect it. Perhaps they wanted to bury their shared secret along with the one who created the secret—that is, Camsap. After all, he found the well and was thus the unspoken "owner" of it in everyone's mind. Perhaps they wanted to bury him along with the rest of it, all of it, everything at once.

Perhaps betrayal for them was a way to forget for all time. Whatever the case may be, humans are prone to the act of betrayal.

* * *

After Camsap realized that he had been abandoned to his fate in this blind well, the hours passed by without hope. Each hour spent waiting is already hopeless, is it not? Then he realized that there was nothing to do but take fate into his own hands. This well he had found was to be his grave, and it took some time for him to fully comprehend this. His rescue required a miracle, so he had to do something besides standing around helplessly. He began to check his surroundings, searching for a way out. For some reason he remembered the joy he'd felt on the day he first found this well. His present captivity felt like revenge for that joy. Perhaps every joy takes its revenge on people after a time. He pawed around in the dirt, trying to dig through the walls of the well with his fingernails. He had to get out of this grave, he had to escape no matter what, even if only to another grave, but he had to get out.

He couldn't remember how long this endless, exhausting effort lasted. After a while he lost his sense of time and place. It was much later that he spotted a light the size of a pinhead coming from one of the walls. At first he thought it was an illusion, a trick of the eye; he shifted his position and looked once more at the same place. No, he hadn't been mistaken. It was a light. He started to dig towards the light. As the light's outline widened, Camsap's hope of deliverance began to grow. At last he was able to open a hole wide enough to stick his head through, then his entire body.

This was his first victory.

A long, wide garden stretched out before him, as far as his eyes could see.

It was a fairytale realm, this place.

That, or a realm's fairytale.

He sensed this from the very first moment: the magic of the garden was like something out of a story. With further scraping and digging, he managed to create a hole he could squeeze through and stepped onto the soil of this new country.

Now the calendar of another time and the climate of another place begins.

The place he stepped into was the land of Şahmeran, but he would only learn of this later.

For now, he was simply experiencing the magic of what he had found, the miracle of his rekindled hope. The garden was stretching, stretching, stretching before his eyes like a magician's illusion.

At this point in the story my master stopped.

"That is enough for today," he said. "Tomorrow we will carry on where we left off."

I didn't say a word.

At night in my bed I imagined the land of Şahmeran. I fell asleep in an instant . . .

* * *

I'm looking at my master's hands. At how he grips the pen, at how he traces a line, at the flexibility of his fingers. His hands flow like a stream above the worktable, skipping suddenly like the flap of pigeon wings. It's as if the lines and the colors are slipping out from under his hand, under his pen. My own hand trembles as I look at his; my tiny hand seems quite pathetic to me. Small, feeble, inconsequential . . . I loved my master, but I deplored the way his hands fluttered above the worktable like beating wings. I was angry with him, envious of him, and jealous of him all at once.

My master had told me, "A master and apprentice must discuss everything— and I mean everything—between them. Nothing can be left unspoken. This is tradition for masters and apprentices."

Yet I remained uncertain whether to tell him my feelings. It caused me shame to feel this way about my master. Then again, I couldn't get the better of my feelings. After mulling it over for a long, long time, I gave up on telling him and put off the truth a bit longer. I thought that I would also grow in skill as time went on, and my hands would skim across the worktable as fast as his. Then I would be neither angry nor jealous.

We would be equal, he and I, and as equals it would be easy to love him; I would be neither angry nor jealous.

That's what I thought then.

As time went on . . .

* * *

"Where did we leave off?" he asked.

"The land of Şahmeran," I said.

This place was a fairytale garden—that, or a garden's fairytale. A courtyard and its wide terraces, all made of fine-grained marble, stretched out as far as the eye could see, erasing one's sense of the horizon, as if there were a sky of another color behind the tall pillars encircling the courtyard, or a second sun slowly setting. In the center of a large pool surrounded by blue and green tiles, a many-colored fountain turned the pool's waters to foam, cooling the nearby air without a sound.

Camsap expected some sort of hope to come out of this silence. He wanted a miracle from within this silence to burst into view and return him to the surface once more. All of a sudden he understood why heaven was depicted as a great garden, a huge one. He understood the hope for heaven. One realizes a great many things at once when one is alone and desperate.

This was an effect of the power of silence.

(He was thinking of gardens and of heaven, while his eyes combed the lawn and the fountain.) Among the vegetation there was not a single apple tree. He thought this was a great oversight, a huge one.

As Camsap approached the center of the garden, step by step, he caught sight of a throne atop a lofty pedestal to the right of the courtyard, resplendent in its size and beauty. The surface of the throne was decorated in various jewels of countless colors, adorned with pearl inlay, worked over with carvings. The throne implied endless and boundless power, everlasting sovereignty. As he reached the steps at the foot of the throne, a host of creatures suddenly swarmed into the garden—demons, snakes, dragons, each quite appropriate for this dream Eden.

They ripped apart the silence in the most terrifying way.

When he found the garden a short while ago, when he stepped out into its silence and coolness, he had been overwhelmed by the feeling that he had been saved. He had even imagined he would be home by nightfall. The fear and the consternation he now felt erased every thought and left a deep desperation in its wake. He felt that heaven was not a very reassuring place, and realized that nothing, nowhere, would be able to alleviate the endless anxiety of mankind . . . Nothing except that stark silence, that is. Nothing except death. There must not be life after death, he thought.

All of a sudden the air filled with colorful trails of smoke, each tracing a delicate and cloudy rainbow before fading and disappearing within the chalk-white fumes. Soon no one could see anything (that is, neither Camsap nor the snakes, demons or dragons) and the whole place was cocooned in clouds of fog. A quilt of whiteness had enveloped the entire courtyard. After a while, as the fumes dissipated and everything started to go back into place, a huge demon appeared from within the fog. It was carrying a silver tray on its head with great solemnity. It took the tray and placed it before the throne, then drew back respectfully.

Upon the tray was Şahmeran.

She—he—glided from the tray onto the throne.

Camsap was mesmerized. He slowly sank to the ground where he stood, until he found himself kneeling.

It was Şahmeran, this being, he recognized it.

He had seen so many plaques adorned with its likeness. Not one of them resembled Şahmeran, but each of them had something that brought Şahmeran to mind. Yet he did not know the story of Şahmeran. He had never heard it, never listened, never even asked out of curiosity. If he'd known this story, known his place in this story, would everything have been different? This is something we cannot know now. Something we cannot ever know . . .

"Welcome to my country," said Şahmeran. "Don't be afraid: all the snakes, demons and dragons you see around you are my friends, my helpers. No harm will come to you here from anyone."

For Şahmeran these are all "someones," thought Camsap, each and every one. Everyone has other "someones" in their lives.

"My name is Yemliha. I am the sultan of all the snakes on this earth. Humans and my subjects know me as Şahmeran. Here, you are under my care, nothing fearful can threaten you. But you must tell me how you came here and what you are searching for."

At this, Camsap found his voice and told Şahmeran everything that had happened to him on his way there, step by step.

Şahmeran, after listening attentively to Camsap's explanations, nodded thoughtfully and said:

"So once more mankind has found where we are. This means that from now on they will never leave us in peace."

Camsap burst out:

"If you're talking about my friends who left me alone in the well and abandoned me to my fate, there's no reason to fear them. What they want most is to forget that well, forget that they abandoned me to my death inside it, forget their betrayal."

"I'm not talking about you or them, Camsap," said Şahmeran. "I'm talking about humankind."

"Aren't you being unfair by lumping us all together?" asked Camsap.

"No," said Şahmeran. "Humankind betrays. For this reason not even a single person must know of our place; they must not share in our secret. We are creatures whose existence depends on secrecy. Think about this: as much as you were frightened by us when you came here, I too was afraid when I saw you. Notice I did not say 'I was afraid *of* you,' I said 'I was afraid when I saw you.'

"I gave up on people once before. Once, many years ago, I trusted a man. I gave him a chance. Later, I paid a very high price for that trust. For this reason, I don't ever want to experience betrayal again, Camsap. To have tasted betrayal even once damages one's heart irreparably; something breaks off from deep, deep within and disappears, never to return. Experiencing the betrayal of someone you loved, someone you trusted, someone in whom you believed, is not a pain you can explain, endure or resist. The heart of humankind is quick to rot. As for me, I have to think not only of myself, but of my subjects. I have to protect them, watch over them. I cannot let my own weakness jeopardize their trust. You understand, don't you? It would be unjust, it would be selfish, it would be evil."

"I would have wanted you to trust me," said Camsap.

"I would have wanted that, too," said Şahmeran.

There was a long sharp silence. The demons and snakes who filled every corner of the garden that was slowly darkening as the sun set, were listening to the discussion with great respect.

The silence continued for some time longer.

It was like internal bleeding, this silence.

Gathering all his strength and hope, Camsap brought up that magical subject they had not discussed but continued to circle around.

"So, are you not going to send me to the surface of the earth, Şahmeran?" he asked.

Şahmeran's silence lasted a long time; Camsap felt the need to try again.

"I swear to you, I will tell no one where you are . . ."

Camsap, who not long ago had been overwhelmed with the feeling that he would be back home by evening when he escaped from that dark well and found this place, now felt as if he were caught in a trap from which he would never escape. He thought about how the things we think are in our grasp escape us in an instant; how quickly we lose the things we hold, the things we seize, the things we touch; how quickly we're able to lose them.

"Just believe me," he said. "I want you to believe me more than I want you to set me free. Believe me, I would rather die than speak of your place, or mention it to anyone. It's enough for you to send me back to the world, to my home, my hearth."

"Consider this: your path here was the result of a betrayal, Camsap," said Şahmeran. "This is not a good beginning. You came here as the result of a betrayal; your path was ultimately defined by wrongdoing. Because once betrayal is born, it changes its clothes and lasts all life long."

"I don't know how to make you believe me," sighed Camsap.

"What would you make us believe?" asked Şahmeran. "You can swear everything as the Camsap you are now, you may even make me believe you; but the one who will betray us someday is not the Camsap you are now. What kind of promise can you make in the name of the Camsap you will become? You don't know him either . . ."

Camsap began to cry in desperation.

"Listen then!" said Şahmeran. "I will tell you the story of Belkıya."

"Belkıya?"

"Yes, Belkıya; the man who first betrayed me. Are you ready?" asked Şahmeran.

"I am ready," Camsap said.

"Are you ready?" asked my master.

"I am ready," I said.

"Then we will continue tomorrow," he said.

* * *

I was still unaware that Camsap was in captivity. I was savoring the adventure of the work. For Camsap, everything had been an adventure up to falling in the well—his life had now begun; for me (or for us, we could say, the listeners, writers and readers), the adventure was everything that happened after falling into the well. Everyone, all of us were spectators of another's fate.

Who knows, perhaps the acts of writing, reading and listening are like spells of protection, keeping the inevitable at a distance.

And sometimes drawing it close . . .

The magic power that stains our hands as we draw or write, the power that stains our hands with what we have created, is for distancing the nearby and drawing the distant near.

That night in my bed, I thought of Camsap beginning his adventure and grew excited; what would happen next was as interesting for me as it was for Camsap.

I thought of Camsap as I drew Şahmeran.

But I wasn't conscious of it yet.

For some reason, when I next went to draw Şahmeran's face, I realized that in this story Camsap interested me more than Şahmeran. What would I place on this face? I drew a number of Şahmerans, but they resembled Camsap more than Şahmeran. The Camsap within me.

Eyes wide with fear, a face that had surrendered its fate to another. A captive anticipation . . .

Later, much later, I realized that the Şahmeran I'd drawn was the right one, knowingly or not. Because Şahmeran was a prisoner too, wasn't it?

Imprisoned by the eccentric identity of its existence. That magnificent, sacred, beautiful creature could find no place in the world of humans or the world of snakes—it remained in limbo, waiting silent and alone in its personal hell. Its subjects would not even awaken until its death.

All the Şahmerans I drew at the time, thinking of Camsap, possessed the truth of a mistake. Sometimes, a person reached the truth by setting off from a mistake . . .

My whole life turned into a Şahmeran story at this point. In the shop during the day (with its sense of reality adorned with colorful threads, spools and plaques), at home during the night (getting ready to sleep in the emptiness thick with darkness), I curled up in the embrace of the Şahmeran story. I couldn't take away anything from this story that related to my own life. Everything was so distant from me. Or else it only seemed distant.

In later years, after greater costs and greater pains, I would finally comprehend that, in fact, my whole life had been a Şahmeran story.

As I came to know beauty and death . . .

I hadn't explored my own well, because I still had not been lowered into one. There was more to come.

From *Lonelinesses* (*Yalnızlıklar*)

By Hasan Ali Toptaş (1993)
Translated by Mel Kenne and Şehnaz Tahir Gürçağlar (2008)

5.

I once thought of loneliness as my grandma
Legends, during those years, would begin as bandit songs.
No thyme-perfumed forests pealing out partridge melodies
resounded in my grandma's voice;
rather, if anything,
mountains;
smoky,
blood-soaked mountains
sentenced to be so by official decree.
Then, rising out of a dry cough
that crumbled like *lor* cheese
bandits would suddenly attack the village;
or from grandma's eyes,
that looked like a pair of olives,
would leap army deserters;
they'd vault over my head
and charge up the mountains,
pulling along their shadows like a great, bloody coat.

Next, the echoing of gunshots . . .
With a shift of her eyelids like two dusty bugs
crushed under the yoke of centuries,
my grandma would say,
your mamma's popping corn
but I never believed her,
for I could still see those gangs everywhere; I would witness them
and I was a child
who understood
that this seeing opened belief's widest gate.

Even when my grandma stopped storytelling and dozed off
the gangs didn't pipe down;
the bullet-whine from mausers at Beşparmak
never let up day or night,
smacking cradles with their evil-eye beads
that ricocheted off the blinders of oxen.
The villagers set aside their shovels, pickaxes
and sieves,
set aside *tarhana* soup and cayenne pepper
set aside the odor of ginger, their voices, their dreams,
set their courage aside and gazed up at the mountains
interminably.

The chimneys watched the mountains,
the doors, the tiny windows, the sheep
watched the purple mountains,
the goats watched the sky-blue mountains,
in other words nature felt curious about itself,
quite curious
and during those years
my eyes were composed of what they looked upon
my hands of whatever they touched.
Don't ask me about my tongue,
it was made out of what I failed to say
and it lay in my mouth like a bloody book.

During those years
I didn't even have my forests inside me
to hide my track,
I wasn't yet even an island
in the sky
I wasn't even a sky.
I had nothing but my grandma
(my dad would stay faithful to her in himself when he went away)
and it was as an island

that I knew my grandma,
then as a father;
as the windows heaved back my likeness,
as my looks, faced by those images
that thrived on my reflection, grew wrinkled,
and as I became short even as I grew tall,
I clung to her.

In the craggy lines of her face
I edged toward myself.
At times I was swept up in the brine of a flood,
other times I scaled sheer heights
in the belief that the nail scratch of a year (who knows which one?)
was the bed of river
and those slopes full of me.

And then, much later, the gory bodies of bandits
were hauled down the slopes
to land right in the midst of my dreams.
When I saw them I trembled (which is how I learned to tremble
even today when I shudder
a bandit drops in me).
Yes, I trembled
and wanted to grab the tired mauser on the floor
and take to the mountains.

But the guards twitched their great moustaches
(each one its own state, founded by the face)
and drove me off;
I began to flee, garbed in my fears, with no mauser,
I would dash off through the birds,
the scent of manure rushing through me,
I would cut under the wings of a chicken
scurry through the bottom of a sack of bulgur
or

slip through the way a sifter hangs from a nail
but
I'd not stop even once to look to turn and look back.

From the way I ran you could see the guards were hot on my trail;
I had to run and so I ran and ran,
until after a while all the running
made running feel like stopping.
At that point the only way I could find to run was to stop;
I stopped and a cliff got tangled up in my ankles.

To be got up in a cliff somehow is what loneliness means.

7.

Loneliness means placing yourself before you,
And talking to the other *yous*.
It means trading looks with your other *yous*;
fighting them.
And, sometimes, it means killing
the one who is most like you,
because that one's not at all like you.

Loneliness is killing.

Loneliness is the rod of Moses,
it is Noah's ark,
the cross of Jesus,
Muhammed's camel.
For the fly
lifting off the scale
to settle on Grocer Hüsnü's shoulders,
it's the fly's wing,
it's my hand,
it's my foot.
It's the instant shiver on my skin,
It's your quick way of looking at me.

Loneliness is you setting out to plod up to yourselves.

Tante Rosa's Animals
(Tante Rosa'nın Hayvanları)

By Sevgi Soysal (1968)

Translated by Amy Spangler (2010–2011)

Tante Rosa found a turtle—the animal that carries its home on its back—the day the war ended. Homes were destroyed. She found the animal that carries its home on its back over by the ruins, liked it and wanted to take it home with her. She remembered that their home had been destroyed, and that they were staying in one of the dorms built, thanks to the Volunteer Pink Angels Hand-in-Hand With the People campaign, by the Society for Helping Victims of the Bombing, and she no longer liked the animal that carried its home on its back. On that day she understood that a home was, that it should be a destructible object, detached from one's person.

After that, she only liked cats and free, predatory forest animals, from a distance. Tante Rosa woke up one morning, understood that her own animal too had awoken, and she liked her own animal. First the glances, then dancing on Saturday evenings. Waltzes, tangos, swing; her animal liked to dance. It liked the love stories in *You and Yours* magazine. She liked the usual male gazes when she entered and left the ice cream shop on the corner of Königstrasse. She liked to adorn herself in the male gazes, one by one.

On a day like this, a Saturday, Saturdays are crazy days, she went dancing at the local bar with Hans, the neighbor's son. She had three glasses of beer. This time, for some reason, Hans paid for all the beers. Hans paid for the beers, this time, for some reason. Rosa sweat a lot during the first dance. She sweat even more during the second dance; after the third and the fourth dance, she was covered in sweat, her cheeks aflame. Hans's hand was shaking. Rosa was bashful, but she was not bashful enough, not enough to avoid leaving together, not enough to avoid walking together on the path leading into the forest. Rosa was not bashful enough.

That animal called sex which is embodied all of a sudden, which suddenly assumes concrete form, emerged from the forest, just like that, and became a Hans, Tante Rosa found herself facing not Hans, but that animal, that cunning animal that lay there waiting in ambush, and she delivered herself into the arms of, not Hans, no, no it could never be Hans, into the arms of that animal. But worst of all, now, that animal which is so suddenly embodied, which assumes concrete form, became Hans once again, stupid Hans, three-dance Hans, Hans who for some reason paid for their beers that day, Hans who could not possibly know, could not possibly comprehend that Tante Rosas might have animals of their own, and that they might sleep with those animals.

Tante Rosa got pregnant.

Tante Rosa got pregnant by Hans. Just like in all those pedestrian love stories published in *You and Yours* magazine, she got pregnant as soon as she slept with him, and she thought that what was written in those love stories was right and true. She thought that it was right and true, and so in order not to become a family girl with "sullied honor," in order not to give birth to a bastard child, she married Hans.

First, she began to like dogs more than cats, dogs, which assumed protecting their owners and their owners' homes to be the sole meaning of their existence, more than cats, which didn't really give two hoots about protecting their owners and their owners' homes. Then she liked canaries, clueless chickens, boring parakeets and all domesticated animals, plus turtles, which carried their homes on their backs—she had forgotten all about those free, predatory forest animals.

She thought she had forgotten, because when she realized that what was written in the love stories in *You and Yours* was not true, when she realized, oh, when she realized . . .

When she started sleeping with her husband unwillingly, she realized what it meant to be a woman of "sullied honor," and as she gave birth to bastard children after unwillingly sleeping with her husband, she realized what it meant to give birth to bastard children, she understood so well, as if physically grasping the fact, she understood that nothing was at all like what was written in the love stories in *You and Yours*.

On the day the war ended, Tante Rosa found a turtle—the animal that carries its home on its back. Homes were destroyed. She found the animal that carries its home on its back over by the ruins, she liked it, she wanted to take it home with her. She remembered that their home had been destroyed, and that they were staying in one of the dorms built, thanks to the Volunteer Pink

Angels Hand-in-Hand With the People campaign, by the Society for Helping Victims of the Bombing, and she no longer liked the animal that carried its home on its back. On that day she understood that a home was, that it should be a destructible object, detached from one's person.

The aforementioned incidents ran through Tante Rosa like water through a sieve and Tante Rosa began viewing the world through the holes of the sieve.

Tante Rosa is Excommunicated
(Tante Rosa Aforoz Ediliyor)

By Sevgi Soysal (1968)

Translated by Amy Spangler (2010–2011)

While Tante Rosa was breast-feeding her third child, it was a Sunday, she watched the people flocking to church. Old women and young women had put on their hats and wiped their children's noses. Men with rough, red, fat fingers took their last gulp of beer at the pub, they wiped their faces with their swollen, red-fingered hands. The hats of their wives struck the pub window, they got up, they exited into the frosty morning weather, they sought the usual dampness of snot in the noses of their children. The sound of bells, murmuring of prayers, songs, embroidery, icons, candles, pictures of angels—pictures of angels. Pink baby boys flapped their wings, they flapped their wings to the sound of the organ. Tante Rosa's husband of seven years recalled the morning they were married. Tante Rosa, whose husband was used to reminiscing to the sound of the organ, could not come to church on Sunday morning because she was now breast-feeding their third child, The prayer lasted a long time; the songs, the sound of bells, the sound of the organ lasted a long time. The Jesuses on the icons grew old. The noses of the children who came to church with clean noses were snotty again—the sound of the bells.

Tante Rosa watched the crowd returning from church. It was snowing outside. The children, throwing snowballs, led the pack. One snowball flew and broke Tante Rosa's window. The house became filled, with the frosty winter weather, with snow, with the presence of her husband come back from church, the child had fed all it was going to feed from the breast, it slept. Tante Rosa filled up the hole in the window with her breast, the frosty winter weather bit her breast, the women returning from church took off their hats and shielded their faces and out of the corners of their eyes they looked at Tante Rosa's husband. Tante Rosa's husband didn't hear a thing, he was thinking of the roasted duck at home, the roasted duck and the apple pie consumed every Sunday, and the hot coffee.

Then the first child cried, the second child cried, the baby cried. Tante Rosa buttoned up her breast, she walked in her robe that swept the floor, the wooden stairs creaked. The cover of a chest opened, faded photos, faded notebooks, dried violets between pages, violets dried before they wilted, purple. She saw a letter, just any letter, the top of the chest closed, it was snowing outside, her husband came home. Sunday's roasted duck was better than ever, the apple pie was really, really good, the house was warm, the tablecloth was starched, the husband's hair was parted down the middle and slicked back with wax. Tante Rosa's corset was of a good brand, the roasted ducks she ate had swollen her stomach, the corset was good, it was tight, it was real tight, she withdrew to her room. She locked the door from inside. Every Sunday afternoon her husband would come, her husband would come every Sunday afternoon, into her bedroom—she locked the door. She tried to remember the letter she had seen, she thought of a man's face, but it didn't work, ships kept passing before her eyes, before her eyes ships passed, train whistles, factory whistles, a droning sound, the droning sounds of crowded big cities, the drone of the city where *You and Yours* was published—the door was being forced opened, hands used to opening the usual doors on the usual days, shocked, were forcing the door. Shock and tyranny, an unexpected tyranny, Tante Rosa's husband was yelling. The man was banging against the door with his fists, with his fists he banged against the door that had disrupted his routine. Upon the door which had broken off the last, loose link of the "morning – church – roasted duck – apple pie – wife's bosom" chain that was his routine, he banged with his fists. Tante Rosa remembered the man's face that she had been trying to remember.

Behind her, Tante Rosa left a letter, she left three children, one still nursing, she left the maid who she'd taught how to cook roasted duck and to bake apple pie, to starch the dining room tablecloths, to arrange the shelves. She left a small garden with margarita plants, a high-ceilinged house with a wooden staircase, and an alarm clock, she left the husband who went to church every Sunday morning, who would come to her bosom every Sunday afternoon, she left women who wear hats and their snotty-faced children, she left their husbands and their lives too with their roasted duck, she left the church, she left the sound of the bells, the sound of the organ, the Christmas carols, she left her left breast that she had used to fill up the hole in the window that was broken by the snowball that the children threw on their way back from church, her left breast that covered her heart with a layer of fat. She left. She left and she went to where the factory stacks and the ship horns were, she went to where everyone steps on each other's feet on the trams without saying sorry, to where people say neither good morning nor hello, it was Sunday afternoon, or evening, she hit the road, behind she left folded letters among faded violets, she left behind wedding dresses and veils.

In *You and Yours* magazine it said, it said that a woman had left her husband, her youngins, a Catholic woman no less, she had left a village, a village full of respectful people, where the most respectful priest of the south gave sermons, a woman of the church, it said, the village church had excommunicated her, it had excommunicated her, you seeee, those women, their snotty-faced children, their husbands who became so suddenly and unbearably manly every Sunday, they all listened to this, on Sunday mornings, the priest always told the story of that woman, the priest told the story of Tante Rosa, that Sunday, her husband, as if he were the village hero, all of the women wearing hats raced to invite Tante Rosa's husband over for roasted duck, they raced to fill porcelain plates with apple pie, to fill them up with more and more. The church, the priest, the husband, the maid, to excommunicate her they raced.

What is expected now is a suicide, a cliff, a fall. What is expected now is for an old hag to die miserably at the end of a life of sin. Or is it the merry life of a sinner, dead (snuff it) before she can make her confession, that is expected now? Is it success, happiness that is expected now?

Is it nothing, or is it nothing? Ship horns, factory whistles, mixing into a crowd of people who step on each other's feet without saying sorry, who say neither good morning nor hello, is that nothing? What is it? If Tante Rosa was excommunicated in a peace-loving Catholic village on a Sunday, what is that, what is the expected ending?

In the big city that she went to, Tante Rosa became a newsagent. And she sold *You and Yours* magazine. Upstairs her husband, her beautiful husband, her new husband played the violin, he played the violin. After she was excommunicated, Tante Rosa earned good money selling *You and Yours* magazine.

Lament of a Working Mother's Child
(Annesi Çalışan Çocuğun Ağıtı)

By Gülten Akın (1976)

Translated by Cemal Demircioğlu, Arzu Eker, Mel Kenne and
Sidney Wade (2007)

I threw them out. What good are paints
For loneliness, apart from black
What color can I use
Dry table, dull ceiling, sulky carpet
My pictures should look pale

My window no longer attracts birds
Daffodils are losing their breath
Even with three brushes, you still can't comb Yuku Lili's hair
I am the child of a mother who goes out to work

Snow on the road and the roof veils
The blue lines left over from last summer
I say nothing. Trying once or twice
The sound of joy will also say nothing
Cat-like wails at the foot of the wall
In the gardens, ugly chrysanthemums should be blooming

Sand (Kum)

By Gülten Akın (1995)

Translated by Mel Kenne and Arzu Eker (2007)

I had a love interest once
who from his hometown mailed me sand
while I was always asking myself
what about its wind
is it soft, is it wild, is it steady?
does it quickly hurl into the skies
whatever it picks up from the ground?

later we took to sharing cities
the wind served as master, I as apprentice
in a rage of coming and going it blew
filling my eyes with sand

From *May I Have a Fly-Sized Husband to Look Over Me* (*Sinek Kadar Kocam Olsun Başımda Bulunsun*)

By Hatice Meryem (2002)

An Imam's Wife (İmamın Karısı)
Translated by Ruth Whitehouse (2010)

If my imam husband cared even an iota for worldly matters like most good imams, everything would be just rosy during our brief time on this earth, just as it was for the wives of other imams. Local women wouldn't whisper "Heretic Nurten" behind the corners of their muslin headscarves. Cheeky kids wouldn't taunt me with chants of "fatty fatty bum bum." The women would think I didn't know what they called me and the kids would think I didn't mind about the taunts. But I would mind and it would make me sad.

Sometimes, when walking home to our two-room house next to the mosque I would sense that I was living through yesterday and today at the same time. Yesterday and today would fuse into one and I would think how time without past or future was God's greatest gift to mankind. Otherwise, how could people grapple with the past and future simultaneously? That is, if they can even grasp the concept of a simultaneous past and future. How else could a woman cope with gaining fifty kilos in five years? How else would anyone believe a woman could be jealous (God forgive me!) of her husband's place in the affections of God?

My imam would spend all his time praying. He would get up in the middle of the night to perform *namaz* and sleepily repeat the ritual during the day in order to show Him that he was a most auspicious slave of God, the truest of believers. My imam would spend little time over meals, but rise from the table having barely eaten enough to keep himself alive. Eventually, growing thinner by the day, he'd select only the nutrients essential for his daily energy. The moment he awoke, he'd perform his ablutions, put on his cleanest clothes and run to Him.

After the children went their different ways in the mornings, I would be totally alone. I'd do a little tidying up before going out. As soon as the gossips huddled outside my door saw me, they'd separate and adjust their headscarves. Then, when I reached the house to which I'd been invited, they'd gather around me, waiting for me to begin my talk.

I would start with the words, "Ladies, Islam is finer than a human hair, keener than the sword," and end with, "Beware of falling prey to vice and immorality!" As I finished speaking, my main concern would be to scoop up any crumbs on the table, which was spread with food prepared for my benefit, and pop them into my mouth.

I would talk with my mouth full of delicious potato pastries, saying:

"Ladies, television is a thing of heresy. Don't fritter away your time in front of the television. You must pray! You must worship! And take care when buying your muslin prayer scarves. There are hypocrite artists who put plus signs in the center of flowers and think we don't see or understand. But we do. They're secretly displaying images of the cross to us. Don't forget, ladies, that to pray in such headscarves is heresy!"

Then I'd inhale the vapors of steaming hot, meat-filled *dolma* and, tossing one into my mouth, continue:

"Be careful when choosing your prayer rugs. They should be neither too flowery nor too decorative. The eye is the most sinful of bodily organs. God gave women eyes in order to test them. Just think, it's said you must control your hands, your hips and your tongue. But if the eyes don't see, the hands, hips and tongue will behave themselves. Isn't that right, ladies? Make sure you control your eyes. If your eyes stray for a moment to a flower, an insect, a twig or a leaf, if your attention is distracted for even one instant, your prayers will be in vain!"

Next would follow the part the women liked best. The husbands of some, in fact most, would want to go to bed several times a day with these unseemly women. What should they do? Was it proper in the eyes of God? The husbands of some, in fact most, would come up from behind and put their arms around the waists of these shrewish women during menstruation. What should they do then? They didn't want to upset their husbands, but neither did they want to commit a sin. In fact, they wanted to gain favor before God. Some of them would say, "Excuse me, Hodja, but we are talking woman to woman here, aren't we?" Then, shamelessly expecting me to turn a blind eye to their sins, they'd say, "My husband's very lazy about trimming the hairs around his private parts.

Does our religion have anything to say about that?" Seeing me blush, they might seek a way out and add, "Or should my husband ask the imam?" These improper questions would come spilling out one after the other—questions so indelicate that women much wiser than me would have difficulty answering them. I would end up pontificating like my husband in one of his ecstatic, divinely-inspired Friday sermons:

"Ladies, your husbands are your salvation and your downfall, your ticket to Heaven or Hell. Never forget that your husband will await you at the gates of Heaven and at the gates of Hell! If your husband sees fit, you will go to Heaven. Otherwise you go to Hell! If you want to gain a place as a woman in Heaven, you must never refuse his needs, even if you're about to give birth. You must respond to his call, even if you're busy cooking dinner at the stove."

While speaking, I'd think of my husband:

Confiding in God,

In God's embrace,

Closer to God than to me.

A Jailer's Wife (Gardiyanın Karısı)
Translated by Ruth Whitehouse (2010)

On winter mornings especially, there'd be no getting up early, no lighting the stove with a few pieces of firewood, no waking him with a kiss on the cheek and gently lifting the quilt at the sound of the kettle boiling, no sorting out the socks scattered about the previous evening, no washing his vests and underpants yellowed from ten days' wear and no folding up his shirts and trousers into neat piles on a chair. I'd lie under the woolen quilt sent by my mother from the village, inhaling the heat, wiggling my butt from side to side and watching my husband with one eye half open, as if I were a stranger to him. From under the quilt, I'd hear this poor clumsy husband of mine trying to warm his cold hands with his breath, looking for his socks and cursing vehemently through clenched teeth, at me for not looking after him, at his kids whose mouths he knew full well he was obliged to feed, at the socks he couldn't find and at his whole bloody lot in life. The moment he put his head outside the door, beautiful Serpil on the top floor would shake out a tablecloth, emptying scraps from the meal she'd prepared for her husband's return from night shift. The olive stones that rained down on my husband's head would provoke yet more curses.

All this would carry on until, one day, my husband, along with ten colleagues and the deputy governor, would be taken hostage during a riot at the prison.

It would go like this. Two gangs at the prison would get into a fight. When the guards tried to intervene, they would be taken hostage. The attorney general would then arrive and speak to a representative of each of the gangs, after which my husband and the others would be released. After days like that, my husband would be in a dilemma. He'd spend the evening pacing back and forth inside the house like a caged wolf.

"What is it? What's the matter?"

"They told me to take the money or I'd be 'dead meat'!" he'd blurt out immediately.

"Who said that?"

"They did."

"Who are they?"

"The gangsters, of course!"

As soon as my jailer mentioned money, the world would suddenly look a brighter place.

"So," I'd say, "Go ahead and take it."

The moment I said that, my poor jailer would roar at me like a lion: What the hell was I saying? Did I think it okay to take money from gangsters? They'd only try to smuggle in telephones, knives and guns. He had no choice but to ask for a transfer to another prison the very next morning.

He'd go on and on until I interrupted and started talking him around. At this point, I'd be feeling sick because it was hateful having to plead with such a spineless oaf.

"Tufan, dear," I'd say. His name had to be Tufan. "Just listen to me. You have to provide for your family. Life is cruel. Don't be so soft-hearted. Be a man. Look, I'll go and make you nice cup of coffee."

As I put two spoonfuls of coffee into the pot, I'd peer through the door to see what was happening. My stupid man would be sprawled on the sofa like a lord. I'd go to the bathroom where, in front of a cracked mirror, I'd adjust the cheap nylon headscarf that kept slipping off my hair and pretty myself up a bit. Anyone seeing me enter the room with the cup of coffee in my hand would think I was a fresh young bride. Without going into detail, even our woolen quilt would take me for a shameless hussy that night.

Needless to say, the next morning I'd wake up early and, with youthful vigor, set about the daily tasks I normally left undone. However, I wouldn't go so far as to sprinkle the traditional water after him to speed his safe return. As he went out through the garden gate, I'd berate that brazen Serpil at the top of my voice and wake the whole neighborhood.

That evening, it would be music to my ears, like the sound of the stream flowing in my village, to hear my husband say he hadn't asked for a transfer. In my most flirtatious voice, I'd say I wanted to buy a five-piece set from the steel saucepan seller who watched over the neighborhood like a village headman, a Tetris for our younger son, a stylish pair of jeans for the older one and a few balls of best quality lace thread for the trousseau of our daughter who'd be approaching marriageable age.

"You can get a couple of pairs of woolen socks for me too, woman." He'd blurt out finally.

That's when I'd realize this man would be a government minister before long.

A Useless Man's Wife (Lüzumsuz Adamın Karısı)
Translated by Mark David Wyers (2010)

To the Useless Man, Sait Faik

If I were a useless man's wife . . . I would be a large-breasted Jewish girl, and as women in the old days used to say, my hands would be so pudgy they would have dimples the size of hazelnuts. You know the kind of girl I mean; you just can't resist the temptation to take another look, and then another. I would have just one flaw, however: a black speck in the iris of one of my eyes. Sometimes I would dawdle on the steps of the apartment building with a newspaper cone full of sunflower seeds, munching away and chatting with passersby.

The first time I set eyes on this useless, jobless tramp from the window, I would have just turned fifteen. I would probably jump to the conclusion that he was a man of literature, because he always had a journal tucked under his arm. In the early evening hours, when the rest of the world was still busy at work, he would storm down our street as if his life depended on it—but, he would never fail to toss a glance up at my window. His expression would be so blank and meaningless, however, that at some point I would wonder if he might be a cop, or a private detective.

Every evening, at the hour when I knew he would pass by, I would put on my loose-fitting, low-cut dress that bared my legendary cleavage, perch in the window and set about like a master tailor mending rips and tears which normally I would never bother with. So there I would be, making all of this fuss for that useless man, and then, what do you know, the meddlesome carpenter across the street would think I was doing it all for him! When our literary tramp passed by, the carpenter would swagger out and bluster, "Look here, fatso, if I see you around here again, I'll knock your lights out!" And then what do you know, after this ill-fated incident, our useless man would apparently forget the way to our street.

Then the solution would dawn on me: I would go straight to the woman who runs the local coffee shop, and tell her everything that had happened. She would titter with excitement, and swelling with the pride of someone assigned a task of national proportions, say, "Now, don't you worry, I'll take care of this," and serve me a cappuccino. Three days later, after waxing off a few stray leg-hairs with the gum I was chewing, I would slip on my favorite violet floral print dress and, slamming the front door of the apartment building behind me like someone who is never going to return, I would jounce and strut right past that meddling carpenter. When I arrived at the coffee shop, she would take me into her back room, far from prying eyes. A few moments later, I would hear her coquettish voice sing out in accented French, "Bonjour Monsieur, comment allez-vous?"—and my heart would start pounding.

When he saw me, what would he do? Would he be overjoyed, or would he get flustered, his little tongue tied in knots? Would he say, "What have you done?" and send me back home? Of course, that's what he would do. He would say, "I'm sorry but I am so much older than you, and I don't even have a job—all I do is wander the streets, and I haven't even had a visitor in seven years. I just don't have the money to look after you, and with me, your youth and beauty would just waste away." And then he would send me packing.

No, that's not how it would happen. If only the Madame's plush bright red armchair could speak! As soon as he came in, that passion of mine, which I wore like a borrowed brooch, would set me free of those feelings that make people shy, coy or ill at ease. I would fidget in the chair, right and left, setting my full breasts aflutter, like two chubby birds that had happened to perch there. After he stood there for a while, however, I wouldn't be able to take it anymore, and I would cheekily say:

"Why are you standing there, come sit by me." When he went on standing like a stick in the mud, I would tense up as well, and fix my gaze on a flower on my dress, like a child who had been caught doing something wrong. After I had counted the leaves of the flowers on my dress God knows how many times, finally he would say, "Get up. Let's go to the tripe soup restaurant just over there. Their tripe is white as snow and clean, and they even have antique bowls."

We would have our soup, soured with plenty of lemon juice, and afterwards we would walk all the way down to Karaköy port, he walking a few steps in front of me like a father taking his daughter to register for school. When we got on the ferry at Eminönü, he would turn and say, "Now look, don't get any regrets about this," and I, without batting an eye, would reply, "I won't." Not until we reached the island would I realize that we had been on the island ferry.

As I kissed the hand of his aged, saintly mother, I also would not realize that the man I had so dreamed of marrying wouldn't come back to this house for nearly three months.

Let me get straight to the point: who would be the wife of such a useless man? That's youth for you. He was an educated man, he could make a living, obviously all he needed was a woman. That's what I thought. But it was useless, he had given up on life.

I would go back home, as if not three months but just three days had passed, as though I had just been visiting my aunt in Fatih. Nobody would really ask any questions, including that nosy carpenter. He would gladly take me in, we would get hitched, and he would put me up on the third floor of the carpentry shop, looking down over the same street—but this time from the other side. Just like before, I would munch sunflower seeds and chat with passersby, and I would thank God that, at the last minute, I had been spared marriage with such a useless man.

A Man's Second Wife (Bir Adamın İkinci Karısı)
Translated by Jonathan Ross (2010)

If I were a man's second wife, I'd know damn sure that the last thing I should do would be to bad-mouth his first wife; I'd realize that the more I maligned that woman, who'd be my rival for the rest of my life, she'd become like ivy, spreading, and smothering our relationship, and this man, who was supposed to be *my* husband after all, would constantly be thinking about her, wondering what would have happened if . . .

Even if my husband were moaning about his ex, I'd say, "Cenap,"—that being his name—, "No one wants to neglect their kids. Who's to say why she didn't breastfeed the baby," demonstrating my respect for that woman whom I'd never actually met. I'd feel that, in doing so, I'd managed to lop off the head of the worm that had been gnawing away at my husband's soul ever since he'd made the mistake of his life. I'd lead him to believe that everything about his first marriage was a matter of fate; I couldn't bring myself to grind him down by taunting him that it had all been his fault.

One evening, when he would be dozing sluggishly in front of the TV, I'd put it to him: "Did you really love her a lot, Cenap?" Having said this, I'd carefully narrow my eyes, which had been staring blankly at the horizon the whole day and home right in on him, as if with a zoom. Should he shuffle about in the armchair, start tidying up around him, think a while, and then say, "No," an ember the size of a millstone would plunge into my heart. But what if, without seeing the slightest need to wiggle his butt and budge from the lying position he had assumed, he grunted, "Let it go, Melek. What are you on about, for God's sake? Just let me have a little nap"? Then, even if I didn't quite catch the mumbled sentence or two that followed, I would believe that he was telling the truth, that his past didn't weigh so heavily upon him now and, with my mind at rest, I would walk over to him, prod him here and there, saying, "Come on, Cenap, let's go to bed." Yet, even if I slept blissfully that night, I would of course know that no second wife could take it for granted that the following night would offer such peace.

Mustafa (Mustafa)

By Gonca Özmen (2009)
Translated by Saliha Paker and Mel Kenne (2009)

I peeled the orange Mustafa
I placed you at my bedside

A bed, look, no wider than a grave
Just like that deep down I'd offered myself

Thin sword, thin blood, slim death
This condemnation I invented myself

Dumma dumma dum in every man a woman

The one romping inside me had black eyes
One, Mustafa, doesn't call out my name any more

They think this one's a love poem too, so let them
Their umbrellas are large
They're not getting wet

These skies must be pulled down Mustafa, pulled down
In people deep down lies their boundlessness

Keep me cool Mustafa
Keep me cool
In being alive lies the word's being

To return, those children in far off homes

Memet (Memet)

By Gonca Özmen (2008)
Translated by Saliha Paker and Mel Kenne (2009)

Take these *ratta-tat*s Memet
Take them to the *ratta-tatta* man

Take this me Memet
Take this me to the meadows

Do I know what to do with me?
To me, I'm always a seabattle Memet

Take this me to the birds
Drop this me to the poor suburbs

Battling's a backpack anyway Memet

Besides can a wound get old
Just keep me waiting again on a pillow bed

Even the apple awaits its time

Just . . . me in an old oil drum . . .
Deeper even deeper Memet

Just watch what a carnival, the human race

Does the *ratta-tatta* man
Ever *ratta-tat* the *ratta-tat*s Memet?

Best if you dump me in with the poor Memet
Take this me, throw this me off the minaret

Snake (Yılan)

By Mine Söğüt (2011)
Translated by Hande Eagle (2012)
Poetic prologue translated by Alev Ersan (2012)

I had a Globe of a mother
Square of a father
Brothers of savagery
Sisters of if-only
We lived in a deep well.
We steeped in the fire
at the core of the Earth
which is why I'm piping hot.
I shall scorch with that fire
anyone who touches me.

When my mother was pregnant with me, every night she dreamed that she gave birth to a snake. It came out worming between her legs and had enchantingly beautiful colors . . . the snake.

Not small like a fetus, but huge.

Then it would coil around my mother's legs. Around her helplessly parted fair, bare, slender, branch-like long legs . . . First it would slither to her feet. In her eyes my mother carried the horror of having given birth to a snake and would look at her baby in fear.

In fear and sadness . . .

Fear at having given birth to a snake, but also sadness as her baby snake glided away from her and towards her feet. She would grieve about the baby snake abandoning its mother. "If she leaves she will die," she thought. "Who will take care of her? She is still a child."

She is still a child.

The snake would read my mother's thoughts. It would return from her fair, bare, branch-like long legs in the same slow motion to mount her breasts. My mother, my helpless mother, lying stark naked on her back on a floor bed with her legs spread, would accept the traverse of her curves by the slippery sensation of the snake exiting her womb . . . She would watch her varicolored baby slither towards her breasts and lean its fork-tongued mouth on her right and then on her left breast, then right again and left again, then right again and left again and then right and right again, then once again on her left breast quaffing her milk at length, and then she would cry. She would pity the snake. She would pity herself. She would get mad at her mother.

WHEN I WAS PREGNANT, every night I dreamed that I gave birth to a snake. Though this wasn't as terrifying a dream as one might assume. It was as if the angels had whispered this into my ears years ago. It was as if I knew I had been carrying a snake in my womb for months but I wouldn't tell anyone . . . for fear of scaring them. I assumed they wouldn't love my baby; they wouldn't want her and would kill her as soon as she was born. It was for this reason that I eluded everyone in my dreams. Sometimes I would be in a cabin in the woods; at home in a room of which no one knew but I; or once, at the bottom of a well in the garden.

In my dream I saw my pains and pangs increase, and then consecutive contractions would begin. The water broke just like that of a fetus . . . whereas it was a snake's water breaking . . . I would at once get up from the bed . . .

I would go to the room, to the nook, to the well without waking anyone . . . I went wherever appeared in my dream on that night. I would strip to the skin and lie down on a narrow bed prepared for this purpose, perhaps by the angels or the snake prophet. Stark naked . . . I would part my legs wide open . . . and wait. Sometimes for hours and sometimes, for a moment . . . Every time my baby snake would glide from my womb very slowly and gently, painlessly.

A long, a very long baby snake . . .

Her eyes were still sealed shut. That is why she couldn't immediately find her direction. She would first mistakenly sweep to my feet. Then she would detect the scent of the milk in my breasts, turn back around, and move towards them, savoring her mother; coiling and coiling, coiling, coiling, coiling, coiling around my naked body. First she would suck on my right breast with her fork-tongued mouth, then on my left breast. Then once again, on my right breast, then on my left . . . She suckled for hours. I would shed tears of joy at the sight of my baby snake sucking my breasts.

WHEN MY DAUGHTER WAS PREGNANT WITH MY GRAND-DAUGHTER, at night she would dream that she gave birth to a snake. She would wake from her nightmare with the first rays of the morning sun. She would walk to the door of my room with venomous footsteps. For a while she would stand in front of the door motionless before gathering her strength, furiously opening the door and taking a step inside. She wouldn't come near the bed. Instead she would stand by the door and shout at me:

"Mom, get up! Get up, don't sleep. I dreamed I gave birth to a snake again because of you."

I would turn a deaf ear. Even though I had been awake for hours and even though my sleep never lasted longer than two hours in the dark of the night, I pretended to be asleep. I wouldn't open my eyes.

I would continue to take deep breaths with my back towards her . . . Deep, deep breaths . . . I would continue to take death-defying deep breaths and;

turn a blind eye to, I would . . .

to her shouting at me, to her baring her soul . . .

to her killing me desperately . . .

by recounting her nightmare every morning . . .

to her wanting to kill me . . .

to her not loving me . . .

to her hating me . . .

to her hating me . . .

to her wanting to kill me . . .

to her killing me . . .

She would tell me she saw a snake in her dream. She would tell me she saw the snake because of me. She used to say that it was I who spawned her with that snake. She wasn't mistaken. It was I who wished this misfortune upon her. She was just a little girl. A girl who didn't know men, who couldn't tell dreams and reality apart . . . I wished this misfortune upon her when she was my little girl who sat by the window and eyed the man across the road from head to toe . . . when she was my little girl who laid eyes on a man with her snake eyes.

In youth, one has clandestine dreams without actually knowing what one's heart desires. Clandestine dreams make young girls grow weary. I didn't want my daughter to be sad. She was still little. I thought that if she grew up a bit more she would surely fall in love with a boy suitable for her age. How could a child of fifteen heave a sigh for a man of forty?

A tall man, very tall, slightly graying hair . . .

the smile of a libertine shadowed by that mustache gray . . .

a luminous gaze . . .

None that should enamor a girl of fifteen . . .

Should not have . . .

If only it had not.

If my daughter had not fallen for that man and if, in the dead of night, she had not spread her legs, by the door and with her back to the wall, to that man, to that old man with the urge of sexual delights she had never known; if she hadn't let out silent shrills as she inhaled the scent of that gray-mustached, tall, that very tall man with the luminous gaze.

"You will give birth to a snake," I had told her. If you sleep with this man again you will give birth to a snake.

AT NIGHT I LIKE TO ENTER women's dreams. I slowly glide between their legs. I coil myself around their naked bodies with my flat, cold, slippery body. First around their legs . . . then around their stomachs . . . and finally around their breasts . . .

They all suckle me. Just as if I were their baby. I thirstily suck milk from their breasts . . . First from the right, then from the left . . . then from their left breasts again and right again . . . then from their left breasts again . . . then from the right and from the left again . . . I quaff . . . until satiated.

Those who think snakes can be sated are mistaken and fated.

Scheherazade (Şehrazad)

By Gülten Akın (2007)

Translated by Ronald Tamplin and Saliha Paker (2007)

From a thousand and one dark nights
Scheherazade reached the fairytale light
voices sheltered by the wind
flew far off within it

with an arrow turned upon yourself
you stood within
tyro, hunter who caught nothing
or if you did in a moment it twisted from your hands
trialled by pain by praise
they tagged you, a lookalike
and some of them said "I saw her I saw
and the halo upon her"

tenderly you wrapped the pieces
that survived hid them in unending light
everything now that's fallen
Gülten then unknown unrevealed

Three Masters to One Captive
(Bir Tutsağa Üç Efendi)

By Gülten Akın (1971)

Translated by Saliha Paker and Mel Kenne (2013)

I spent the summer in tremors, dear master
Reading omens, divining dreams, conversing with water
I don't see, but I can tell. A heavy weight on my chest
Perhaps it's a tiny woman not I
A bait for the falcon chained to your arm
A frightened sparrow for its mouth

The bird flew off, you mounted a pure Arabian stallion,
Your horseblock a live shoulder,
Riding pillion, three ivory girls and a dark boy
"Mama" they'd call out to me
Their faces wore your image and mine
Therefore, with hardly a doubt,
You were my husband, my precious master.

I can't remember but it was said
One day you came home listless
"Sweet are the street fountains, bitter is home
Sweet are the streets, bitter is home
Sweet is the meal spread by others, bitter is home"
—Oh just let me die, master—
You picked me up hurled me to the ground
I was not a little girl, perhaps some stone
For fathers love their little girls
As I've seen in others

You were the city's dark outlaw, beloved master
Off to the mountains your falcon on your arm

You rode your horse, held your whip
Your voice, churchbells heralding a holy day
A clear bugle call for the barracks, shepherds' whistle to the water
I loved you so much, oh so much
Then one day, with bared teeth, a dark look in your eyes
—Oh just let me die, master—
"This is no joke," you said. "As your son,
 I am your supreme master from now on."

The Poetry of Memory and Books with a Backbone

Excerpt from a Talk by Birhan Keskin (2011)
Translated by Şehnaz Tahir Gürçağlar (2011)

As someone who has read Bachmann and Neruda in Turkish, I am thankful that poetry translation is not impossible after all.

Let's start with a question. Why am I working with something so old, so ancient? We all know that poetry is one of the oldest activities of humankind. It was born before all other genres and even before writing came about. I think that when it comes to writing, poetry started everything; poetry is right at the heart of it all. Perhaps that's why all genres aspire to poetry . . . a novel, a short story, a film, they all want to be poetic. So although poetry is not a field appreciated or followed much by the masses today, the actuality that everything aspires to become poetic means that it is still a longing within us.

Because poetry is as old as humans, I believe it is the shortest path both leading to and coming from humans. Not only do I believe it is the shortest path but also that it is the most crystallized one. That is basically why I work with poetry.

Why do I have so much regard for nature in my poetry? Because humans haven't been able to develop a language that can explain itself solely through its own means, if we didn't have nature and its multitude of creatures around us, our language would be blind. The language humans created for themselves is incapable of expressing who they are entirely through themselves. In this language we can only express ourselves by looking at other living beings, by taking our lead from other living beings, by comparing ourselves to other living beings. If our language becomes concerned with humans alone, it remains powerless, weak and blind.

A young fellow poet said that I write the poetry of memory. This person may have been referring specifically to *Yeryüzü Halleri* (*Earth Moods*), but to tell the truth, this is something that runs through all of my poetry, or that is the main axis of all of my poetry: memory or what becomes a memory. I think that in my poetry everything is there either to come from a memory or to arrive at a memory. And sometimes this reaches such extremes that I think I have no present or future tense. Present, future and past tenses only exist to be used in daily language. At least that's how it seems to me. All these different tenses are doomed to become a part of the past. Memory is what we reconstruct and redesign through the things we select from these different tenses. What remains for us is a simple tense, a tense I call "genişgeçmiş" (simple pastpresent). My poetry often takes off from that tense and takes place in it. Everything, all our times, our possessions, our adventures, are there, as if to create one great big memory.

Except for my first book, all my books have a backbone. It's because I don't like to see my books as only a collection of poems that I always give them a backbone. Sometimes I know what that backbone will be or sometimes it's experience or life itself that implants this backbone which may be created through personal experiences I am having. Or it may be created by the state of the world, what's happening in it during a specific period. If a book happens to lack a backbone, I can wait a long time to write more poetry that will give it one, and I am very patient.

As a person who has read the major poets of the world in Turkish, my conclusion is that poetry and translation do not really agree. No matter how well it is translated, poetry loses a lot when translated into another language. Think of poetry as a rose with many layers of petals. When poetry exists in its own mother tongue, in the codes of its own culture, it is a beautiful and rich rose, but when it is translated into a foreign language it starts to look like a faded rose. That is why I think poetry translation is one of the most challenging tasks in the world. However, I believe it is a worthwhile challenge, and having read Bachmann and Neruda in Turkish, I am thankful that poetry translation is not impossible after all.

From *Yol*

By Birhan Keskin (2006)

The book-length poem *Yol* consists of two parts. The first part is entitled *taş parçaları* (literally "stone pieces"), and the second part is entitled *eski dünya* (literally "the old world"). The following three translations are of sequential sections excerpted from the first part of the book. The first translation, by Elizabeth Pallitto and İdil Karacadağ, consists of the first six sections of *taş parçaları* ("Pieces of Stone"); the second translation, by Mel Kenne and Saliha Paker, consists of a sequence of seven sections from the middle part of *taş parçaları* ("Broken Bits of Rock"); and the third translation, by Murat Nemet-Nejat, consists of the final eight sections of taş parçaları ("casting pebbles"). While the sections in the three translations follow the sequential order in which they appear in the book, the poet chose to have the Roman numerals designating them follow an unconventional numerical order. The form of the Roman numerals used by the poet is also unconventional at times.

From *A' way*: **Pieces of Stone**

Translated by Elizabeth Pallitto and İdil Karacadağ (2011–2012)

III
Since you thought that even my crying after you was too much,
Take these stones, then, they are yours . . .
From now on, considering that,
Let all the drums beat,
Let the *saz* strings break, let them shout into the void together.
We'll retch blood,
We'll retch blood,
Since the world is so cruel,
Since it doesn't suit our hearts.

Let all the drums thunder,
Let the one who comes from the void
Shoot those who fill up the void,
Who scream into the void,
Shooooot!

Look! How the one who sleeps in ashes is coughing up blood.
Let the world witness.

IV
I am everyone.
Whatever it is that life can teach ashes,
That is what it taught me.

For a long time, I slept in ashes.
I slept in ashes for a long time.

II
Just before dawn,
the scream that is blocked inside moans outside
Sleep rejects me

From somewhere outside
A looooooong moan bursts.
Inside me, the walls of cruelty.
Sleeeeeep,
Take me to bed with you.

As I get up,
staggering to the bathroom, sounds are pouring forth from my eyes.
Inside,
it says,
these silently flowing tears are yours.
On the walls inside me
these stones sit;
there is a sound I cannot voice
in the silence of stone.
it gets extracted from me:
thick, primitive, heading into the void, out of the hollow of the night,
Facing *out*ward:

Finally, I've released you, set you free into this lie of a world.
It hurts a lot.
A *lot*,

VI
Always, my love, I always read you
from the waves rippling over your face.
In your eyes, I read love, in your hands, compassion.
Your mother had disowned you,
I took you and wove you into my flesh.

V
Don't expect me to burn
You know how much I have burned
I can't burn, I can't
I can't burn my ashes are flying away

The razors you stuck into my skin in my dream
Are still there
It doesn't bleed, it doesn't hurt
It doesn't hurt
This world is made of ice
In this ice
Nothing hurts.

These are lies,
What I said were lies
What you said were lies
These words only suit the world

I was reduced to ashes already
Ashes already
alllreadyyyyyy
If any humanity was left
Among the ashes
It is rising up now

Let the world witness now,
The world white as snow
The one who devoted herself to you
is coughing up blood
on the ice.

I
As they stand apart, one by one,
one calls the other who is not yet by her side.
When those two come together, side by side,
or one underneath the other,
the world grows greater.
One offers fire to the other
And a new meaning grows out from the old book
Carrying their being with them, and their becoming

In a verrrry old book, she sets the fairytale in motion
To make it warmer.
Still, yet another tale spills out
Over the boundaries of their being
She calls the other who is not yet by her side
This is how enchantment is created
Another calls the one who is not yet by her side
Were they a story, she asks . . .
a fairytale?

From *a/waY*: Broken Bits of Rock
Translated by Mel Kenne and Saliha Paker (2011–2012)

IX

She threw me into a world I didn't know

Without a full sentence, I'm scattered all ooooover, that's why.

We had a dream, "growing old together" is what we called it,
it hurts so much, maybe that's why.
Do you expect a statement of love from me.
Dooon't wait.
Two women who make jam in the kitchen. Red peppers and all that.
A sort of windy and hilly place. Looking out, from both sides
oohhoooooooorizon, and all that.
The world seems elliptic rather than round.
In any case, two women with no sense of that roundness.
Just so. I'd believed in her as much as I had in myself.
To speak of love beyond whatever love is, aaaaaaaaaah
A conviction, should I say.
That's why I'm in so many pieces, why
I seem to feel flung into this world now.
What do you expect me to say
With each breath there's a throbbing tooth inside me
That's why I'm silent, it's why I talk.
Not dying with that first pain, I was already cross with life.
Only then did I first become human.
Or having ruined me from birth, they remade me a newborn.
When I gave myself up to pain I remembered
there was no dying, I remembered
No dyiiiiiiiiiiiiiiing

XI

Be fair even when you're suffering, she tells me.
Be fair. Aren't you the one who believes

that life is a great destiny,
that even the directing of destiny lies within that great Destiny,
and all that stuuuuuuffffff.
Given that, now be fair.
Hush. Don't talk that way! Be fair.

You doubt it, don't you?
She threw me into a world I didn't know
I'm sayyyyyyying.

Here's what I'm saying,
It's all only words. Just woooords.
And yet it's *I* who should be fair, you say.

X
Oh you who don't heed the human,
Oh great flaw they call life.
. . .
Oh for no one else would I trade
Your separation, why is it so heavy?

Where is justice?
From one November to another November
I'm blind on one side deaf on the other.

XIII
I'm strewn all around.
Strewn all aroooooound and
The gang's all here: Aprın Çor Tigin
Haşim, Kadı Burhaneddin
Everyone's here, blind, lame, grim
Shooooooouuuutting:
Let it cool down,
letttttt it cooooooooool
let your bits cool off

when they come back together
you'll become something else.

XV

I doooon't want to be anything other
I wanted nothing else.

With patience my love with patience
So in this city may our pains be evened out
said again, again.
In this city passing flesh to reach heart
with patience. With patience alone.

How many people in this city are there
who out of their souls just for you a dome
a dooooooooooooome
have made!

XIV

Within one's great grief, I've seen, I've found
affection in passing from flesh to love.
Beside this my love beside this
fleshly betrayal is, in short
nothing.

XII

Now a fairy from a fairytale
Should listen to me quietly,
Should take my tired head

Take me, my self's whole sentence
And place it gently in her heart.

What strength have I got left to bear all this
noooooooooone.

From *at the bifurcation becoming*
Y
why
"casting pebbles"

Translated by Murat Nemet-Nejat (2011–2012)

XXXXIII

You are too human, my darling, too human,
whereas I'm a barbarian, a beast
my tongue talks of forgiveness, for giving it
for free and yours of justice
revenge

Is there a need to say it, my love
to say it now
the ace sniper I raised shOOOOt me
the snows of Kilimanjaro my love
snows of Kilimanjaro
sliiiiiding down

XXXIV

If you love someone, don't kill her, saying it
is easy whereas each love is first to herself
then the other an executioner.
and in love death has a meaning, "an act in style
must have its disruption," let us say
every fire first grazes its side

so from now on every time you see the shadow of a poet
darkened by the smoke left after a fire,
aimless, restless, passive, static, **still**
still smoldering
or a sister weeping to her partridge,
far away, with the sound of clarinet on her breast wandering

XXXVI

After such a long time why I didn't touch her
why I didn't pull out my weapons
tucking everything that happened into my heart and withdrew
you ask me . . .
if i have not touched her,

not touched her
is only for one reason . . .

barbarians lay hands only on equally barbarians.

XXXVII

I resemble grass lying aslant in the flowing street
branches pulling left and right by the wind.
because of love wounding with betrayal is it love?
oh, the nook of my liver, burning burning
my heartstrings breaking, tie me.

XXXXI

If I had left one breath of life I'd breathe it on you
They will say: the dungeon in her was too high
should've seen, touched, caressed, without teaching
without telling her to put wings and arms to her fate, I
having lost her, I burn now, I burn particularly
for that.
I could not fix the places I broke
I could not fix the places I broke

I had clung to you with a last breath.
That was the worst, the worst.

XXXIX

Love, between two people is what is never =
I am not a Divan poet darling

to chisel lines for you
nevertheless, on the spur of the moment,
I'd like people to know my attraction for your eyes, your hands, your feet.
I'm of this mad times, this venomous moments
the poet, in smithereens. What can I say,
still, in me, from very ooold times,
Ah, Lei . . . Ah, Leilaaaaa
I left your name on a cold desert night.

XXXVIII

There are two cherries on a branch
between love and anger
burning *a*burning, parted *a*part.
Let this love stop. Love, take five!
Oh, the wild one!
Insurrection
InsurrectiOOOn!

Tie the space between my legs.

XXXX

My love, as if she's staying
All words, as if they're staying
Because love, love because
it wants a path, an ideology for itself.

I know, some ages are tumbleweed in the desert wind,
you my love, ahead, a bit ahead in time
you will start your history, that place
starts with my history.

And count, backwards, one by one
let them stay with you now, take them
these stones.

The Yellow Notebook of Dreams
(Sarı Rüya Defteri)

By Ahmet Büke (2010)

Translated by Nilgün Dungan (2011)

I.

The old palm tree at the entrance of our neighborhood grew nuts!

Of course I didn't believe it. But Auntie Sourpuss didn't stop banging on my door. When I didn't open it, she threw stones at the window. When finally she riddled the front tire of my bicycle with her crochet needle, I couldn't stand it anymore. I pulled back the curtain.

"I swear; it has dark, hairy nuts this big."

Grandpa the Inventor came out of his door beneath the road.

"Hang on there, lady! Don't be so rude. At least call them testicles."

"Ah, you and your testicles. I'm telling you, they're as big as my head. If they were to burst, the whole neighborhood would be covered in molasses."

Grandpa the Inventor couldn't stand there any longer. He went back inside.

The neighbors congregated. All together they walked towards the beginning of the street and disappeared.

There is no knowing what will become of these people. Living in poverty, they've all gone nuts. A herd of barefoot children scurried behind.

"A palm tree with nuts, only we have it."

The long, dirty black kitchen chimney of Grandpa the Inventor took off in smoke.

Another poor rocket left the neighborhood and flew off towards the orbit of the moon.

* * *

Bad dice—Aunt 3&1—rolled in for a visit.

Before I started writing, I didn't know how to cry. Ever since I took pen and paper in hand, we, the whole family, became crybabies. I wet the pen on the tip of my tongue, and my grandma begins to rue. She has floral print underpants. Made of two yards of cotton flannel. Granny style. Tiny white daisies in bloom on a dark background.

"My dear son," she says. She pronounces the "o" kind of funny. You see, my grandmother is an immigrant from the Balkans. In the past, kids used to mock me.

"Greenhorn, undies torn."

You know I said we're crying; my grandpa, my father, our cat Damsel, my mother's bootees take turns. Those are the only things left of her. They took my mother away. They washed her with hot water. I didn't see it. My grandma told me. She cried as she kept tugging at her floral underwear.

Tonight bad dice rolled in for a visit again: Aunt 3&1.

She'll say three; I'll write one.

We'll cry altogether.

* * *

t
a
n
a
b
a
tanaba
entububa entububa
arabina varabina
paluha
inşai

* * *

The World Cat Convention will be held in our backyard, they say. Are you kidding me! Double Tail, friend of our Damsel, came and told me about the preparations. What fell to my share was meatballs with kashar cheese.

"Aye-aye," I said. "I take it as my duty."

"Don't be so modest, bro. It's not a duty at all. It's just a humble request."

A sound boy, this Double Tail is.

The other day, though, he aspired to be the muezzin. He's had a few. White dust on his whiskers and such. Let's put it this way, he was raring to go. In any case, he wanted to go up there and do the Friday call to prayer. Everyone stood in front of him. They didn't let the boy do it. I brought him to our place just so he wouldn't get upset. He and my grandma recited the *salâh* opposite each other. We all got teary-eyed. Including my mom's bootees. What praise for a life spent and the end of your time.

I never hurt Double Tail. As I said, he's a good boy. A bit on the loppy side. But no one's perfect.

"I hope your convention is successful. May God guide you to a fruitful completion," I said.

"Amen," he said.

He was planning to recite *yasin* from the Qur'an at the closing ceremony.

If my grandma heard this, she'd cry from emotion. But I haven't told her. She has tachycardia. We're afraid she'd drop dead.

* * *

I found an awesome taphouse: Yavuz Abi's Place. Supposedly, he knows me. Says I used to ditch school and go there while I was in high school. What a lie! I got pissed off and left. I went into Kalyon Pub. Boy, what a terrible welcome they gave me. Beer, nuts and money up front, they said. I put on a bold face, couldn't just leave. The waiter was a hulk of a man. I didn't have the nerve. Didn't have the guts. I guzzled the mug in two gulps. I ran out and went inside Yavuz Abi's.

"Son," he said. "Fuck it, so what if you don't have money. You're on us today."

First I was embarrased. Then I didn't dwell on it.

"Squid, *rakı*, sardines, crack open ten stuffed mussels."

Man, it was as if I just rattled them off! It was like they were locked up in a room in my mind, and all of a sudden I found the key and let them all out into the open air, into the chill, away from clouds and moisture. Yet, I was as alone as a spaceship in this world.

"The worst part is there's no one to treat me to rakı."

Yavuz Abi, who bore, right on his forehead, a tattoo of a woman carrying silvery bombshells on her back, said this.

He sold his wife for twenty-five kurus. In Hilal Station. His friends forced him to kneel under the acacia. Bringing in the blind tattooist lady, they forcibly embossed a tattoo on his forehead. Tattoo of twenty-five kurus.

Then Yavuz Abi shot both his wife and the man he sold her to.

Even if it was a story, people still listen to it in the taphouse.

"I know you. But I wonder if you know yourself," he said.

Do I really know?

I broke away from space and came here. I must have caught fire as I flew through the air like sandpaper. My feet burn the most. The smell of kindling.

Who the heck launched me, man?

Gotta find Grandpa the Inventor. If not, I'll read the previous pages again.

Who the heck am I, man?

What's this scar running from my forehead almost to my lip-line?

Yavuz Abi said, "What's this, man?"

That scar wasn't there before.

* * *

I'm just walking casually, you see. I seem to have come to a place like a bus terminal or something. My arms are tired. You see, I swing them like a soldier as I walk. Whereas it's normally one's feet that hurt, with me it's the other way around.

Tramp, tramp, tramp. Thank our Lord . . .

What's the difference between thanks and gratitude? Let me ask this to Long Tail. Or was it Double Tail? Ah, this muddled state of mine. My mind is just like my pocket. Jackknife, tissue, token, dry prune, adage, ticket to Daday. Anything you're looking for, there. Inside my head is like this too.

I was talking about the bus terminal.

The best ones go to the Town. In deep blue stripes, their tires resembling dark rain clouds.

I'm tired, I just said to myself. Weariness doesn't come instantly. Everyone knows that. It builds up in drips. Just like those drops falling serenely from the faucet into a cup. Drip, drip. First you don't hear it, but when it builds up, it plays the drum inside the house. Before you say you're tired, you begin to groan first . . . Then you know what lies ahead.

But I'm not like a normal human.

Pulling away from the crowd, I just sat on the sidewalk.

If you're tired, you sit. But you don't plop down like a jackass. You sit gentlemanly, quietly. You put your hand on your knee and you say, "Woe is me."

"What are you doing here?"

"Who?"

"Who am I talking to?"

"I just sat, you see."

"Can do no such thing."

"And why's that?"

"This is my sidewalk. You go over there by the corn guy. Go on!"

"You apparently have the place registered to your name. You bugger off over there."

"No way."

"Why not?

"The corn guy's farts smell like rotten eggs."

"Good heavens," I said and got up. Two kids spat on the ground and shoved each other around in front of me. A man who came out of one of the offices shouted at them. The children turned into timorous sparrows. They walked on air.

By the time I got there, the corn guy had lifted his cart on two wheels and scat. I sat in the space left by his departure. I smelled the air. No, it doesn't smell like fart or anything.

This boy came over to me again. He rested his dull gray, empty tray on his knees.

"This place also belongs to you or what?"

"No, it's free."

"In that case, you fuck off now."

He seemed miffed. He went to the opposite sidewalk and sat down.

I couldn't bear it. I went up to him.

"You're not offended, are you?"

"No."

"What do you sell?"

"Peppermint. To the passengers."

"You one of those who get on the busses and sell things?"

"Yup, you got it."

This boy has no front teeth. The sandals on his feet are filthy. So are his dirty feet.

"You have no peppermint left?"

"No, finished yesterday."

"So, you walked around with nothing today?"

"Yup, you got it."

The boy spent his earnings yesterday. And the grocery store didn't sell on credit, either. Today he felt like making a tambourine of his tray and playing it.

I sang, and he beat on the back of the tinned tray. Passengers looked back. One woman disapproved. An old man belly danced in front of us.

I guess he'd got tired. When he stopped, I asked:

"Now where?"

"Home. What about you?"

"Dunno."

"Where's your home?"

"I can't think of it now. Maybe I'll find it when I think a little bit."

He didn't find me odd at all. He didn't give me a blank stare like others do. I stood up. I walked. One can find his home on the way too.

* * *

I found my mom's letter written in my handwriting. It fell from among the pages of the notebook as I was fleeing the police. My heart was almost at my throat, but still, I went back and picked it up. Besides, I realized that I can run pretty fast.

I wonder why, when I see a uniform, I take to my heels?

I did damn well, it looks like. My handwriting, bless it, is like a string of pearls.

Son,

I remember you throwing your backpack on your shoulder and leaving. With each step you took until you reached the end of the street, I burned up and cooled down inside. I kept hoping that maybe you'd come back.

Don't be mad at me and please read the back of the page.
Your mom

It looks like I tore the back of the page and threw it away.

Me. The spaceship with burning feet. The police chases. My mom's page keeps hovering in front of my eyes. Filled with black scratches.

* * *

I found a large guestroom for myself. Two hundred steps by I don't know how many steps. I measured the width quite easily. I got bored when it came to the length. Also, I was wary of the stones under my feet. There are pebbles and stuff everywhere. But it's clean and empty. It's as good as mine. On the door, it's written in big letters "Closed for Burial Services. Don't Forget Your Prayers." A kind of guestroom where there's no one. In that case, it must be everyone's, I said, and threw my jacket over into a corner that lets in the sun but not the wind. Heaviness filled with void came and perched on my little heart. I feel sluggish. But I'm sensitive and understanding. I appreciate the value of silence here. At night a whistle with a hat goes by—only his hat is visible over the wall—I know him and respect him. The quieter I am, the more this guestroom belongs to me. Or everyone. Night after night, using this soundlessness as an excuse, actually, I think about continuity. For instance, take this ant. On its back, actually I should say in its mouth, it's carrying a sunflower shell, like countless others I see, to the anthill through the same path.

Let me tell you more slowly and articulately:

Sunflower shell – – – will be carried to the anthill.

Sunflower shell – – – each time it will be carried to the anthill by only one ant.

Sunflower shell – – – each ant will follow the same path.

Sunflower shell – – – where it is now – entrance to the main path – passing over the same broken piece of marble along the path – reentrance to the rest of the main path – arriving at the opening of the anthill.

Now, let's say that all this continuity just breaks at one point. Let's say, for instance, as soon as the ant touches that piece of marble, it finds itself closer to the anthill, but still on the main path. Well then, how do we express that discontinuity?

You see, while I was thinking about this in everyone's living room, which is quiet, I came to realize that time is actually discontinuous. Am I not the biggest proof of this, too?

Time for whistle and hat. Must wrap up well and be quiet now.

* * *

Around me I hear comments like this:

"You're not caught up in the familiar race. That's why you smile at all of us."

I don't get this. Just like I don't get anything that anyone says. In my hand, I have a half-wound audio reel. I open it from its shiny sharp edges, so sharp that I scrape my thumb a few times. So frantic am I in my attempt to unwind it that I think I'll be relieving all those sparrows, garbage bags and good people watching me.

Then when I go back and look at the notebook, I realize that I don't get any of it.

Well then, am I opening in vain these recordings made of voices and images—we briefly call moments—most of which we forget when we're done with them, opening them in full view of everyone. In the big square, now among the stands selling plums and cherries.

What in the world does "familiar race" mean anyway, my brothers?

Or is it that I possess forcibly memorized skin? No, you say. Then why do you look at me as if to say he won't understand it but he'll do. If I were more dangerous, for instance, if I broke into your home and increased your electricity consumption, if I tossed around in your beds, if I retched in your pillboxes, you'd find it hard to look at me pityingly, like I'm a puppy, cute but with five legs.

All the asphalt you poured onto your roads is melting, peeling like pieces off a bone. I see the old stones showing from underneath, some resentful and shy, but quick to say they're ready to be pounded once again, seeing how they're given the task.

You think you're afraid of death the most. Wrong! It'll be impossible for you to touch it, feel and understand it. That's actually why you get chills down to your spine. Then don't turn around and say all this behind my back. I hear it all.

* * *

Come on now, I'm falling apart. I read it and my eyes got kind of damp. Does a person create his memories himself? Actually, that's what everyone does. But it's different with me. Is it exciting? No. Painful, sad, tattered, sandy, windy? I don't know anything that profound.

I found this place on the hill. When it got hot, I had to get out of the nook. I walked not caring about the sweat and tears. Girls with fluttering skirts came down, cats ran away in front of me, the sun slid down. I didn't quail. I finally made it to the flat place. Two clouds and me.

They call it Old Man Cedar's place. Its crisp airiness carried me away. Another sparrow over my head. "Hello," I said. They all nodded. Everyone, all of us, all humanity, even the creatures who contemplate, have a cedar in this world. "Those who wish can tow one over. We'll lie side by side. We'll watch the meadow," they said.

First I got a little embarrassed. No cedar, no cushion? Looking at my hands I felt like crying. It turns out they had a makeshift one in the attic for those sentimental types who arrive suddenly and unknowingly. They took it out. Someone rolled out for me the old cushion that was under the rug.

I sat down next to them. Wind, wind, wind. By the time the hot air comes rolling in, it loses its load. What's left for us is its frivolous side. We just lay there side by side. No interrogation, no question. Old Man Cedar, may he rest in peace. His subjects are happy. The lame one sang a song. I fell asleep before he was finished. I opened my eyes and there's a grayish-blue darkness. They put over us the most tender sheet after having poked holes in it. What seeps through the needle eyeholes is not light but mother's milk, you'd think.

II.

They didn't actually understand what was going on. Not before, not later. They were walking down the İkiçeşmelik road. A. and 970. When the vendors of secondhand goods—the smell of secondhand chairs, spongy couches, retired refrigerators, stools sat on by God knows who, partial chests—started on both sides of the street, they began to run.

When A. arrived at the mosque, it jumped; then 970 landed on the minaret.

There, on the hand-sized ledge, on the stone platform, they stopped.

Strange things were happening below.

The two pre-Gods, A. and 970, sensed something, but they could not explain it to each other.

Neither the shadows of the minaret nor those of the buildings were getting any taller. They looked at the sun. It was stuck in mid-afternoon. The longest summer mid-afternoon of the world.

They caught one of the escaping pictures. They cut its insides and poured it out:

How are all the fathers of the world? Slightly paunchy, the sleeves of his shirt rolled up, a person who rocks back and forth while laughing in the direction of his children. That creature we call a father looks nice under the grapevine. If it's summertime, he sets his sights on the unripe grapes. He'll sprinkle blue vitriol with one hand, the other hand on the kerchief covering his mouth and nose.

Then we went to the afternoon prayer together. Because he said "come" with his eyes. Actually we used to go to the Friday prayer together when I was little. My grandfather prays next to the muezzin. Before the Sunna, he mumbles the *ezan* through his lips. When my grandfather's knees act up, he pushes the visor of his cap back, they bring him a chair and he performs *salaat* sitting. His hands on his knees, he monitors us with his eyes. With his son and grandson in front of him, he sits cross-legged on the floor where the light green rails end. My eyes are on the prayer beads, multicolored, all hung up on the timber legs with very thin nails. When I prostrate myself, I turn my head halfway. Acacias flutter outside.

A. said: "Time has got stuck."

970: "I don't remember earlier. I don't think later will happen either. Eternal's just started."

They looked at the young man below, sitting down and watching people. His feet have caught fire, crackling away amidst the sparks.

They caught another picture:

He drew a large circle on the wall. He marked five points. He drew the sharp tips that touched the four points, then he made that into a star. Then he quickly turned the last remaining point into a fist. His friend on watch in the dark jumped. Leaving the paintbox in the middle of the road, he began to run. Sometime later, he remembered the brush he was holding and threw it towards the garden of the houses with a low wall. As he turned the corner under the electric pole, a white car confronted him.

"The rest is swollen. As if sunburnt . . ." (A.)

"How about that. A huge well." (970)

No one should touch anyone. When the bookmarks were finished, our wrist bones snapped. Hungry crows ripped each other apart inside us. Everywhere smelled of dead cats. Still, we were mumbling in the direction of life. Out there in the distance there was space. We knew of good planets with their ships and smiling navy uniforms, that face of humanity which still prevailed, and black holes that would cool our foreheads off despite the shadows flushed by hot indicators. They could not kill us without anyone hearing it or caring about it; that's what we were thinking. Layer upon layer of snow fell on us. With ember and hot waves. They tore their own walls down on us with their own steps, with their own machines, treading and roaring.

Erasing all my memories, I started from scratch, a clean stretch of road.

My insides hurt so bad that I simply stopped time one mid-afternoon.

I can't just sit here and tell you about all my corpses. Instead, I'm leaving the eternal present. I have to do that in order to start over.

III.

I woke up. Two praying mantises by my side. BLESS YOU, boys! They stare at me befuddled. A chill came over my forehead. I wrapped it up with my arms. "I'm Grandpa the Inventor," said the man running down from the neigborhood up the way. Everything about him got younger as he spoke. He turned into an old friend. You know how half of his face got shriveled up and burnt like an old newspaper when they poured some cream-colored powder off the roof. It's him. My face got cold, my feet reignited, but I still couldn't remember his name.

"I'm leaving to you the longest encyclopedia in the world. Don't you read it now. You can have a look sometime after you get out," he said.

I folded up the paper and placed it at the very back of my notebook, but now the outside stands before me like a splinter stuck in the way of time. Perhaps when the words that jumped over me and used me like a bridge take away my weakness, this infinity will come to an end and hours will start flowing.

IV.

–encyclopedia of social details

a.

b. "back to life": 19 december 2000. time 05.00[1]

c.

d.

e.

f.

g.

h.

i.

k.

l.

m.

n.

o.

p.

r.

s.

t.

u.

v.

wernicke-korsakoff: Balance disorder, disturbed vision, involuntary muscle spasms, memory loss, learning and long-term memory transfer disorders, numbness and burning of the hands and feet, complaints such as burning feet syndrome. Permanent memory loss and transfer disorder, amnesia, difficulty in walking, inability to move about on one's own, and inability to remember due to the extensive loss of brain cells. Failure of overall physical condition due to serious nutritional deficiency in prolonged hunger strikes.

---

1. Operation Back to Life was the official name given to the December 19, 2000 operation in which security forces simultaneously occupied twenty prisons, after some detainees and convicts turned into a death fast on November 19 the hunger strike they had begun on October 20 to prevent the transfer of political prisoners into F-type high security prisons. Thirty-two died and hundreds were injured in the operation carried out by more than ten thousand security officers.

Afterword: The Path Leading to Cunda

The idea of collaboration to facilitate translating, in the case of Turkish literature, which in the past had very few fiction translators into other languages, emerged from experiences during my years in London in the 1980s, particularly when I was teaching part time at the University of London's School of Oriental and African Studies (SOAS). At the time, Yashar Kemal's corpus of fiction was the only one available in English, the first translation of his work having been done by Edouard Roditi, with subsequent translations by Thilda Kemal, Yashar Kemal's amazingly productive first wife. As colleagues and students in SOAS often pointed out, there was need for fresh, innovative Turkish voices to be heard in fiction translation.

Latife Tekin had recently made her début in Turkey with some widely acclaimed but controversial narrative works, one of which was *Berci Kristin Çöp Masalları*. I introduced the novel to Ruth Christie, a great poetry translator who, at the time, was collaborating with Richard McKane on translations of poems by Oktay Rifat, and she agreed to collaborate with me on translating this challenging work of fiction. When the English edition *(Berji Kristin: Tales from the Garbage Hills)* was published, it was blessed with a glowing preface by John Berger. Gradually a network emerged, which included other well-known translators of the time, such as Nermin Menemencioğlu *(Penguin Book of Turkish Verse)* and Feyyaz Kayacan Fergar *(Modern Turkish Poetry)*, as well as a group of dedicated independent publishers of literature in translation.

Involvement in this intercultural network was an experience in itself, a learning experience not only about collaboration and diverse ways of practicing literary translation but also about the economics of publishing translated work, specifically the need for funding. The one dire fact facing us all was the lack of any subvention from Turkish sources; some publishers of translated literature pointed out that this was the main reason why they had to turn down finished and in-progress translations.

The situation began to change slightly in the 1990s, when the first translations of books by Orhan Pamuk, and the abovementioned poetry and fiction titles, were published in Britain by whatever means available. In Turkey, Şenay Haznedaroğlu and I brought out a special Turkish–English issue of

Nar (1996), one of the leading literary magazines of the time. Yapı Kredi Publishing was instrumental in publishing *Mediterraneans. Istanbul, many worlds/Méditerranéennes. Istanbul, un monde pluriel* (1997). This refreshing English–French issue on new Turkish writing, edited by Ken Brown and Robert Waterhouse, carried many translations of works by leading authors. Fellow translators from Britain, Ruth Christie and Celia Kerslake, but also new American colleagues resident in Istanbul, Virginia Taylor Saçlıoğlu, Clifford Endres and Mel Kenne, contributed to the translation of poetry and fiction for this special issue. Clifford Endres and I had already collaborated on the translation of a recent collection of poetry by Enis Batur, *The Sarcophagus of Mourning Women*, which was first published in Kemal Silay's *Anthology of Turkish Literature* (1996). By the end of the 1990s, I was working with Mel Kenne on *Dear Shameless Death*, a translation of Latife Tekin's first work of fiction. I had come to realize that collaborative practices could lead to a greater number of literary translations in less time, and in some cases, to better translations in terms of quality, so long as some harmony was established between the collaborators' views on stylistic interpretation. So the time seemed ripe for starting a literary translators' workshop of the kind I had in mind. However, though the international network of translators and publishers interested in Turkish literature had expanded over the years, no substantial means seemed to exist for setting up such a workshop.

The turning point came in 2005, when a special translation subvention project was launched by the Turkish Ministry of Culture and Tourism: now well-known as the TEDA Program, it turned out to be a groundbreaking enterprise for the translation and publication of Turkish literature worldwide. Heartened by this unexpected development and with the enthusiastic and dedicated support of my colleague Şehnaz Tahir Gürçağlar from Boğaziçi University, we decided to apply to the Turkish Ministry of Culture and Tourism for funding. Poet and translator Mel Kenne, my colleague from Kadir Has University (now retired) was with us from the start, wholeheartedly supporting the project, as was Cemal Demircioğlu from Okan University. The Cunda International Workshop for Translators of Turkish Literature (CWTTL) was thus initiated for experienced and new translators to collaborate on rendering Turkish poetry and literary prose into English in an annual workshop.

Meanwhile, my friends Şinasi Tekin, Professor of Turkish Studies at Harvard

University, and his wife Gönül Alpay Tekin, also a professor in the same field, suggested a beautiful home for the prospective workshop on the island of Cunda, off Ayvalık, in northern Aegean Turkey. This old island house, renovated as the Sevgi-Doğan Gönül Research Building, was donated to the Harvard-Koç University Ottoman Studies Foundation and, since 1996, has served as the venue for the Intensive Ottoman and Turkish Summer School founded by the Tekins.

The idea of a literary translators' workshop that focused on English must have greatly appealed to Professor Mustafa İsen, who was then the Counsellor of the Ministry of Culture and the Head of the TEDA Advisory Committee. With his and Mr. Ümit Yaşar Gözüm's support, our application for the CWTTL was accepted as a joint project led by the Department of Translation and Interpreting Studies of Bogazici University and sponsored by the Turkish Ministry of Culture and Tourism. In June 2006, we held our first workshop in the Sevgi-Doğan Gönül Research Building, and we have continued to do so since then with the kind permission of the Rector of Koç University.

Since 2006, translators have come to our workshops from Britain, the US, Turkey, Greece, Norway, and Sweden, and some have attended more than one time. In 2009, we began our partnership with Literature Across Frontiers (LAF), through which we have received European Union funding, and translator participants from the Czech Republic, Finland, Latvia, Poland and Romania. All in all, we have hosted forty-five translators and eighteen guest writers, poets and speakers. As you probably have gathered by reading this collection, for us, the translators, the Cunda experience has been more than worthwhile.

Regarding the workshop's future, our first and foremost goal is to maintain the continuity of CWTTL, with support coming from old and new participants as well as from Turkish authors and poets, who have been showing an ever-increasing interest in our translation activities and who, we believe, will continue to produce exciting work worth translating. We hope that publications resulting from our collaborative efforts will rise in number over the years and complement our ongoing production of good translations, for this will encourage our sponsors to ensure the survival of the workshop in the years to come.

My warmest thanks to Mel Kenne for proposing such a book in celebration of the workshop's seventh year and to Sedat Turhan who visited us during the 2012 workshop while we were compiling the book and showed a spontaneous interest in publishing it for Milet. Thanks also to Şehnaz Tahir Gürçağlar, our General Coordinator, to Cemal Demircioğlu, and to Amy Spangler, who joined our team in 2007 and since then has made herself indispensable. Their generous support and unflagging dedication have ensured the continuity of CWTTL from one year to the next. Finally, my special thanks to you, reader, for choosing to add this rather unconventional volume to your library. Indeed, your decision to do so is a testament to our shared passion for literature and translation.

—Saliha Paker

Cunda International Workshop for Translators of Turkish Literature: Translators and Guest Writers

As a reference for readers, here is a list of the translators and guest writers who participated in the Cunda workshops from 2006 to 2013.

2006 Guest Writers	Translators	
Gülten Akın	Jean Efe Carpenter	Mel Kenne
Haydar Ergülen	Ruth Christie	Murat Nemet-Nejat
Nurdan Gürbilek	Clifford Endres	Saliha Paker
Müge Gürsoy Sökmen	Selhan Savcıgil Endres	Angela Roome
Murathan Mungan	Engin Geçtan	Jonathan Ross
Zeynep Uzunbay	Erdağ Göknar	İpek Seyalıoğlu
	Şehnaz Tahir Gürçağlar	Ronald Tamplin
	Kurt Heinzelman	Nilüfer Yeşil

2007 Guest Writers	Translators	
Latife Tekin	Cemal Demircioğlu	Mel Kenne
Hasan Ali Toptaş	Nilgün Dungan	Saliha Paker
	Arzu Eker	Amy Spangler
	Erdağ Göknar	Ronald Tamplin
	Güneli Gün	Sidney Wade
	Şehnaz Tahir Gürçağlar	

2008 Guest Writers	Translators	
Gökçenur Ç.	İdil Aydoğan	Kurt Heinzelman
Murat Gülsoy	Cemal Demircioğlu	Suat Karantay
	Nilgün Dungan	Mel Kenne
	Arzu Eker	Saliha Paker
	Clifford Endres	Deniz Perin
	Selhan Savcıgil Endres	Jonathan Ross
	Şehnaz Tahir Gürçağlar	Amy Spangler

2009 Guest Writers	Translators	
Behçet Çelik	İdil Aydoğan	Petr Kucera
Gonca Özmen	Alexandra Büchler	Murat Nemet-Nejat
	Gökçenur Ç.	Saliha Paker
	Ruth Christie	Deniz Perin
	Cemal Demircioğlu	Bengisu Rona
	Nilgün Dungan	Jonathan Ross
	Arzu Eker	Amy Spangler
	Clifford Endres	Annika Svahnström
	Selhan Savcıgil Endres	Ronald Tamplin
	Mel Kenne	Ruth Whitehouse

2010 Guest Writers	Translators	
Guest Writers	İdil Aydoğan	Tuula Kojo
Onur Bilge Kula	Zane Bruvere	Saliha Paker
Hatice Meryem	Ruth Christie	Elizabeth Pallitto
Murathan Mungan	David Connolly	Arzu Eker Roditakis
	Cemal Demircioğlu	Jonathan Ross
	Ahmet Ergenç	Amy Spangler
	Şehnaz Tahir Gürçağlar	Ronald Tamplin
	İdil Karacadağ	Ruth Whitehouse
	Mel Kenne	Mark David Wyers

2011 Guest Writers	Translators	
Ahmet Büke	İdil Aydoğan	Saliha Paker
Birhan Keskin	Gökçenur Ç.	Elizabeth Pallitto
	David Connolly	Arzu Eker Roditakis
	Kenneth Dakan	Jonathan Ross
	Cemal Demircioğlu	Donny Smith
	Nilgün Dungan	Amy Spangler
	Şehnaz Tahir Gürçağlar	Annika Svahnström
	Sheila Iaia	Ruth Whitehouse
	Mel Kenne	Mark David Wyers
	Murat Nemet-Nejat	

2012	Guest Writers	Translators	
	Mine Söğüt	Sunia Iliaz Acmambet	Suna Kafadar
	Güven Turan	İdil Aydoğan	Mel Kenne
		Abigail Bowman	Saliha Paker
		Alexandra Büchler	Elizabeth Pallitto
		Ruth Christie	Arzu Eker Roditakis
		Kenneth Dakan	Bengisu Rona
		Cemal Demircioğlu	Amy Spangler
		Nilgün Dungan	Ronald Tamplin
		Hande Eagle	Venke Vik
		Alev Ersan	Ruth Whitehouse
		Şehnaz Tahir Gürçağlar	Mark David Wyers
		Feyza Howell	

2013	Guest Writers	Translators	
	Haydar Ergülen	Arzu Akbatur	Izzy Finkel
	Ruken Kızıler	Alexander Dawe	Şehnaz Tahir Gürçağlar
	Suha Oğuzertem	Cemal Demircioğlu	İdil Karacadağ
		Nilgün Dungan	Mel Kenne
		Clifford Endres	Saliha Paker
		Selhan Savcıgil Endres	Amy Spangler
		Alev Ersan	Caroline Stockford
		Kate Ferguson	Mark David Wyers

Biographies of Authors and Translators

Gülten Akın was born in 1933. In a 2008 survey of Turkish writers and publishers, she was selected as "the greatest living Turkish poet." She studied law at Ankara University and worked as a lawyer and a teacher in different parts of Anatolia. Her poems have been translated into Arabic, Bulgarian, German, English, Flemish, Danish, Hebrew, Italian, Polish and Spanish. Her major poetry collections include: *Rüzgâr Saati*, *Kestim Kara Saçlarımı*, *Sığda*, *Kırmızı Karanfil*, *Maraş'ın ve Ökkeş'in Destanı*, *Ağıtlar ve Türküler*, *İlahiler*, *Sevda Kalıcıdır*, *Sonra İşte Yaşlandım*, *Sessiz Arka Bahçeler* and *Uzak Bir Kıyıda*. Akın won the Turkish Language Association Poetry Award in 1961 and 1971, and the Sedat Simavi Literature Award in 1992. Her first collection published in English is *What Have you Carried Over? Poems of 42 Days and Other Works* (Talisman House, 2013).

Oğuz Atay was born in İnebolu in 1934, and studied and lived in Ankara for many years before moving to Istanbul. Undoubtedly one of the most influential authors of twentieth century Turkish literature, Atay's first novel *Tutunamayanlar* was awarded the TRT Novel Prize in 1970. It was followed in 1973 by a second novel *Tehlikeli Oyunlar*, and later, the short story collection *Korkuyu Beklerken*. His biographical novel *Bir Bilim Adamının Romanı* was published in 1975. His play *Oyunlarla Yaşayanlar* has been staged at theatres throughout Turkey. Atay died in 1977, before finishing his greatest project, *Türkiye'nin Ruhu*.

İdil Aydoğan was born in London and grew up in both London and Izmir. She completed her BA in English language and literature at Ege University and received her MA in comparative literature from King's College, London University. Her English translations of Turkish short stories by Hatice Meryem, Behçet Çelik and Ahmet Büke have been published in various books and magazines and in the special edition of *Transcript Review* on Turkish literature. Most recently, her translations of short stories by Erendiz Atasü, Müge İplikçi, Nazlı Eray, Menekşe Toprak, Mine Söğüt and Oya Baydar were published in *Istanbul in Women's Short Stories* and *Europe In Women's Short Stories from Turkey* (both, Milet Publishing, 2012).

Barış Bıçakçı was born in Adana in 1966 and has lived in Ankara since 1969. He graduated from the Department of Engineering, Middle East Technical

University (METU), Ankara, but has never practiced engineering. He is the author of seven works of fiction. Bıçakçı's novel *Bizim Büyük Çaresizliğimiz* (2004) was adapted into a film by the same title (*Our Grand Despair*, 2011); the film met with critical acclaim both in Turkey and abroad. Bıçakçı's work has been published in Bulgarian, Dutch, English, French, German and Norwegian.

Abigail Rood Bowman, born in 1989, is an MA candidate in history at Sabancı University, Istanbul. Originally from Johnston, Iowa, Bowman graduated magna cum laude from Princeton University in 2011 with a BA in Near Eastern studies and a certificate in creative writing for translation. Her senior thesis, *The Legs of Şahmeran: A Translation of Murathan Mungan*, which was advised by Robert Finn, received the Ertegün Foundation Thesis Prize and the Francis LeMoyne Page Creative Writing Award. After graduating, she received a 2011–12 Fulbright Scholarship to study and translate modern Turkish literature at Boğaziçi University. Her translation of Semra Topal's "The Silence of Sevinç Duman" was published in *Istanbul in Women's Short Stories* (Milet, 2012), and an article based on her thesis research was published in the 2012 issue of the *Journal of Turkish Literature*.

Ahmet Büke was born in Gördes, Manisa in 1970. He published his first short story collection *İzmir Postasının Adamları* in 2004, followed by five more collections, including *Alnı Mavide* (2008), for which he was awarded the Oğuz Atay Short Story Prize, and *Kumrunun Gördüğü* (2010), for which he received the prestigious Sait Faik Short Story Award. His stories have been published in English translation in *Transcript Review* and *Absinthe*, and in German translation as well.

Gökçenur Ç. was born in Istanbul in 1971 and spent his childhood in various Turkish cities. He graduated from the Faculty of Electrical and Electronic Engineering, Istanbul Technical University and has an MA in business administration from Istanbul University. His first two poetry collections *Her Kitabın El Kitabı* (2006) and *Söz'e Mezar* (2010) were published by Yitik Ülke. His third book *Onüç Kuşa Bakmanın Tek Yolu* (2011) was published bilingually in Italian and Turkish by I Libri Del Merlo. His poems have been translated into Bulgarian, Croatian, French, German, Greek, English, Hebrew, Japanese, Latvian,

Lithuanian, Macedonian, Portuguese, Romanian, Serbian and Swedish. He has translated Wallace Stevens, Paul Auster and a modern Japanese haiku anthology into Turkish, and is currently preparing an anthology of modern American poetry.

Behçet Çelik was born in Adana in 1968. He graduated from the Faculty of Law, Istanbul University in 1990. Çelik's story "A Cold Fire" was translated into Dutch and published in the collection *Stad en Mens*, and his story "So Very Familiar" was featured in the collection *Istanbul Noir* (Akashic Books, 2008). He is the author of six short story collections, including *Gün Ortasında Arzu* (2007), for which he received the Sait Faik Award, and *Diken Ucu* (2011), for which he received the Haldun Taner Short Story Award. Former editor of the literary journal *Virgül*, Çelik is also the author of two novels, *Dünyanın Uğultusu* (2009) and *Soluk Bir An* (2012), as well as one children's book and two collections of essays.

Ruth Christie was born and educated in Scotland, taking a degree in English language and literature at the University of St Andrews. She taught English for two years in Turkey and later studied Turkish language and literature at London University. With Saliha Paker she translated *Berji Kristin, Tales from the Garbage Hills*, by Latife Tekin (Marion Boyars, 1993), and in collaboration with Richard McKane a selection of the poems of Oktay Rifat, *Voices of Memory* (Rockingham Press, 1993), as well as a major collection of Nazım Hikmet's poetry, *Beyond the Walls* (Anvil Press, 2004). Her translation of Bejan Matur's poetry collection *In the Temple of a Patient God* was published in 2004 (Arc Visible Poets). Her recent translations, with Richard McKane, include *Poems of Oktay Rifat* (Anvil Press, 2007) and *The Shelter Stories* by Feyyaz Kayacan Fergar (Rockingham Press, 2007). Her translation of Bejan Matur's *How Abraham Betrayed Me* (Arc Visible Poets) was awarded the Poetry Book Society's Recommendation for 2012.

David Connolly was born in Sheffield, England, and is of Irish descent. He studied ancient Greek at the University of Lancaster, medieval and modern Greek literature at Trinity College, Oxford, and received his doctoral degree for a thesis on the theory and practice of literary translation from the University of East Anglia. A naturalized Greek, he has lived and worked in Greece since 1979 and has taught translation at the undergraduate and post-graduate levels for many years. He is currently Professor of Translation Studies at Aristotle University of Thessaloniki. He has published over thirty books of translations featuring works by major Greek poets and novelists. His translations have received awards in Greece, Britain and the United States.

Kenneth Dakan was born in Salt Lake City, Utah in 1964 and is a freelance translator and voice-over artist. His published translations of fiction and non-fiction include: Mehmet Murat Somer's *The Prophet Murders* (Serpent's Tale, 2008), *The Kiss Murder* (Penguin, 2009) and *The Gigolo Murder* (Penguin, 2009); Ece Temelkuran's *Deep Mountain: Across the Turkish-Armenian Divide* (Verso, 2010); Perihan Mağden's *Escape* (Amazon Crossing, 2012); Ayşe Kulin's *Farewell: A Mansion in Occupied Istanbul* (Dalkey Archive, 2012); and Buket Uzuner's *I Am Istanbul* (Dalkey Archive, 2013).

Cemal Demircioğlu is Assistant Professor of Translation Studies at Okan University, Istanbul. He completed his BA and MA in modern Turkish literature at Boğaziçi University, where he also worked as lecturer and later obtained his PhD in translation studies. His main research interests concern the history of translation in Ottoman and modern Turkish society. Among his published articles is "Translating Europe: The case of Ahmed Midhat as an Ottoman agent of translation" in *Translation and Agency* (John Benjamins, 2009). He has co-translated the poetry of Murathan Mungan, Gülten Akın, Gökçenur Ç., Gonca Özmen and Birhan Keskin.

Nilgün Dungan is a lecturer and translator based in Izmir. She studied English language and literature at Ege University and received an MA in management from Bowie State University in Maryland. She is currently pursuing her PhD in translation studies at Boğaziçi University in Istanbul and teaching in the Department of English Translation and Interpreting, Izmir University of Economics. Her English translations of articles and short stories have been published in various journals and magazines. She is also the translator of the novel *Mount Qaf* by Müge İplikçi (Milet, 2013).

Hande Eagle was born in Istanbul in 1984. In 2006, she completed a degree in sociology at the University of Leicester. A regular contributor to the arts and culture pages of the Turkish national newspaper *Cumhuriyet*, she works independently with several publishing houses and authors on both fiction and non-fiction projects. Translation projects she undertook in 2011 include *Mosaics of Anatolia* by Gürol Sözen, and *Samatya: Colour, Flavour and Nostalgia* (Boyut Publishing). Currently, she is working on the translation of a selection of short stories by Yekta Kopan. Her research interests include contemporary art and architecture, and music, as well as literature.

Jean Carpenter Efe received BA and MA degrees in archeology in the US. She worked for many years as a field archeologist in Turkey before joining the Department of Translation and Interpreting Studies, Boğaziçi University, where she taught for over ten years until her death in 2007. She translated from Turkish to English many books on archeology. Her works of literary translation include *Tales from the Taurus* (2006), a collection of short stories by Osman Şahin, and *One Cat, One Man, One Death*, a novel by Zülfü Livaneli.

Clifford Endres has taught at the University of Texas, Austin, and in Turkey at the universities Ege, Boğaziçi, Başkent and Kadir Has. He is the author of *Johannes Secundus: The Latin Love Elegy in the Renaissance* (1981) and *Austin City Limits* (1987). Together with Selhan Savcıgil Endres, he has translated the Turkish poets Güven Turan, Enis Batur, Gülten Akın, and the novelist Selçuk Altun. His translations and articles have appeared in, among others, *Agenda, Chicago Review, Edinburgh Review, Massachusetts Review, Near East Review, Quarterly West, Renaissance Quarterly, Seneca Review, Southwest Review* and *Texas Studies in Language and Literature*.

Selhan Savcıgil Endres has taught at Hacettepe and Başkent universities and has written on various Turkish and American authors, including Paul Auster, Toni Morrison and Orhan Pamuk. Selhan and Cliff Endres live in Istanbul, where in 2000 they established the Department of American Literature and Culture at Kadir Has University. Their translations have appeared in a variety of anthologies, such as the *Anthology of Turkish Drama* (Syracuse University Press, 2008), and journals including *Quarterly West, Seneca Review, Talisman* and

Translation Review. Other published translations include *Ash Divan: Selected Poems of Enis Batur* (Talisman House, 2006), and the novels *Many and Many a Year Ago* (Telegram, 2009) and *The Sultan of Byzantium* (Telegram, 2012) by Selçuk Altun.

Haydar Ergülen was born in Eskişehir in 1956. He graduated from the Department of Sociology, METU. He has lectured on Turkish poetry at Anadolu University and worked as a copywriter and columnist for *Radikal* and *Birgün* newspapers. He currently writes a column for the literary journal *Varlık*. He was in the group that produced the literary magazines *Üç Çiçek* (1983) and *Şiir Atı* (1986). His first book of poems *Karşılığını Bulamamış Sorular* was published in 1981. Since then, he has publsihed over a dozen poetry collections, including most recently *Yağmur Cemi* (2006), *Üzgün Kediler Gazeli* (2007) and *Zarf* (2010), and is the winner of several prestigious prizes for his poetry. Since 2000, he has also published ten collections of essays.

Alev Ersan was born in Turkey in 1980, and raised between Kyrenia and Istanbul. After completing her BA in English literature at Boğaziçi University, she moved to Canada in 2006 and studied with Miranda Pearson, Betsy Warland and Wayde Compton at the Simon Fraser University Writer's Studio in Vancouver. She was also involved with the Kootenay School of Writing. In 2005, Alev cofounded *Thrice Upon*, an installation theater group based in Vancouver which produced five interactive plays. Most recently, she collaborated with artist Tejal Shah to create an animated work for *Between the Waves* for *dOCUMENTA(13)*. She has published poetry and prose in *emerge* anthology, *CanLit* and *FRONT* magazine, and translated into Turkish the novel *Automated Alice* by Jeff Noon. Alev currently teaches English at Kadir Has University and special topic courses focusing on experimental writing at Boğaziçi University. She is also working on her first book of fiction.

Şehnaz Tahir Gürçağlar, the Coordinator of the Cunda International Workshop for Translators of Turkish Literature (CWTTL), studied translation at Boğaziçi University and media studies at Oslo University. She holds a PhD in translation studies and teaches literary translation, translation theory, history and criticism, and interpreting at Boğaziçi University. She is the author of *Kapılar* (2005), a book exploring different approaches to translation history, *The Politics and Poetics of Translation in Turkey, 1923–1960* (Rodopi, 2008), and *Çevirinin ABC'si* (2011), an introduction to translation and translation studies in Turkish. She has been involved in the organization of CWTTL since its launch in 2006, and during the workshop she has translated works by Nurdan Gürbilek, Hasan Ali Toptaş, Murat Gülsoy and Hatice Meryem. She has also published translations of works by Haydar Ergülen, Melih Cevdet Anday, Derviş Zaim and Hür Yumer.

Erdağ Göknar is Assistant Professor of Turkish Studies at Duke University and an award-winning literary translator. He holds a PhD in Near and Middle Eastern studies (Turkish literature and culture) and has published various critical articles on Turkish literary culture, as well as three book-length translations: Nobel laureate Orhan Pamuk's *My Name is Red* (Knopf, 2001) and Ahmet Hamdi Tanpınar's novel of Turkish modernity *A Mind at Peace* (Archipelago Books, 2008), both translated from Turkish, and from the Dari, Atiq Rahimi's *Earth and Ashes* (Harcourt, 2004). He has received the Dublin IMPAC literary award and a US National Endowment for the Arts translation award for his translations. He is the coeditor of *Mediterranean Passages: Readings from Dido to Derrida* (University of North Carolina Press, 2008). His most recent project is a book of cultural criticism entitled *Orhan Pamuk, Secularism and Blasphemy: The Politics of the Turkish Novel* (Routledge, 2013). He directs the Duke in Turkey exchange program with Boğaziçi University.

Murat Gülsoy was born in 1967. He studied engineering and psychology and has a PhD in biomedical engineering. He began his literary career in 1992 as a publisher and writer at the literary journal *Hayalet Gemi*. The author of over a dozen published works, Gülsoy has received some of Turkey's most prestigious awards for his novels and short fiction, such as the Sait Faik Short Story Award, the Haldun Taner Short Story Award, and most recently, the Notre Dame de Sion Literary Award. Gülsoy's short fiction has been published in German translation as well as in English translation in various journals and anthologies, while his novel *İstanbul'da Bir Merhamet Haftası* (*A Week of Kindness in Istanbul*) has been published in Albanian, Arabic, Bulgarian, Chinese, Macedonian and Romanian, with English excerpts featured in *Transcript Review* as well as this volume. He presently works at Bogazici University as a life science researcher and creative writing teacher, and chairs the Bogazici University Press editorial board.

Güneli Gün lived with her family in towns all over Turkey, but she grew up mainly in Izmir as a boarding student at the private American School for Girls. She completed her liberal arts education at Hollins College, Virginia, followed by graduate degrees at Iowa Writers' Workshop and Johns Hopkins University. Gün has taught at METU, Johns Hopkins University and Oberlin College. She is the author of two works of fiction, *Book of Trances*, and *On the Road to Baghdad*, the latter of which was translated into a dozen languages and put on stage in London at the Sadler's Wells Theatre. She also translated Orhan Pamuk's *The Black Book* and *The New Life*, for which she was awarded a translation prize by the American Literary Translators Association. Gün has published criticism and short fiction in various publications.

Nurdan Gürbilek is one of the foremost cultural critics in Turkey. She is the author of *Vitrinde Yaşamak*, an analysis of the cultural dynamics of the 1980s in Turkey, as well as other essay collections, including *Kötü Çocuk Türk*, an analysis of some of the significant images and tropes in modern Turkish literature and popular culture. *The New Cultural Climate in Turkey: Living in a Shop Window* (Zed, 2010) combines selected essays from both of these collections. Translator and editor of a collection of essays by Walter Benjamin in Turkish, Gürbilek has received some of Turkey's most prestigious awards for her own writing, including the 2010 Erdal Öz Award, an annual award for lifetime literary achievement in literature, and the 2011 Cevdet Kudret Award for her most recent book, *Benden Önce Bir Başkası*, a comparative study of works from Turkish and world literature.

Kurt Heinzelman is Professor of English at the University of Texas. His critical articles on topics such as British Romanticism, modern poetry and cultural economics, and his poems and translations have appeared in numerous journals. In addition to his many scholarly publications, Heinzelman has published three books of poetry: *The Halfway Tree* (Verser, 2000), *Black Butterflies* (Mulberry Press, 2004) and *The Names They Found There* (Pecan Grove Press, 2011). A nominee for the Pushcart prize numerous times, Heinzelman was founding coeditor of *The Poetry*

Miscellany, a journal he edited for ten years, and is currently editor-at-large for *Bat City Review*. He is also editor-in-chief of *Texas Studies in Language and Literature* and is on the board of directors of the Dylan Thomas Prize.

İdil Karacadağ is from Istanbul. She completed her BA in Literature at Kadir Has University in 2013. Her translations of Murathan Mungan have been published in the online journal *Fox Chase Review*. She has worked on translations of other contemporary Turkish poets, such as Zeynep Köylü and Necmi Zeka, which are published in the 2013 issue of *Turkish Poetry Today*.

Mel Kenne is a poet and translator who has lived in Istanbul since 1993. A founding member of the CWTTL, he has translated much Turkish poetry and prose into English. Kenne collaborated with Saliha Paker on the translation and editing of the collection of poetry by Gülten Akın, *What Have You Carried Over? Poems of 42 Days and Other Works* (Talisman House, 2013). Again with Paker, he translated the novels *Dear Shameless Death* (Marion Boyars, 2000) and *Swords of Ice* (Marion Boyars, 2007) by Latife Tekin. Six collections of his poetry have been published, most recently *Take* (Muse-Pie Press 2011), and a bilingual collection in English and Turkish, *Galata'dan / The View from Galata* (Yapı Kredi, 2010), translated into Turkish by İpek Seyalıoğlu.

Birhan Keskin was born in Kırklareli in 1963. She took her degree in sociology from Istanbul University in 1986. Her poetry was first published in 1984, and from 1995 to 1998 she was joint editor of the magazine *Göçebe*. She has since worked as an editor for a number of prominent publishing houses in Istanbul. Her first five poetry collections were reissued in a single volume titled *Kim Bağışlayacak Beni* (2005). Her most recent collections are *Ba* (2005), for which she won Turkey's prestigious Altın Portakal Award, *Yol* (2006), and *Soğuk Kazı* (2010), for which she received the Metin Altıok Poetry Award. *And Silk and Love and Flame* (Arc Visible Poets), a selection of her poetry translated into English by George Messo, was published in 2012.

Hatice Meryem, born in 1969, is an Istanbul-based novelist and short story writer and former editor of the literary magazines *Öküz* and *Hayvan*. Her books include the novel *İnsan Kısım Kısım Yer Damar Damar* (2008), her most recent book *Beyefendi: Erkeklere Methiye* (2013), and the surprise bestseller short story collection *Sinek Kadar Kocam Olsun Başımda Bulunsun* (2002), in which the narrator imagines herself as the wife of a variety of different men from myriad walks of life; the latter title has since been published in Arabic, Bulgarian, German and Romanian.

Murathan Mungan is one of the most prominent and prolific contemporary writers of Turkey. Mungan has published poetry, short stories, plays, novels, screenplays, radio plays, essays, film and theater criticism, and political columns. A selection of his poems was translated and published in Kurdish. His works have been translated into Bosnian, Bulgarian, Dutch, English, Finnish, French, German, Greek, Italian, Norwegian, Persian and Swedish. Mungan's play *Mesopotamian Trilogy, Geyikler Lanetler* (1992) was staged by the Arca Azzura Theater in Italy. His play *As on the Page* was published in *Solum and other plays from Turkey* (Seagull Books, 2011), and the English translation of his novella *Evening Gown* is forthcoming from City Lights.

Murat Nemet-Nejat is a poet, translator and essayist. He edited and largely translated *Eda: An Anthology of Contemporary Turkish Poetry* (Talisman House, 2004), translated Orhan Veli's *I, Orhan Veli* (Hanging Loose Press, 1989), Ece Ayhan's *A Blind Cat Black and Orthodoxies* (Sun and Moon Press, 1997; Green Integer Press, 2012), Seyhan Erözçelik's *Rosestrikes and Coffee Grinds* (Talisman House, 2010), and Birhan Keskin's poem *Yol* (Imprint Press, 2013). Nemet-Nejat also wrote *The Peripheral Space of Photography* (Green Integer Press, 2004), the memoir/essay "Istanbul Noir" in *Istanbul: Metamorphoses in an Imperial City* (Talisman House, 2011), and the poem *The Spiritual Life of Replicants* (Talisman House, 2011). His poems, translations and essays have appeared in multiple journals, such as *Mirage, Zen Monster* and *Karaub*. Nemet-Nejat is presently working on the long poem *The Structure of Escape* and preparing a selection of Sami Baydar's poetry in English translation.

Gonca Özmen was born in 1982 and graduated from the Department of English Language and Literature, Istanbul University in 2004. Her first poem was published when she was fifteen years old, and the same year she was judged "a poet worth paying attention to" by the Yaşar Nabi Nayır Youth Award committee. In

1999, she was awarded the Ali Rıza Ertan Poetry Prize. Her first book of poetry *Kuytumda*, published in 2000, won the Orhon Murat Arıburnu Poetry Prize, and in 2003 she received the Berna Moran Poetry Prize. Her second book *Belki Sessiz* was published in 2008. She helped to initiate *Ç.N.*, a magazine of literary translation, and she edits the monthly literary journal *Palto*. Her poems have been translated into English, Farsi, French, German, Slovenian and Spanish. A selection of her poems translated into English by George Messo, *The Sea Within* (Shearsman Books), was published in 2011.

Saliha Paker holds a BA (Hons) degree in English and a PhD in Classics from Istanbul University. She is Professor of Translation Studies and part-time translator of Turkish poetry and fiction into English. After retiring from Boğaziçi University in 2008, she served as Head of the Department of Translation Studies at Okan University, Istanbul, for two years. She continues to teach courses in the MA program at Okan as well as in the PhD program at Boğaziçi University. Her special field of study is literary translation history in Ottoman and modern Turkish society, on which she has written numerous essays in international publications. She has also worked on the history of Turkish literature in English translation. In 2006, she founded the Cunda International Workshop for Translators of Turkish Literature, which has been running since then, under the sponsorship of the Turkish Ministry of Culture. Her translations include three novels by Latife Tekin, *Berji Kristin Tales from the Garbage Hills* (with Ruth Christie), *Dear Shameless Death* and *Swords of Ice* (with Mel Kenne), all published by Marion Boyars (1993, 2001, 2007, respectively). She edited *Ash Divan, Selected Poems of Enis Batur*, brought out in 2006 by Talisman House, which is also publishing *What Have You Carried Over? Poems of 42 Days and Other Works* (2013) by Gülten Akın, coedited with Mel Kenne.

Elizabeth Pallitto has lived in New York, Boston and Istanbul, where she was a visiting assistant professor at Kadir Has University. She received a PhD in comparative literature from the graduate center of City University of New York (CUNY) and an MA in creative writing from New York University. Dr. Pallitto teaches creative writing, rhetoric and literature at CUNY. She has published translations from the Italian of poetry by Campanella, Velardinello, Fioravanti, and the Iraqi exile Thea Laitef. In 2007, she published *Sweet Fire: Tullia d'Aragona's Poetry of Dialogue and Selected Prose*, the first English version of d'Aragona's 1547

Rime. Her articles have appeared in *Hybrido: Arte y Literatura, Comitatus,* and *Renaissance Quarterly,* translations in *Philosophical Forum* and *Forum Italicum;* and original poetry in *Litspeak, Fox Chase Review* and *The North American Review.*

Deniz Perin, a poet and translator, is the recipient of a Lannan Writing Residency Fellowship and the Anna Akhmatova Fellowship for Younger Translators. Her work has appeared in *Atlanta Review, Poetry International, Words Without Borders,* and several other journals. Her translation of Ece Temelkuran's *Book of the Edge* (BOA Editions, 2010) was a semifinalist for the National Translation Award. Her translations of Nazım Hikmet's poetry were anthologized in the *Ecco Anthology of International Poetry* and in *Tablet & Pen: Literary Landscapes from the Modern Middle East.* A frequent participant in the CWTTL, she teaches English and creative writing at the University of San Diego.

Arzu Eker Roditakis has a BA in communication studies from Istanbul University and an MA in translation from the Department of Translation and Interpreting Studies, Boğaziçi University, where she also began her doctoral studies and gave courses on translation theory, practice and criticism. Her MA thesis *Publishing Translations in the Social Sciences since the 1980s: An Alternative View of Culture Planning in Turkey* was published by Lambert Academic Publishing in 2010. She currently resides in Greece, where she is working at Aristotle University of Thessaloniki on her doctoral dissertation on the English translations of Orhan Pamuk's fiction. In collaboration with Saliha Paker, she produced an English translation of a chapter from Cemil Meriç's *Bu Ülke,* which was published in the *Journal of Levantine Studies* in 2011.

Bengisu Rona was born in Ankara and studied English language and literature at Istanbul University. She did her PhD in linguistics at the School of Oriental and African Studies (SOAS), University of London, on the phonetic and phonological structure of Turkish. After teaching for ten years at Boğaziçi University, she joined the staff of SOAS, leading Turkish studies there until her recent retirement. Her specialist fields are Turkish language and nineteenth and twentieth century Turkish literature. Her translation work includes poems by Tevfik Fikret and Nazım Hikmet, and prose works of Orhan Kemal, Sabahattin Ali, and Sait Faik Abasıyanık. Recent publications include Orhan Kemal's *In*

Jail with Nazım Hikmet (Saqi Books, 2010) and *Puzzles of Language*, edited with Eser Erguvanlı Tayla (Harrassowitz Verlag, 2011).

Angela Roome was born in England and completed her BA Hons in English at Durham University and her MA Ed at Bristol University. She taught at Guildford High School for Girls before moving to Turkey, where she taught English language and literature at Ankara High School and Robert College, Istanbul. She now lives in Istanbul where she works as a freelance editor and translator from Turkish into English.

Jonathan Ross was born in London and studied German and politics at the University of Edinburgh before going on to do a doctorate in East German literature at King's College London. He now teaches in the Department of Translation and Interpreting Studies, Boğaziçi University. His research interests include the translation of film titles, and community interpreting in Turkey. Among his published translations are two collections of articles for the Turkish Ministry of Culture, several books on Turkish archaeology, the English subtitles for the musical documentary *Lost Songs of Anatolia*, and Gaye Boralıoğlu's story "Mi Hatice," which appeared in *Istanbul in Women's Short Stories* (Milet, 2012).

İpek Seyalıoğlu was born in 1976 in Istanbul and received her MA in translation studies from Boğaziçi University. She is the author of a poetry-play called *Bakır Kalkan*, and her poems, short stories and translations have been published in a number of journals, such as *Kitap-lık, Isırgan, Ç.N., Sonra, Cogito* and *Eurozine*. Also an actor, Seyalıoğlu continues to work as an English language instructor at Boğaziçi University.

Sevgi Soysal was born in Istanbul in 1936. She grew up in Ankara with her father, an architect-bureaucrat originally from Salonica, and her German mother. She studied archaeology in Ankara. Soysal's first volume of short stories was published in 1962. She went on to write *Tante Rosa*, a novel of interconnected stories based upon the life and personality of her aunt Rosel. *Yürümek*, her novel addressing male-female relationships and the issue of marriage, was banned upon charges of obscenity. In 1974, Soysal won the prestigious Orhan Kemal Award for *Yenişehir'de Bir Öğle Vakti*. Her novel *Şafak*, in which she criticized the coup of March 12th by way of the story of a woman exiled in Adana, was published in 1975. Her memoirs of prison life, originally published in the newspaper *Politika*, were published in a single volume as *Yıldırım Bölge Kadınlar Koğuşu* in 1976. Soysal died of cancer in 1976. She left behind an incomplete novel, *Hoşgeldin Ölüm*.

Mine Söğüt was born in Istanbul in 1968. She received her BA in Latin from the Department of Classics, Istanbul University in 1989. In 1990, she started to work as a courtroom reporter for the newspaper *Güneş*. She went on to work as a journalist for periodicals such as *Tempo, Yeni Yüzyıl* and *Öküz,* and screenwriter for the television documentary *Haberci.* In 2005 she completed her graduate thesis on Latin theatre entitled "Polemic Elements in Terentius's Prologues." Among her literary works are four novels, *Beş Sevim Apartmanı* (2003), *Kırmızı Zaman* (2004*)*, *Şahbaz'ın Harikulade Yılı 1979* (2007*)*, and *Madam Arthur Bey ve Hayatındaki Her Şey* (2010*)*, as well as the short story collection *Deli Kadın Hikâyeleri* (2011). Her work has been published in Arabic, English, German and Romanian translation.

Amy Spangler was born in 1978 in Ohio, US, and is a graduate of Bryn Mawr College, with BA degrees in Near Eastern and classical archeology and German language and literature. Cofounder and director of AnatoliaLit Agency (www. anatolialit.com), Spangler is the translator of *The City in Crimson Cloak* by Aslı Erdoğan (Soft Skull Press, 2007), and the coeditor and co-translator of *Istanbul Noir* (Akashic Books, 2008). Her English translations of Turkish short stories and novel excerpts have been published in various books and magazines, including the collection *ReBerth* (Comma Press, 2008), *Best European Fiction 2010* (Dalkey Archive Press, 2011) *Edinburgh Review, Words Without Borders* and *Transcript Review.* She teaches a literary translation course at Boğaziçi University.

Ronald Tamplin was born in London in 1935. He was educated at Merton College, Oxford, and taught English literature at various universities in Britain, France, Turkey and New Zealand from 1961 to 2003, including Bilkent University (1996–2003) and the University of Exeter, where he was also honorary university fellow. His books include: *Wynkyn de Worde's Gesta Romanorum* (Exeter

Univeristy Press, 1974), *A Preface to TS Eliot* (Longman, 1988), *Seamus Heaney* (Open University Press, 1989), *Rhythm and Rhyme* (Open University Press, 1993), ed. *The Arts: A History of Expression in the 20ᵗʰ Century*, (Oxford University Press, 1991), and *Famous Love Letters: Messages of Intimacy and Passion* (Readers' Digest, 1995). His poetry has appeared in many magazines and anthologies around the world, and in three collections, the most recent, *Checkpoint* (2010). He has won a number of prizes, including the Eugene Lee Hamilton Sonnet Prize (1956), The City of Winchester John Keats Bi-Centennial Prize (1995), The Wells International Poetry Prize (2009), and prizes in the Poetry Society's National Poetry Competition (1998) and in the Bridport Poetry Competition (2002). Among his published translations of poetry are sections of an ongoing modern verse version of the 14ᵗʰ Century Middle English poem *Piers Plowman*, which have appeared in several anthologies, and, in collaboration, poems from a number of Turkish poets, including Enis Batur, İlhan Berk and Edip Cansever.

Latife Tekin was born in 1957. Her first novel *Sevgili Arsız Ölüm* (1983), about the struggles of a family that had to migrate to the big city, told in fairytale style from a young girl's point of view, was later published in English translation as *Dear Shameless Death* (Marion Boyars, 2000). Her other novels to appear in English are *Berji Kristin: Tales from the Garbage Hills* (Marion Boyars, 1993) and *Swords of Ice* (Marion Boyars, 2007), while her other books published in Turkish include *Gece Dersleri* (1986), *Aşk İşaretleri* (1995), *Ormanda Ölüm Yokmuş* (2001), *Unutma Bahçesi* (2004), and *Muinar* (2006). She also wrote the screenplay for the film *Bir Yudum Sevgi* (1984). Her work has been translated into many languages, including Arabic, Dutch, English, French, German and Italian. Tekin is the director of the Gümüşlük Academy Foundation, which she cofounded in 1995 as a cultural center and writers' residence in Bodrum. A branch was established in 2013 in Arnavutköy, Istanbul.

Hasan Ali Toptaş was born in Çal, Denizli, southwest Anatolia, in 1958. After completing his military service, he survived by doing odd jobs until he found a position at the Turkish government Office of Inland Revenue. He worked in various small towns as a bailiff and treasurer, and finally as a tax officer. Following the publication of a few short stories in journals and anthologies, he paid for the printing of his first volume of stories *Bir Gülüşün Kimliği* in 1987.

He submitted his second novel *Gölgesizler* (1995) to the Yunus Nadi Prize jury, and won. This novel was later adapted into a feature film (2007). Toptaş has received many other awards, including the Cevdet Kudret Literary Award for his novel *Bin Hüzünlü Haz* (1999) and the Orhan Kemal Award for Best Novel for *Uykuların Doğusu* (2005). *Yalnızlıklar* (1990), poetic texts he constructed as a series of encyclopedia entries, has been successfully adapted to the stage. Toptaş retired in 2005, and since then has dedicated himself fulltime to his writing. His most recent book, the novel *Heba* (2013), will be published in English by Bloomsbury in 2015, and is to be followed by the English translation of *Gölgesizler*. Toptaş's work has been published in many languages, including Dutch, French, German and Korean.

Güven Turan was born in Gerze, Sinop, in 1943. He studied English and American literature at Ankara University and holds an MA degree in American literature. He worked as an instructor at the same university, wrote programs for the "Voice of Turkey," which broadcasts for Turkish nationals living abroad, edited literary reviews, and, from 1976 to 1995, worked in advertising. His first poem was published in 1963, and since then he has published many poems, short stories, novels, art and literary critiques, and translations of English and American poets. To date he has produced nine books of poetry, three novels, three books of essays and criticism, and a book of short stories. A number of his poems and short stories have been translated into English and French. He has participated in the International Writing Program at the University of Iowa; in the Cambridge seminars; and in the Voix de la Mediterranée, in Lodéve, France. He is now a consultant editor for Yapı Kredi Publications.

Zeynep Uzunbay was born in the Karaözü district of Kayseri in 1961. She graduated from the Vocational High School for Health and served as a nurse in Turhal and Tokat. In 1985, she received her BA in Turkish literature from Gazi University, Ankara. Since 1995, she has published five collections of poetry: *Sabahçı Su Kıyıları* (1995), *Yaşamaşk* (1998), *Kim'e* (2003), *Yara Falı* (2006), and *Geri Dönüşüm* (2010). She has also written two story books for children and a study of Gülten Akın's poetry, Aydınlığım Deliyim Rüzgarlıyım (2011). In 1995, 1998 and 2003, she received awards for her poetry, some of which has been translated into English and Italian. After teaching in several schools, she retired in 2006. Uzunbay presently lives in Izmir, where she continues to write her own poetry and articles on the poetry of others.

Venke Vik studied at University of Oslo and the University of Cambridge. Her thesis, submitted in 1973, was *The Thematic Function of the Social Structure in Shakespeare's Plays*. Her work experience has been connected to primary and secondary education, first as a teacher, but also in the 1980s through her involvement in union work at the county and national levels. For the last 20 years, she has worked as the principal of a secondary school, a project leader, and an advisor to the director of secondary education in the county of Nordland, Norway. Vik has written extensively on various aspects of education. She has translated Latife Tekin's novel *Dear Shameless Death* into New Norwegian.

Sidney Wade has six collections of poems, the most recent of which are *Straits and Narrows* (2013) and *Stroke* (2008), both published by Persea Books. Her poems and translations have appeared in a wide variety of journals, including *Poetry, The New Yorker, Grand Street* and *The Paris Review*. In 1989–1990, she taught at Istanbul University as a Senior Fulbright Fellow. She has translated many works of Turkish poetry into English, including works by Melih Cevdet Anday and Yahya Kemal. She has served as president of the Association of Writers & Writing Programs and secretary/treasurer for the American Literary Translators Association. Since 1993, she has taught poetry and translation workshops in the MFA@FLA creative writing program at the University of Florida, where she is poetry editor of the literary journal *Subtropics*.

Ruth Whitehouse took a PhD in modern Turkish literature at the SOAS, London University. She has participated in the CWTTL since 2009. Her published translations include *Ali and Ramazan* by Perihan Mağden (Amazon Crossing, 2012), and the crime fiction novels *Hotel Bosphorus* (Bitter Lemon Press, 2011) and *Bakhsheesh* (Bitter Lemon Press, 2012) by Esmahan Akyol. *The Last Tram*, her translations of a collection of 22 short stories by Nedim Gürsel, was published by Comma Press in 2011. Her translations of short stories by Esmahan Aykol, Yıldız Ramazanoğlu, Karin Karakaşlı and Stella Acıman were published in the anthology *Istanbul in Women's Short Stories* (Milet, 2012). Whitehouse's other published translations include "The Perforated Amulet" by Sevgi Soysal

(*Texas Studies in Literature and Language*, 2012) and "Fig Seed" by Feryal Tilmaç (*Transcript Review*, 2009). The latter was also broadcast on BBC Radio 4 in a series called "Young Turks." Ruth also served as the Turkish–English translator for the 2010 Royal Court Theatre International Residency for Emerging Playwrights in London, working with Turkish playwright Berkun Oya.

Mark David Wyers was born and grew up in Los Angeles, California, and received his BA in literature from the University of Tampa. He lived in Kayseri, Ankara and Istanbul for a number of years, and in 2008 completed his MA in the field of Turkish studies at the University of Arizona. His book *"Wicked" Istanbul: The Regulation of Prostitution in the Early Turkish Republic*, a historical study of gender and the politics of urban space, was published in 2012, and a number of his translations of short stories have been published in journals and collected works. Currently, he is employed as the director of the Writing Center at Kadir Has University in Istanbul, where he continues to work on historical research as well as literary translations from Turkish and Ottoman to English. In addition to his translations in the *Women's Short Stories* collections published by Milet, Wyers is currently working on a translation of Selim İleri's novel *Yarın Yapayalnız* (Milet, forthcoming).

Acknowledgements

On behalf of the Cunda International Workshop for Translators of Turkish Literature (CWTTL), we would like to thank the Turkish Ministry of Culture and Tourism for making our workshop possible with their generous sponsorship; the distinguished members of the TEDA Advisory Committee, for supporting the publication of this collection with a grant; the Rectorate of Boğaziçi University and its Deparment of Translation and Interpreting Studies, for their institutional sponsorship; the Rectorate of Koç University, for permission to use the Harvard-Koç Sevgi Doğan Gönül Ottoman Research Institute as home base for our workshop over the years; Professor Gönül Alpay Tekin, for her friendship and encouragement; Alexandra Buchler, Director of Literature Across Frontiers (LAF), for all her efforts as our partner to keep the workshop running with funding from the European Union since 2009; Professor Şehnaz Tahir Gürçağlar of Boğaziçi University, our General Coordinator with LAF and the Ministry, for her ever resourceful contribution to the organization of our workshop and painstaking bookkeeping, as well as for her superbly professional interpreting services at all our workshops; all our dedicated colleagues in translation from the USA, the UK and Turkey; all the Turkish poets and writers who have so enthusiastically participated in our workshops; the translation colleagues of the 2012 workshop for their gracious, generous input in the selection and compilation of this volume; our assistant editors, Arzu Eker Roditakis, who never hesitated to offer a helping hand from Greece, and Nilgün Dungan in Izmir. Our great thanks go to the highly dedicated team at Milet Publishing, including its founder, Sedat Turhan, who has devoted his career to supporting Turkish literature and education, and whose company has long been a trailblazer internationally in publishing texts in these fields; our wonderful editor Patricia Billings, who led us in our journey through the maze of decisions involved in producing a book of this size and complexity, and with boundless patience and resolve helped us surmount the host of difficulties we faced along the way; and the designer Christangelos Seferiadis, who brought his Aegean sensibility to bear in conceiving the beautiful cover and overall design of the collection, thus fusing his vision with ours. And, finally, we thank all those other friends and colleagues whose names our space here does not permit listing and whose help and encouragement contributed to making our dream of this book come true.

—Mel Kenne, Saliha Paker and Amy Spangler

Permissions Acknowledgements

We are grateful for the permission to reprint in this volume the following translations that first appeared in other publications:

Absinthe 19, Spotlight on Turkey (Summer 2013): "Railway Storytellers—A Dream" by Oğuz Atay; "Lakeshadow" by Ahmet Büke; "Death Imagines Stars as the Night's Scabbed-Over Wounds" and "Flour Soup, Cherry Raki, a Pinch of Time" by Gökçenur Ç.

Excerpt from *A Mind at Peace* by Ahmet Hamdi Tanpınar, Archipelago Press (2008).

Blue Lyra Review, Issue 2.2 (August 2013): "Lost Brother" by Haydar Ergülen; "In a Way" by Murathan Mungan; "5." from *Lonelinesses* by Hasan Ali Toptaş; "San Gimignano" by Güven Turan; "wet" by Zeynep Uzunbay.

CALQUE (2010): "Stain" and "Lament of a Working Mother's Child" by Gülten Akın.

The Dirty Goat, No. 20 (2009): "The Spokesperson of Words" and "Death Thinks of the Stars as Night's Scabbed-Over Wounds" by Gökçenur Ç.

Istanbul in Women's Short Stories, Milet Publishing (2012): "Why I Killed Myself in the City" by Mine Söğüt.

Muse-Pie Press, 2010 (*www.musepiepress.com*): "Moon Time," "Autumn Chills," "Blemish," "Shadows," "Start Again," "Mustafa" and "Memet" by Gonca Özmen.

Strange Harbors, Two Lines Press (2008): "Done with the City" by Gülten Akın; "With Your Voice" by Zeynep Uzunbay (the version translated by Saliha Paker and Mel Kenne).

The Near East Review (2007): "I Cut My Black Black Hair" by Gülten Akın;

"Carry Us Across" by Haydar Ergülen; "voice" and "you gotta go when you gotta go" by Zeynep Uzunbay.

Texas Studies in Literature and Language (Winter 2012): "The Perforated Amulet" by Sevgi Soysal; "The Balcony" by Hasan Ali Toptaş.

Transcript Review, Issue 30 (www.transcript-review.org/en/issue/transcript-30-poetry-from-turkey): "Flour Soup, Cherry Rakı, a Pinch of Time," "Nothing in Nature Says Anything," "A Monument to the Impossibility of Utterance" and "Death Thinks of the Stars as Night's Scabbed-Over Wounds" by Gökçenur Ç.; "Moon Time," "Shadows," "Start Again," "Mustafa" and "Memet" by Gonca Özmen.

Transcript Review, Issue 31, Autumn Shorts (www.transcript-review.org/en/issue/transcript-31-autumn-shorts): "My Big Brother" by Behçet Çelik.

Transcript Review, Issue 32, New Prose Fiction from Turkey (www.transcript-review.org/en/issue/transcript-32-new-prose-fiction-from-turkey): "Equilateral Hell," "Give Me Your Mother" and "An Older Woman" by Barış Bıçakçı; "Do Teardrops Cover Three Quarters of this Earth?" and "Factor of Solitude and Ego Fusion" by Murat Gülsoy.

Excerpts from *What Have You Carried Over? Poems of 42 Days and Other Works* by Gülten Akın, Talisman House, Publishers (2013): "Garden Vines," "19," "20," "22" and "23" from *Poems of 42 Days*, "Poem of the Girl Who Died Alone," "Baroque," "Stain," "Done with the City," "Lament for a Working Mother's Child," "Sand" and "Three Masters to One Captive."